ALICE CAMPBELL

FLYING BLIND

Alice Campbell (1887-1955) came originally from Atlanta, Georgia, where she was part of the socially prominent Ormond family. She moved to New York City at the age of nineteen and quickly became a socialist and women's suffragist. Later she moved to Paris, marrying the American-born artist and writer James Lawrence Campbell, with whom she had a son in 1914.

Just before World War One, the family left France for England, where the couple had two more children, a son and a daughter. Campbell wrote crime fiction until 1950, though many of her novels continued to have French settings. She published her first work (*Juggernaut*) in 1928. She wrote nineteen detective novels during her career.

MYSTERIES BY ALICE CAMPBELL

1. *Juggernaut* (1928)
2. *Water Weed* (1929)
3. *Spiderweb* (1930)
4. *The Click of the Gate* (1932)
5. *The Murder of Caroline Bundy* (1933)
6. *Desire to Kill* (1934)
7. *Keep Away from Water!* (1935)
8. *Death Framed in Silver* (1937)
9. *Flying Blind* (1938)
10. *A Door Closed Softly* (1939)
11. *They Hunted a Fox* (1940)
12. *No Murder of Mine* (1941)
13. *No Light Came On* (1942)
14. *Ringed with Fire* (1943)
15. *Travelling Butcher* (1944)
16. *The Cockroach Sings* (1946)
17. *Child's Play* (1947)
18. *The Bloodstained Toy* (1948)
19. *The Corpse Had Red Hair* (1950)

ALICE CAMPBELL

FLYING BLIND

With an introduction
by Curtis Evans

DEAN STREET PRESS

Published by Dean Street Press 2022

First published in 1938 by W. Collins & Sons

Cover by DSP

ISBN 978 1 915393 02 9

www.deanstreetpress.co.uk

To

ACEITUNA GRIFFIN

Whose kind sympathy encouraged my first hazy gropings towards a plot.

ALICE IN MURDERLAND

Crime Writer Alice Campbell, The Other "AC"

In 1927 Alice Dorothy Ormond Campbell—a thirty-nine-year-old native of Atlanta, Georgia who for the last fifteen years had lived successively in New York, Paris and London, never once returning to the so-called Empire City of the South, published her first novel, an unstoppable crime thriller called *Juggernaut*, selling the serialization rights to the *Chicago Tribune* for $4000 ($60,000 today), a tremendous sum for a brand new author. On its publication in January 1928, both the book and its author caught the keen eye of Bessie S. Stafford, society page editor of the *Atlanta Constitution*. Back when Alice Ormond, as she was then known, lived in Atlanta, Miss Bessie breathlessly informed her readers, she had been "an ethereal blonde-like type of beauty, extremely popular, and always thought she was in love with somebody. She took high honors in school; and her gentleness of manner and breeding bespoke an aristocratic lineage. She grew to a charming womanhood—"

Let us stop Miss Bessie right there, because there is rather more to the story of Alice Campbell, the mystery genre's other "AC," who published nineteen crime novels between 1928 and 1950. Allow me to plunge boldly forward with the tale of Atlanta's great Golden Age crime writer, who as an American expatriate in England, went on to achieve fame and fortune as an atmospheric writer of murder and mystery and become one of the early members of the Detection Club.

Alice Campbell's lineage was distinguished. Alice was born in Atlanta on November 29, 1887, the youngest of the four surviving children of prominent Atlantans James Ormond IV and Florence Root. Both of Alice's grandfathers had been wealthy Atlanta merchants who settled in the city in the years before the American Civil War. Alice's uncles, John Wellborn Root and Walter Clark Root, were noted architects, while her brothers, Sidney James and Walter Emanuel Ormond, were respectively a drama critic and political writer for the *Atlanta Constitution* and an attorney and justice of the peace. Both brothers died untimely deaths before Alice had even turned thirty, as did her uncle John Wellborn Root and her father.

Alice precociously published her first piece of fiction, a fairy story, in the *Atlanta Constitution* in 1897, when she was nine years old. Four years later, the ambitious child was said to be in the final stage of completing a two-volume novel. In 1907, by which time she was nineteen, Alice relocated to New York City, chaperoned by Florence.

In New York Alice became friends with writers Inez Haynes Irwin, a prominent feminist, and Jacques Futrelle, the creator of "The Thinking Machine" detective who was soon to go down with the ship on RMS *Titanic,* and scored her first published short story in *Ladies Home Journal* in 1911. Simultaneously she threw herself pell-mell into the causes of women's suffrage and equal pay for equal work. The same year she herself became engaged, but this was soon broken off and in February 1913 Alice sailed to Paris with her mother to further her cultural education.

Three months later in Paris, on May 22, 1913, twenty-five-year-old Alice married James Lawrence Campbell, a twenty-four-year-old theatrical agent of good looks and good family from Virginia. Jamie, as he was known, had arrived in Paris a couple of years earlier, after a failed stint in New York City as an actor. In Paris he served, more successfully, as an agent for prominent New York play brokers Arch and Edgar Selwyn.

After the wedding Alice Ormond Campbell, as she now was known, remained in Paris with her husband Jamie until hostilities between France and Germany loomed the next year. At this point the couple prudently relocated to England, along with their newborn son, James Lawrence Campbell, Jr., a future artist and critic. After the war the Campbells, living in London, bought an attractive house in St. John's Wood, London, where they established a literary and theatrical salon. There Alice oversaw the raising of the couple's two sons, Lawrence and Robert, and their daughter, named Chita Florence Ormond ("Ormond" for short), while Jamie spent much of his time abroad, brokering play productions in Paris, New York and other cities.

Like Alice, Jamie harbored dreams of personal literary accomplishment; and in 1927 he published a novel entitled *Face Value*, which for a brief time became that much-prized thing by publishers, a putatively "scandalous" novel that gets Talked About. The story of a gentle orphan boy named Serge, the son an emigre Russian prostitute, who grows up in a Parisian "disorderly house," as reviews often blushingly put it, *Face Value* divided critics, but ended up on American bestseller lists. The success of his first novel led to the author being invited out to Hollywood to work as a scriptwriter, and his name appears on credits to a trio of films in 1927-28, including *French Dressing*, a "gay" divorce comedy set among sexually scatterbrained Americans in Paris. One wonders whether in Hollywood Jamie ever came across future crime writer Cornell Woolrich, who was scripting there too at the time.

Alice remained in England with the children, enjoying her own literary splash with her debut thriller *Juggernaut*, which concerned the murderous machinations of an inexorably ruthless French Riviera society doctor, opposed by a valiant young nurse. The novel racked up rave reviews and sales in the UK and US, in the latter country spurred on by its nationwide newspaper serialization, which promised readers

> . . . the open door to adventure! *Juggernaut* by Alice Campbell will sweep you out of the humdrum of everyday life into the gay, swift-moving Arabian-nights existence of the Riviera!

London's *Daily Mail* declared that the irresistible *Juggernaut* "should rank among the 'best sellers' of the year"; and, sure enough, *Juggernaut*'s English publisher, Hodder & Stoughton, boasted, several months after the novel's English publication in July 1928, that they already had run through six printings in an attempt to satisfy customer demand. In 1936 *Juggernaut* was adapted in England as a film vehicle for horror great Boris Karloff, making it the only Alice Campbell novel filmed to date. The film was remade in England under the title *The Temptress* in 1949.

Water Weed (1929) and *Spiderweb* (1930) (*Murder in Paris* in the US), the immediate successors, held up well to their predecessor's performance. Alice chose this moment to return for a fortnight to Atlanta, ostensibly to visit her sister, but doubtlessly in part to parade through her hometown as a conquering, albeit commercial, literary hero. And who was there to welcome Alice in the pages of the *Constitution* but Bessie S. Stafford, who pronounced Alice's hair still looked like spun gold while her eyes remarkably had turned an even deeper shade of blue. To Miss Bessie, Alice imparted enchanting tales of salon chats with such personages as George Bernard Shaw, Lady Asquith, H. G. Wells and (his lover) Rebecca West, the latter of whom a simpatico Alice met and conversed with frequently. Admitting that her political sympathies in England "inclined toward the conservatives," Alice yet urged "the absolute necessity of having two strong parties." English women, she had been pleased to see, evinced more informed interest in politics than their American sisters.

Alice, Miss Bessie declared, diligently devoted every afternoon to her writing, shutting her study door behind her "as a sign that she is not to be interrupted." This commitment to her craft enabled Alice to produce an additional sixteen crime novels between 1932 and 1950, beginning with *The Click of the Gate* and ending with *The Corpse Had Red Hair*.

Altogether nearly half of Alice's crime novels were standalones, in contravention of convention at this time, when series sleuths were so popular. In *The Click of the Gate* the author introduced one of her main recurring characters, intrepid Paris journalist Tommy Rostetter, who appears in three additional novels: *Desire to Kill* (1934), *Flying Blind* (1938) and *The Bloodstained Toy* (1948). In the two latter novels, Tommy appears with Alice's other major recurring character, dauntless Inspector Headcorn of Scotland Yard, who also pursues murderers and other malefactors in *Death Framed in Silver* (1937), *They Hunted a Fox* (1940), *No Murder of Mine* (1941) and *The Cockroach Sings* (1946) (*With Bated Breath* in the US).

Additional recurring characters in Alice's books are Geoffrey Macadam and Catherine West, who appear in *Spiderweb* and *No Light Came On* (1942), and Colin Ladbrooke, who appears in *Death Framed in Silver*, *A Door Closed Softly* (1939) and *They Hunted a Fox*. In the latter two books Colin with his romantic interest Alison Young and in the first and third book with Inspector Headcorn, who also appears, as mentioned, in *Flying Blind* and *The Bloodstained Toy* with Tommy Rosstetter, making Headcorn the connecting link in this universe of sleuths, although the inspector does not appear with Geoffrey Macadam and Catherine West. It is all a rather complicated state of criminal affairs; and this lack of a consistent and enduring central sleuth character in Alice's crime fiction may help explain why her work faded in the Fifties, after the author retired from writing.

Be that as it may, Alice Campbell is a figure of significance in the history of crime fiction. In a 1946 review of *The Cockroach Sings* in the London *Observer*, crime fiction critic Maurice Richardson asserted that "[s]he belongs to the atmospheric school, of which one of the outstanding exponents was the late Ethel Lina White," the author of *The Wheel Spins* (1936), famously filmed in 1938, under the title *The Lady Vanishes*, by director Alfred Hitchcock. This "atmospheric school," as Richardson termed it, had more students in the demonstrative United States than in the decorous United Kingdom, to be sure, the United States being the home of such hugely popular suspense writers as Mary Roberts Rinehart and Mignon Eberhart, to name but a couple of the most prominent examples.

Like the novels of the American Eber-Rinehart school and English authors Ethel Lina White and Marie Belloc Lowndes, the latter the author of the acknowledged landmark 1911 thriller *The Lodger*, Alice Campbell's books are not pure puzzle detective tales, but rather broader mysteries which put a premium on the storytelling imperatives of atmosphere and suspense. "She could not be unexciting if she tried," raved the *Times Literary Supplement* of Alice, stressing the author's remoteness from the so-called "Humdrum" school of detective fiction headed by British authors Freeman Wills Crofts, John Street and J. J. Connington. However, as Maurice Richardson, a great fan of Alice's crime writing, put it, "she generally binds her homework together with a reasonable plot," so the "Humdrum" fans out there need not be put off by what American detective novelist S. S. Van Dine, creator of Philo Vance, dogmatically dismissed as "literary dallying." In her novels Alice Campbell offered people bone-rattling good reads, which explains their popularity in the past and their revival today. Lines from a review of her 1941 crime novel *No Murder of Mine* by "H.V.A." in the *Hartford Courant* suggests the general nature of her work's appeal: "The excitement and mystery of this Class A shocker start on page 1 and continue right to the end of the book. You won't put it down, once you've begun it. And if you like romance mixed with your thrills, you'll find it here."

The protagonist of *No Murder of Mine* is Rowan Wilde, "an attractive young American girl studying in England." Frequently in her books Alice, like the great Anglo-American author Henry James, pits ingenuous but goodhearted Americans, male or female, up against dangerously sophisticated Europeans, drawing on autobiographical details from her and Jamie's own lives. Many of her crime novels, which often are lengthier than the norm for the period, recall, in terms of their length and content, the Victorian sensation novel, which seemingly had been in its dying throes when the author was a precocious child; yet, in their emphasis on morbid psychology and their sexual frankness, they also anticipate the modern crime novel. One can discern this tendency most dramatically, perhaps, in the engrossing *Water Weed*, concerning a sexual affair between a middle-aged Englishwoman and a young American man that has dreadful consequences, and *Desire to Kill*, about murder among a clique of decadent bohemians in Paris. In both of these mysteries the exploration of aberrant sexuality is striking. Indeed, in its depiction of sexual psychosis *Water Weed* bears rather more resemblance to, say, the crime novels of Patricia Highsmith than it does to the cozy mysteries of Patricia Wentworth. One might well term it Alice Campbell's *Deep Water*.

In this context it should be noted that in 1935 Alice Campbell authored a sexual problem play, *Two Share a Dwelling*, which the *New York*

Times described as a "grim, vivid, psychological treatment of dual personality." Although it ran for only twenty-two performances during October 8-26 at the West End's celebrated St. James' Theatre, the play had done well on its provincial tour and it received a standing ovation from the audience on opening night at the West End, primarily on account of the compelling performance of the half-Jewish German stage actress Grete Mosheim, who had fled Germany two years earlier and was making her English stage debut in the play's lead role of a schizophrenic, sexually compulsive woman. Mosheim was described as young and "blondely beautiful," bringing to mind the author herself.

Unfortunately priggish London critics were put off by the play's morbid sexual subject, which put Alice in an impossible position. One reviewer scathingly observed that "Miss Alice Campbell . . . has chosen to give her audience a study in pathology as a pleasant method of spending the evening. . . . one leaves the theatre rather wishing that playwrights would leave medical books on their shelves." Another sniffed that "it is to be hoped that the fashion of plumbing the depths of Freudian theory for dramatic fare will not spread. It is so much more easy to be interested in the doings of the sane." The play died a quick death in London and its author went back, for another fifteen years, to "plumbing the depths" in her crime fiction.

What impelled Alice Campbell, like her husband, to avidly explore human sexuality in her work? Doubtless their writing reflected the temper of modern times, but it also likely was driven by personal imperatives. The child of an unhappy marriage who at a young age had been deprived of a father figure, Alice appears to have wanted to use her crime fiction to explore the human devastation wrought by disordered lives. Sadly, evidence suggests that discord had entered the lives of Alice and Jamie by the 1930s, as they reached middle age and their children entered adulthood. In 1939, as the Second World War loomed, Alice was residing in rural southwestern England with her daughter Ormond at a cottage—the inspiration for her murder setting in *No Murder of Mine*, one guesses—near the bucolic town of Beaminster, Dorset, known for its medieval Anglican church and its charming reference in a poem by English dialect poet William Barnes:

Sweet Be'mi'ster, that bist a-bound
By green and woody hills all round,
Wi'hedges, reachen up between
A thousand vields o' zummer green.

Alice's elder son Lawrence was living, unemployed, in New York City at this time and he would enlist in the US Army when the country entered the war a couple of years later, serving as a master sergeant throughout the conflict. In December 1939, twenty-three-year-old Ormond, who seems to have herself preferred going by the name Chita, wed the prominent antiques dealer, interior decorator, home restorer and racehorse owner Ernest Thornton-Smith, who at the age of fifty-eight was fully thirty-five years older than she. Antiques would play a crucial role in Alice's 1944 wartime crime novel *Travelling Butcher*, which blogger Kate Jackson at *Cross Examining Crime* deemed "a thrilling read." The author's most comprehensive wartime novel, however, was the highly-praised *Ringed with Fire* (1943). Native Englishman S. Morgan-Powell, the dean of Canadian drama critics, in the *Montreal Star* pronounced *Ringed with Fire* one of the "best spy stories the war has produced," adding, in one of Alice's best notices:

> "Ringed with Fire" begins with mystery and exudes mystery from every chapter. Its clues are most ingeniously developed, and keep the reader guessing in all directions. For once there is a mystery which will, I think, mislead the most adroit and experienced of amateur sleuths. Some time ago there used to be a practice of sealing up the final section of mystery stores with the object of stirring up curiosity and developing the detective instinct among readers. If you sealed up the last forty-two pages of "Ringed with Fire" and then offered a prize of $250 to the person who guessed the mystery correctly, I think that money would be as safe as if you put it in victory bonds.

A few years later, on the back of the dust jacket to the American edition of Alice's *The Cockroach Sings* (1946), which Random House, her new American publisher, less queasily titled *With Bated Breath*, readers learned a little about what the author had been up to during the late war and its recent aftermath: "I got used to oil lamps. . . . and also to riding nine miles in a crowded bus once a week to do the shopping—if there was anything to buy. We thought it rather a lark then, but as a matter of fact we are still suffering from all sorts of shortages and restrictions." Jamie Campbell, on the other hand, spent his war years in Santa Barbara, California. It is unclear whether he and Alice ever lived together again.

Alice remained domiciled for the rest of her life in Dorset, although she returned to London in 1946, when she was inducted into the Detection Club. A number of her novels from this period, all of which were published in England by the Collins Crime Club, more resemble, in tone and form, classic detective fiction, such as *They Hunted a Fox* (1940). This event may have been a moment of triumph for the author, but it was also something of a last hurrah. After 1946 she published only three more crime novels, including the entertaining Tommy Rostetter-Inspector Headcorn mashup *The Bloodstained Toy*, before retiring in 1950. She lived out the remaining five years of her life quietly at her home in the coastal city of Bridport, Dorset, expiring "suddenly" on November 27, 1955, two days before her sixty-eighth birthday. Her brief death notice in the *Daily Telegraph* refers to her only as the "very dear mother of Lawrence, Chita and Robert."

Jamie Campbell had died in 1954 aged sixty-five. Earlier in the year his play *The Praying Mantis*, billed as a "naughty comedy by James Lawrence Campbell," scored hits at the Q Theatre in London and at the Dolphin Theatre in Brighton. (A very young Joan Collins played the eponymous man-eating leading role at the latter venue.) In spite of this, Jamie near the end of the year checked into a hotel in Cannes and fatally imbibed poison. The American consulate sent the report on Jamie's death to Chita in Maida Vale, London, and to Jamie's brother Colonel George Campbell in Washington, D. C., though not to Alice. This was far from the Riviera romance that the publishers of *Juggernaut* had long ago promised. Perhaps the "humdrum of everyday life" had been too much with him.

Alice Campbell own work fell into obscurity after her death, with not one of her novels being reprinted in English for more than seven decades. Happily the ongoing revival of vintage English and American mystery fiction from the twentieth century is rectifying such cases of criminal neglect. It may well be true that it "is impossible not to be thrilled by Edgar Wallace," as the great thriller writer's publishers pronounced, but let us not forget that, as Maurice Richardson put it: "We can always do with Mrs. Alice Campbell." Mystery fans will now have nineteen of them from which to choose—a veritable embarrassment of felonious riches, all from the hand of the other AC.

Curtis Evans

CHAPTER ONE

Too late Thomas Rostetter cursed himself for accepting his nephew's luncheon-invitation. He should have remembered Troy, Franklin's man with the axe to grind, or more concretely the recent occasion when Rankin Rostetter, popping over to Paris, had by suave flattery wangled the loan of a flat, with a thousand francs—unrecoverable—thrown in.

As usual, there had been little to put the victim on guard. Rank's approach had been disarming, the restaurant, bijou but modest, looked well within even his precarious means, and when all was said was it not fitting that some recognition be paid a visiting and generous relation? So Tommy argued when, confronted by a choice of lamb cold and lamb curried—for the ritual of Saturday shop-closing had delayed the meal till a late hour—he resigned himself to the mild boredom any well-intentioned uncle must now and then expect. He accepted the apologies for past neglect, agreed that Rank was wise to abandon the flower-business recently embarked on, and—since it left him free to pursue his own thoughts—let the lad maunder on at will.

"Crowded out's my story," Rank informed him. "All very easy to say every one buys flowers. The fact remains you can't heave a brick in Mayfair without damaging an arum lily or a gift-pot of hibiscus. Bilfilian and I have worked our fingers to the bone. What with hot-footing it down to Covent Garden at the crack of dawn—"

"Have you done that?" demanded the uncle, roused.

"Every other morning," said Rank firmly. "We've taken it in turns. Choosing, pricing, window-dressing—I'm rather good at that, you may have noticed; serving customers who don't know their minds, making up set piece for funerals and what-not . . . sheer slavery, that's what it is, and for what?" A pause, while Rank bitterly inspected a slab of mango-chutney to determine whether the hairs adhering to it were its own or the waitress's. "Forced to sell at a loss. Shoved off to Madeira—and just when I've a most urgent reason for sticking in London."

Having heard the whole, stark tragedy from his brother, Tommy did not crave a rehash. It remained matter for wonderment that even a besotted parent could have parted with five hundred of the best to install Rankin Rostetter in any enterprise requiring acumen and concentration; yet glancing towards the speaker he did certainly observe a marked improvement over the Oxford days. Hair once ragged was pommelled till it shone like dark, ruddy copper. Tweed coat and creased bags had been replaced by the trimmest of lounge-suits, while the midnight blue shirt, if a thought precious, was undeniably becoming. Yes, much as Tommy might flout this story of early rising and constant grind, Peter's brat looked distinctly on the up and up.

"When do you start in on the wine-business?" he asked carelessly.

Between set teeth Rank muttered, "Tuesday evening. Slow boat, no news reaching me till I land." He fell moodily silent, to add with a jerk, "It's why I had to get hold of you to-day. There's darned little time."

Time? Tommy shied, and momentarily expecting a touch stiffened for refusal. Rank, however, was stealing a watchful glance at the only other lunchers the Snuggery contained—to wit, a pair of ultra-smart, hollow-chested young women with apricot make-ups and the voices of Balham, who, after fiddling with a faded salad, were now stowing away strawberry ice.

"Mannequins," Rank mumbled. "Won't do to let them hear what I'm about to say. These trade-joints, you know, are a regular forcing-bed of gossip, and Rosemary's aunt wants this thing kept dark."

Tommy frowned.

"What, my boy, is this jargon about Rosemary and aunts?"

"Jargon?" Rank opened puzzled eyes. "Surely I told you I wanted your help on a rather worrying matter?"

"You did not," said Tommy curtly. "And if it's another loan—"

A pained gesture cut him short.

"More curry? Oh, well, I'll just mop up the overflow, so we can move forward. It's like this," the whisperer proceeded, glutinously, through a mouthful of rice. "Something decidedly grim has been happening to a friend—I should say to two friends—of mine. Knowing your clever flair for mysteries and so on, I suggested calling on you for advice. No objection, I hope?"

"Every objection," snapped Tommy with the finality of a slammed door. "If you dimly imagine you're going to haul me into your friends' messes, just get this into your head: I'm a newspaper man, not a detective; and I know when I've had enough."

"Modesty," approved Rank, calmly chewing. "All the same, who plunked that French kidnapper a few years back? Who got the low-down on Dodo Quarles's murder and saved a pure young girl's reason if not her life?"

"Incidentally getting socked on the bean and cold-storaged in a rusted tank. Like to inspect the scar that marks my limit?"

Turtle-fashion Tommy thrust forward the sleek, black sheath of his head and tenderly stroked a crescent-shaped scar. Rank surveyed the souvenir but did not weaken.

"Stout fella," he admired. "So I was saying to Rosemary a moment ago. Wait, my girl, I said, till you see this uncle of mine. Unlined—practically speaking; not one grey hair—"

"And why in hell should my hair be grey?" retorted the hero, stung. His fresh-coloured face had hardened, his eyes, blue as flax-flowers, were ominously bleak. "Will it close the issue if I tell you I'm pushing off home to-morrow?"

An untrue statement, and a wasted one, for Rank, with a broad tolerance wholly exasperating, merely remarked that the police here seemed a muddle-headed lot, and that however the victims might joke about it the situation was frightening.

"When it comes to revolver-shots being bunged in at windows, isn't it about time something drastic was done?"

Tommy flickered an eyelash in Rank's direction. Then his lips tightened, and he fixed a resolute gaze on the trio of smart shop-fronts which faced the restaurant. One, a bright vision of tulips, forget-me-nots and azaleas, represented the ill-starred venture of his nephew and a repulsive youngster named Bilfilian. Another, chastely displaying a bleached chair, a length of shimmering puce satin, and a dead-white jar, marked the decorating establishment of young Lord Hollings, while that between bore the gilt caption of Anatol Ltd., and contained a solitary hat. On the last, for no obvious reason. Tommy concentrated his attention, absently held by the strange concoction of black, glazed straw and glycerined ostrich feathers which formed its central feature. It looked, he thought, like a chimney-pot on which a draggled rook had roosted. . . .

"Spill it," he growled churlishly, "if you must; but I warn you, I'll have no truck with it. Who's Rosemary? A mannequin? Or is she a manicure?"

"Rosemary," said Rank with dignity, "happens to be a Miss Bellamy-Pryce. Yes,"—as Tommy glanced at him, "the vicar's one and only daughter, from your own abandoned home-town. Grand-daughter of old stick-in-the-mud Bellamy-Pryce, who's dug himself in at Black Gables. You know that beam and plaster atrocity on the north slope of the downs."

"The tea-merchant? He's been dead for years."

"•Oh, no! Only dying; but that's beside the point. Rosemary scarcely knows the old skinflint. Neither do his own sons; and as for Boggie—"

"Who's Boggie?"

"Why, Mrs. Bellamy-Pryce—widow of James. The aunt Rosemary lives with in Kensington. She's the core of our problem—or so she believes. I'm not so sure."

"Why Boggie?" demanded Tommy, cantankerously.

"Why anything? She's the sort of woman who does get called Boggie. Affectionate nickname. When you see her—"

"I shall not."

Rank nodded benignly to the waitress, pressed on his guest the one, melting ice, and when it was declined applied himself to it with relish. Tommy, occupied with Cheddar, saw in his mind's eye the Sussex village he so rarely visited and was even now nerving himself to pay a duty call. Broughton-Elmtrees, tucked away in a fold of green downland; somnolent High Street—church-bells—inertia; self-satisfied inhabitants, in antiquated clothes; the red glory of a May-tree, beside the Sheep for Shearing. So the vicar had a daughter. News, but uninteresting.

"Works over there," Rank explained, indicating the hat shop. "This spring, when Boggie's husband pegged out on the way back from Ceylon, it seemed the obvious thing for the two of them to team up. They've a small furnished house in Victoria Grove. Boggie's a cheery soul. As she says, a woman that's spent half a lifetime in God-forsaken holes takes a lot of daunting; but I can tell you this much: They're both of them scared stiff."

Tommy consulted his watch. Rank gathered speed.

"Wednesday evening," he said, "at exactly ten o'clock, a shot was fired bang through the front window of Boggie's drawing-room. It whizzed past Rosemary, playing the piano, not four feet away; and if Boggie, writing letters, hadn't moved her head at the correct moment it would definitely have transplanted her to Kingdom Come."

The narrator paused dramatically. The listener yawned. "Well, and what of it? Had they the sense to call the police?"

"Obviously. Rash though it sounds, they ran out almost at once. Garden empty, street empty. The constable they flagged came back and gave the place a thorough comb-over. Fat lot of good that was!"

"No one outside had seen a man running?"

"No one was about to see anything. The shot, let me tell you, was discharged so close to the curtains that the stuff was scorched."

Tommy eyed him briefly.

"Oh? And the police opinion of all this?"

"On Thursday a Yard inspector called round with a fairly satisfactory yarn. This house, mark you, is number ninety-six Victoria Grove. Now, then, just round the corner, at ninety-six Victoria Road, lives Mr.

Justice Wainbridge. Last week he gave a thundering long sentence to a fraudulent bookie; and this chap's pals have been ringing him up from call-boxes saying they were going to bump him off. Headquarters believed—oh, blast!"

Breaking off with a mutter, Rank glued a gaze of dark hatred on the mirror at his uncle's back. Tommy, facing him, perceived the reason, in the person of an upstanding, broad-shouldered man who had just sauntered casually—arrogantly, one might say—into the restaurant. The newcomer was in the mid-thirties, well dressed, though in a style more pronounced than that of the two Rostetters. Superabundant vigour struck one like a blow from his red-bronzed skin and bold, hot brown eyes. His dark hair, crisply corrugated, retreated from a sunburned forehead, his thick scrap of moustache was clipped to reveal an aggressive, self-indulgent mouth. All in all, in a slightly coarse, over-masculine way, he was good-looking—arrestingly so. Military, was Tommy's thought, to which was added the rider, from overseas.

Disappointedly he glanced at the empty tables, exchanged a word with the waitress, and lounged towards the two mannequins who at sight of him had preened expectantly. Now, as he dawdled beside them, their shrill giggles gave earnest of their pleasure; but while he talked, jocosely familiar, he stared hard and provocatively at Rank's unturned head. His eyes, encountering Tommy's, held an inquisitive challenge. Once it seemed as though he were going to approach for conversation; but he checked the impulse, roamed discontentedly away, and having bestowed an absent caress on the waitress's bare arm, lit a cigarette, stuck his bowler on at an angle, and departed into the June glare of Brackham Place.

"Bounder! Checkmated for once." Rank was giving vent to grim explosions under his breath. "Well, and where were we?"

"The police," Tommy wearily reminded him, "assume that the shot was intended for the judge, only an error was made in the street. On the face of it, I'd say they were right."

"Oh, yeah? Then listen: Next evening—Thursday—at the same time, precisely the same thing occurs. Another shot plunges in through the window. Again it's a near thing for both of them."

"Rubbish."

"It's true. Ro rang me up, laughing and gasping. Round I hiked, found the pair of them furnishing details to the inspector behind drawn blinds. The Yard man didn't laugh. He knew damned well his theory was out. Whoever it was saw jolly well who was in that room. Just a second spot of luck for one of them—which one, we don't know. A third try may bring it off."

"Not with that aim."

"You think so? Then let me tell you the tag-end of a scarf Ro was wearing was nipped off. Boggie's hair, above the left ear, was singed. Can you explain that away?"

"I am not attempting it," said Tommy callously. "I am not interested, and if I were it would be ridiculous to imagine a person like myself could . . ."

It was Tommy's turn to suspend his remarks. Directly opposite, the door of Anatol's Ltd. had opened, and from its shelter a girl peered guardedly forth. She seemed fairly tall, with a slenderness healthily rounded, and her summer frock was blue, of a shade just deeper than the cloudless June sky. It was her hair Tommy chiefly noticed. It floated, it swam, pale roseate gold, in the dusk of the entrance glimmering as of its own light, a small, radiant sun. He did not know when he had seen hair so alive, so ardent, or so captivating to the imagination. If her face lived up to it—but that was hardly likely.

She had ventured out and frowning a little was stepping tentatively off the pavement. From her bare hand dangled a wide, shallow hat of the shepherdess type. She was heading in this direction, with purpose in her eye. . . .

"Any personal reason," Tommy hazarded, "for worrying your head over this affair?"

"Certainly." Rank settled his tie. "If all goes well with this new job. I hope to marry Miss Bellamy-Pryce."

"Has she accepted you, then?"

The girl, midway the street, was dodging a Bentley. She reappeared, walking slowly, as in doubt.

"She hasn't said yes," stated the lover carefully. "But on the other hand she hasn't given me a definite no."

"What, may one ask, has she said?"

"Let's keep to the subject. I may mention, though, that her being a trifle my senior is simply twaddle. She looks a mere child, as you'll presently see."

"Look out! What are you up to?" barked Tommy, for at this juncture Rank, with execrable clumsiness, had swept the entire cruet-stand on to the floor.

"Only a small signal," soothed Rank, calmly swabbing vinegar from his uncle's shoes. "I told her if you were interested I'd chuck something down."

"Signal!"

Too precipitately Tommy leapt to his feet. His chair, a skeleton of steel curves, capsized with a crash, and mortification burned red-hot wounds in his self-esteem. No escape now. On the girl came, swinging her shallow hat by its elastic, her manner nicely balanced between anticipation and diffidence. Her face, he saw, accorded admirably with her hair; but be she Cleopatra and the Queen of the May rolled into one, this scoundrelly betrayal justified any rudeness.

"Ro, my sweet, I want you to meet Tommy." Thus the blackguard spoke, smugly confident. "It's quite okay, darling. He's going to look after you."

"It's not true!" The vicar's daughter gasped, opened lovely eyes, and stared in a puzzled fashion. "Are you really Rank's uncle?" she demanded bluntly. "That is, I'd expected some one different. Older. Oh, do forgive me! I'm being stupid. How do you do?"

With a little laugh she held out her hand. It was long-fingered, firm, cool to the touch. As Tommy took it she ventured a second glance, searching, suspicious, and her colour rose.

"Rank's done the dirty on you," she said quickly. "I can see he has. Oh, don't lie! Oh, Rank!" She turned stormily on the culprit. "How could you be so perfectly foul, after what you promised?"

"Now, listen," began Rank, capturing her arm, but she shook him off.

"I won't! Oh, Mr. Rostetter, I'm so frightfully ashamed! This is all Rank's doing. We don't want help. What are the police for, I ask you? I'm not the tiniest bit funked. I swear it. Please let's forget anything's been said about our troubles. Shall we?"

Her eyes, earnestly beseeching, were grey-blue, flawless, with long upturned lashes. In them Tommy read independence, lurking humour, generosity; but there was something else, valiantly seeking cover. If she had tried less determinedly to hide it, if she had not made it easy for him to repeat his fib about the immediate return to Paris, all might have ended; but the damage, alas, was done. Once again Tommy felt himself slipping. He met her clear gaze, and his wrath turned to compassion.

"Actually," he protested, "I was just saying that as I'm not here for long I'd better get in touch with you at once and talk things over. Won't you sit down and tell me all about it?"

Rank smiled and heaved a sigh.

CHAPTER TWO

MISS Bellamy-Pryce had had lunch, but she would take coffee.

"I mustn't stop long," she declared. "I'm on my own to-day, and I've got to close up the shop."

"I'll go across with you," said Rank grimly. "I don't half like this hopping off for week-ends and leaving you by yourself."

"Darling, don't be an ass!" she retorted. "Clover's there now, cleaning up. She's my real reason for not dawdling. In fact, it's just come over me I've left the gin-bottle out—and you know what Clover is."

"Gin-bottle?" Tommy raised his brows. "I must say this sheds a happy light on the milliner's trade. Do you serve out drinks before hats are tried on, or after purchase, as a reward of merit?"

"Neither." She laughed light-heartedly. "Oh, we do throw cocktail parties fairly frequently! You must come to the one we're having on Tuesday, to inaugurate the Sale. No, this is our private bottle, just to help us through the frightful tedium of the day. Personally I loathe gin, but the other girls seem to find it most cheering. So does the countess, if Saturn's in the ascendant, or she's got a tummy-ache after lobstering at the Ritz."

"The countess?"

"Our aristocratic proprietress—Countess Rakovsky. She's by way of having a temperament."

"Go on, be honest about her," muttered Rank truculently. "Tell him that tight or sober she's a hell-cat and hates you like poison."

"Must you be childish, Rank?"

The flushing of her cheeks revealed the fact that the delicate tint Tommy had been admiring was as much her own as the trail of faint freckles traversing her nose. She squared her shoulders, dispensed the coffee with a negligent hand, and stated with great firmness that the countess was not at all a bad sort, and on the whole most decent to her.

"Rakovsky," mused Tommy, ignoring the by-play. "I've run across her, I think, in Paris. Slim, exotic, raven-black hair?"

"It's red this year. She's beautiful and utterly fascinating. Now, then, let's get on. Rank's told you, hasn't he? Then I'm afraid I've very little to add. We've been shot at twice—and we don't know which of us is wanted, or who's after us. Maybe it's all finished. He may give up the attempt, in which case—"

"He!" Rank put in doggedly. "You will have it it's a man. Can't a woman fire a gun?"

"Rank, you're only holding us up. Mr. Rostetter, what do you want me to tell you?"

Tommy roused. He had been thinking how fresh, how natural she was, though every whit as carefully-groomed as the two enamelled mannequins who were now licking their eyelashes and plastering their mouths with magenta in preparation to depart. It occurred to him that this hare-brained nephew of his had thundering good taste; and to atone for the startling pang of annoyance which shot through him he adopted a woodenly-practical tone.

"I understand," he said, "that the wrong-address theory is virtually shelved."

"Oh, quite—or so we think."

"It's all-important then, to know which of you is being attacked. Any notions on the subject?"

"Not the foggiest. No, Rank, I won't have it!" This in a stern aside. "I've no enemies; nor has Boggie. At least, I don't see how she can have. She's such an absolute duck."

Watching her closely, Tommy fancied some slight reservation.

"But your aunt? What does she think?"

Rosemary knit her smooth brow and studied the bubbles on her coffee.

"That's the puzzling part," she answered hesitatingly. "Without actually saying so, she seems to take it for granted she's the one. I keep wondering if she isn't hiding something from me. Neither I nor Rank can get a word out of her. She just refuses to take the matter seriously; but I can't help thinking she's putting up a magnificent bluff, to keep me from seeing how—how really terrified she is."

"What about my having a talk with her?"

"Oh, would you?" Her eyes lit with gratitude. "I didn't dare suggest it! Somehow I feel you might succeed where we've failed. If we knew, you see, it might make all the difference."

"I'll have a try, anyhow. Shall we make it now?"

"Angel." She gave his arm a quick squeeze which, to his renewed chagrin, sent an alarming shock through him. "I'll ring her up this minute, to make sure she's in. Shall we go over to the shop?"

They rose, and Rank, according to custom, began a futile rummage of pockets, terminating with the expected murmur of, "Do you awfully mind, Tommy, old thing? We'll settle up later."

Rosemary, hearing, promptly denounced him for a low hound, and in the same breath snatched away the hat he had picked up from the floor.

"Hands off! I've only borrowed it for Ranelagh, and on Monday it goes back into stock."

Tommy, at the cash-desk, heard Rank imparting a piece of information which met with a shrug.

"Oh? Well, I'm not interested."

"You'd locked the shop-door, I suppose. Anyhow, he prowled in here hoping to find you. As usual—the swine!"

She did not answer. Head high, she led the way towards Anatol's, Rank at her heels like a moody puppy.

"Come in," she invited, holding the shop-door wide. "Don't tread on the hats. If I don't catch Boggie at once she'll be off to her bridge club . . . Oh, Clover!" The last was a cry of reproach. In the small, super-luxurious interior a stringy charwoman, posed before a mirror, jumped like a rabbit and hastily removed from her head a mauve feathered toque.

"Shyme to leave these 'ere light-coloured 'ats mucking abaht, miss," she remarked, turning on the accuser a bleared but ingratiating eye. "You don't mind me putting 'em away before I start in on my dusting?"

"I'll attend to it," said the girl severely. "You get going with the other room."

As the inner door closed on the unabashed Mrs. Clover, Rosemary made a dive among the jumble of hats and catching up a quart bottle held it to the light.

"I knew it. No trusting her. Rank, be a pet and stow these things away while I do my telephoning."

She lifted an ivory hand-microphone from a little silvered table. Rank obediently began disposing the stock in a cupboard, and Tommy, left idle, surveyed the room. The walls were cerulean blue, peppered over with silver stars. The carpet was black and an inch thick, and the furniture consisted of low stools fashioned of mirror-glass and matching cabinets in which were displayed a ravishing collection of evening-bags, scent-sprays, and head-ornaments. Everything looked expensive, and the whole atmosphere was permeated with an insidious, cloying perfume.

"I doubt if any of this is paid for," confided Rank, pausing in his labour. "How the woman carries on God alone knows. She couldn't, but for—"

"Hush, you!" Rosemary ordered as a rich, cheerful contralto hummed over the wire. "I've just got through." After a few minutes' eager explanation she hung up the receiver and announced that it was all right. "She's asked us to tea. Will you two amuse yourselves while I do my last jobs?"

She dashed into the rear room. Taking advantage of her absence, Rank hurled a rose-pink crinoline on to a shelf, and drew close to his uncle with the air of portentous conspiracy Tommy invariably found irritating.

"If she clears out," he hissed darkly, "this show will fall apart in a fortnight. She will clear, too. Getting fed up with the false customs declarations and the bad cheques handed out. Rakovsky knows that, and she's got the wind up properly. Wednesday afternoon there was a row in here that raised the roof. You can't fool me what it was about. Some gilt-edged goof of Rakovsky's been making passes at Ro. They all do, one after the other. Stick around, and you'll see. Rakovsky's losing her grip—but she can still grip a revolver. Now are you getting it?"

"Not quite," Tommy answered coldly. "You are suggesting that this girl is indispensable to the success of the shop. If that's so, why should the countess want to murder her?"

"Rakovsky's not normal," insisted Rank. "She'll be shrewd five days and bust a cylinder on the sixth. Ro knows enough to jail her. Besides, if she leaves and goes to another shop, won't it mean the collection of boy-friends will camp there instead of here? It's not so mixed as it may sound. Just you chew on it a bit while I dodge into my own premises. I won't be long."

Left alone, Tommy lit a cigarette, and strove to piece together what he had heard in Paris of Anatalia Rakovsky. He could remember little save her vaguely Rumanian origin, her succession of marriages all terminated, and her reputed skill in ensnaring the rich of both sexes for the financing of her multifarious schemes. There had always been odd stories about her: but why waste time on them till it was definitely established which woman, aunt or niece, was the object of attack?

Suddenly he realised that herein lay his weakness. Had he been assured it was the aunt whose life was imperilled wild horses yoked together to drag him one step farther would have sweated and given up. Unfortunately he had seen the girl—and he did not, could not, know if it were she who might suffer extinction.

He was a fool, of course, to stick his amateur oar into other people's muddles. He had sworn fierce oaths never again to be tempted; but if at his age and after his searing experiences he was still not proof against brave eyes and apple-blossom complexions—no benefit from which was in the least likely to accrue to him—why, then, he was past praying for, and might as well accept his fate. He would just satisfy himself. If it was the aunt, then *fiche le camp.*

Rosemary was back and had dumped on the carpet an armful of expensive oddments which she proceeded to pack into an attaché-case. He saw a rainbow of delicate scarves, powder-compacts, an assortment of glass and porcelain animals.

"Side-line, from Paris," she explained. "Comes over by 'plane. I have to hawk this lot round the big shops on Monday morning, so I'm carting it home to save time." She held up a minute, grotesque dog, wrought in glass, and gently stroked its ears. "Nice, isn't he? He's Cuthbert—because, you see, he's so exactly like my father. Notice his sweet, wool-gathering look?"

Eyeing the dog, Tommy abruptly recalled the vicar of Broughton-Elmtrees. It was true, here was the same trusting vacancy of expression, the same tousled forelock. "Then you're like your mother," he remarked candidly. "So they say," she laughed gaily, "but I hardly remember her. He's rather a love, I think. I hate sending him away, but he's a sample, so he'll come back." Tenderly she wrapped the dog in tissue-paper and put him to bed on a scarf. Then she sat back on her heels, shook her hair out of her eyes, and said earnestly, "I know what Rank's been saying. It's just sheer bilge, all of it. Don't listen to him, will you?"

"You mean about the countess?"

"Certainly. There's nothing in it. She knows perfectly well I wouldn't touch one of her boy-friends with a barge-pole. She goes off the deep end quite often, but it's not serious. We all know that. I—it's just that I hate having you get wrong ideas. And you mustn't suppose I'm frightened. On my own account, that is. I don't say I enjoy being shot at, but was it me? I can't believe it was."

He did not answer, held in thrall by the astounding loveliness of her frank, clear face and bright halo of hair against the blue, starred wall. With a start he came to, knelt on the floor beside her, and helped her with her task; and while they were thus occupied Rank blundered in, so cumbered with carnations, posies bedded in moss, and a potted hydrangea four feet high that he seemed at first glance to be moving shop. Rosemary turned with a groan.

"Fool!" she scolded. "Take those back—all of them! That's stock, that is. You can't go on squandering it on me—and besides, it'll mean a taxi."

"Tommy's got a car of sorts," Rank placidly informed her. "They'll be gone by Monday, so why bother?"

"It's not business, you know. Easy to see why you've hashed things up. Oh, well, get them out of here. You're dropping petals wherever you go."

Though she tended to haul her feckless lover over the coals and order him about like an errand boy, Tommy detected an almost wifely touch in her manner towards him. With a nagging persistence he wondered what feelings lay behind her casual front. All this young lot lacked sentiment; and she had not said no. . . .

The car, lent Tommy for the duration of his visit, was indeed of sorts. Solely by painful compression could the front seat hold three, yet hold them it must, since the half-portion seat behind, designed presumably for a legless person, was entirely crammed with the floral offerings. The smaller fry, that is—for the hydrangea, to Tommy's disgust, had of necessity to be bound to the running-board, and clutched by Rank through the window. In such wise, without dignity or comfort, the party erupted from Brackham Place, chugged through quiet, Saturday Mayfair, and thence amidst the cool greenery of the Park to respectable Kensington. They looked, Rosemary declared, like Bank Holiday on the Heath.

"One good push, and our pod will burst. Oh, dear, why do I feel so silly? Is it because I've got a nice shoulder to lean on, and somehow I know—oh, I do know! —everything's going to come right?"

Her hand, for want of space, rested on Tommy's knee, in a warm patch of sunlight. Her hair tickled his cheek, and her joyous patter turned the whole excursion into a rag. Maybe it was a rag. It was less and less possible to believe that somewhere in brilliant, mid-season London an assassin was lurking and watching his chance to slay an innocent victim. A thing like that could not be on this first day of a glorious June, with the park teeming with harmless faces, summer warmth enticing bathers into the Serpentine, and the whole world in festive form. The suspicion grew on Tommy that he was being hoaxed. He was just the person to have this sort of game played on him.

The thought strengthened when they turned into the short, sequestered retreat of Victoria Grove. Every house was smugly conventional, none more so than number 96, near the end of the row. A crazy-pavement, bone dry and starred with vivid blue scillas, spanned the space between gate and indigo-painted door. Crisp net curtains swayed gently inward at the open windows, cleanliness and order gave guarantee of a life conducted on die-hard, unimaginative lines. Already Tommy could picture Mrs. Bellamy-Pryce, widow of James—who, if he remembered rightly, had been a judge—Anglo-Indian pillar of Empire, conservative to the core. She would play excellent bridge, hold unprogressive views, handle servants firmly. Was it likely she any more than her niece had been marked down for slaughter? Either it was a mistake, or else a somewhat elaborate practical joke at his expense. He must be on his guard.

The two-and-a-half seater disgorged its load. Leaving Rank to extricate the flowers, Rosemary fitted her latch-key into the door, remarking as she did so that their one maid had been sacked a few days before.

"So you mustn't mind pigging it. It's a furnished house," she explained, showing Tommy into the narrow hall. "My aunt's belongings haven't yet come over from Ceylon. Here's the drawing-room. Is Boggie there? Oh, well, I'll call her." She lifted her voice and shouted a lusty, "Boggie! We've come."

There was no answer. A second summons roused only echoes from what, all at once, seemed a remarkably empty house.

"That's funny," said Rosemary. "She must have run out for a moment. I'll look, though, to make sure."

Lightly she sped upstairs, while Tommy examined the moderate-sized, two-fold room into which he had wandered. All the anticipated furnishings—shining mahogany, pleasant chintz, glittering brass fender before a grate banked with birch-leaves; silver and china ornaments, a grand piano draped with a Chinese shawl. Irreproachable, well-kept, and agreeably dull. Boggie's own household affects, when they arrived, would look precisely the same.

In the silence a gilt clock ticked clearly. Tommy noticed a tea-tray, trimly disposed on a little gate-legged table covered with a starched, lace-edged cloth. Flowered Worcester—silver kettle—a stand bearing thin bread and butter, and two kinds of cake. He moved to the window and studied the curtains. Plum-coloured damask, thinly-lined—and yes, just above the sill, two round holes, charred brown at the edges.

Those at any rate were genuine.

Rosemary returned, more slowly, with Rank behind her, balancing his hydrangea.

"Tea's all waiting, I see," she said absently. "Now where can Boggie have got to? Rank, do set that thing down, before you knock a picture off the wall. It's so unlike her to . . . *Oh!* what was that?"

The three stood riveted, straining their ears for a repetition of the sound which had just reached them. An ominous, gurgling sound, close at hand—but coming from where?

"There!" whispered the girl. "Did you hear?"

Tommy had heard—and his hair stirred at the roots. Once before he had heard a noise like this. The man had lain in a shell-hole, a gaping void in his carotid artery. It was here, within these four walls; but how could that be? Again it came, choking, agonised, the gasp of a person very near death. Rosemary clutched his arm and pointed.

"Look—oh, look! Don't you see?"

He saw, at the farther end of the room, a bare mahogany table, decorated by a bowl of roses. Half blocking the archway was a sofa. Then, looking down, he received his second shock. From beneath the sofa-valance protruded the toe of a woman's shoe.

"It's Boggie!" wailed Rosemary, plunging towards it. "Oh, my God, how horrible! Quick, help me!"

Swiftly Tommy and Rank lifted the sofa, set it clear, and bent over the prostrate form of a woman clad in a black coat and skirt, her arms tightly bound to her body with row upon row of stout cord. Her mouth was gagged. Above it eyes bloodshot and semi-glazed stared up at them. The moaning had ceased.

On her knees Rosemary sobbed, "Boggie! Speak to me! See, I've got that beastly thing off. Oh, poor, poor, Boggie, what have they done to you?"

In the dreadful pause a gruesome whisper came from the younger Rostetter.

"So it was Boggie, after all!" he muttered.

Tommy detected the distinct relief in his nephew's voice, and to his shame found its echo in his own breast.

CHAPTER THREE

"SHE can't be dead!" urged Rosemary frantically. "Quick, the carving-knife. In the buffet drawer. Let's cut away these horrible cords."

In a moment the victim was hacked free and laid on the sofa. The purple bruise on her temple would account for her dazed condition. No other injury could be found, and almost at once she struggled to articulate. Tommy asked if there was any brandy. Rosemary had it ready, and together, raising the heavy head, they administered a little. Presently, groaning, Mrs. Bellamy-Pryce began stiffly to stir. As they watched anxiously her mottled colour merged into an even, brickish hue. She was not only coming round, but was in better case than had been expected. Viewing her robust person, Tommy decided that it must have taken considerable force to overcome her. Since there was no sign of a tussle, the knock-out must have taken her totally unawares. He examined the gag, loose on the floor. It was a man's white linen handkerchief, absolutely new and unlaundered, bearing neither initial nor mark. Then he touched a bit of the cord to his lips. It was salt to the taste.

"She's trying to speak," said Rosemary, hanging over her aunt. "Boggie, darling, can you manage it? Who did this horrible thing?"

Mrs. Bellamy-Pryce blinked, shook her head, and muttered indistinctly. "Don't know. Didn't see." As they stared at one another she groped towards her forehead, winced and gave another slight groan. With a rueful twist to her mouth she murmured: "Hadn't I a hat?"

Tommy picked up the wide, unfashionable black straw he had seen lying near her. She eyed it with the ghost of a humorous smile.

"I was wearing it," she said thickly, her lips still stiff. "Good old Edwardian habit. Saved me, didn't it?"

As she spoke her eyes rested on Tommy. Her expression changed, and with a commendable effort she essayed the amenities.

"Mr. Rostetter? Good of you to come. I didn't dream, though, you'd have such a reception."

She offered her hand. Tommy noticed its surprisingly capable grip, the unbeautified nails, the almost rough texture of the skin. The whole accorded with her type. She was evidently not a woman given to vanities.

"That'll do, dear, keep quiet," Rosemary begged. "We'll get a doctor . . . and . . ." in a swift whisper to Rank, "The inspector. Quick!"

"Inspector?" Boggie had understood. "Yes, by all means; but who wants a doctor? Stuff and nonsense, my girl! I don't seem to have any broken bones. When I've got my bearings, I'll be right as rain."

Rosemary sought counsel of Tommy. He felt the injured woman's pulse, looked again at the bruise, and decided medical attention was not really required. They bathed her head, but at the first suggestion of getting her up to bed she strongly rebelled.

"No! I'm going to sit up now und pull myself together. Believe it or not, it takes a lot to down Boggie. Get me a cup of tea. Then I'll tell you all about it—or as much as I can."

When the young people had raced on their errands, she hoisted her ample form into a sitting posture and began righting her tumbled dress. Over her broad chest the white silk blouse she wore had fallen open in a V. Observing a small strand of real pearls Tommy remarked encouragingly that at any rate she had not been robbed.

"Robbed?" she echoed, obscurely startled.

She had not thought of this, evidently. She fingered the pearls, glanced down at the two rings she wore on the same finger with her gold wedding-band. One was the classical half-hoop of diamonds; the other an unimpressive emerald in an ugly setting. A queer expression hovered in her eyes.

"Well!" she said with a short laugh, "I must be thankful for small mercies! There, I'm feeling much better." She made a confidential appeal. "We don't want to make a song about this, you know," she resumed in an undertone. "My niece, poor child, has had quite enough shocks! She'll begin to think she's taken up with a bird of ill omen. A good thing I've a thick skull and no nerves. Once in Darjeeling . . . but that, as dear old Kipling would say, is another story. . . . Have you a cigarette?"

A true sport, Tommy reflected, as he hastened to supply her; but her manner puzzled him, and he fancied her intrepid self-command hid agitation of no common sort. He was beginning to understand the feeling the girl had about her. Unquestioningly she seemed to accept this latest outrage as part and parcel of an organised persecution directed on her and her alone. At the moment, as she puffed stoically at her cigarette, she was thinking with great concentration. He took the occasion to study her a little.

She was a sturdy, deep-bosomed woman in the latter forties—neither good-looking nor exactly plain, merely ordinary. Her face was weather-beaten and good-humoured, without vestige of make-up, her eyes light hazel-grey, with wrinkles of fun round them. There was a hint of a double chin, and at the back of her neck a firm horizontal crease, just below the clean clipped ending of her hair, which at some distant period had been brightened with henna, but was now growing out a drab brown, dry and crinkly from excess of hot waving. She struck him as eminently practical, and above all wholesome—the sort of women who has few flights of fancy, but is a good sort, living by an excellent if dull code.

Through spirals of smoke she smiled at him, warding off the questions he was wanting to ask; but he had not long to wait. Further revived by tea, she leant back in the big arm-chair to which she had been helped, and gave her story bluntly, with odd, abrupt pauses.

It was soon told. Shortly after her niece's telephone call, just as she had done preparing the tea, a postman's knock had drawn her to the door. As no letters fell through the slit, she had assumed there was a registered letter requiring signature; so she opened the door. On the threshold stood a man, but before she could form any clear impression of him he had pressed forward und struck her a powerful blow. Consciousness left her, and from then on till she heard voices in the room she had known nothing at all.

"And that," she ended whimsically, "is that. Can you clever people make sense of it?"

There was a dead silence. Rosemary drew in her breath, her eyes painfully troubled.

"And you didn't see him? His face I mean?" she asked with a strained tenseness.

"Couldn't. The sun was in my eyes."

Firmly as the answer was given, Mrs. Bellamy-Pryce seemed embarrassed. The others looked at her.

"It's fantastic!" muttered Rosemary. "Nothing taken, nothing disturbed—oh, I've had a good look, upstairs and down! Only Boggie knocked down and tied up!"

"But not killed, mark you," pointed out Rank, starkly logical. "So what, I ask you, was the object? It's not like the shootings. I, for one, fail to see any connection between these various affairs. See here, Boggie, old thing. You got some sort of glimpse of this chap. Surely you can give us a line on him?"

She shook her head—confusedly, Tommy thought—and dabbed her temple with aromatic ammonia.

"It happened so quickly," she faltered, not meeting their eyes. "Like a thunder-clap, I tell you."

"But you must have noticed something," Rank persisted. "Was he tall or short? A gentleman, or—the other kind?"

The victim moistened her lips, tried to laugh, and glanced round in a hunted fashion.

"Shabby," she admitted reluctantly. "Undersized. I . . . I rather think he was dark, and . . . and dressed in dark clothes. Yes, that's right, rather queer, shabby black clothes. There . . . there was a dirty look about him."

"Do you mean he gave you a dirty look?" hammered Rank, bent on explicitness. "Or that he looked simply unwashed?"

"Unkempt, certainly," said Mrs. Bellamy-Pryce with a chuckle to cover that seemed a growing uneasiness. "I really didn't have time to see. With my hat knocked over my eyes. . . ."

"Tramp?" Rank pursued, grinding over her like a steam roller. "Sort of customer who might mean to steal, but got the wind up over some interruption?"

Rosemary caught his arm. "Don't!" she whispered. "Can't you see she just doesn't know?"

"Well, there's no harm asking, is there? Go on, Boggie. Tell us any little thing you may have noticed."

Rosemary's aunt again exhibited that suggestion of the badgered quarry seeking to elude a pack in full cry. She had small, kindly eyes, not keenly intelligent, yet with flashes of shrewdness, and these eyes now cast furtive, worried glances at the girl on her right.

"He didn't seem exactly a vagrant," she said hesitatingly. "He might have been a gentleman—but no, it's no use! I've said all I can say, except . . . well, one little thing I did notice, now you mention it. As his arm shot out, I saw he had on gloves. Very shabby, black ones. It seemed so odd in this weather. . . ."

There fell another and far more difficult silence. Tommy saw that his nephew was quelled, and that Rosemary's face had suddenly become drained of all colour. In the strained atmosphere Mrs. Bellamy-Pryce made desperate efforts to appear natural. Reaching her capacious handbag from the piano stool, she took out a powder-pad and rubbed it energetically over her perspiring features. She then fished up a small aspirin bottle, shook it, and murmured:

"Na poo—and I would like something for this head of mine, before that inspector gets here. Children, would you mind running out and fetching me some more tablets?"

Rosemary opened her lips to speak, changed her mind and quitted the room. Without a word Rank followed. They moved, Tommy thought, like two automatons.

"Nice babes, both of them," commented Mrs. Bellamy-Pryce. "What I'd have done without them this dreadful week I can't bear to think!" She paused, watching her guest, who had wandered mechanically to the front window, and with a little gleam in her eyes continued casually, "Mr. Rostetter, I understand you come from my husband's part of Sussex. Do you happen to be acquainted with any of his people?"

"Your husband's people?" Tommy turned back contritely. He had been striving to account for his feeling of depression. Since it could not arise from the sight of the two burnished heads moving away in such intimate proximity to one another, it must, he supposed, be due to his nephew's commandeering, without leave, the borrowed two-seater. "Only, I think, your brother-in-law, the vicar. I used to spend my holidays abroad, and it's now eighteen years since I've been in Broughton-Elmtrees for more than a few days."

"Dear, woolly-lamb Cuthbert!" She smiled with indulgent affection. "Head full of butterflies. I dare say if I ran into him in Bond Street he wouldn't know me; but I spent a pleasant week at the vicarage only this

Spring. An odd lot, the Bellamy-Pryces," she mused. "A mixed bag, I call them. You've never come across . . . but no, so you've said."

Tommy had been about to mention that he used to see another brother prowling about Oxford in his own time; but Boggie, fingering a bunch of keys taken from her bag, caught his eye with a queer, guilty expression. With sudden resolution she said:

"While those two are gone, I . . . I think I'll just take a little look in my own room, upstairs. It's these keys, you know. My bag was in my hand at the time. Suppose they were borrowed and put back?"

"Do you think you can manage the stairs?"

She had risen, taken a few steps, and stopped, with a grimace.

"If you'll lend me your arm. Those wretched cords seem to have touched up my old sciatica."

Limping a trifle, but making light of it, she mounted the stairs, leaning on him for support. At the top she turned straight into a large bedroom, sunny and well-furnished, running the depth of the house and situated directly over the room they had left. At once she sank heavily on to the stool facing a silver-laden dressing-table. She unlocked a long drawer, pulling it towards her with such eagerness that her next action seemed surprising. Instead of prodding about amongst the contents, she merely sat still, gazing hard into the interior.

Tommy, behind, looked up and caught sight of her reflection in the oval mirror. The face he saw was purple and splotched with anger. Her lips were compressed, and veins at her temples stood out. Was she on the verge of a stroke? At any rate he knew that for the second time that hot June afternoon Mrs. Bellamy-Pryce, widow of the judge, had been dealt a paralysing blow.

CHAPTER FOUR

WATCHING, Tommy saw her nod, as though grimly accepting a thing half expected, but which, till positive proof confronted her, she had been loth to believe. Now, with shaking hands, she took from the drawer a worn leather brief-case, marked with the initials J.B.P. She laid it on her lap, and absently began rubbing it all over with her handkerchief.

"Don't do that!" warned Tommy sharply. "What about fingerprints?"

She jumped and for the first time met his eyes in the glass.

"What a prize idiot I am!" she cried with compunction. "I simply wasn't thinking."

Her laugh sounded unforced, but all the same he wondered. . . .

"My husband's," she explained, touching the briefcase. "I knew the moment I looked at it that it had been moved and opened with one of my keys; but if he had on gloves, there wouldn't have been any finger-prints, would there?"

"Maybe not." He was thinking that whatever marks might have been on the leather were gone by now. "But why don't you look inside the case? Something may have been removed."

"Oh, no!" She gave a shrewd chuckle. "I will look, to please you, but I can tell you in advance nothing's been taken. What he may have hoped to find simply wasn't there." She unlocked the case, shuffled through a collection of papers, and closed it again. "All in order," she declared triumphantly. "Just as I thought. I'd have given something to see his face. Really, it would have been a treat!"

Was it possible she did not realise her astounding admission? It was on the tip of Tommy's tongue to retort: "But I'm certain you did see his face—and what's more that you recognised him." The words, however, remained unspoken. It is not easy to accuse a woman who is almost a total stranger of deliberate fibbing. Besides, if this woman was fibbing, she was probably doing so from the worthiest of motives. Not very cleverly, to be sure; and if she would insist on furnishing him with proofs of her duplicity, she must take the consequences. For the moment he decided to allow her more rope.

"Do you mind my taking a mild survey of the other rooms?" he asked.

"Not in the least. I can promise you won't find anything disturbed. That is," she hastily amended, "my niece did look, didn't she?"

No, Rosemary's aunt was not an adroit liar. She did know a great deal more than she cared to say, though whether it was going to be easy to corner her he seriously doubted.

There was a bathroom next door. Tommy paused and looked in, keeping his ears alert for sounds from the adjoining room. He did not expect to make any discoveries, but he wanted to know what would happen if he left his hostess to herself. He guessed that she had got rid of their companions so as to conduct this little investigation without their knowledge. Why, then, had she permitted him to witness it? It suggested she meant to make him an ally. On the other hand, he had seen something he firmly believed was not intended for him to see—her sudden paroxysm of rage, which she had not attempted to explain. Altogether—and with particular reference to the wiping off of the brief-case—her conduct presented a rather irritating riddle. It was to be hoped the inspector in charge of the case would be less mystified than himself.

Nothing in this bathroom, with its clean mauve-bordered towels, mauve soap, bath-salts like amethyst crystals, and grey linoleum, shining like glass. Nothing at all, except . . . He stepped inside and bent over.

Below the rim of the basin lay a fluffy heap of grey ash, fallen from a cigarette. Hers? He scanned the bare spaces for a corresponding stump, found none, and started to gather up the ash and preserve it for analysis. Then he remembered that he had no right to touch possible clues. He let it lie, and turned into the smaller bedroom on the other side.

Rosemary's, obviously. It was a little untidy, but fresh and smelling faintly of the same scent pervading the hat-shop. Scarlet mules under the bed, from whose coverlet protruded the tag-end of a filmy blue nightdress. Red roses in a jar dropped petals on the carpet, letters were scattered about, and on the mantelshelf were two framed photographs—one of Rank, looking picturesque and superior, the other of the Reverend Cuthbert Bellamy-Pryce, bearing a petrifying likeness to the dog his daughter had named for him.

As he stood examining the two faces he heard the splash of water in a basin. Two minutes passed, and then, through the open door, he saw Mrs. Bellamy-Pryce emerge from the bathroom, humming to herself, and with a firm step descend the stairs.

Back he stole to the bathroom door, took a rapid glance inside. Gone! Where the pile of ash had lain all he saw was a faint, dull smear. He swore under his breath, realising that by his conscientious scruples he had perhaps lost the police a valuable clue. But had he? There was no way of knowing, any more than there was with the possible fingerprints. Maybe it was her ash.

Suddenly it seemed to him that Mrs. Bellamy-Pryce, excellent woman though she might be, held every ace in her hand. If she did not choose to be frank, what could be done about it? Nothing. Her coolness roused his antagonism. Had she not invited him here for an understood purpose? Certainly she had. Very well, then, on her head be it if what he now planned to say displeased her. He resolved to say it at once, before she attempted further tricks.

He found her in the drawing-room, sniffing at smelling salts, and gazing thoughtfully down at the handkerchief-gag and knotted cord, laid ready on a table for the police to examine. The handkerchief, probably got for sixpence out of a slot-machine, was not likely to prove helpful.

The cord, however, was another matter, for its purpose advertised itself. He was relieved to find her not touching it.

"Mrs. Bellamy-Pryce," he began quietly. "I suppose you must know the sort of impression you're giving me?"

"I beg your pardon?" She paused warily in the act of lighting a fresh cigarette. "What exactly do you mean?"

"Just this: that . . ."

There was no good going on. The gate had clicked, and through the window both saw a visitor approaching. Tommy, with slight surprise, recognised the broad-shouldered, sunburned man who had come into the restaurant, presumably scouting for Rosemary. As before he sauntered casually, with the trace of a swagger which proclaimed him, in his own estimation at least, the cock of the walk. Boggie's ragged brows met in a frown, though whether her annoyance over the interruption was real or assumed it was impossible to tell.

"Oh, dear, we can't talk much now, can we? He's seen me, so I'll have to ask you to let him in. Yes, he does know about the other affairs. Perhaps I'd better explain who he is. His name is Argus. He's quite a nice Australian my poor husband and I met on the boat. He was very decent indeed to poor old Jimbo, and naturally I've been glad to be friendly with him, particularly as he knows so few people in London."

Tommy opened the front door. He saw that the recognition was mutual, though he could not account for the curt nod and hard, suspicious stare with which he was favoured. Later he was inclined to think that this manner and the bold, off-hand way in which the Australian pushed past him into the drawing-room were defence tactics to cover an awkward self-consciousness. Mrs. Bellamy-Pryce's boat-acquaintance seemed anxious to ram home the fact that he had the right of way here. Perhaps their hostess was not altogether pleased at seeing him. At any rate, despite her explanatory words a moment before, her greeting sounded brusque and a trifle cold.

"Captain Argus, Mr. Rostetter."

Thus baldly she performed the introduction. The captain jerked his head again in Tommy's direction, perceived the presence of something amiss, and looked interrogatively at the woman seated in the arm-chair with her bottle of smelling salts to her nose. All at once his face altered.

"I say," he blurted out brusquely. "How did you come by that bash on the forehead?"

Mrs. Bellamy-Pryce shrugged ironically.

"Oh, so you have noticed it? Well, then, you may as well know our latest. The children and Mr. Rostetter arrived for tea and found me tied up and suffocating under that sofa. Oh, it's only a bruise, but . . ."

"What!"

The exclamation rent the air like a revolver shot.

Stock-still, with dropped jaw, the Australian glared in a hostile manner first at the speaker, then at his fellow-visitor.

"Are you pulling my leg?" he demanded angrily.

"Tell him," bade Mrs. Bellamy-Pryce with a brief nod to Tommy. She seemed, for some reason, to be exercising great self-control.

Tommy recounted what had happened. Captain Argus, breathing hard, kept his brown eyes glued to the other's face. He looked sceptical, accusing, and when finally convinced seemed too confounded for immediate comment. As Tommy had previously observed, he was a fine, commanding specimen of manhood, with rather an over-allowance of the animal in his make-up. The room seemed smaller since he had entered it; warmer, too, as though all the heat of outdoors were stored in his body. As he listened, a trickle of sweat ran crookedly down his forehead. He dabbed at it with the knuckles of a large, sun-reddened hand.

"What's wrong with you, Jack?" Mrs. Bellamy-Pryce prodded him with a curious, half-bantering malice. "You ought to be pleased, surely. At least we're now certain which of us they're after."

He brushed the badinage aside.

"They!" he repeated recalcitrantly. "You talk as if it was a corporation. Who the hell is this fellow? What's his filthy object in . . . in making a parcel of you, and then not . . ."

"Not finishing me off?" She stared back at him coolly. "Well, there you are. Possibly he considers me more useful alive than in my coffin. It's an idea, isn't it?"

For a second the two regarded each other unflinchingly.

"What precisely do you mean by that statement?" Argus demanded.

She shrugged again. He continued slowly: "I'm beginning to think you had considerably more than a glimpse of this blighter. No? Then it's got me beat. If any human soul can show me the connection between firing guns at your head and this last crazy business—"

He subsided into angry mutters, in the midst of which he wheeled towards the window, fists doubled, eyes lurid with resentment. The footsteps of two persons resounded on the crazy pavement outside.

"Only our inspector, complete with aide-de-camp," announced Mrs. Bellamy-Pryce calmly. "They hunt in couples, it seems. You might just fetch in the whisky and soda, Jack. I dare say we could all do with a mild nip."

At a sign from her Tommy admitted the two officers from Scotland Yard. The inspector proved to be a large, slow-moving man, dull looking, with small, uneventful blue eyes, and a heavy nose with a wart on the side. He and his younger companion declined the offer of drinks, seated themselves, and without more ado prepared to listen. This time Mrs. Bellamy-Pryce told her story with less hesitation; but she failed signally to mention her discovery upstairs. Tommy said nothing, feeling that however strange her behaviour the matter for the moment was out of his hands. The cord and gag were examined, the victim was requested to put on the hat she had been wearing when the blow was administered and the inspector's eyes were just resting meditatively on her when Rank and Rosemary appeared, stopping dead on the threshold.

At a glance Tommy knew that they had been holding grave and perturbed discussion. The girl was still very pale, her air tense and distrait. From a seat behind Mrs. Bellamy-Pryce's chair Captain Argus had risen, and tumbler in hand was gazing eagerly at her. She met his stare with blank eyes, hardly, it would seem, observing his presence. With ears grown fiery, he gulped down the remainder of his drink and sulkily turned away.

Remarks had been suspended. Without speaking Rosemary crossed to her aunt, laid a small parcel in her lap, and sat down on a straight-backed Sheraton chair close to the window. Rank took up his station by the fireplace, sent the Australian one baleful look, and then ignored him. Mrs. Bellamy-Pryce unscrewed her new bottle of aspirins, swallowed two tabloids, and pensively removed her hat. Fingering the ornament on it she said, with evident anxiety to end the ordeal:

"Well, Inspector! I suppose that's all?"

"Not quite," answered the detective stodgily. "I'd like the sergeant here to read over his notes. Will you just confirm them?"

"Oh, yes, certainly!"

She was looking nervous again. In the tone of a schoolboy reciting a lesson, the sergeant complied. By the time he reached the description of the attacker Mrs. Bellamy-Pryce had begun to fidget with her bag, looking at no one.

"I failed," droned the younger officer, "to take in any further details of his appearance, owing to the dazzling sun in my eyes, and the fact that as he struck out his left arm was thrown up in front of his face."

"Stop!" ordered the inspector. "Now, then, madam, you say this person was a little shorter than yourself. Possibly five foot four inches in height; that he seemed to be dark, wore shabby dark or actually black clothing, black gloves—and you can definitely state he threw up his arm as if to cover his face from your view?"

Rosemary's eyes were fixed steadily on her aunt, who had grown a deeper brick colour, the flush spreading down her neck. Perhaps she was only just realising that in her original account she had not mentioned this last item.

"Yes . . . oh, yes, it's quite true," Mrs. Bellamy-Pryce stammered, obviously suffering.

Rank also stared at her. Captain Argus, hand on the whisky decanter, paused, suspicion in his eyes. Rosemary, on her stiff chair, remained motionless and rigid, a figure carved in wax.

The mute anguish in her attitude went home to Tommy. There was something here which affected her far more intimately than it did her aunt, strange though it might appear—something, moreover, which he felt the police were going to find it extremely difficult to get at. From this moment onward he studied her closely and with sympathy. By the time the interview was over he had evolved a plan.

CHAPTER FIVE

ROSEMARY had not at first seen how she could manage a free evening. Sick from the shock she had received, she would have liked nothing better than to do as Rank's uncle suggested—go out, have a quiet meal, and talk matters over; but what was to be done about Boggie? It was unthinkable to leave her alone.

"It's true there's been a plain-clothes man watching the house every evening since Thursday," she whispered in the doorway. "But after all this she must want looking after a bit."

"Can't you get some one to come in for a few hours?"

"Not on such short notice, I'm afraid. You see, my aunt's been back in London only three months, and doesn't know many people. Besides, she'd have to give some explanation—and she's particularly against having this talked about. It's not been in the papers, you know, about the shootings. Both she and I didn't want my father to hear."

As though she had made an involuntary admission she dropped her eyes and felt the colour mounting to her cheeks. She wished Tommy wouldn't keep looking at her so closely. That inspector, too, seemed to have noticed something. Oh, how ghastly this was!

"See what you can do about it," Tommy said with an encouraging pressure of her hand. "You know where I'm staying. If you find you can leave her, give me a ring."

He was gone, and in another minute or so the two detectives also departed, taking the cord and handkerchief with them; and almost directly Boggie, Spartan woman, made things easy for her by announcing that after she had lain down for an hour she intended to dine at her bridge-club in Thurloe Square and play her usual game of contract.

"But, Boggie, you mustn't think of it! After that shattering experience! I gave in to you about the doctor, but I'm not sure even now I did right. I've just told Mr. Rostetter I wouldn't go out with him, because I meant to get you straight into bed."

Boggie laughed sturdily.

"Do I look such a crock? I shall be, certainly, if I start humouring myself. Don't coddle me, I know what's best. Jack's taking me and seeing me home. It was the plan in any case, wasn't it, Jack? We were going to ask you and Rank to come along with us, for dinner at least; but if you'd rather go with Mr. Rostetter, it'll come to the same thing, won't it? We'll both be in good hands."

There was no arguing with her, and really it might be the best thing, seeing she had so ably recovered, to have pleasant distraction. Captain Argus, with whom Boggie for some reason had seemed a little short, did not look overjoyed at the arrangement, but that was only to be expected. He wanted, of course, to spend the evening here with the two of them, on the chance of wangling a few moments alone with Mrs. Bellamy-Pryce's niece. Not so good, perhaps, as carting her along to one of his rather foul little night-clubs; but that feature, he must realise, was definitely out. However, he acceded with a good grace for which Rosemary felt grateful. Not a bad sort, she supposed, if only he didn't hang around so persistently and have to be held at arm's length.

One obstacle was surmounted; but there still remained Rank, perversely wanting to cancel a most important engagement in order to join his uncle and her. It was necessary to take a firm line with him.

"Idiot!" she scolded, shaking him by his neat lapels, "if you don't see that man to-night, you may lose your one and only chance of selling your interest in the shop. Of course you're seeing him—and if you don't get it all down in black and white I'll be horribly cross with you. Now go, this instant. If you don't, I'll not lunch with you to-morrow."

Rank went, like a whipped dog—and Rosemary heaved a long sigh.

She had the best of reasons for keeping Rank out of this evening's discussion. Ever since this trouble cropped up it had been touch and go his sailing for Madeira at all. Jobs were hard to come by, and if he lost this one it would be tragic. All the time they were out together this afternoon she had striven to convince him it was not she who was in danger, and that the notion he had got was a gross and preposterous mistake. She had nearly succeeded, but she felt exhausted with the effort.

Hauling people about for their own good, coaxing or manhandling them to prevent them committing blunders! Just now it seemed her chief rôle in life, and for once, worn out with the strain, she wanted to cling, be guided. Those in her vicinity had always leant heavily on her. Her father, Rank, the countess, the two girls at the hat-shop. . . . Boggie hadn't, of course. That was one reason it had been so comfortable to live with her. Boggie was staunch, independent, and usually right—so right that it made her present behaviour all the more terrifying; and yet on this single occasion, mightn't even she be misled by a tricky resemblance? Any one may imagine things, particularly if a strong prejudice is already rooted in one's mind. Too bad Rosemary herself had made it impossible for her aunt to tell her the thing she now ought to know.

"She's sacrificing herself on my account. Oh, that's perfectly evident! I can't let her go on doing it; but then, supposing she is wrong?"

In spite of the heat, cold sweat broke out all over the girl's body. Maybe it wouldn't do to let Rank's uncle know the dreadful idea which had come to her this afternoon. She wanted time to think it over. If it meant only herself—but it didn't, it involved the happiness of other people. Either way it was fraught with difficulties, for if she did not drop some hint . . .

"I'll do it," she decided in a sort of rash desperation, and going to the telephone in the hall put through her call.

As she lay in her bath, she tried gropingly to think things out. Why hadn't Boggie been killed outright? Was her being left alive the outcome of mere lucky accident? It might be, but somehow she felt there was more to it than this simple explanation. Why, even Argus had looked as though he considered the episode decidedly peculiar! She wondered if he knew a good bit more than any one else, except Boggie herself. After all, he had been on the boat. Maybe Boggie wanted to seek counsel of him this evening. That might be why she was so determined to take him off to her bridge-club. Possibly he had warned her against being alone in the house, even in daytime, and this accounted for Boggie's treating him with unusual stiffness. Good-natured though she was, very seldom ruffled, she wouldn't like having people say, "I told you so." Yes, that was probably it. At the thought Rosemary's heart sank more heavily than before.

In her own small room she dressed hurriedly in a thinner frock. She was just tidying her hair and from pure habit dabbing a spot of Anatol's especial scent—got at cost price—behind her ears, when she heard her aunt go downstairs.

"Do you honestly feel equal to going out?" she called through the open door.

"Me? Oh, I'm fit as a fiddle! Jack's just mixing a White Lady. Sure you won't have one? It will buck you up."

"Thanks, darling, you know I never do."

It was perfectly true, she hated spirits in any form; but it was also true she didn't want, just now, to have to face either her aunt or Captain Argus. Since she knew they would not leave the house till she had gone, she delayed her descent till the hands of her watch stood at eight, then slipping down went straight out to the gate to watch for Tommy Rostetter's coming.

Tommy for his London visit had taken over from a barrister-friend a small flat in the building known as Albany, facing Piccadilly, but retired into a nook. He had hardly returned thither when the telephone trilled, and picking up the receiver he heard Rosemary's voice.

"It's all right," she said briefly, "I can come."

"Eight o'clock, then," he answered, and with a feeling of deep satisfaction hung up.

He indulged in a quick shower, and had not finished dressing before another summons came, this time from the front door. He was expecting it, and therefore was not surprised to find on the threshold the large, phlegmatic figure of Inspector Headcorn.

"Come in, Inspector. I was about to concoct a dry Martini. Will you break your rule and join me?"

The call being unofficial Inspector Headcorn gratefully accepted. In the green-walled sitting-room, he lowered his bulk on to a deep sofa, and watched his host's operations with a preoccupied frown. When an iced glass was handed him, he took a sip, and began.

"I'm very glad to be having a private word with you, Mr. Rostetter. In a case of this kind it's most helpful to get the personal angle which is apt to be withheld from officials. Might I ask, first of all, how long you have known these two ladies?"

Tommy explained. His visitor looked disappointed.

"And you know only a little of their family connections?" he inquired searchingly. "Well, well! It can't be helped. However, you can at least tell me something I didn't care to go into more closely in Mrs. Bellamy-Pryce's presence. You were right, of course, about the cord being the sort used for deep-sea fishing, and about its having been in salt water. What I want to know is, how were the knots placed?"

"Behind the body," answered Tommy promptly and without astonishment. "They'd have taken some undoing."

"I see." A dull blue eye swivelled round on him. "Should you say, then, that it was an utter impossibility for the victim to have tied them herself?"

"A total impossibility," declared Tommy firmly. "As a matter of fact, I've considered it, and when you said you were coming round to see me I guessed you would ask that very question. It's no good, Inspector, those strands of cord were too tight to have been tied in front and slipped round. She couldn't have managed it."

"Humph!" grunted the other in the discouraged tone of one for whom a tentative theory has been knocked out. "And you think when you released her she was just recovering consciousness?"

"She gave me that impression. She seemed genuinely dazed, though less injured than I expected. It's a fairly nasty bruise, of course."

"Oh, quite!" The inspector rubbed the wart on his nose and looked as though trying to reconcile various rather glaring discrepancies. "Oh, well," he continued, "I suppose we must take it the attack occurred in some such manner as described, and that the blow, supplemented by moral shock, rendered her unconscious for a short period. What I'd like to make sure of is the accuracy of her statement. Have you any ideas on that subject?"

Tommy hesitated. Supposing the good woman was suppressing facts in order to spare her niece some painful knowledge? If so, he would feel a scoundrel to betray her. Yet, on the other hand, he had only to recall the girl's stricken face to realise that any such attempt on the aunt's part had already defeated itself. By unskilful manoeuvres Mrs. Bellamy-Pryce had made matters worse instead of better. It was this thought which decided him.

"I think you ought to know," he said quietly, "that a portion of what happened has been kept from you. I'm quite positive, all else aside, there was a man in that house this afternoon, just before we arrived. I am also convinced beyond a doubt that Mrs. Bellamy-Pryce knows who he was."

"Ah!" The inspector set down his glass and leaned forward. "And how have you come to that conclusion?"

Tommy gave a detailed account of what happened while he and Mrs. Bellamy-Pryce were alone in the house, added the rather cryptic passage at arms between his hostess and her Australian caller, and having done waited curiously for comments. The Scotland Yard man had leant back, looking half asleep. He had missed nothing, however, as his questions presently proved.

"This is very interesting, Mr. Rostetter," he rumbled. "You say she seemed to expect to find this brief-case had been opened. You are sure she was genuinely angry?"

"It's one of the few things I am sure about," replied Tommy. "She didn't know I was watching her in the glass. Oh, that reaction was absolutely spontaneous! About her rubbing off the brief-case I simply don't know what to think. She may have done it mechanically—and that goes equally for the cigarette-ash. What chiefly puzzles me is her allowing me to go upstairs with her at all. Knowing you had been sent for I was perfectly prepared to leave everything to you."

"I am very glad you went with her," declared the Inspector, adding dispassionately that women were often capable of extremely foolish conduct, and that it would not be the first time he had been called in on an investigation involving personal safety only to find his efforts deliberately balked. "Purposely," he said, "I did not take this occasion to question the niece very closely. I thought, though, she looked very badly upset—naturally enough, in the circumstances, only I got the idea there was some reason beyond the obvious one."

It was a feeler, thrown out in hope of more admissions. Again Tommy hesitated, and again he decided that in both women's interests it was better to be frank.

"Yes," he said, "and I can place exactly the moment when the shock occurred. You see, in the beginning, her aunt assured us she had no notion whatever what this man was like. It was only when my nephew kept insisting that she let out the description she later repeated to you. That description did the damage."

The inspector's face seemed to clear. With a sprightlier air, he got up from the sofa and shook Tommy's hand.

"That is precisely what I wanted to know," he said with more animation than he had yet shown. "I'll leave you my card, in case you should wish to get in direct communication with me—though I hardly suppose, now, it will be necessary. Good-evening, Mr. Rostetter; I am greatly obliged for your help."

With these words he picked up his bowler hat and rather quickly, for one of his lethargic movements, quitted the flat. Now he was gone Tommy wondered if he ought to have mentioned his coming talk with the niece, and his fixed intention of getting from her what it seemed impossible to get from the older woman. On the whole he was not sorry he had kept silent about it. As it was he might have done a deal of mischief. Better find out a little more before he ventured further with his meddling.

Had he time far a shave? In the bathroom again he had his safety-razor in his hand when his face hardened.

"No!" he muttered determinedly, "who the hell am I to her? Merely an uncle—nearly decrepit, from her standpoint. That bit about expecting me to be older was pure eye-wash. I knew it at the time."

It cannot be denied, however, that he hunted out his favourite tie, and adjusted it with unwonted precision; and human contrariness being what it is, he had not trundled far on his way to Kensington before he was stroking his chin, clean-shaven that morning, with dubious regret. Into his mind had come the tall Australian, left a short while ago in full possession of the field. Why, he asked himself, had he conceived this brooding antipathy for a man with whom he had exchanged hardly a remark? True enough he regarded this Captain Argus as a bit of a bounder. He disliked his crude manners, still more his air of a prowling tom-cat; but were these facts sufficient to account for his present feeling of acute annoyance?

"Tommy, old son," he muttered, "you know the real reason. It lies in the other fact that this same Argus, bounder or not, chances to be the sort of male every other male distrusts on sight, simply because women of all ages and types are drawn to him as flowers to the sun. Sex-appeal, my hat! Why, the damned stuff's bursting from him at every pore! There were three wilting women in that restaurant to-day—the mannequins and the waitress. The minute he swaggered in they all livened up as though they'd been given a sniff of cocaine. What if this one girl was off-hand with him? She was worried to death—and he hadn't got her alone. That whelp Rank was watching her, jealous as blazes. What you're wondering is, has either of those two a reasonable chance?"

Whatever the case, he reflected, it could not concern him, so he would do well not to waste his speculations, and keep to the matter in hand. The mystery, he believed, would very soon be ended. Once the All Clear signal had sounded, his interest in Rank's lady-love would end too.

The sight of Rosemary, waiting by the gate, was a little disturbing to these resolutions. It was not only the fresh, powder-blue of her frock and the warm white of her bare arms which moved him. It was the glad eagerness with which, almost before he had stopped the car, she had slid in beside him, her deep breath of relief as she cast her white, woolly coat on the seat behind, and snuggled down as though his coming had taken a weight from her shoulders.

"Good work!" he said. "We'll talk as we go—and by the way, where shall it be?"

"Oh, anywhere that's cool! The river—unless you're pining for food." As they moved off she closed her eyes and sighed again, luxuriously. "Oh, what heaven to be out of it all, if only for one evening! If you don't mind, I'd rather not speak of things till we've got where we're going."

"Right, there's no hurry. But what's happening with your aunt?"

She told him how matters had worked out. Argus, he perceived grudgingly, had his uses. As for Mrs. Bellamy-Pryce, whatever her faults, she was the true sport he had believed her.

At Bray they found an inn of the sort that was unlikely to contain any of their acquaintances, and managed, as it was late, to secure a table by the railing of a verandah overlooking the river. The water, twilit and laced with the dark shadows of trees, flowed noiselessly below. Dinner had been ordered, but still Rosemary had not made her disclosure. Now the moment had come, she was finding her task very difficult.

"Now, then," said Tommy quietly. "Why did that description upset you?"

She had taken a crusty roll in her hand. Her fingers tightened on it till it crumbled into bits.

"What a lot you notice!" she murmured almost inaudibly, and sat staring down at the fragments beside her plate. Rather breathlessly she added, "Poor old Boggie! She never meant to make that floater. It just slipped out in spite of her. I expect you noticed that, too?"

"Certainly I did. From that and other things I've come to believe she's hell-bent to shield this person, whoever he may be. Are you going to let her? Because there's danger in it, you know. The next time may succeed. If he's sane, he must be locked up. If he's a lunatic, then we must have him certified. Who is he? For of course you know."

"It's not so simple as you think," she muttered, painfully distressed. "Boggie may be only guessing about it, and if that's so, my saying anything will make things ever so much worse. Give me just another minute to think."

She had lowered her head so that her face was hidden from him. A pale, sleepy moth drifted in from the outer night and lit on the floating tendrils of her hair. Psyche with her wings, he thought, and could not bear to disturb either the frail visitor or her. Presently she looked up. The moth flew away. She straightened her shoulders, ate a bit of the crust, and spoke as steadily as though she were remarking on the weather.

"Have you ever," she asked, "come across my uncle Gavin?"

CHAPTER SIX

GAVIN! That was the name Tommy had been lashing his memory to recall. Gavin Bellamy-Pryce, an odd, wizened figure of a man, dodging furtively in and out the Bodleian Library. . . .

"He used to be one of our exhibits at Oxford," he told her. "I never met him, though. He'd some sort of archaeological hobby. What was it—totems, tabus?"

"Yes, primitive devil worship. It's his life passion. I believe the book he's preparing, if he ever finishes it, will be about twice as long as *The Golden Bough*. It's all about the rule of fear. I've made him tell me about it, when I've caught him in the right mood."

"Then you do see him?" asked Tommy, watching her.

"Oh, yes; but he's very seldom in England. I've always been rather fond of Uncle Gavin, whatever some of the family may feel about him. You see, he's an eccentric. I personally don't mind that. In fact, I've been rather proud of having an eccentric for an uncle, seeing he's one who does interesting things and gets about the world on twopence in the most extraordinary way. Maybe he is a bit screwy, but what of it? I can't call a man mad simply because he won't cut his hair or trim his nails, and mooches about looking like a—a funeral mute that's been left overnight in the rain."

The little, nervous rush of the last words drew Tommy's eyes towards her with quickened curiosity. She avoided them, continuing with a rather strained casualness.

"I sometimes wonder if many families are like ours—you know, all seething with hate and queer, petty jealousies."

"Are the Bellamy-Pryces like that?" he inquired.

"Are they! Ask your brother—ask any one who knows them. Let's take them in turn, just to show you what I mean. First, there's my grandfather—bitter against all his children, hasn't spoken to one of them for years. Even now, mewed up at Black Gables, with a trained nurse looking after him—practically dying, in fact—he still manages to send abusive letters to each of us—through his solicitor, as a rule. Boggie's had them, though she's only a daughter-in-law. Even I, whom he scarcely knows, had one forwarded to me only the other day."

"You? But that's fantastic, surely!"

She had laid down her fork, for a moment wrapped in her own troubled thoughts. He had the feeling she did not want to pursue the subject of her letter.

"Grandfather is fantastic," she said presently. "Hatred of his kin has become an obsession with him. Take that away, and he'd crumble to dust in two minutes. He can't not leave us his money. It's all tied up in an unbreakable entail; so he takes it out in keeping his sons on the shortest possible commons, and hurling abuse at them. Oh, Grandfather's not really important! I mention him merely because I consider him answerable for so much. Hatred breeds hatred, doesn't it?"

"You think his has done that, do you?"

"I'm sure of it. Take my uncles. The oldest was Charles, whom I never saw. He was naturally expected to follow his father in the tea business—take orders for twenty years or so, and by painful degrees, like the frog jumping out of the well, attain the dizzy eminence of a company director, sit on boards, wear a top hat. Well, Charles wouldn't—and that did for him. He shipped for the colonies, and was lost sight of, and very soon he died. He'd a wife, I believe, but no children. I think the wife died, too; so that wipes Charles out.

"Next, Uncle James—Boggie's husband. He likewise incurred wrath by turning down tea, only he distinguished himself by becoming, in time, an Indian judge. I dare say he was a good man. Boggie says he was; but oh, he had a fish's blood in his veins—cold, carping, self-righteous. He sneered at my father, loathed his brother Gavin like poison, and led poor Boggie a hell of a life. Or so I imagine. Boggie's far too loyal to admit it. More hatred, you see."

"But your father?" suggested Tommy. "Don't tell me he shares in the family sport."

"Daddy?" Rosemary's eyes grew soft. "Daddy's utterly incapable of hating any one, even his own father. It just wouldn't occur to him, poor lamb! No, he's the exception. He sympathised with Charles, admired James, is absolutely devoted to Gavin. He wants protection, of course. Any one as unsuspecting as that does want it. My fear these past few days has been that some misguided busybody will tell him what's going on here and bring him trotting up to town all frightened and bothered.

You'll not write him, will you? Promise you won't?" Rosemary begged with sudden anxiety.

Touched by her attitude towards the father who seemingly occupied the position of a helpless child, Tommy gave his word, and gently led her back to the main theme. Was Gavin full of this same unreasonable hate?

"Undoubtedly." She whispered it with reluctant conviction. "Though I've never known whether it was directed towards any one person in particular. Uncle Gav's a mystery man. All very easy to call him mad. Boggie, with her conventional outlook, would think that of a person who travelled steerage when his own brother, a judge, was on the same boat in first class; but . . ."

"Hold on!" Tommy interrupted. "Was this the last voyage back from India? The one your Uncle James died on?"

"Yes, but that's nothing to do with it," she answered so firmly that it was evident he had touched a sensitive spot. "Uncle James died of heart failure. He was already in a very groggy condition, or he wouldn't have come home. Uncle Gavin came aboard at Bombay. He'd been poking about those dead cities on the—what's the river I mean?"

"The Indus?"

"Yes—the cities they're excavating. If he went steerage it was because he'd no money. I understand he and Uncle James met only once, and . . . and before anything happened. Boggie, when she first landed—I hadn't ever known much about her till this time—started telling me how she came into her husband's cabin and found the two brothers spitting at each other like cats on a back fence. They always did, it seems, and I don't think Boggie knew what they were quarrelling about. She shut up directly she saw how I felt about Uncle Gavin, and hasn't uttered a syllable since. I had nearly forgotten it till this afternoon. The . . . the black gloves . . . he will wear them, you know, even in the hottest weather; and then her unwillingness to tell us anything, her getting so flustered. . . . She didn't want me to know he'd tried to hide his face from her. Oh, Mr. Rostetter, now do you see?"

"You mean," said Tommy slowly, "that if it should turn out to be Gavin it would cause a particularly ugly scandal."

He was thinking with discomfort of the inspector's confident leave-taking. If Gavin were arrested, his would be the blame. . . .

"Oh, worse than scandal!" Rosemary's voice shook. "How would you feel if your own flesh-and-blood uncle, whom you've stuck up for and thought of as a wonderful scholar, suddenly developed into a fiend who wants to murder another person you're fond of? And that's only the smallest part of it. My poor little father! It would break him up, utterly. I don't think he'd ever get over the grief and shame of it. Oh, the whole thing's too hideous!"

"It seems fairly evident your aunt doesn't want to bring a charge against her brother-in-law," remarked Tommy thoughtfully.

"She doesn't—and surely you understand why? She's hoping it's just a sort of brain-storm. She's trying to say nothing rather than make the rest of us miserable. The trouble is, of course, that if she goes on being noble she may be killed. Oh, don't think I don't realise it! That's why I'm telling you."

"Your aunt has iron nerves," commented Tommy dryly.

"Boggie? She's marvellous!" Unexpectedly Rosemary broke into laughter. "I wish you could have seen her when that first shot came crashing in on us. My instinct was to burrow. I did it, too, right under the piano; but Boggie didn't. I can see her now, standing up straight, her face as red as a turkey cock. I could have sworn she wasn't frightened so much as furious. I had to hold on to her to keep her from rushing out at once—and it was much the same the second evening. I've never seen such pluck. I didn't know it existed."

Tommy watched her slightly hysterical mirth subside. Had Boggie known Gavin was likely to attack her? Anger instead of alarm looked queer; but it was anger she had displayed when she discovered the brief-case had been tampered with. He wondered if there was any connection.

"I believe you said there were no footprints in the garden. Not likely to have been, on that dry stone pavement. What about the two bullets?"

"Oh, those were dug out of the wall at the back. They went through the other window, you know. The inspector has them. I heard him say they were fired from a Smith and Wesson revolver—a '45."

An American gun. It might prove a useful clue. He was silent, once dwelling on the seeming paradox of Mrs. Bellamy-Pryce's latest escape from death, and on the enigmatic answer given to the Australian. He roused to ask whether, if it was her uncle, she could think of any motive. She shook her head, not very convincingly, he thought.

"I don't know anything more than I've told you. No one pretends to understand Uncle Gavin. One thing's certain: Only Boggie can help us. You hadn't a chance with her to-day, had you? I was thinking you might have another go at her to-morrow morning—if it's not too much to ask. Would you awfully mind?"

He intended this very thing, as the hard glint in his eye showed.

"But if she says it was your uncle, what then?"

"I. . . . I can't imagine what we ought to do! Couldn't you look Uncle Gavin up, sound him very discreetly, and . . . but need we look further ahead than that? I'm sure you'd know the best course to pursue."

Tommy's mouth twitched. He longed to retort: "My good girl, if I find your uncle suffering from maniac depressive insanity, my best course will be through the window." However, he did not say it. For one reason, her trust in him was too flattering; for another, he saw too clearly how much she needed help. He contented himself with inquiring when she had last seen the relative in question.

"About six weeks ago. I suppose daddy must have told him where we were. Anyhow, one Sunday, early in the afternoon, he paid us a short call. It wasn't a happy occasion."

"Did he quarrel with your aunt?"

"Oh, no, he hardly spoke to her! It was what one felt under the surface. I couldn't think why he came. He was in one of his most biting moods. Satanic, Boggie called him, but as I've said she's prejudiced. Captain Argus was there. He'd been lunching with us and he went away at the same time as Uncle Gavin. I remember that, because . . . but it's of no consequence," she ended hurriedly.

"Why do you remember it?" Tommy insisted.

"It's just that I caught what Captain Argus whispered to Boggie the moment before. He said, 'I don't care two hoots who he is. I'm jolly well going to see that chap off the premises!' It made me absolutely furious. What business had he to speak like that of my uncle?"

Tommy had taken out his fountain-pen and was drawing squiggles on the menu.

"This Captain Argus," he hazarded idly. "A fairly frequent occurrence, isn't he?"

She flushed faintly and looked away, over the darkening river.

"Captain Argus is Boggie's friend, not mine," she answered with reserve. "I've tried to be decent to him, naturally, on her account."

So it was like that! Tommy felt distinctly cheered as he asked what the Australian was like at close range.

"How should I know?" She kept her eyes averted. "I suppose you ask that because you saw how Rank detests him. He does hang round rather a lot, maybe because he's at a loose end, hunting a job, and has nowhere better to go. Boggie's bighearted and hospitable. She'd mother any stray dog; but of course Argus does play awfully good bridge. She and Uncle James played with him every evening on the boat, that is when Uncle James felt well enough. After Uncle James died, he fetched and carried for her. She's grateful to him, I suppose; but then in any case she likes having young people around."

"Young! I don't know that I'd call this Argus a fledgling."

"He can't be more than thirty-five or six. That's young, surely."

More exhilarated than he would have cared to admit, Tommy carefully drew two horns on his last squiggle and shifted his reflections to another quarter.

"By the way, you tell me your servant was sacked shortly before the shootings occurred. What was the reason?"

"Why on earth do you want to know that?" she opened amused eyes. "It was because Boggie discovered her wearing one of my hats on her afternoon out. I'd have winked at it. Vera wasn't a bad girl; but you see Boggie's got strict notions. I came home and found her already gone."

"I was wondering," said Tommy, "if she had noticed any strange man loitering about. She may have done, you know. How can one get hold of her?"

"Let me think . . . Boggie engaged her through . . . yes, I remember, it was Mrs. Coates' Agency, in Sloane Street. Maybe they would know where she's gone. Her other name is . . . I've got it! Coldbottom."

"I refuse to believe it."

"It's a fact, I saw it on her reference. Vera Coldbottom."

Having jotted down this information, Tommy inquired where Gavin was to be found; but on this point Rosemary was quite ignorant. Her uncle, as part and parcel of his oddity, always kept his domicile a dark secret.

"I don't like asking daddy. I can only tell you he's a member of the Symposium Club."

Tommy folded the menu and slipped it into his pocket.

"You won't like what I'm going to say now," he resumed diffidently. "I must say it, all the same. Smoke?"

She accepted a cigarette, let him light it for her, and eyed him apprehensively.

"Well, what is it?" she whispered.

"Just this: Wouldn't it be a good notion if you went to live somewhere else?"

For perhaps thirty seconds she made no reply. Her eyes, fixed on the glowing tip of her cigarette, slowly gravitated towards his.

"No!" she declared firmly. "Do you think I could leave Boggie at a time like this, after she's been so splendid to me? It would be worse than cowardly. It would be inhuman."

"But surely she could find another friend to live with her?"

"But could she? I doubt it. I've told you she's stayed out of England too long to have many friends here. No, I simply couldn't let her down. For one thing, till my grandfather dies, she's not any too well off. She took this house on the understanding that I'd share expenses. It's not for long, anyhow, because she's giving it up in August, and going into the country. Are you worrying about me? There's no need, now we've got the plain clothes man stationed out in front."

"He can't be kept there forever," Tommy objected.

"I know, but we'll be getting in a new maid almost any day now. Oh, it'll be all right! I'm not one tiny bit frightened, really I'm not."

"Then you won't consider making a move? I'm sorry. I was only thinking that Rank will be gone after Tuesday, I'll very soon have to shove off to Paris, and . . . but I'm forgetting Argus. He'll be on the mat, I suppose?"

"He's offered to sleep at the house," remarked Rosemary detachedly. "Only Boggie won't hear of it. I say, what's the time?"

He showed her his watch. It was still not late, but he could see she wanted to change the subject. There was no good arguing any more. She was resolved to stick by her aunt and if more danger came to share it. As she leant back and rested her arm along the balustrade, her eyes, however troubled, were determined. Tommy, gazing at her white, trailing hands and the ruffled gold of her hair, reflected that here, in this slender girl's body, dwelt courage and loyalty of no mean order. What a wife she would make! Rank, if he got her, would be lucky beyond all deserts. Was she thinking of Rank now? She had not said no. . . .

CHAPTER SEVEN

"*UGH*, it's like an oven in here!"

The drawing-room they had entered was hermetically closed. Boggie had not returned, and all was as she had left it, even to the empty cocktail glasses on the piano. Tommy threw open the front window, and a welcome breeze blew in. He paused, watching the flutter of the damask curtains.

"See here," he said suddenly. "Was there any wind on the nights those shots were fired?"

"Was there?" Rosemary tried to recall. "I think so. Yes, I seem to see the curtains blowing apart, as they're doing now. Each time I was playing on the piano. I do it very badly, but Boggie likes hearing me. The second night, you see, we felt so certain the other shot had been meant for some one else we weren't being careful."

"Just sit down on that piano stool," he suggested.

"That's it. Now, where was your aunt sitting?"

She pointed towards the lower portion of the room. "She was writing letters at the dining-room table. It was the purest luck she happened to move—reaching out for her address book, I think. Where are you going?"

"Don't stir," he said. "I want to take a look in from outside."

The crazy-pavement extended to a narrow area, between which and the wall was a space of perhaps three feet. When he had knelt down on the edge he could not only with ease reach inside the window, but had only to wait for a puff of wind to see most of the room beyond through the central parting of the curtains. The place Mrs. Bellamy-Pryce had occupied was plainly visible; but the girl at the piano he could almost have touched!

"Come out!" he called briskly.

"What is it?" Rosemary asked as she joined him. "You sound tremendously pleased over something."

"I am. Just take a look—now, while the curtains are moving. He must have been aiming at your aunt. If it had been you, he couldn't possibly have missed."

"But had you any doubt of it after this afternoon? I hadn't."

"Well," he excused himself lamely, "it's good to have this proof."

To be candid, he had felt a doubt, till this moment. Now, he was thinking, he would be perfectly content if only Rosemary could be persuaded to separate from her aunt. The trouble was it would be so easy for her to become involved, perhaps disastrously, in her companion's danger.

He remained crouched down, examining speculatively the two bullet holes in the curtains. Rosemary had knelt beside him, so close that her bare arm brushed his shoulder, and the scent of her hair was in his nostrils. In the warm darkness a bond seemed to have knit them together. So strongly was he conscious of it that it was hard to resist the impulse to slip his arm round her body and press it to his own. Not to do so seemed denying nature; yet he did not dare, as he would have done with so many girls—far too many, in these free and easy times!

"I suppose," she said thoughtfully, "that moving curtain deflected his aim. Why didn't he use the open space?"

"It would have been surer, certainly," he admitted. "But in that case you might have caught sight of his hand."

"I hadn't thought of that."

She looked suddenly at him, then away. He knew what was in her mind. If she had seen a hand in a shabby black glove, she might have guessed whose it was.

A step sounded on the walk behind them. Something clicked, and with startling abruptness they found their two figures picked out by a shaft of dazzling light. With a gasp, Rosemary scrambled to her feet, and now, without offence, Tommy's arm closed round her. As they stared, half blinded by the glare, an apologetic laugh reached them, and in the same instant the light vanished. An obscure form creaked forward.

"Sorry, miss! I thought I'd best see what was going on. Nothing wrong, I hope?"

It was the plain clothes man. They reassured him, and he told them he had been keeping under cover of the carriage-way two houses below. He lingered, evidently glad to break the monotony of his vigil, and commented on the number of cars which had been backfiring in the neighbouring streets.

"If it was like that those two nights," he remarked, "it's easy to see how it was no one paid attention to the shots. All these radios, too, make a difference. I notice," he continued glancing at the darkened house opposite, "that they all keep their curtains drawn in this street, even on a warm night. That will explain why your chap wasn't seen making off. What one would like to know is, was he counting on that fact?"

Rosemary glanced at Tommy, but said nothing. Their visitor took it upon himself to make his meaning more clear.

"What I'm getting at is, there's a deal to suggest he knew this neighbourhood well, and not only that but the run of this particular household. It's not up to me to mention it, but that maid that was dismissed—think she might have tipped him off a bit?"

"Oh, I can't believe that!" cried Rosemary decidedly. "She was a very simple sort of girl, perfectly honest. Or rather," she corrected herself, "it's not as though we'd had anything stolen, is it?"

"You never know. She might have given information without realising, say in the event of his being a . . ." The Yard man had broken off to listen. Along the quiet length of Victoria Grove voices approached. They sounded earnest, and that of the man held a note of sulky protest. The two speakers came abreast of the gate, stopped still, and peered suspiciously into the scrap of garden. A jovial laugh rang out. It was Boggie's. As though a brief alarm had been removed, she finished an interrupted sentence, throwing it over her shoulder to her stalking escort.

"It had to be a spade," she said dogmatically, and then, walking a little stiffly, she entered her domain and chaffingly greeted the group inside. "You three did give me a turn. Is this a secret conclave? Oh, I see, Mr. Rostetter is doing a bit of detecting. And is this our watch dog? Good-evening."

She held out her hand. The plain clothes man took it and congratulated her on her lucky break. As she stood there solid and self-assured, it was hard to believe that only eight hours ago she had been taken for dead.

"A boring job for you, isn't it, officer?" she went on cheerfully. "And a thirsty one, I dare say. What do you say to joining us in a glass of ale?"

The plain clothes man grinned and succumbed to the temptation. As the party filed indoors, Tommy saw that Argus's hot brown eyes remained fastened on Rosemary with an expression lustful, fascinated, but baffled.

"Look lively, Jack!" Mrs. Bellamy-Pryce jogged her companion's elbow good-naturedly. "You know where the ale is kept. Fetch some up, will you?"

She led the way into the drawing-room, offered her guests cigarettes, and settled comfortably into her favourite chair.

"Well!" she exclaimed. "And what new theories have you been concocting? Stop, though! Don't tell me, or I shan't sleep a wink. I've come in feeling on top of the world, with two pounds twelve in winnings which I mean to lay out on a hat, if my niece's precious sale can furnish me a bargain. Nothing can happen while you're outside, eh, officer?"

Tommy looked thoughtfully at her complacent features and firm, weather-beaten throat. She was neither young, handsome nor smart, but her wholesome vigour and fine jauntiness sent out a magnetic attraction, like a warm handclasp. He was sure that most men would feel instantly at ease with her—expand, be at their best, even as the gratified Yard man was now doing. It was a quality he had often observed in Anglo-Indian women. As he listened to the jolly patter of platitudes, he found himself according her honest admiration. Commonplace she might be, too limited in ideas and a shade hearty for his own taste, but after her fashion she was a thoroughly likeable woman. He did not relish the prospect of bullying her, as he might have to do to-morrow. Still, if she would persist in her wrong-headed altruism, she must be brought to book. . . .

Just as the cold ale was foaming invitingly into glasses, Rank walked in with a face of concentrated gloom. Rosemary who had hardly spoken, laid hold of him with a fiercely "whispered inquiry."

"Oh, yeah?" he retorted. "Well, then, you're wrong. I've got his cheque in my pocket. Does that satisfy you?"

"Oh, Rank, then there's nothing to stop you getting off!" Her eyes shone softly as she squeezed his unresponsive hand. "Thank God, for that!"

Captain Argus looked smoulderingly at the pair, in his face a medley of emotion struggling for first place. Tommy understood, for he likewise was wondering just what meaning to attach to the girl's evident relief. Was she glad to be rid of Rank, or pleased at this new step towards final union with him? Suddenly deflated, he finished his drink and said good-night; but as he reached the gate Rosemary ran after him.

"You will come to-morrow?" she begged anxiously. "If I promise to leave Boggie alone with you?"

"Certainly. I'll be here at eleven."

"Oh, darling, bless you!"

Her voice broke, and her hand clung to his with a swift caress. Then she was gone.

In bed, too keyed-up for sleep, Tommy tingled in every section of his body—tingled as he had not done since—but no, even then it had not been like this.

A moment later, revulsion took him. These darlings skimming lightly back and forth—what did they mean? Merely the small currency of to-day . . . except when spoken to one's self. Which was absurd. Here was a supremely desirable girl, not more than twenty-three, a girl he had reason to know was dallying with thoughts of his own callow nephew. Was she in the least likely to think of him as anything but an obliging, middle-aged . . .

But was this so? Vain delusion though it might prove, she treated him as an equal in age. She called thirty-six young, and he was only thirty-eight. Moreover, despite her youth, she was not one of the young things falsely termed "bright." She did not share their blank stares, pity-ingly raised brows, damning silences. Sophisticated, perhaps; but it was impossible to think of her as stale. On the contrary, she had enthusiasms, a heart brimming over with kind impulses, and no insincerity that he could detect. Therein, of course, lay the danger. It was as well he had seen it in time, for his was a free spirit, and he had no wish to disarrange the agreeable serenity of his life. Anyhow, he hadn't the suspicion of a chance. Was it that thought which was keeping him awake?

A cold shower and a punishing rub-down worked wonders. Under the influence of these and a stiff whisky his iron-set jaw relaxed, and in another twenty minutes his slumber was sound.

*

Mrs. Bellamy-Pryce, at sight of her Sunday morning caller, wore the air of one trapped for a fell purpose. When her niece sauntered parkwards and Tommy settled down again her nervousness increased.

"It's really topping of you to let us take up so much of your time," she said rather too heartily. "Isn't your stay in London almost over?"

"Unfortunately, yes," he admitted, adding that Paris would be scorchingly hot. "But you, I imagine, don't trouble about heat?"

"Me?" She gave her infectious chuckle. "Why, I was just going to try a little snifter to thaw me out. Will you join me?"

She took a long time over the mixing, staving him off, as he well knew. At last, glass in hand, she resumed her seat and chattered animatedly about Ceylon. He waited till she paused, and then mentioned her husband's death aboard ship.

"It was heart, wasn't it?"

"Yes," she answered, and took a sip of her gin and vermouth.

He was relieved to find she could touch on the sad event quite easily. Poor old Jimbo, she said, would slog too hard. Over-conscientious, always. Only the certainty of collapse had forced him to apply for sick leave, and even so he had left it too late. Hearts do turn wonky when you've lived on quinine for thirty-odd years. Jimbo's had been in a very serious state for some time.

"It was in the Red Sea it happened." James's widow gave a thoughtful twitch to her hat and wiped the moisture from the coarse down at the corners of her mouth. "He'd been feeling better, and after a sizzling day we'd just had a jolly foursome of bridge—Jimbo, the ship's doctor, Jack Argus, and me. Jimbo went to his cabin. I took a short turn on deck, then went below to mix him his little night-cap. I found him doubled over the wash basin, gasping for breath."

"Did he die quickly?" asked Tommy as she halted.

"In an hour's time. He never spoke again, although he wanted to badly, poor dear!" Boggie hesitated, choosing her words with care. "I got him into his berth and sent the steward racing for the doctor. While I was measuring out the drops we kept for these attacks, he made the most pathetic efforts to tell me something. He got quite cross when I couldn't understand. Somehow he'd managed to get hold of an old briefcase from the floor and push it into my hands. I suppose that was too much for him. He fell back unconscious, just as the doctor came in. So you see, I never have known just what he had on his mind."

With slightly unsteady fingers Mrs. Bellamy-Pryce lit a cigarette. Although she had given her account with the strict avoidance of emotion typical of her caste, her manner now suggested she had let slip rather more than she had intended, and that she was hoping it had passed unnoticed.

"This brief-case," said Tommy bluntly. "Was it the one I saw?"

He half believed she was going to deny it. However, with a doubting glance, she answered: "Well, as a matter of fact, it was," and sat drumming on the arm of her chair. "I kept tight hold of it," she went on. "And in the morning I gave it to the purser to lock up in his safe. It stayed there till we landed."

"But you looked through it, I suppose?" inquired Tommy. He was thinking that for all her feminine contradictions Boggie was a practical woman.

"Oh, yes! There was nothing in it except a few old deeds and purely personal letters. Why my husband wanted me to have it I couldn't at all make out. Still, he was an exceedingly cautious man."

Had she totally forgotten her admission? It would seem that she had.

"There must have been some paper you thought it wise to remove," Tommy objected. "You certainly gave me that impression yesterday. Mightn't it help matters if you told me what it was?"

"Did I say paper? I can't have done!"

"Perhaps you didn't specify a paper. We'll call it an object. Anyhow, there was something you took out, something the person who attacked you hoped to find."

She was eyeing him with all her former confusion.

"I . . . I may have been utterly mistaken," she stammered. "Really, Mr. Rostetter, it can't do any good to . . ."

"You wanted my advice," he broke in firmly. "If you refuse to be frank with me, how can I give it?"

"Well, then, it was a knife," she burst out hurriedly. "Not my husband's. I'd never seen it before. I could swear it hadn't been there that morning when I put away a transfer slip Jimbo asked me to take care of. How it had come to be in the brief case I haven't a notion."

"A knife! What sort of knife?"

"Oh, just a cheap, sharp, dagger sort of knife. One sees scores of them in the native bazaars."

She had upset her glass. Energetically she set about wiping the sticky drops from her skirt.

"I see. And where is this knife? I'd like to have a look at it."

"I'm afraid that's impossible. That is . . ." she laughed apologetically, "I've such a horror of knives. I chucked this one overboard."

CHAPTER EIGHT

"YOU what?"

Tommy glared at her. Overboard!

"Was it idiotic of me?" Mrs. Bellamy-Pryce murmured contritely. "Jack Argus was extremely annoyed about it; but really what was the object of keeping a thing like that? There was no reason to suppose my husband had been attacked. I didn't even know if it was the knife he was trying to tell me about. There was nothing to suggest it."

"The idea evidently occurred to you," said Tommy dryly. "May I ask why?"

"Only because the doctor—all of us, in fact—wondered if Jimbo had been given any kind of shock. He'd been feeling so much better."

Tommy was wearying of all this. But for his promise to Rosemary he would have felt tempted to walk straight out of the house. Tersely he informed her that he had heard about the judge's quarrel with his younger brother Gavin, noted her startled expression, and asked pointedly when the meeting between the two had taken place.

"Oh, quite three days before! I admit my husband seemed upset at the time, but he had got comfortably over it."

"Do you think there can have been another quarrel, ending in the heart-attack?"

"At midnight? I don't see how. My brother-in-law was travelling steerage, you know. It wouldn't have been possible for him to visit the upper cabins as late as that—or indeed at any time, without the captain's permission."

"Then you did inquire into it?"

"Rather naturally, I did. Having seen them going for each other hammer and tongs that other time, I—well, I shan't say I didn't think of it. However, I couldn't prove anything."

"And you can't tell me what the trouble was between them?"

She shook her head, uncomfortably, he thought.

"Jimbo wouldn't say. He was very close about certain matters. I knew, of course, how put out he had been to see his brother coming aboard at Bombay with a pack of native riff-raff. After that one talk he declared he never wanted to set eyes on Gavin again; and he also said that if Gavin supposed any member of the family would lend him money he must be madder than we imagined."

So Gavin had tried to borrow money!

"See here, Mrs. Bellamy-Pryce," Tommy said quietly. "I am going to ask you to give me a perfectly straight answer. Was it your brother-in-law who attacked you yesterday afternoon?"

She gave a dismayed gasp. In one instant all her fictitious composure had deserted her.

"Oh, what a fool, what a miserable fool, I've been!" she lamented. "I see now exactly why you're asking me these questions. Something I've said has given my niece this notion, and she's sent you to tackle me about it. Poor little Ro, she has a child's romantic attachment for her uncle. I guessed that, a bit too late, I'm afraid; but if I've let her imagine—"

"Then it was Gavin?"

Her eyes wavered from his.

"But I don't know who it was!" she protested wretchedly. "Really, my dear man, we've no right to jump to conclusions. I described him as best I could, but—" She broke off, dabbing her warm face with her handkerchief. "Fancy," she muttered, "the horrid mess for all of us if I brought a—an accusation against my husband's next of kin, and then found I was mistaken!"

He was sure that in her own mind she was convinced it was Gavin. It was her unwillingness to admit it that put him in a quandary. Could he by any possibility pin her down to one concrete statement? He was beginning to doubt it, but he tried again.

"If, as we're assuming, these three attacks were perpetrated by the same person, it's very hard, as you must see, to make sense of them. We can say the two failures with the revolver were due to mischance. Yesterday, however, it would have been a simple matter to kill you, if that had been the intention—simpler, indeed, than binding you up in that elaborate fashion. There's hardly any need to go into it in detail. What I'm trying to point out is that if it was Gavin, and he merely wanted to recover his knife, shooting you from outside wouldn't have helped him accomplish his purpose. He would have had to shoot your niece as well, and then risk being found on the scene by any neighbours who rushed in. Now then, can you offer any explanation which will make these contradictions hang together?"

He saw he had only succeeded in confusing her still further.

"I'm afraid I can't," she said ruefully. "God knows I've tried! All I really know is my brother-in-law's very odd reputation. After the things one's heard, one could believe anything of him."

"Should you say he was doing all this merely by way of sadistic persecution?"

"Perhaps. We've always said Gavin was Satan in the flesh," Boggie stirred uneasily in her chair. "Although, to be sure, there might be an explanation. No," she pulled up in haste, "better call him mad. It will save a deal of trouble."

"What reason?" urged Tommy unyieldingly, "don't forget, the motive's all important."

"Must I—? Oh, well! Apart from detesting me—why, I've never known, except that James and I were one—it is certainly true that if I were got rid of Gavin would reap a material advantage. After my father-in-law dies, of course."

"Oh! So that's how it is? I'd rather imagined Gavin Bellamy-Pryce as not at all a mercenary person."

"Then why try to borrow from my husband?" she retorted shrewdly. "No, Gavin may doss with natives and disgrace his relatives in other ways, but these expeditions of his do cost money, you know. Central Africa, the South Seas—why, he's always on the move! When Sir Osmund's estate is divided up—death duties will carve a big slice off it, make sure of that—all Gavin will get will be a much-depleted third. If one of us dies, he'll come in for half."

Tommy at last saw daylight. It did not clear up everything, but after a moment's thought he believed it could be made to serve. At all events his own course lay straight before him.

"See here, Mrs. Bellamy-Pryce," he said gravely, "if what you're telling me is fact, you are still in very serious danger. In justice to yourself you ought to make a clean breast of this to the police, and without delay. You may say I have no right to interfere, but whatever risks you may choose to take on your own account, there's always your niece to consider. Surely you realise how very foolishly you're behaving towards her?"

"Rosemary? But Gavin wouldn't harm her! There'd be no point in it. Till her father dies, she doesn't touch a penny."

"While she continues to live with you, there's bound to be danger. Suppose she had moved a few inches either of those nights? She'd have got the bullet meant for you. However, that's not entirely what I'm referring to. I understand perfectly that you're trying to spare her feelings. Well, it's too late for that now. She knows. And in addition, what if you are murdered? That would cause her infinitely worse pain than having her uncle arrested."

Mrs. Bellamy-Pryce looked badly shaken by these arguments. Incoherently she muttered that she had not quite faced up to the possible outcome.

"I've felt a brute to let the poor child in for this; but what can I say to her, even now? It's not as though I were sure. Believe me, Mr. Rostetter, I'm not. Only last night I begged her to leave here, just in case of more disturbances. It was no good, she wouldn't hear of it."

"You don't surprise me," said Tommy. "Well, then! That very refusal of hers must show you your responsibility."

"It makes it even harder to hurt her and her dear, loyal little father," faltered Boggie in deepening distress. "Harder, too, to risk having both of them turn against me, as they might so easily do, if I were to accuse Gavin and then fail to prove anything. Incidentally, Gavin might sue me for libel. Maybe he would win his case. Oh, you really don't know what he's like! Cunning as a monkey, and so fiendishly malicious. I somehow feel," she went on with a look of dread in her eyes, "that if it is Gavin—which I devoutly pray it isn't—he's simply egging me on to some public action he can use against me to my utter ruin. If that's his object, he'll be protected at every point. I'm not usually a coward, but quite frankly I'm terrified to do anything at all. Oh, if only Jimbo was here to decide for me!"

Tommy eyed her with sympathy. Still self-controlled, she made a faint gesture of wringing her hands.

"I think you must be taking an exaggerated view," he remarked reasonably. "I quite appreciate your difficulty, but I ought to tell you that the time for fooling the police has gone by. In one way and another you've given the impression that you are deliberately shielding a criminal—which is true, isn't it? It will look bad for you if he's caught and proved guilty—and I am fairly certain he will be caught, very soon. Something Inspector Headcorn said to me showed he was already on the right track."

"On Gavin's track?" She gripped the arms of her chair and stared at him apprehensively. "Then he'll know I've given him away."

"Don't worry. The police are as anxious as you are not to make a wrong arrest. Gavin won't suspect what is happening till they've secured pretty clinching evidence. What I want you to do now, is to let me ring up the inspector and get him to come round. Never mind whether or not you are sure it's Gavin. Just tell Headcorn all you've admitted to me. It will strengthen your position, and save you future embarrassment."

"I—I suppose I'll have to, after what you've told me. I always was a hopeless liar! Couldn't you speak to him for me? I—I shall feel such a fool."

"Certainly, if you prefer. Do you mind if I use your telephone?"

Determined to act quickly before she changed her mind, Tommy made for the hall. It had been easier than he had expected; but there was still a good deal he was dissatisfied about. In the doorway he turned to ask:

"You're quite sure, I suppose, about the disposition of Sir Osmund's property?"

She was lighting a fresh cigarette with unsteady hands. Her ragged brows shot up humorously.

"I'm only going by what my husband told me. Jimbo's word was good enough for Boggie."

Good enough for any one, reflected Tommy, thinking, however, that it might be as well to make a full investigation into the entail. He got on to the inspector, arranged to see him at two-thirty, and returning suddenly realised that if he went away now he would be leaving Mrs. Bellamy-Pryce alone in the house. He offered to stay, but was assured there was no need.

"Ro's not coming back," she said, "but some Columbo friends of mine are calling for me almost at once, to take me to Ranelagh. Ro'll be joining us for tea, and we'll be together from then on. Besides, I shan't be nervous any more. Look!" Triumphantly she lifted the cushion on which she had been seated, and displayed a serviceable revolver. "Actually, I had this here yesterday, only I had no time to get hold of it. It's Jimbo's. I got it out of storage on Friday morning to have by me."

"Oh! And do you know how to use it?" he asked, fingering the weapon thoughtfully. It was a Colt's '45, cleaned and loaded.

"I'm not a bad shot, for a woman. I used to practise, out East. I haven't told Ro about it yet. I didn't want her to think I was taking this matter too seriously. Don't give me away, will you? I'm told I ought to have a licence."

It would come cheaper, he reminded her, than a hundred pound fine; and somewhat dubiously deciding that from now on she could look after herself, he took his leave to drive slowly and meditatively towards Hyde Park.

Had it been the hope of seeing Rosemary again that had prompted his wish to remain a little longer? At any rate the prospect of not laying eyes on her for a full twenty-four hours if not more was singularly depressing. As he turned into the first park gate he knew just how small a chance there was of spying her, unless she happened to be along the main drive, looking out for him. His heart therefore gave a bound when almost at once he caught sight of her, bolt upright on a bench, gold head bare to the sun, eyes fixed expectantly on the passing cars. So she had wanted to see him; but even as she leapt up and came towards the roadway, his elation suffered a check. Captain Argus was with her, following doggedly in her wake.

Tommy stopped his engine. Rosemary's eyes searched his swiftly.

"No, you needn't say it," she whispered in despair. "It was Uncle Gav. Oh, how utterly awful!"

All her colour had ebbed. He tried to comfort her.

"She still insists she doesn't know," he explained, with a guarded glance at her companion. "Though personally I think there's little doubt as to who it was. I've got her consent to speak openly to the inspector, who is meeting me directly after lunch. It seems the only thing to do."

She had grasped the reason for his reticence. With a jerk of the head in Argus's direction she muttered, "Oh, he knows. Boggie's told him," and silently listened while Tommy supplied further details of his conversation. She glanced at him with a swift intake of breath when he mentioned the money part of it, but made no comment.

There fell a strained silence, during which Tommy cogitated on the best means of getting rid of the third member of the party. Possibly the same thought was in Rosemary's mind, but if so it was abandoned.

"Well," she said fatalistically, "there seems nothing for it but to just wait and see. I'll have to rush away now. Rank's waiting for me," and with a brusqueness which betrayed her misery turned on her heel and made rapidly for the interior of the park.

Tommy watched her lithe figure till a bank of flowering rhododendrons hid it from sight. Argus, not looking round, stood scowling down at the hot gravel. Presently he blurted out that it was a thundering good thing some one was at last making a move. Rousing, Tommy inquired what he meant. Argus explained, moodily:

"It's what I've been on to Mrs. Bellamy-Pryce to do since that first shot was fired. She wouldn't listen to me."

Tommy looked at him curiously. It occurred to him that Argus, as a fellow-passenger on the P. & O. boat, might be worth sounding.

"I'm going to Piccadilly," he said. "Can I offer you a lift?"

"Thanks," returned the Australian carelessly, "I'm heading that way myself, as it happens. Comic cut of a car you've got," he remarked, as he heaved and squeezed his stalwart frame into the vacant place. "Don't know how you've got the nerve to drive such an object. Not yours? Oh, I see. Well, it seems to go, doesn't it?"

"After a fashion. By the way, you're settling in London, are you?"

"Don't know," grunted Argus. "It's blasted hard to land jobs. So it is everywhere. I picked the wrong time to get de-mobbed."

"Were you long in the service?"

"Joined up at sixteen—calling it eighteen, you know. There's nothing in it in peace-time, though. Now if another war broke out . . ."

"What sort of work is your choice?" asked Tommy, strongly suspecting that the ex-captain would be apt to find any routine tedious.

"Choice! That's a good one." The Australian gave a barking laugh. "My old governor," he continued, "wanted to take me on at his show. Building-contractor he was, out in Sydney; but like a fool I shinned out. When I landed back, the governor was gone, and so was the business. There was a small spot of cash. I tried hydraulic mining, selling cars, oh, what you like. It was no good, the slump was always there before me. So I thought I'd have a go at London. It's livelier, anyhow."

He drew on the pipe he had lighted, and stole a sidelong glance.

"Well," he challenged, "and what's your notion about these affairs?"

"I rather wanted to ask you that same question," answered Tommy. "I'm only a newcomer."

His companion shrugged. "I only know what I've heard—and the small bit I've seen," he made cautious return.

"On the boat, you mean?"

"That's as may be." Argus paused, eyes to the front, then demanded, "Just what has a certain party been telling you?"

"Only enough to rouse my curiosity about Judge Bellamy-Pryce's death. I wanted to inquire where you were at the time it happened. Can you recall?"

"Now, what the hell's that got to do with it?" blazed the captain, as though cut on the raw.

There was no accounting for the sudden bluster of his tone. Astonished, Tommy could only suppose that he had run foul of some hidden sensitiveness. However, he had already noticed Argus's chip-on-the-shoulder attitude, compounded, no doubt, of vanity and underbreeding. He hastened to smooth him down.

"I was merely wondering if you or any one else was near enough to the judge's cabin to have overheard voices coming from it."

"Oh, so that's your idea!" the Australian grumbled scornfully. "Not so damned original, either. Well, then, I was nowhere about. In the bar, or on deck—according to when the seizure took him—which, of course, nobody knows. If he had a visitor, he wasn't able to say so. You may be sure it was gone into thoroughly, but nothing came of it. It's too late now, that's a dead cert."

"On account of the sea-burial?" suggested Tommy blandly.

"Sea-burial? What the hell! That's not the ticket. Don't you go running off with the idea that there was anything wrong about the death itself." As though realising his vehemence was uncalled for, Argus took a quieter note. "What I mean is, it was a straight case of heart. The ship's doctor would have told me, if there'd been any doubt. He and I were great pals. I had it from him the judge was unlikely to last the journey. He said he'd never seen a worse heart. The darned thing was missing on both cylinders, ready to go phut for no reason at all."

"Even a mild shock, then, would have done for it?"

"If he had a shock, we can't prove it now—whatever some of us may have thought."

Struck by the tone, Tommy asked whether it was as impossible as Mrs. Bellamy-Pryce supposed for a steerage passenger to get to the upper decks after nightfall.

"So they'll tell you. I happen to know otherwise." The captain grinned and waxed confidential. "I berthed steerage on one voyage," he explained. "There chanced to be some one—of the other sex, I need hardly say that—with a cabin on Deck A. Oh, I soon found I could wangle it!" The conquering hero burst out in a reminiscent guffaw. "Meant spending the night and watching the right moment to sneak below next morning, but it wasn't too hard. The bigger the boat the less notice taken—or so I've discovered."

"Have you any reason to think the judge's brother did that? In plain language, is there anything to suggest the knife Mrs. Bellamy-Pryce found was his?"

"Oh, so she's told you about that, has she?" Argus cocked a wary eye at his inquisitor and mused dispassionately. "Might have been his. Anyhow, it was damned silly to get rid of it; but you know what women are. What was the other thing you were asking? Oh, yes! It was all rather indefinite. It's just that I fancied I saw this brother that very evening, slinking behind one of the life-boats. Directly we'd left off playing bridge it was. Maybe I was wrong. I certainly saw some dark, slimy little brute with much the look of him, but as I started after him to make sure a chap I knew stopped me for a light and said had I heard the news about the judge. I barged below to offer my services and what-not and clean forgot the brother till the question of shock came up. I can't see it matters two hoots—unless you think it might shed light on this later business?"

It was glaringly plain that the Australian, for all his cautious indifference, shared Mrs. Bellamy-Pryce's doubt.

"Tell me this," resumed Tommy. "Apart from the brother, should you say the judge had managed to rouse any ill-feeling on board?"

Sceptically Argus replied that it seemed improbable. The man was too near his grave for picking quarrels.

"Not but what he'd a cruel tongue when the fit took him—a nasty, cold-blooded way of getting right under a person's skin. His wife came in for the worst of it, though. Funny it never seemed to faze her. Always a jolly comeback; but she's like that. Darned good-natured."

A tinge of bitterness in these remarks seemed to hint that on some occasion the speaker himself had suffered from James's caustic sarcasm. As though to counteract it, Argus added that no doubt ill health excused much, and that the judge had been held in high esteem by all who knew him.

They had reached Piccadilly Circus.

"Then you can't swear," said Tommy as he drew up by the kerb, "that this man you saw on deck was Gavin Bellamy-Pryce?"

"N-no. I couldn't take my oath on it. It was pitch-dark, remember, and he slid away like an eel directly he saw me looking at him." The wave of a pipe-stem graphically illustrated the vanishing-act. "Will this do me? Oh, Lord, yes—quite good enough."

During the short drive Argus had expanded a trifle and lost some of his moroseness. Now, as he alighted, antagonism returned, and Tommy, meeting the hard-gazing eyes, suddenly read the meaning of it. Jealousy!

It was an unexpected and subtly flattering tribute. Its recipient even thought that the lift had been accepted less for the purpose of imparting certain items of information than for the opportunity it offered of studying and measuring a potential rival. Did Argus seriously consider him in that capacity? In quest of food, Tommy smiled broadly to himself.

Meanwhile, in his empty flat, the telephone was ringing its head off, with no one to answer it.

CHAPTER NINE

ROSEMARY raced as though devils pursued her. Although it was still early for her rendezvous with Rank, she had to escape and be alone in order to think—think desperately, against time. When she had reached a green space in the very middle of the park, she sank down, breathless, and pressed her fingers hard over her eyes. Her head buzzed as she tried to command her reasoning powers.

There must be a way out of this horrid impasse! Her uncle, the rather peculiar idol of her youthful fancy, could not possibly be an utterly callous murderer. If he was, she had not exaggerated in saying that her father, staunch, innocent partisan, would be crushed by the revelation. What was going on must be stopped. That went without saying; but the remedy as shown to her seemed almost more appalling in its consequences than the ailment itself. Boggie, of course, had been feeling the same.

If not Uncle Gavin, then who could it be? Some one presumably—though not certainly—acquainted with the ways of their household. Some one reasonably like her uncle, maybe—here was an idea—got up to resemble him. A hired assassin? That, in the England she knew, sounded absurd; but then wasn't the whole sequence of happenings bordering rather closely on the ridiculous? Thus far, only failures—and about yesterday's episode, in particular, there had been a touch of—yes, the amateurish. She still could not understand how it was Boggie had not been killed. It looked very much as though, this time at least, no murder was intended. . . .

"A private enemy of Boggie's? No, that's equally wild-sounding. Good old Bog can't have an enemy. Or rather . . ."

But the truth was Boggie had.

One enemy, though not to be taken seriously. The proof of it was here, in Rosemary's white handbag, the snag being . . . oh, there were a number of snags! In fact, it was only now that she had her back to the wall that she recalled the shadowy suspicion she had dismissed as nonsensical.

Looking furtively about—how the hateful habit had grown on her!—she took from the back pocket of the bag a folded letter which no eyes but hers had seen. Boggie, bless her, had no knowledge it existed. Several times she had been on the point of burning it, but somehow she had refrained. Here it had stayed, reminding her of a repulsive toad she could not bring herself to crush. She flattened the paper out and forced herself to reread its typed enclosure. The familiar, cramped signature at the end she pored over with unwonted concentration. It seemed a bit wobbly. For the simple and obvious reason? Experts, she supposed, could decide; but even so, would that help towards a solution?

She had not believed these vile sentences could still enrage her, but they did, all over again. At the same time, the warning they contained seemed slightly less insane than at her last reading. If it was not insane at all, then here, in this typed page, was her answer. It might mean the saving of Uncle Gavin—and of her father.

All at once she saw that she would be foolish indeed not to place this letter straight into Tommy Rostetter's hands. She strongly disliked doing so. Tommy might read the wrong meaning into it; but in a real crisis, oughtn't she to risk it? She would do it, at once, before her resolution weakened. Besides, it must be done at once, before Tommy saw the inspector.

Up she sprang, crammed the letter back into its hiding-place, and made at full speed for the telephone booth at Marble Arch. Rank would be champing at the bit. She might even have to let him down on this, their last free day together; but he would have to be sacrificed. Poor Rank! Of late the playmate she had hectored and coddled by turns had got somewhat tiresomely under foot. If only he hadn't turned soft on her! As it was, his going would be a relief, despite the fact that she would be deprived of a substantial buffer against Argus, likewise—but more ominously—getting out of hand. She wished Tommy didn't live in Paris. It was stupid how, in so short a time, she had grown to depend on him—she who never before had depended on any man. . . .

The telephone rang and rang. Of course, Tommy was out lunching. Ought she to go and camp on his doorstep till he came in? The taxi she signalled passed oblivious of her. Three more whizzed by, with their flags down. A fifth approached. She had raised her hand, but now she let it drop—for her decision, so firm a moment before, had collapsed like a pricked balloon.

"I daren't—oh, I daren't!" she muttered. "It might do more harm than good." She turned laggingly back into the park, took a few slow steps, and whispered to herself: "At least, not yet. . . ."

Inspector Headcorn showed little astonishment at Tommy's disclosures.

"More or less what I had expected," he said. "You've saved me considerable time and trouble; but I'd like to ask you this: Do you think the lady may be drawing rather freely on her imaginations?"

After a moment's thought, Tommy answered in the negative.

"She strikes me as a very literal-minded woman, not at all given to flights of fancy. You yourself remarked on the crudeness of her attempts to fool us; and she was almost trapped into giving that description. I believe she's genuinely terrified of bringing what may be a false accusation, for quite understandable reasons. Mind, I'm not sure she's yet told the entire truth. I think, though, there's likely to be a good basis of fact in what she says, and that she herself is morally convinced the man who attacked her was Gavin. I suppose, like me, you've no doubt the two shots were aimed at her?"

"That was fairly certain at the outset." The inspector dismissed the point briefly. "And this Captain Argus," he went on, "you say he's in love with the niece?"

"I haven't his word for it. I formed my own conclusions."

Headcorn grunted, indicating that he also had gathered the same impression.

"A bit thin," he brooded, "the brother-in-law's expecting to find his knife still in the brief-case."

"Decidedly, but he may have had reason to think it was still there. Possibly it was his intention to use it on his victim and then take it away with him. You think that's thin, too? Well, so do I; but I doubt if you'll get her to admit there was anything else in the briefcase to interest Gavin. I also doubt if at this date you'll discover that the judge's heart attack was caused by being set upon by his brother, though it's evident some talk of it arose at the time."

The inspector grumbled on the length of time it would take to secure statements from the ship's captain. The sum total of wireless messages received would probably elicit no new information and while one was waiting for them another murderous attack might be perpetrated. From these observations Tommy concluded that it was the speaker's intention to have Gavin watched and his recent movements investigated.

"I trust you won't have difficulty in finding him. He seems an elusive bird."

"Symposium Club, you said? That's good enough."

Within the next hour Tommy pitied Inspector Headcorn for his optimism. After a telephone canvass of various Oxford acquaintances, he himself called in at the august portals of the club in question, only to be met with a shocked refusal. The elderly porter looked aghast that any one with the outer appearance of a gentleman should be so ignorant as to imagine a member's private address could be had for the asking. Tommy met the fishy eye brazenly, grinned and dealt the reprimander a punch in the ribs.

"Well, Henry!" he greeted him. "Filling out the waistcoat a bit more, aren't we? Is it tummy, or chest?" A startled gulp, a pop-eyed stare, and gratified recognition relaxed the other's features.

"Mr. Rostetter! Dear me, sir, I'm extremely sorry. It's my eyesight, I think, because I can't say you've changed. It must be a good eight years, sir, since I had the pleasure of taking in your letters at The Alpine?"

Henry coughed apologetically and drew closer. "I hope you'll pardon me, sir, for having to give you that answer. Unbreakable rules it is. If you'd care to . . ."

"Write a letter here, it will be forwarded. Yes, I know; only I don't care to. Now, then, Henry, as man to man, are you or aren't you going to hand over that address?"

Henry looked acutely embarrassed. "Mr. Rostetter," he protested in a suitably hushed whisper, "I can't. No, sir, I mean just that. I'd willingly oblige you, if it was possible. Maybe you noticed I seemed a bit startled-like when you spoke that gentleman's name?"

"Startled, was it? And why?" asked Tommy with quickened interest.

"It was on account of me being asked that same question not twenty minutes ago, and getting in a hot argument about it. Some people," he continued with acrimony, "won't believe you on oath. They seem to think if they show you some badge or other tucked away under a lapel it'll get blood out of a stone. The cold fact is . . ." the whisper now betrayed mortification, "the member referred to always collects his letters himself. The committee may know where he lives, but there's nothing on our books. Never has been—and that's the Lord's truth. It's not my place to pass remarks, but—well, sir, I did say to myself just now, 'Henry, my boy, you've many a time said there was something queer in that quarter. It's long odds you're right.'"

It began to look as though the Criminal Investigation Department was going to be severely taxed in the matter of locating a man evidently desirous of remaining in obscurity. However, on Monday morning a stroke of pure luck enabled Tommy once more to render service.

Calling early at Anatol's and finding Rosemary not yet arrived—he had totally forgotten her intention of bombarding the big shops with Parisian samples—he dropped into his nephew's flower-shop. Rank, still lord of this one domain, was as usual issuing orders. His partner, Bilfilian, quietly disregarded them, going his own loathly way. In a past not remote, the latter had been the instrument of rescuing Tommy from a particularly vile death. In addition, like the younger Rostetter he was changed, translated—not only daintily garbed but excessively clean; but with his squeaky voice and reptilian movements it was still hard to feel affection for him, and if the irritated Rank had chucked a flowerpot at his head instead of calling him the God-forsaken son of a flatfish, he would have met with his relative's unqualified approval.

"Drop that hamper!" Rank was bellowing. "Our last day, new owner coming any minute to look us over, and the place like a warehouse! Look slippy and clear that muck away. They've rooked you for this lot, anyhow. My God, what lupin—gone grey round the gills! Are we in Whitechapel?"

"Pity we aren't," piped Bilfilian, furtively continuing to abstract carnations from a bed of shedding fern. "In Wapping Great Stairs you should have seen the camellias I used to buy for a penny. They looked just like wax flowers on my black table."

"You'll have some on your coffin if you don't leave off making this mess. How many times have I told you . . . Oh, it's Tommy. Heave that blasted pail out of the way, can't you? Water slopping about. . . . Well!" The erstwhile dawdler of Balliol mopped a heated brow, and addressed his uncle, now picking his way round piles of debris. "You look pretty idle. Got a cigarette on you?"

As Rank sighed moodily, Bilfilian sidled forward to extend a wet hand like a crayfish's claw, and retreating to his task shook a shower of dewdrops over the visitor's nicely polished shoes. Tommy inquired the latest news from Victoria Grove. Rank, who had called there the night before, reported an atmosphere of strain.

"Would be, while this uncertainty's about," Rank muttered this, conveying with elaborate winks that his partner was not apprised of events. "Oh, I got it," he continued *sotto voce*, "the minute that description was let out. Ro's tried to fool me, but it's plain enough who it was. Well, sickening as it is, it's good they've found out. Have you got hold of him yet?"

"Gavin? No. He seems to have dug a hole and crawled into it."

"You're telling me! And he'll stay hid, depend on it. I . . . What's wrong with you?" The last was hurled at his partner, accusingly. "Get on with your job!" Over the hamper-lid a face like a dark tadpole's, all eyes, was regarding them strangely.

"Were you trying to find Gavin Bellamy-Pryce?" squeaked Bilfilian surprisingly. "Because if so I can put you on to him. I dare say I'm one of the few people who can."

Rank rounded on him unreasonably.

"You? All along you've known Gavin's address and were letting it die on you? Out with it, you . . . you milkweed! Wapping Great Stairs, is it? Limehouse Causeway? Houndsditch . . . ?"

"Lambs' Conduit Street, Bloomsbury," said Bilfilian meekly. "I forget the number, but it's a room over a bake-shop. Only last week I went there. He was showing me his fragments of Sumerian pottery. Three marvellous bits from Ur . . ."

"Lambs' Conduit Street!" Rank raised arms to Heaven. "My own partner!"

"Cuniform, you know." Bilfilian was uncorked. "He's hoping they'll turn out a paean to Astaroth, but they may be only part of a laundry list. He's a great man, Gavin. It'll take a full century before he's appreciated. It's a crying shame some one doesn't die and leave him the money to carry on with. All his life he's been hampered by poverty. If he had a location of his own . . ."

"Could I mention your name," interrupted Tommy, to whom an idea had come, "in case I want to get an article out of him on the Indus cities?"

"Oh, certainly!" Bilfilian eyed him with deep respect. "But you'll have a job to catch him. He spends most of his time at the museums."

Tommy thanked him and departed somewhat hastily. He had just seen Rosemary approaching from the farther end of Brackham Place, dejectedly carrying her attach^ case and shepherdess hat.

"You!" she greeted him in relief. "With this awful day in front of me, I was afraid I shouldn't see you at all. Every blessed hat to be spot-cleaned and furbished up for the Sale—the countess has worn most of them, and her powder does stick so—then the cocktail binge to be planned for, and not a thing done. . . ."

"Don't worry, it'll soon be over."

"Yes, I know; but what, what do you think's happened?" She came to a standstill before her own entrance and sank her voice tragically. "Some one's told daddy. He'll be in town this morning—and what am I to do with him?"

CHAPTER TEN

"YOUR father? But who told him?"

She shrugged despairingly. "God knows—but, oh, I could kill whoever it was! He only knows about the shootings. I had a line by the first post, simply saying he was much disturbed over the news, and was coming straight up; but wait, that's not the worst of it. He says he means to look up Uncle Gavin first thing, and get his advice about it. Could anything be more perverse?"

Tears had sprung to her eyes. She wiped them with her knuckles, and with a little hysterical laugh accepted the loan of Tommy's handkerchief.

"Boggie's as upset as I am," she whispered. "She's ready to meet every train, only she and I both know he's more than likely to come by motor-coach, that being cheaper. I bunged off a wire saying it was all a mistake, and to stay at home; but he probably won't get it in time to stop him. You know Broughton-Elmtrees. Telegrams have to wait till the grocer's boy is making a round, or some neighbour happens to pass."

"Couldn't you have telephoned?"

"Daddy's had his telephone taken out. He always hated it, and he wants the money to have his housekeeper's daughter's legs straightened. I'm afraid it's no use. He knows Uncle Gavin's address if we don't, and he'll go straight to it. You don't see how awful that is. I didn't, till something Boggie hinted gave me a most terrible jar. She said that she was all right, because she was warned; but that daddy wasn't warned, and that if it was an advantage to have her out of the way, the same thing applied to him. It's true, isn't it? As she sees it," the shaken voice went on, "Daddy may be the unsuspecting fly walking right into the spider's web."

"Nonsense! I've just found out where your uncle is, and—"

"You've found out? But how?" she demanded eagerly.

He told her, and sketched out his scheme. She showed no vast astonishment on learning that Bilfilian was acquainted with her uncle. The two were Balliol men, they had much the same grubbing-underground tastes and leanings towards the macabre. Bilfilian was a queer, secretive sort of boy. . . .

"Then you'll go to Lambs' Conduit Street now and try to be there when daddy arrives? Oh, I should feel so much happier! You might say something about the fact that Scotland Yard is making investigations. If Uncle Gav is doing this, it may scare him off altogether."

Her face had brightened noticeably. He asked if she could lunch with him and hear his report.

"I shan't have time to eat properly," she said. "If you'll make it The Snuggery over there, I'll manage to pop across for a moment. Yes, Cybele, darling," she called to the flaxen-haired maiden now beckoning frantically from the shop-door, "I'll find it, whatever it is. Oh, Mr. Rostetter—"

"Better make it Tommy."

"Thanks, Tommy—I am so grateful to you! Don't leave them alone, will you? Steer daddy over to Boggie. She'll take care of him."

She vanished into the shop.

Lambs' Conduit Street proved to be a dingy turning off the tram-clanging Theobald's Road. It contained but one baker's establishment, beside which yawned an entrance which gave on to a dark, stale-smelling staircase. Tommy went up, and after two flights reached a door bearing a dirty visiting card. As there was no bell, he knocked. Receiving no answer, he tried the knob. The door did not yield.

In the premises below the stout woman of whom he made inquiries shook a mulish head. Tommy bought buns. She shovelled them into a bag, sized him up anew, and said to a girl with chocolate-smeared mouth and lank hair tumbling Garbo-fashion about her shoulders, "Not seen Mr. Bellamy go out, I suppose?" Licking her chin with phenomenal stretch of tongue the girl replied, no, nor for the matter of that she hadn't seen him come in—not for days. The woman nodded, planked down change, and remarked conclusively, "That means he's gone off again. No good asking where, nor when he'll be back. He never says."

"Is there any restaurant near here where he goes for meals?"

"Mr. Bellamy don't have meals," he was informed. "As a rule he just fetches in a loaf and a bit of cheese, maybe a bottle of milk. We say he lives mainly on air."

"Now and again he stews an eel on 'is gas-ring," volunteered the girl, exploring a tooth-cavity. "We smell the onions down here, don't we, Ma?"

"If his window's open," agreed the stout woman, and steadfastly turned her back.

Caution warned Tommy to put no more questions. They might be repeated to the lodger on his return. Making straight for a telephone-box, he gave the inspector the address, together with the information that Gavin seemed to be away from home. He then rang up Rosemary, told her there was little likelihood of her father and uncle coming into immediate contact, and having lifted a load from her shoulders drove to Somerset House, in the Strand. Here he paid the customary shilling and requested to examine the last will and testament of—but here he was hung up. Which Bellamy-Pryce would it be? Boggie had not said, and he had not thought to inquire.

The grizzled attendant who met him came to his rescue. The name mentioned was an uncommon one. Wasn't he wanting the will made by James Luther Bellamy-Pryce, founder of the famous tea-importers firm, and father of the present head, Sir Osmund?

"Quite correct. May I ask how you guessed?"

Smiling, the attendant answered that it was a natural conclusion, seeing this was the fifth application for the document within a period of two years.

"The fifth!"

"That's so, sir. The last was only about an hour ago."

Headcorn, without doubt; but the others? When the will had been produced, Tommy detained the old man in conversation, and pretending idle curiosity put a few inquiries. It appeared that in each instance the applicant for the will had been a man. The first had come in slightly more than two years ago—James, perhaps, for he had been in England about that time, as Boggie had mentioned yesterday; but it was impossible, after so long a time to learn any details concerning him, and the same was true of the second, who had arrived much later—in February or March of the present year. He might, Tommy conceived, have been a solicitor representing one of the beneficiaries—or the vicar, though this he doubted. This morning's arrival was, of course, fresh in memory. He had been a large, heavy gentleman, with a big wart on his nose.

"And the last before him?" Tommy asked.

"He came along soon after the second," said the attendant, smiling again, reminiscently. "I'm not likely to forget him, for I said to myself he was the only one of the lot that didn't look as if he could have been one of the family. That is to say," he explained, "I used often to see Sir Osmund, when my stepson was working for the firm in Tower Hill. Tall, sandy-grey, hatchet-faced he was. You might call him distinguished. This chap was hatchet-faced, but not sandy, and not tall—nor distinguished. Dark as a native—a little, weazoned runt. Rather a queer customer he struck me."

"Not a gentleman, you thought?" suggested Tommy, noting the disparaging tone.

"Well—I wouldn't quite say that. He spoke like one. It was his clothes—shabby's not the word; and unusual-like. I seem to picture him in one of those real, old-time overcoats, such as you don't often see nowadays. Cape attached to it. Yes, and black gloves. Never took 'em off the whole time he was studying the will. I took particular notice."

Black gloves!

Again they had cropped up, sinister, significant. During the half-hour Tommy spent in poring over the mass of legal verbiage and fixing in his mind certain damning facts, Gavin's black gloves hovered like liver-spots before his eyes. They followed him out into the dazzling Strand, hung suspended in mid-air all the way to Mrs. Coates' Servants' Registry in Sloane Street, and superimposed themselves on the powdery face of the very grand lady who answered his next inquiries. Vera Coldbottom, he learned with disappointment, had quitted London for a post in Essex. He took down her new address, left the office, and suddenly remembered that just round the corner in Cadogan Gardens lived Lord Downside, the amateur archaeologist who, according to the porter of The Symposium, was almost the only club member to whom Gavin ever spoke. It so happened that the aged peer had been a friend of Tommy's father. Thinking a call on him might throw some illumination on Gavin's character, Tommy presented himself, and was courteously received.

"I've little more than a confrere's acquaintance with Gavin Bellamy-Pryce," said Lord Downside. "I should doubt if any one knows him really well. He's a very odd fish indeed—difficult, secretive, and with but one passion in life. I'm inclined to think he would barter anything for research—or anybody," he added with humorous tolerance. "Rather an inhuman sort of chap; but this much can be said for him—however poor he may be, he never borrows, and never sponges. I've reason to know that. Recently I offered to put him up at my Wiltshire place. I wanted him to be present at the opening up of some prehistoric barrows in the district. Suspecting, I fancy, that having him as a guest might stand in the way of letting the house—I am forced to do that now and then in these thin times—he gave a point blank refusal.

"His scholastic reputation is of the soundest. He's never published anything, though, and it's quite on the cards this monumental work of his will never be finished. He'll peg out, first, from sheer poverty and self-neglect."

"Not, surely, if his old father dies and leaves him money?"

Lord Downside made a wry face.

"If you'd known Osmund Bellamy-Pryce as long as I have," he retorted, "you'd have doubts of his doing any of his children so good a turn. I'm told he's dying now, but it wouldn't astonish me if he hung on till Domesday, out of pure spite. Twice this year he's been on the point of death—the second occasion, I believe, was when he received the news of his son James's decease. However, my solicitor, who happens also to be his, assures me he makes marvellous recoveries. So he may well outlive Gavin, whose health is always precarious."

Tommy left in a pensive mood. It seemed likely that both James and Gavin had hurried home in anticipation of their father's end, which for Gavin in particular would mean the fulfilment of an imperilled desire. It was not unnatural for Gavin, on his arrival, to want to refresh his memory of the will by which he hoped soon to benefit; but circumstances combined to give his call at Somerset House a suspicious aspect. As to his never borrowing—well, his sister-in-law's story flatly contradicted Lord Downside's belief.

"And no belief can alter the fact that with both James and Boggie dead, Gavin comes in for considerably more money. If the vicar and Rosemary die . . . but good God, that's fantastic!"

Was it? Tommy wondered—and cold shivers ran along his spine. Instantly, however, he cheered up. Whatever wholesale clearance of relations might have been in contemplation, not one death was likely to happen now. The police were too well warned.

He had a long wait at The Snuggery before Rosemary appeared. In the meantime Captain Argus had prowled in, made halting conversation with a weather-eye on the hat-shop, and finally, in disappointment, roamed away. It was after two o'clock when Anatol's door opened, and like a cyclone the girl Tommy was expecting rushed in.

"How long has he been gone?" she whispered, sinking into the chair at Tommy's side.

"Your uncle? No one seems to know. Probably for some days."

Hope and doubt alternated in her face. Her thoughts were clear reading.

"Daddy's come," she announced, nibbling the remnant of a roll. "And when, or where, do you think he's putting up? The Shaftesbury Palace Hotel. He just would," Irrepressible mirth took her. "Oh, Tommy, can't you see sweet little daddy all alone in that God-awful place—getting lost in corridors, apologising for being barged into in that Chamber of Horrors lounge? And never once seeing how funny it is!"

Helpless with laughter—due largely to reaction, he imagined—she waved aside the menu pressed on her.

"Girl," said Tommy sternly, "you must eat. Have a chop, have a—"

"I've had two eclairs and a square of rum chocolate. That'll do beautifully till dinner, when daddy's coming to us."

"Have you found out who told him?"

"He simply won't say." She had sobered, and was frowning a little. "Whoever it was has sworn him to secrecy. He's too honourable to go back on his word, but it *is* rather queer, isn't it? I haven't seen him yet. He rang Boggie up, and she got on to me. She and I have agreed to suppress Saturday's event entirely; and we're letting him think both those shots were meant for Victoria Road. You see why, of course. If he believes there's no danger for us he'll turn round and go home again."

To safety. Tommy understood.

"Perhaps it's just as well," he returned. "It wouldn't help matters to alarm him. Hold on!" He caught her on the wing. "Does this mean I shan't be seeing you before to-morrow?"

"Not, I'm afraid, till the cocktail party. You will come, won't you? It'll be an awful scrum."

Hardly had she regained the shop when a taxi halted outside Anatol's entrance, and from it alighted a slim reed of a woman, black-clad and of Parisian chic. With her was a male escort. He followed confidently, but at the door was turned back by an imperious hand. *"À demain, mon cher,"* cooed a thrilling voice, recognisable even at this distance. Tommy took another look, and above the escort's bent head—a sulky head, he would have said—discerned immense dark eyes burning from thick rims of what might be kohl, a smile of peculiar seduction, and side-locks of hair luridly suggestive of the Inferno's flames. Anatalia Rakovsky had arrived. She had not been at the shop this morning—only two charming girls, of whom one was an honourable, the other a dean's daughter; but he remembered now that she never did appear till after lunch, the preceding period—so Rosemary had explained—being given over to the manufacture of her face. He could well believe it. Fifty if a day, but a complexion smooth as Canton enamel—kiss-proof, tear-proof, one might almost say bullet-proof.

It was the firm barring of the door which brought back Rank's tale of jealousy. Tommy reflected that Countess Rakovsky might have fired shots which missed. If she fired shots at all they probably would miss; but granting the absurdity of her adopting a male disguise was it possible for her to have downed a woman of Boggie's proportions? Hardly; and besides, what would have been her object? Boggie was not her rival. Definitely, the countess was out.

His thoughts turned back to the fishing-cord. Had Gavin possessed such a thing? Had he been absent from London for six whole days, and if so could the fact be established? It was up to the inspector to answer these questions. He, a simple journalist, had no business to interfere in routine procedure; but it irked him to sit here idle, gazing at a garden-hat priced two guineas—reduced—purely because of its association with a certain week-end wearer, and though there was plenty of amusement to be had the prospect of tennis at Queen's or golf at Walton Heath left him singularly cold. With a feeling that after all there might be some trick about Gavin's disappearance, he got into his car and paid a return visit to Lambs' Conduit Street. He climbed again the dingy staircase; but the second floor door was still locked.

CHAPTER ELEVEN

SCRUM aptly described the gathering into which, at six-thirty the next afternoon, Tommy insinuated himself. At first glance the minute interior of Anatol's presented the congested, seething slow-motion observable in a magnified segment of ripe Gorgonzola.

Here, tightly jammed, were some fifty of those pleasure-seekers, familiar to readers of *The Tattle* and *Sketch*, who frequent race-meets, first-nights and the newest clubs, and dart restlessly to and fro, mostly by air, in quest of raiment, seasonal sport, or simply the sun. A polyglot tendency prevailed. French, Austrians, white Russians and Spaniards mingled with the taller and handsomer British. Among the men Tommy counted two ambassadors, five minor diplomats, and three captains of heavy industry. The women celebrities included a tennis champion, several revue artists, two opera singers and an aviator. As for the titles, he did not attempt to count them, but he imagined they overbalanced all else.

He looked about for Rosemary, but could not see her. Probably she was hidden from view in the far corner from which a steady hand-out of drinks was being propelled over heads and shoulders. Some one thrust a sticky glass on him. He grasped it firmly, and flexing his muscles prepared a putsch. As he did so, the countess, till then invisible, emerged from a gluey tangle, much as a queen bee on occasions comes out for a breath of air.

She was wearing the draggled-rook hat last seen in the window, and round her eyes she had laid an extra wide band of—yes, undeniably it was kohl. She did not recognise him; he had hardly expected she would, but with hospitality unimpaired by that fact she squeezed his hand fondly, and assured him that not only was all he saw for sale at bargain prices but that his cheque would be honoured now or at any future time. She then slipped lithely from the embrace of a Scandinavian minister slightly the worse for potations, and turning her back on the new arrival fastened like a limpet on to a man whose magnificent head towered well above the mob, and whose shoulders from a rear view struck a familiar and slightly discordant note. Tommy moved to a better position, and saw that the countess's prey was indeed no other than Captain Argus.

Gate crasher? No reason to suppose it. Rosemary had no doubt felt obliged to invite him—or perhaps the countess herself had done so. At any rate, her predilection for crude virility was too well known to astonish. In Paris, a few years back, it had been a heavy-weight boxer.

Thus far Tommy had seen no one else he knew, but now he caught the friendly eyes of the nice flaxen-haired dean's daughter beaming recognition. He was edging towards her when a hand gripped his arm, a plate of caviare capsized against his waistcoat, and over the debris he beheld Boggie's jovial features.

"Oh, I'm here!" the humorous chuckle greeted him. "Just made it, too. Will you look at that sky outside?"

Even as she spoke there came a snick of pale lightning through the darkening room, an ear-splitting crash of thunder, and then the deluge. Wall-flights flooded on. They spread pools of milky radiance over the blue, starred paper, and revealed the thick fog of cigarette smoke, all wreathed and streaked above the massed heads. Boggie righted her black straw hat, which had got knocked over one eye, evaded a wobbly youth who armed with a scent spray, was playfully showering those in his vicinity with costly fragrance, and asked where her niece was.

"I only braved this on her account. She'd have been so disappointed. Oh, there's Jack. Here, Jack, have you seen Ro?"

Argus, the countess still hitched on, shook his head. His companion, vaguely catching the drift, murmured that she believed darling Rosemary had gone out after more gin. It was always so, she explained in her atrocious English. These dear, silly girls simply would not order sufficient. Some one invariably had to run out.

"And we can just guess who that some one always is," whispered Boggie in Tommy's ear. "Ro has all the dirty jobs to do."

Argus scowled and exploded. "Out in this rain? Where'd she go? To the Running Horse, I suppose?" and without waiting for an answer he made an angry movement towards the door.

The countess held on to him.

"Oui, il pleure," she commented indifferently. "It is a good thing, *n'est ce pas? Formidable, ce chaleur. Ah, la voilà!"*

The shop door had burst open, and through it panted a drenched figure—Rosemary, her plumbago-blue frock soaked and clinging to her, her eyes for one brief instant looking—so Tommy thought—as though they had just seen a ghost. The expression vanished. Laughing, her armful of bottles clutched to her breast, she paused a moment to recover breath. Rain trickled from her lashes, her cheeks were like washed peonies.

The countess had darted forward, seized hold of her, and with ferocious energy was thrusting her towards the bar.

"Look out, countess, darling!" cried the girl, unperturbed by the onslaught. "I'm dropping the stuff. Rank, do leave go!" For Rank, appearing from nowhere, was trying to relieve her of her burden. "No, Captain Argus, I can manage nicely, thanks. Just clear a passage for me, will you?"

She steered an intrepid course, her thin pumps leaving puddles. Various male guests turned after her with livened interest. The countess shrugged, and Boggie good-humouredly bade Argus remain where he was.

"Better leave the child alone," she advised. "There's already a hopeless jam in that bar corner. Oh, well, if you must help, see if you can fetch me a bracer." She shook her head as she watched the Australian doggedly shouldering his way past obstructions. "It's no use, he'll only spill it," she said to Tommy. "Suppose we go too and try our luck?"

It crossed Tommy's mind that if the countess had meant to remove her youthful rival from masculine attention she had gone the worst way to achieve her purpose. Rosemary, busy with her mixing, was surrounded six deep by stationary men who resisted all efforts to be restored into circulation. With the greatest difficulty he secured Boggie her cocktail, and together they retired to a less crowded spot.

"Well," said Mrs. Bellamy-Pryce in a whisper. "Have you heard anything more?"

"Nothing, except that I've discovered your brother-in-law's address. I've been there, but his room seems to have been empty for some days."

"Seems!" she repeated sceptically. "Let's hope he isn't fooling us. With Cuthbert in town—well, it's a bit of a strain. The inspector called on me this morning. He's inclined to think we must do all we can to prevent the two brothers from meeting. Still, if Gavin really is away, it makes one less bother, doesn't it?"

Absently she finished her drink, murmuring that she loathed crowds, and meant to go once the downpour had stopped. Tommy, however, hardly heard her. Through the mass of heads he had just caught from Rosemary what he took to be an S.O.S. signal. He left his companion and managed to wedge in behind the bar, where his nephew and Argus were competing with an Italian naval attaché for the privilege of opening bottles. At once he saw what the annoyance was. All three men, having freely imbibed, were urging Rosemary to drink something to avoid catching cold after her soaking, and Rosemary was determined not to oblige them. The Italian was gaily persuasive; Rank, whom anything above three cocktails rendered preternaturally solemn, was by turns demonstrating that hers was the infallible road to pneumonia, and beseeching her, as a parting favour, to do this one small service to please him. Argus had reached the stage of inebriety when repetition replaces eloquence. Over and over he kept up the stubborn growl:

"How can good liquor make you sick? Just nonsense, that's what it is." She had been brushing them off like troublesome flies, going steadily on with her task; but now Argus elbowed the others away and tried to enforce his argument by laying masterful hands on her shoulders.

"That'll do, thanks!"

She twisted herself free, an angry scarlet in her cheeks, and in her eyes a dangerous glitter. Tommy got between her and the Australian, who edged sullenly to the side. In the clamour and confusion round them no one else had taken note of the episode, which had brought Tommy a gloating contentment. Constituting himself assistant bar-tender he remained, and presently discovered that both the Italian and his nephew had melted into the throng. It must have been some five minutes later that he saw Rosemary, shaker in hand, leaning forward with a stare of comic dismay.

"Daddy!" she whispered. "Oh, dear!"

"Your father? Impossible! Where?"

"Just inside the doorway. Don't you see him?" Her laugh had a catch in it. "It's entirely my fault. I told him to drop in if he had nothing better to do. It never entered my head he would. Shall we rescue him, poor lamb?"

The vicar of Broughton-Elmtrees had not yet spied a familiar face, but that fact seemed not to disturb him. Battered and jostled, there he stood, blinking in pleased wonderment at what for his eyes must have been an unaccustomed and extraordinary scene. Not one whit had he altered since Tommy's last glimpse of him. His Small person still displayed the fictitious bulkiness of waistcoat which results from amplitude of woollen underwear; his cheeks retained the waxed rosiness of an early apple, his fuzz of blond hair, imperceptibly fading to grey, continued to thrust forward so that he peered as from under a pent-roof. His expression at the moment indicated that sooner or later he might rouse to conclude he had strayed into the wrong place, but that meantime, enjoying what he found, he was not indisposed to linger.

"Come with me!"

Rosemary seized Tommy by the hand to begin pushing through the mob. Midway the room, however, she stopped, drew in a sharp breath, and dug her nails into her companion's palm.

"Look!" she gasped. "There, behind him!" Tommy looked. Over the vicar's shoulder hung a visage of dark sallowness, almost green in the shadow of a villainous black hat. A pinched, sinister face it was, with uneven streaks of jet hair trained before the ears, a long nose, and bilious, sunken dark eyes which glinted with a saturnine humour. The neck supporting it was scrawny. Round it was folded a black stock, very greasy and ancient, with no trace of relieving linen.

Not the least need to ask the identity of this weird and repellent apparition. Gavin gone away? On the contrary, he was here, in their midst.

CHAPTER TWELVE

TOMMY took firm hold of Rosemary. After all, he argued, in an undertone, there was no reason for alarm. She nodded and whispered back, "No, I suppose not. It's just their being together; but Boggie isn't absolutely sure, is she? I keep hoping it's just a horrible mistake."

In another moment they had reached the newcomers. Even as Tommy caught sight of Mrs. Bellamy-Pryce gazing in startled fashion at the two brothers Rosemary was introducing him with gay nonchalance.

"Surely you remember Mr. Rostetter, Daddy darling? He's Rank's uncle, from Paris. Uncle Gav, this is a surprise! You'll neither of you like this, you know. It's more beastly than I thought. Stay put, and I'll fetch you some sherry." In Tommy's ear she muttered a fierce, "There *is* sherry, thank goodness—one bottle. Find it!"

The vicar beamed with vacant amiability. Gavin, having jerked his head the merest fraction of an inch, let his eye travel in malevolent, bored amusement over the company. Both were perfectly at ease, and though the vicar made vague murmurs about not remaining he expressed his willingness to partake of refreshment. Tommy therefore set off to find the sherry, but his progress being stayed by the entanglement of a diamond bangle in his cuff-link he was a witness to Boggie's new exhibition of sang-froid.

"Well, old stick-in-the-mud!" cried Mrs. Bellamy-Pryce, surging up and bestowing, on the way, a careless nod in Gavin's direction. "Not going to cut me, I hope, after the good curry I gave you last night?"

The Reverend Cuthbert started out of his rapt dream. "Honoria? Dear me, so it is." He summoned his vagrant thoughts. "You slept well, I trust? No—er further disturbances?"

Boggie laughed robustly.

"Not a bit of it!" she declared. "Our little excitement's fizzled out. False alarm, as I told you."

"Yes, yes, so I was explaining to Gavin. Most unnerving, though, and might, to be sure, have led to serious results. Similar street-names. Oh, quite understandable!" The vicar's attention was momentarily caught by the enchanting spectacle of an English viscount dribbling the dregs of a cocktail down a Chilean plutocrat's neck. "Well, well,"—with a broad smile—"this is certainly most delightful; but tell me,"—his gaze once more arrested—"what do you suppose those two ladies are doing with the hats? Is it some game?"

He was looking interestedly at the Lady Primrose West-Cornforth and Emily, Duchess of Dwight, who were balancing a number of bargain purchases in towers above their present headgear. Boggie chuckled joyously, and Tommy, just extricated from the bangle, noticed that Gavin was watching her with an evil, penetrating smile. That smile remained when, in an effortless, detached way, he began to worm towards the bar. Tommy, fishing up the sherry-bottle from the corner, found Gavin facing him, and there he still was, darkly sipping his drink, and rolling it thoughtfully over his tongue, when Tommy conveyed a second glass of sherry to the vicar. In fact, it was one of the few impressions which stood out clean-cut when the time came to reconstruct past happenings—Gavin stationed close to the regiment of bottles, calmly enjoyed his Amontillado, his dingy caped overcoat buffeted by the smart, surging crowd, but his puny figure immovable as a crab stuck to a rock. He had kept on his gloves—nearly green with antiquity. That also Tommy was able, afterwards, to recall.

The family group was as he had left it—Rosemary, absent and tense, fondling her father's arm, Boggie alongside keeping up her lively patter, the vicar himself gazing fixedly at the beautiful ladies who passed, spellbound by their charms and uncritical as a boy of six seeing his first bevy of circus queens. Tommy remained for a few minutes, but was dragged away and into the other room by a woman acquaintance who firmly assured him he had been at school with her latest husband; and it had only just come out that the husband's school had been Eton, not Winchester, when a dishevelled Rosemary brushed against him with a scarcely-audible, "They've gone! Oh, quick, see where they're off to!"

Into the subsiding drizzle Tommy dashed—and stared blankly up and down the street. In this short interval the pair of brothers had completely disappeared. He sprinted round one corner, doubled back and tried the other, and too late sighted yet a third exit to Brackham Place—a cobbled alley-way leading in the general direction of Oxford Street. This likewise he explored, and a portion of the populous thoroughfare beyond. In the end he had to give up and go back to report failure.

Rosemary, again at her post, made no comment. She had gone suddenly quite white, and from the frown on her forehead seemed to be thinking rather desperately. The Italian attaché had his plump olive hand on her elbow, and was obviously beseeching her for an answer. "And why not?" he purred with gentle insistence.

Mechanically bright, she replied, "I'm most frightfully sorry, Signor Grimaldi. Really this evening I'll be too done up to think of anything but bed." She turned back to Tommy, carefully measured Cointreau into the shaker, and murmured, "They may, of course, have gone to daddy's hotel. Oh, could you find out?"

For a second time Tommy made off, just as Captain Argus hot-eyed and smouldering, once more shoved towards the bar.

It was after eight-thirty when he regained the shop, sufficiently emptied now to reveal the litter of cigarette-ends and broken biscuits underfoot. Only the countess and a few intimates lingered, and these, blissfully comatose, took no heed of him. The bar-table was deserted, but as he looked about, Rosemary came in from the rear room, her hair freshly combed, but her whole air that of exhaustion.

"No luck, I suppose?"

"None. I've tried the Shaftesbury, and the Lambs' Conduit Street place. They've probably made for some restaurant. By the way, what became of Rank?"

Gone, she told him. Didn't he know? This had been Rank's farewell indulgence. She hoped he hadn't been too tight to make his boat-train.

"And Argus?" he asked, recalling the dogged look last seen on the Australian's face.

"Oh, he went, too—in a huff. Imagine expecting me to come out and dance!"

"That other fellow, the Italian, seemed to cherish similar hopes."

"S'sh!" She sent a warning glance towards the countess, picked up her hat and bag, and moved listlessly towards the door. "Well," she sighed, "I've done all I could. Now I'm going home to turn in."

"Not home," Tommy spoke dictatorially. "To a restaurant, for food. I'm taking you there now."

"In this wreck of a frock?" She glanced down at her rough-dried clothing. "Oh, no, I'd disgrace you!"

"Now then, no back-chat. Step on it!"

He took her arm. Limply she gave way.

In the car she said, "Boggie, of course, was wonderful; but did you see her face when they came in together?" Not waiting for a reply, she continued: "She tried to persuade daddy to dine with us again, but he simply wouldn't. He'd got his heart set on hobnobbing with Uncle Gav. Oh, Tommy, how horrible this is!"

He pinioned her hand for a second.

"Stop thinking," he ordered. "Not another word till you're fed. What do you say to an iced melon to start with, a beautiful trout to follow, and after that a little duck with green peas, asparagus on the side, and—"

She laughed brokenly and slid her arm through his.

"Oh, Tommy darling, what a comfort you are! Why must you live in Paris, when I could do with so much more of you?"

Comfort! That, in a nutshell, was what he represented to her—and with the warmth of her young body sending electric currents along every nerve! Even as a comfort he might have let her down. It would be cruel, he felt, to delude her with false hopes about this uncle of hers. To his relief, however, she did not ask him his own opinion. Instead, when she was revived by an Epicurean meal, she led the talk into an unexpected channel.

"I told you, didn't I, what a queer family ours was?" Munching a marron glace, she gazed past him at the shaded lamps of the restaurant. "There was one bit, though, I didn't mention. I don't know now if I ought to do it. On Sunday I had my mind made up. Then I weakened. This afternoon I saw something which changed me back again—though even now I can't quite see—"

"Has it to do with your uncle?"

"Oh, no! But it's because of him, now he's in danger of being accused of things he may not have done. If there was some one else. . . . You remember what I said about my grandfather's sending us all abusive letters? Well, I've got mine here in my bag. It came straight from Black Gables—typed, but with his signature. So he must have dictated it."

"You sound doubtful."

"Wait." She laid aside the marron, unfinished. "I must tell you to begin with that it's a beastly letter. Not attacking me—I could have borne that—but saying the most vile, unspeakable things about my aunt. Stupid, impossible things," she insisted vehemently. "Warning me—yes, warning me, to keep clear of a harpy who'd ruined my Uncle James's life, and—just fancy!—would ruin mine if I let her. It actually hints—but here, read it yourself. Boggie—hardly known to my grandfather; Boggie, the perfect wife and the greatest dear . . . oh, what's the use? It's too preposterous!"

She thrust the letter across to him and watched, on tenterhooks, while he ran through its amazing contents.

"Well?" she demanded. "Isn't it all I said? Without reason or the smallest atom of excuse?"

Laying the communication aside, but still glancing at it, Tommy answered, with truth, that her grandfather sounded a mixture of Jeremiah, Cassandra on a bad day, and the ghost in *Hamlet*.

"With a spice of individual venom thrown in. Yes, I'd say one assertion he's made might constitute grounds for a legal action."

"You mean where he accuses Boggie of causing her husband's heart-attack on purpose, so she could have his money to herself?"

"Exactly. And what does she say to it?"

"Boggie? She doesn't know. Do you imagine I'd let her see a thing like this? She may joke about his letters to her, but she mightn't think it funny when he tries to poison my mind against her. Suppose she started wondering if I believed these fiendish accusations? I couldn't risk that."

Suddenly he realised the reason for her acute anxiety, and hastened to remove it.

"And you've been afraid I also might get wrong notions? Don't worry. Even if your aunt were a different woman from the one I judge her to be, I shouldn't dream of connecting her with her husband's death. Your Uncle James, by all accounts, was likely to die very soon in any case. It would have been taking a stupid risk to hurry things."

"Naturally. Oh, thank God you take a sensible view!"

"As for the rest of this tosh," Tommy went on, "just look at the facts for a moment. Thus far your aunt has been the sufferer, not you, and whatever the explanation she happens to be the one person who can't possibly benefit by any family death except your grandfather's. If the lot of you died to-night, Mrs. Bellamy-Pryce would still inherit only her husband's portion of the estate—and only the income, at that. I've found this out from examining your great-grandfather's will. So, you see, she's actually cleared of all suspicion."

"Does the inspector know this, too?" she asked eagerly.

"Oh, certainly; but I can see you've more to tell me. What is it?"

"This letter," she said slowly, "reached me about a month ago. On the very next Saturday I went down to Sussex, and without saying anything to daddy sneaked up to Black Gables. I meant to have it out face to face with my grandfather. My blood was up."

"And—?"

"I didn't see him. The nurse who's been his dragon bodyguard for seven years quite literally turned me out of the house. Oh, she was most plausible! She declared my grandfather had taken a turn for the worse; but that same afternoon I met your brother, Doctor Rostetter, and he told me grandfather's solicitor had been down during the morning for a business conference. So I wondered—as we've all wondered, at times—whether this nurse didn't exceed her instructions. There's simply no way of knowing. And then, since these awful things have been happening in Victoria Grove, I keep asking myself how could my grandfather predict calamities, unless"—she picked up the bitten marron and examined it—"unless he meant them to happen."

"But why should he want them to happen?" objected Tommy.

Rosemary shrugged. "You might ask that about any of his actions towards us. He might want to punish Boggie for an imagined evil deed. Warning me to leave her might be done to prevent my running into her danger—or to remove a damaging witness. But," she added, frowning, "I also asked myself if my grandfather really did write this letter? His signature might have been traced. I thought of it again this afternoon when I ran bolt into Nurse Claiborne, coming out of a dressmaker's in South Audley Street. She was just getting into my grandfather's Rolls."

Tommy gave sharper attention.

"The woman who barred you out? Tell me this: Is she young, good-looking?"

"Neither, especially. Very hard, highly efficient. I'd describe her as a lady-like sergeant-major in skirts. Gives herself airs, so they say in the village. She's supposed to see eye to eye with my grandfather. So, of course, she detests his family."

"How long has she been in town?" asked Tommy pointedly.

"Whitechurch, the chauffeur, told me she came up last Wednesday, to be with her mother, who's ill. It was his saying Wednesday that made me sit up; and it seems my grandfather really is sinking rapidly. He's got a night-nurse now, otherwise Claiborne wouldn't be away. I can't quite see her firing revolvers at us, still less disguising herself as a man and knocking Boggie out—though she's strong enough, Heaven knows. Still, if she had some one acting for her?"

"On her own account, or your grandfather's?"

"It might be either—that is, if she's anything to gain by it. Does it sound very silly? She was wearing an awfully posh silver fox—and South Audley Street's high-stepping for a nurse. There was I, bareheaded, clutching gin-bottles. She gave me such a glare; but she'd a funny look in her eye. You say you've seen that will. Is there any possible way that Boggie's dying could make a difference to my grandfather?"

Tommy took out the note-book in which he had jotted down the main points of the entail, and read out what he had written. The estate left by James Luther Bellamy-Pryce took the form of a closely-guarded trust-form—no capital to be released till the third generation.

"Which is you, I gather. No other great-grandchildren, I suppose?"

"I'm the one and only. Well?"

The will had been drawn up after the birth of Osmund's four sons. In accordance with its terms neither Osmund, sole direct heir, nor his children in their turn, could enjoy more than a life-interest on income derived from property largely invested in the tea business. At Osmund's death this income was to be apportioned amongst the legitimate offspring and the widow, if surviving. The distribution was to be equal, unless one of the sons took on the business, in which event the son so electing would receive considerably more than his co-heirs. The death of any of Osmund's sons would increase by redistribution the income of his brothers; but the childless widow of a son would, at Osmund's decease, receive only that portion to which her husband would have been heir at the time of his death. Thus Boggie, having no children, was now due to receive an income on one-third of the estate.

"That's plain enough, isn't it? Your grandmother predeceased her husband. So did your mother. Now, then! If a childless widow dies, her income reverts . . . Hold on, though. Does it revert? By Jove, here's something I'd overlooked."

Tommy bent over his scribbled notes. He must, yesterday, have been hypnotised by the obviousness of Gavin's motive to have paid so little attention to this altering clause. He looked up suddenly.

"That's odd. If Boggie dies before either your father or your uncle, her income is divided between them; but supposing she dies while your grandfather also is alive, the capital from which her income is derived is set free, and four-fifths of it passes to—"

"To whom?" demanded Rosemary tensely.

"Why, to your grandfather! Here, let's have another look at that letter. . . ."

CHAPTER THIRTEEN

WEDNESDAY morning, nine-forty. Brackham Place washed clean by a night of rain, and inside the hat-shop three yawning maidens rehashing yesterday's foray.

"Let's pray their cheques are good," sighed the Honourable Joan Walford, rubbing a bruised ankle. "All considered, we made a fairly clean sweep. Ro, my pet, where do you get your stockings? Mine never look half so alluring."

"It's the filling, my poppet," murmured Cybele Tarrant, ruffling her flaxen hair and chewing the pencil with which she was endeavouring to tot up recent sales. "Help! What's eight and eleven? My head's stuffed with wool." She obtained a result by means of her fingers, wrote it down, and relaxed. "Why so pensive, Ro darling? Are you thinking of him?"

"Which him?" drawled Joan, studying her inch-long lashes in the nearest glass. "I rather fancy this new eye-black of mine, don't you? It's got an oil-basis."

Rosemary stirred.

"Sorry, Cyb! I was half-asleep. I see the mauve horror's gone. And the Baku the countess got ink on. Good business, whoever managed it; but I expect they were all blind."

Her tone was absent. As a matter of fact, she had been ruminating depressedly over Boggie's strangely-irritable manner last night. Such a thing had never happened before. Poor Boggie, her nerves must be badly on edge. Entirely natural, of course. If a person has had three narrow escapes from death within four days, you expect them to blow up. Still, it had been a shock. Was it really due to her coming in so late and never telephoning to say what she was doing? She did hope it was only that.

She cast her mind back to the moment when, having said good-bye to Tommy, she had entered the dark hall, and not bothering about lights started up the stairs. All at once the door at the top had opened, and a voice so hoarse she had scarcely recognised it had called down, "Who's there?"

It was the combined anger and fear of the tone which had startled her into momentary speechlessness. Looking back she realised what a fool she had been not to guess how Boggie, alone in the night, would find herself an easy prey to the terrors she so ably kept under during the day. At the time all she had thought of was that she was being accused of some criminal action.

"Me, of course. Why, what did you think?"

"You!"

The anticipated chuckle had not come. Instead there had been a pregnant pause, curiously like the pall preceding yesterday's thunder-clap. In the half-light from the door she had seen her aunt's solid form, shapeless without stays, and swathed in the mandarin coat its owner wore for a dressing-gown. The capacious bosom had heaved with some inexplicable emotion, the lips twitched to keep back the bitterness all too soon to burst forth.

"Indeed! And have you any notion what time it is?"

"Late, isn't it? Nearly one. We got talking, and—"

"We?" Boggie had interrupted in sharp anxiety.

"Why, yes, Tommy and I. He gave me dinner at Scott's. Is there anything wrong about it?"

"I expected you home," her aunt had said shortly. "When you didn't come I got worrying—rather naturally. All this time I've not closed an eye."

"But Boggie!" In her utter astonishment she had omitted the dear. "I don't understand. I usually do go on somewhere after a cocktail party, don't I? I thought you'd know I wasn't coming home. I suppose I ought to have rung up, but it simply never occurred to me. I'm so sorry!"

For a second Boggie had stood there gripping the balustrade with her firm, cushioned hands and breathing with difficulty.

"After this afternoon," she had said, "anything might have happened. I should have imagined you'd appreciate the state of mind I'd be in."

With this cutting reproof Boggie had gone back into her room and banged—yes, banged the door behind her. If a friendly Newfoundland had suddenly bitten her, Rosemary could not have been more stunned. There had been so much she had wanted to talk over, but the finality of that banged door had made her afraid to venture on further discussion.

"Seeing Uncle Gavin with daddy upset her rather badly," concluded Rosemary, determined not to make mountains out of molehills. "Every one's got a temper. She took hers out on me. Yes, of course, that's it."

It must be, for after all what harm was there in going off to be fed, bodily and spiritually, by the one unexigent man of her acquaintance? Tommy Rostetter—old enough to make no tiresome demands on her; young enough to understand her point of view. Last evening had bucked her up enormously. She had come home soothed and with the edge of her fears blunted—which was probably why being met with unmerited reproaches had bowled her over. Well, it was over now, so she must think no more about it. Boggie at breakfast-time had been her usual serene self, and her father, as they had found out by telephoning the hotel, was perfectly safe. The incident was merely one of the little squalls any two people who live together are liable to meet with sooner or later. . . .

"What were you saying, Joan?"

"Only that we'll never get the stickiness out of this carpet. And do look at that small rubbish-heap, just swept in a corner and left! If you ask me, I'll say Clover found some drink knocking about. Ought we to sack her?"

"The stuff was drained to the last drop," answered Rosemary. "So it can't have been that. I must say she's done a hit or miss job of it, though. Here's broken glass, and there's—oh, help! Must we hear this? It's the Spectre of the Rose, coming in to bother us. David, dear," she addressed the visitor in the doorway, "we're all dead in here. Couldn't you possibly leave the bodies in peace?"

The Earl of Hollings paused, hand gracefully on hip. In deference to their mood he hummed the main theme from the *Pavane pour Une Infante Défunte*, and swayed with Spanish dignity into their midst—an admirable performance, from which all three damsels rigidly averted their eyes.

"Why," Cybele demanded in a tone of scientific curiosity, "this virulent eruption of ballet? It's a disease, I tell you—like hay-fever, or groupiness. Every man I know has gone ballet-minded. Why, even little Lizard's fallen for it! He climbs to the upper circle every night."

"Too true," murmured Joan. Bilfilian, it seemed, was actually composing a ballet based on troglodytes—whatever they might be—with music to be scored for bassoons and penny-whistles. It was all rather sickening.

"Pitch me a cigarette, David, there's a good boy. No, don't come any closer. Your setting-lotion smells simply foul."

"A guinea a bottle, darling—and now we're exchanging compliments, you really should do something about your spots. I suggest arsenic. Ro, my sweet, I'm sorry I can't offer you a smoke. These are all I've got left. Where are you going, with the blood all oozing from your finger? Is it where he bit you?"

Not troubling to reply, Rosemary removed the splinter of glass from her hand, pushed Lord Hollings aside, and disappeared into the back room. Lord Hollings with a spent sigh eased himself to a languid posture on the floor, inhaled his cigarette, and criticised the neck-line of Joan's blouse. Joan in return made scathing comment on his immaculate suède shoes, and a homelike atmosphere was fast establishing itself when from the inner regions Rosemary called out.

"I can't get this door open. Why's that, I wonder?"

"It's locked, darling," answered Lord Hollings. "Which door?"

"The lavatory door, you ass. How could it be locked? It's got wedged somehow, from inside. Come help me shove, can't you?"

"My sweet one, your muscles are equal to mine any day." Grumbling, Lord Hollings rose and lounged to her assistance. "Now, then, why all this pother? When I say shove . . ."

The obstruction behind the door gave suddenly. Rosemary and Lord Hollings tumbled headlong over that which blocked the tiny floor-space within. One gasped, the other turned a faint pea-green and slumped where he stood. The two girls came running, took one look, and shrieked.

Before them, back stiffly arched, grinning mouth upturned, lay Mrs. Clover, stone-dead.

CHAPTER FOURTEEN

TOMMY, over his breakfast coffee, studied again the letter handed him the night before. The phraseology, Rosemary had said, was typical; the signature? With the aid of a reading glass he fancied he could detect a faint doubling of the downstrokes. He, however, was no expert. Headcorn must see this, and decide if the matter was worth following up.

He had just dug from his pocket a crumpled handkerchief he had found in the car and was holding it shamefacedly against his nose when the telephone rudely shattered his daydream. What he heard over the wire sent him speeding, stern-eyed, to Brackham Place, to meet, on the very doorstep of Anatol's, Mrs. Bellamy-Pryce, just going in. She greeted him with her broad smile.

"Well met!" she said breezily. "I'm come to buy that hat. Didn't feel like it yesterday. As you're here, I shall ask your advice. Some of these extreme models—Heavens!" She recoiled a little, as a six-foot, youthful police constable blocked the entrance. "What's going on inside? Not bailiffs, I hope?"

The constable said firmly: "You can't come in, madam. Not for another hour."

"My good man," retorted Boggie with energy. "Of course I'm coming in! What nonsense is this?"

Rosemary appeared, her face chalk-white.

"It's my aunt, and a friend," she explained evenly. "Please let them in. No, Boggie, that's only David." For Mrs. Bellamy-Pryce, now inside, was staring goggle-eyed at the prostrate young man stretched in her path. "He passed out, but he's just coming round. The trouble's over there. It's Clover; but don't look. It's not nice to see."

Boggie did look, uttered a smothered cry, and sank heavily on one of the mirrored stools. A doctor, bending over, glanced up, and resumed his scrutiny of the woman's body, clad in rusty black and calico apron, which occupied the centre foreground. It was a repellent object. Strangely flexed, it supported itself by the head and down-trodden heels, all between curved upward in an arc. Tommy went close and examined it.

"Strychnine, I suppose?" he asked in a low voice.

"Oh, certainly!" The doctor muttered the words without raising his head. "A thumping big dose of it, too. Must have died very quickly, ten to twelve hours ago, I'd say. Where she got hold of the stuff is another question."

Tommy inquired where the body had been found. Rosemary told him, and the constable, holding converse with the two shaken girls, creaked forward to add his own information.

"Came along about eight in the evening. . . ."

"Nine," Cybele corrected him, "because of the party."

"Nine, then—to clean up. Seems to have started work and left off. The party you mention was in the nature of . . . ?" He turned back to the assistants.

"Cocktails," said Joan. "But Mr. Rostetter knows. He was here. The drink was all finished. You said so, didn't you, Ro?"

Rosemary, in a dream, pointed to the array of bottles stacked in the inner room.

"All empty, I noticed, but you can look to make sure. There was a bit left in some of the glasses. I dumped it all in the ice bucket."

The constable produced the ice bucket. It was empty and clean. He replaced it, and disappeared for a moment, to return with a small glass held in gingerly fashion by its stem.

"What about this?" he asked. "On the shelf above the wash basin it was. Seems sticky inside."

It was a glass slightly larger than the ones now washed and ranged in rows on a table. It was also of better quality, with a line of cutting round the bowl. They all stared hard at it. Rosemary had begun to frown when a gulping sound drew the company's eyes in her aunt's quarter. Mrs. Bellamy-Pryce's colour had gone blotched, and her fingers were picking clumsily at her lips.

"Anything wrong, madam?" inquired the constable, and then, as the object of his interest remained mutely gazing: "Pardon me, but were you present as well?"

She murmured confusedly: "Yes—oh, yes, I came. Don't mind me, it's nothing." She fumbled for her handkerchief and mopped her brow. "You say this glass was on the . . . the shelf?"

"In the lavatory—where the body was lying." The constable sniffed at the glass and handed it to the doctor. "Smells like gin."

The doctor stooped his long nose over the glass and made a sour face.

"And strychnine," he said shortly. "Analysis will show it; but that's not my affair."

Straightening up he asked if there was such a thing as a dust-sheet handy. Rosemary produced one from a cupboard. The remains of the luckless Mrs. Clover were decently shrouded, and the doctor, having left his professional card, went away.

"Any idea where she lived?" inquired the constable. The three girls looked blankly at one another. Somewhere in the Seven Dials district, Joan hazarded vaguely; or was it King's Cross? Rosemary, without speaking, rummaged in the silver-lacquered desk, found a scrap of lined paper with a pencilled scrawl on it, and gave it to the officer, who read it aloud.

"Amanda Clover, nine Orkney Mews, Kentish Town. That'll do nicely, miss; and now I'd better take down the names of you ladies. Who runs this place, by the way? Countess . . . ?" He grinned. "You'll have to spell that one . . . I suppose," writing laboriously in his notebook, "no other casualties was noticed?"

A little blankly he was assured that nothing untoward had happened—not, at least, during the progress of the party. The Norwegian minister had been sick, but that was not untoward. The constable, after a stare which lightened to another grin, took down such names as were known, and putting away his book declared that all empties must be left untouched for examination. Bilfilian had now edged in, to gape, vast-eyed, on the gathering. At a word from Rosemary he undertook to guide the still nauseated Lord Hollings back to a pleasanter atmosphere, and meeting the ambulance orderlies outside gave rise to a slight confusion as to identity. In a few minutes every vestige of horror had been removed. Even the scattered fragments of glassware were sealed in one of the firm's crested envelopes and deposited with the various articles awaiting examination. Tommy took the constable aside and informed him that Inspector Headcorn, from Scotland Yard, would be in charge of the case, and that when he arrived it would be as well for him to have a private word with Mrs. and Miss Bellamy-Pryce.

"Inspector Headcorn, sir?" The young officer pricked up his ears. "You mean you've got in touch with him yourself?"

"As soon as I heard." Tommy kept his voice low. "But don't noise it about. I'm going to take the two ladies I've referred to somewhere nearby. The inspector will want to interview all three of us, but not in public, I think." He turned to Rosemary, who had come within earshot. "Where could we go? Your aunt is looking rather faint."

Rosemary understood. Boggie had something to say, but was unwilling to utter a syllable before the others.

"We'd better get her along to David's. His place will be quiet, and it's only two doors below."

"David?" echoed Tommy doubtfully.

Joan Walford had heard and hastened to explain.

"You've just seen him. David Hollings, inferior decorator." She giggled, and then looked conscience-stricken at her own levity. "Poor Mrs. Bellamy-Pryce!" she added, with a sympathetic glance at her friend's relative, now making strenuous efforts to pull herself together. "I don't wonder she feels like a limp rag. If you take my advice, you'll make David cough up that bottle of Johnnie Walker he's so stingy over. What she wants is a stiff peg."

Tommy advised the constable as to where they would be found when wanted, and offered Mrs. Bellamy-Pryce his arm. In the decorating establishment no one was visible, but retching sounds from the rear regions indicated that the proprietor was still far from recovered. Rosemary shut the communicating door firmly, and returned to find her aunt subsiding on to a Regency sofa. Tommy noticed that her own face was rigid. It seemed to him that she was being tom in two, as by instruments of torture.

"I know where David keeps his whisky," she said in a leaden tone. "Shall I fetch her a drink?"

"Drink!" Mrs. Bellamy-Pryce shook her head with repugnance. "Don't let's speak of it. I'm quite all right. It did give me rather a turn, but it's quite over now."

Very quietly Tommy said: "That was your glass, I take it?"

She hesitated and gave a nod, but avoided his eyes.

"Y-yes, so it was. Or one exactly like it." She moistened her lips. "It had neat gin in it. After a . . . a certain thing happened, I felt decidedly wonky. There was no brandy, and I didn't dare risk any more mixtures.

So I just poured myself a little plain gin. You saw me do it, didn't you?" she appealed to her niece, who did not seem to hear her. "Oh, well, perhaps you didn't. You were very busy at the time."

"You didn't drink it, of course," pursued Tommy. "I suppose you set it down and forgot about it?"

"Must have done. There was so much confusion . . . I do certainly remember setting down the glass when I saw my brothers-in-law leaving; and I noticed, I don't know why, that it was different from the others. A scrap larger, with cutting round it. Rather a good glass. There must be more like it?"

A poignant silence, and then: "There aren't," said Rosemary detachedly. "It's an odd one that belongs to the countess, all the plain ones were hired."

Before more could be said, Inspector Headcorn pushed open the street door, and moved across the thick grey carpet. He had stopped at Anatol's, learned the initial facts, and, as had been supposed, was now come to obtain closer information. With a face more stern than its wont he settled down determinedly to his task, and Tommy, thinking it wiser to leave him alone with Mrs. Bellamy-Pryce, withdrew to a distance and made a pretence of studying a very choice selection of glass pictures. Rosemary touched his arm, and beckoned with her head. In another moment the two of them had slipped quietly out of the shop, and with one accord were moving towards the corner.

A small group, composed of errand boys, the waitresses from The Snuggery, and three children sucking lollypops stood gazing ghoulishly at the hat window. It was temporarily dispersed by the arrival of a taxi, which hurtled up and set down a woman in black, whose slenderness seemed wrought of steel wires. It was Countess Rakovsky—evidently interrupted midway the enamelling process, for her cheeks had the look of a stripped wall, while the black round her eyes had been laid on with a frantic hand. In the doorway she wheeled, saw Rosemary, and clutched hold of her fiercely.

"Who says this is murder?" she hissed. *"Vite, dites-moi!"*

Rosemary coolly extricated herself. "I don't know what you've been told," she said. "Clover took strychnine out of a glass with gin in it. That's all we know."

"Strychnine! *Tiens . . .*"

The burning eyes searched the girl's, then turned on Tommy and without a trace of recognition bored holes in him. The countess demanded further details, listened tensely, and relaxed with a smile of bitter, secret triumph.

"De Vries warned me of this," she muttered. "It was to happen in June; but if I wore cat's eyes I should be protected. I have worn cat's eyes—you see?" Ripping off her suède glove she displayed a crimson nailed hand on which a cat's eye gleamed dully in a circlet of brilliants. "To-day is the third—and three, as you know, is my lucky number. De Vries is never wrong."

Swiftly abandoning the metaphysical, she remarked that a thing of this kind was tragic on the first day of the Sale, but properly handled might mean big business.

"Ecoute, ma chèrie!" She seized Rosemary again. "You must wire Victor . . ." Stopping, she bit her lip, and murmured: "No, I'll attend to it myself. A chance like this won't come twice. While the sun shines, we must make lots of hay!"

She swept into the shop.

Speaking as though in a trance, Rosemary answered Tommy's question.

"Who's De Vries? Oh, a tame astrologer she carries round in her pocket. Could you have believed it?" She laughed oddly. "She's taking it for granted that stuff was meant for her. She would, of course. I wonder how many others will think the same?"

To Tommy it appeared a cogent question. He was revolving it dubiously while the girl walked slowly beside him, mused aloud:

"Poor Clover! She liked her little drop of gin quite as much as the countess does. And now Clover's dead, and no one thinks of her at all."

They wandered on aimlessly in the hot, close air, past puddles which reflected the blue sky. Beyond earshot of the group—augmented now by a fishmonger's boy and a sweep—they halted to turn back.

"Wait." Rosemary slid her hand through Tommy's arm. "I think I'd better tell you . . ."

"Well?" he asked, pressing her hand close against his side. "What is it?"

"That glass," she whispered dryly. "Boggie's mistaken about it. You see, Tommy dear, it happened to be mine."

CHAPTER FIFTEEN

TOMMY's heart turned a handspring.

"Yours? Are you quite sure about it?"

"Oh, quite!"

"But you weren't drinking," he argued with heat. "I heard you say no a dozen times."

"I started shivering," she explained. "It wasn't with cold. Captain Argus and Grimaldi began badgering me again. It always seems to bother men if you won't drink. Anyhow, I said I'd take a little plain gin, and I poured myself some in a glass. That glass." She paused, her breath spent. "I remember saying I'd fill it up with water from the tap and just gulp it down like medicine."

"Only you didn't do it. Why was that?"

"I put it off. I really do loathe spirits, you know. Then I saw Daddy and Uncle Gav about to go, so I ran after you. When I got back I saw the glass standing on the table where I'd left it. I took it back into the lavatory, meaning to mix water with it, and—yes, I distinctly recall setting it down on the shelf while I washed my hands. After that it just passed out of my mind."

A few minutes earlier, Gavin had been standing by the bar . . .

"You saw your uncle near you, I suppose?"

"I did. He said nothing, just smiled at me in that queer way he has. I couldn't find anything to say to him. With all these horrible ideas nagging at me . . . oh, Tommy, why can't we *know*?"

"We shall know, very soon." His face was hard. "First, though, let's straighten out a point or two. Your aunt seems thoroughly convinced it's her glass. You didn't actually see her help herself to the gin?"

"No. She must have done it when the ice-bucket got kicked over. I was down on my knees behind the table for several minutes, mopping up the mess. It's all most odd, because when I came to clear away I didn't notice a single glass with plain gin in it. Of course, the light wasn't too good, and when it comes to that some one else may have . . ." Rosemary clapped her free hand over her mouth in terror. "Oh, what if there were two lots poisoned, and some other person's died?"

"Not a chance. We'd have heard by now. Besides, there'd have been symptoms almost at once. Tell me this: Why, just now, didn't you correct your aunt's impression?"

She hesitated. "I couldn't decide off-hand whether it mightn't make it more awful to know both of us were blacklisted. For that's what it comes to, doesn't it? And then there'd be daddy. It wouldn't do any good to kill me and leave him. Oh, Tommy," she cried distractedly. "What is one to do?"

Tommy, still staggered by what he had heard, could think of no suitable answer. His immediate impulse—impracticable, on a populous corner in Mayfair—was to take her forthwith into his arms and chance the consequences.

"The inspector must advise us," he said slowly. "It may not be necessary to say anything at all to your aunt. We'll get her away, so you can talk with him alone. Personally, I don't believe there were two lots of gin poisoned. I think she drank hers, and forgot about it. With the other attacks fresh in her mind, it would be natural enough to mistake this particular glass for hers."

"Oh, most natural! We've five almost exactly like it. We keep thorn at the shop. No outside person would be apt to notice the little difference between those and the odd one. I . . . I don't want any arguments cropping up," Rosemary said suddenly. "Poor old Boggie's not quite herself just lately. I feel the best thing is to be very tactful."

"You mean you'd rather not cross her," he remarked, struck by the embarrassment of her manner. "Now we're getting it. Has there been trouble?"

"Certainly not," she denied with some asperity. "It's only that—how shall I say it? You see, till all this began happening she and I were so comfortable together. We've each led our own life, and been quite happy and independent. I suppose it couldn't go on quite the same, with Boggie believing some devil was trying to murder her. One can't blame her for being a bit—well, edgy. I ought to remember and not give her cause to . . . to blow up."

"When?" Tommy asked, his face drawn closer to hers.

"Last night," she admitted, ashamed. "Oh, it was nothing! She rather went for me for being out so late and not letting her know. I shouldn't have thought anything of it if she weren't always so good-tempered."

"You felt, just for a moment, it might be better to part company?"

"Nonsense! Of course I didn't. You know how it is when for so long you've had no one to call you to account for your actions. I'm arrogant. It serves me jolly well right to be ticked off once in a while." She squared her shoulders. "Let's forget it. She needs me more than ever now, and it begins to look as though I needed her. Whatever happens, we'll stick together and see things through."

Tommy said no more as with a thoughtful expression he steered her back towards the shops. Into Anatol's a young man in horn-rimmed spectacles was just lithely vanishing. A reporter, obviously.

"In case the press gets hold of you," said Tommy. "Be extremely careful what you say, won't you?"

"I shan't say anything." Her frown lingered. "See here," she continued desperately, "Our chief concern is daddy. He mustn't know, but he must be safeguarded till he goes home. There'll be to-day and to-morrow. . . . I know," she exclaimed with sudden inspiration, "Boggie must take him to lunch, and then on to the flicks. Marlene Dietrich, at the New Gallery. He'll adore that. Then we'll Jill three dine together at his hotel, and have drinks in the lounge, right up till time to send him to bed. That's one day settled. After that . . ."

"I don't know if your father's the one to worry about. After all, didn't he pass an entire evening in his brother's company and come to no harm?"

"So he did. They had bamboo-sprouts and what-not at the Chinese restaurant in Greek Street. It's perfectly true he'd have swallowed any amount of strychnine in those messes and put it down to the foreign flavour; but that doesn't mean he'll go on being safe. It did occur to me that Uncle Gavin might have been intending the strychnine for daddy, but when the opportunity to dish it out to me came along he just switched over. He mightn't have had any more on him—for the moment." She shuddered.

Tommy was thinking of the words lately spoken by Countess Rakovsky: *"A chance like this won't come again."* How aptly they could be applied to an indiscriminate gathering of more or less tipsy persons! Still, as he pointed out, it is one thing to drop strychnine tablets into a glass at a cocktail party, quite another to resort to the same method of killing when dining alone with the proposed victim. Strychnine was a poison unmistakable in its effects. It could be used with impunity only on very especial occasions.

"I quite see that," Rosemary agreed reluctantly. "If Uncle Gavin hasn't gone entirely mad, he won't use strychnine again—at least, not unless he sees another good opportunity, which isn't likely. There are plenty of other ways, though—ways that can be made to look like accident. That's what I'm afraid of, for daddy, of course, not for Boggie and me. Don't you think, though, this last sensation may bring things to a head?"

Tommy said Yes, mainly to comfort her. Actually he doubted it. Indeed, he had seldom known of a case where responsibility promised to be so difficult to pin down. He hoped some one had seen the transfer of the poison to the glass. If so, then the matter would be simplified.

At the hat shop entrance Tommy halted.

"I'm going to butt in while that reporter is getting his story. However, I won't be long."

Rosemary walked on, revolving her plans. It seemed to her that with any luck there was only this one short interval of time, like a dangerous channel, to be negotiated. With her father back at the Sussex vicarage, her worst anxiety would be relieved; and surely, oh surely, some way would be found of ending this torturing suspense before another catastrophe could happen! Even with the evidence of her eyes confronting her, she found it hard to believe she had missed a horrible death by mere inches. At the same time she was shaken—badly so. It seemed impossible to breathe normally, or to relax her tightened muscles.

Entering the decorating shop, she still saw no sign of its owner. How few young men of to-day had any guts! The business between her aunt and the inspector was concluding, and Boggie, roughly powdering her warm face, looked as though she had just had a four-pronged molar extracted. She saw the wisdom of Rosemary's suggestions, and gallantly agreed to take Cuthbert in tow for the rest of the day.

"Better ring him up now," she advised. "Tell him I'll come and fetch him."

Luckily the Reverend Cuthbert was in. After an early sortie, he had returned, and was just about to potter off again for a tour of the city churches, his ultimate objective Simpson's restaurant, in the Strand.

"It's all right," sighed the daughter, hanging up. "He'll wait for you, Boggie dear, and I'll meet you at seven, as we've said. Oh, heavens, what a load off our shoulders!"

Mrs. Bellamy-Pryce, her jauntiness recovered, sailed off on her mission. Rosemary, having watched her passage down the street, turned to find the inspector's dull blue eyes resting on herself in a meditative fashion.

"That was very well engineered, Miss Bellamy-Pryce," the calm accents approved. "And now let's hear your version of things. I take it the glass was yours?"

CHAPTER SIXTEEN

WHEN the interview was over, Rosemary decided to hurry along, by taxi, to Simpson's, where her father and aunt were lunching. For one thing, the noon editions of the papers were out, and she wanted to see just what had been printed. These were the posters which glared at her from the street-corners:

"MAYFAIR POISONING"
"DEATH FOLLOWS COCKTAILS"
"STRYCHNINE IN HAT-SHOP"

She bought the three papers and anxiously scanned them. In not one did the name of Bellamy-Pryce appear. She breathed a sigh of relief and gratitude. Tommy had managed this. Very adroitly he had allowed the full limelight to play on the two persons always greedy for publicity—David Hollings, and the countess; though to be sure his task had been made easier by the fact that Joan and Cybele—darlings, both of them, but such hopeless chatterers—had known nothing whatever about the excitement in Victoria Grove. Now her father need not guess the real meaning of Clover's death. Perhaps the whole affair would peter out without ever ruffling the placid surface of his mind. Such was her thought when she watched him working his way through his vast plateful of the celebrated roast beef, and giving vague attention to her edited version of the calamity.

The inspector—how uncannily sharp of him to have spotted her secret!—had advised her to say nothing about the glass being hers. There might have been two lots of gin poisoned—which, of course, she could not deny. The light had not been too good. She might have poured away a colourless liquid thinking it a White Lady.

Anyhow, the inspector had agreed it would do no good to add to her aunt's panic. Boggie, for a bit, had lost all her Spartan composure.

It was a strain, nevertheless, to keep up light patter all during lunch, and an almost worse strain, back in the shop, to endure the countess's probing questions. Talia, wretched woman, seemed to possess a witch's sixth sense. She had stopped hinting that she had been the intended victim, and was now at her other famous game—that of sadistically tormenting those who worked for her. Not for long, fortunately; for calling a taxi she dashed off on one of her mysterious errands, the nature of which was revealed when she arrived back, at five, with a consignment of atrocious, cheap hats, into which Paris labels had hastily to be sewn. That was Talia all over. Business, however badly handled, came first.

Dinner brought a new shock. The vicar, ordinarily like plasticine, all at once disclosed the stubborn streak which at rare moments made his daughter realise he actually did have a mind of his own and could use it. In short, he liked being in London at this season. It was his first visit since the big ecclesiastical conference two years ago, and he proposed to make the most of it. He would remain till Saturday.

"But what will you do with yourself, Daddy?" wailed Rosemary in despair.

She could have shaken him; but it was plain he had not even heard her question, being entirely fascinated by the bewildering assortment of cheeses just extended for his selection.

"Now that," he remarked, blinking benignly at the one under his nose, "looks to me very like a Double Gloucester. One seldom meets them nowadays—I don't know why. Is it a Double Gloucester? No, I was afraid not. . . ."

Boggie's eye, meeting Rosemary's, seemed to say that however one may wish it, one can't take a middle-aged cleric by the scruff of the neck and bundle him off home like a refractory child. On the other hand, Rosemary telegraphed, seeing it was daddy one couldn't enlighten him. She set her lips and asked for the bill.

Her head throbbed with the worry of it. To add the final fly-sting to her wretchedness, they had hardly found a place in the lounge and settled to their coffee before Captain Argus, taciturn and in one of his black moods, stalked in to join them. She knew quite well why he had come. It flattered his vanity to play the constant watch-dog; but it was particularly disagreeable just now to find him turning up, unasked and behaving, for some inexplicable reason, like a sullen hobbledehoy. Oddly enough, his ill-temper seemed directed at Boggie. If it had been herself, she could have understood, for last evening she had been decidedly short with him. That was because he would keep asking for it. Why couldn't this Australian get it into his thick head she was simply bored and bothered by his attentions? She felt like apologising to her father for the bad manners of Boggie's friend, but to her relief saw there was no necessity. Daddy, bless his vagueness, seemed scarcely aware that another man had been added to the party. He was far too absorbed in the throng of new faces, and in the hectic gyrations of the band-conductor. Daddy was thoroughly enjoying himself.

She kept her eye on the doors, hoping Tommy would come along. He, with his agile wits, might solve this latest difficulty—though it was impossible to see how. Half-past nine—and still no sign of him. Maybe he wasn't coming at all. After all, what right had she to expect Rank's uncle to shelve every interest of his own on her account? He had not wanted to get mixed up in this business in the first place. She had guessed that all along. . . .

*

Tommy, on the point of quitting his flat, had been surprised by a visit from the inspector. He was glad to see Headcorn, for he was burning to know what steps had been taken. After his first sharp inquiry, however, his face fell with disappointment. Although the inspector had spent an incredibly active day, it would seem that nothing decisive had been accomplished. He was here not to impart information, but to confirm certain details. Tommy repeated what he had hastily sketched that morning.

"Yes, Gavin kept his gloves on. He stood about for several minutes within reach of the bar, and was in the room, I should say, about twenty minutes in all. Of course, there were plenty of others with an equal opportunity. Notably there was Captain Argus—and I think I mentioned the Italian, who, I'm told, is one of the countess's very especial hangers-on. Foots the bills, I rather , suspect."

"And you heard Miss Bellamy-Pryce refuse to dine with him?"

"She did, most firmly. I think she found his amorousness offensive." Tommy nearly added, "I know I did," but refrained.

"Could the countess have heard?"

"Possibly. I saw her, at intervals, trying to dislodge the various men from that corner. They stuck like flies round a jam-pot."

Headcorn grunted and rubbed his wart.

"It's been illuminating," he remarked, "to see how many of those present instantly connected the strychnine with themselves. I fancy the King's Proctor enters into one case of funk; but the mention of plain gin brought relief. No one remembers having it. So to some extent it's narrowing down."

"I thought it would," declared Tommy tersely. "Have you got any replies from the wireless messages you sent off?"

"I've heard from the boat, and also from Colombo. There was never anything at all questionable about the judge's death. Shock was pure surmise, not substantiated; and as far as is known the brother remained locked below decks. So you see, Captain Argus's belief carries no weight. As for Argus himself, Australia House vouches for him in every particular. He comes from Sydney, joined the Anzac forces in '18, and paid his first visit to England shortly after the Armistice." The speaker paused, then asked, "Are you still of the opinion that he's fond of the niece?"

Tommy met the dull blue eye with understanding.

"I am convinced of it," he answered with authority. "The fellow's jealous as hell of every man who looks at her. He was another who wanted her to go out with him last evening. Not likely he'd poison her first, is it? Besides, he went away not knowing whether or not that gin had been drunk. If he'd doctored it and meant it for her, my idea is he'd have made sure some one else didn't get hold of it. That might easily have happened, you know."

"Quite," assented Headcorn, with a tone which washed the Australian out of all calculations. "Yet whoever did do it wasn't troubled with any such scruples. Now then, I want to make sure about the list of people who knew Miss Bellamy-Pryce's objection to spirits. First, her aunt. Next, Argus; then we have the countess, the two young lady assistants, and a few intimate friends, none of whom were at the party. There's your nephew, of course, but he doesn't figure. He got off, I understand, before the drink was ever poured out. The uncle had no previous knowledge of Miss Bellamy-Pryce's likes and dislikes, but he may, on this occasion, have heard her say she took spirits only as medicine, and was in the habit of bolting the stuff as far as possible without tasting it. The same holds good with Signor Grimaldi and several other guests—perhaps a dozen. Is all that correct?"

Tommy agreed that it was.

"She also thought that most of the people round the bar were too fuzzy-headed to take in what she said, even if they heard it. However, this I can positively state; Gavin Bellamy-Pryce was one hundred per cent, sober. All he drank was a glass of sherry, and he had all his wits about him."

"Muddle and confusion!" complained the inspector. "What if he had? No one saw him tinkering with a glass. I've only found three people who remember him at all. It's a great pity. That remark of Miss Bellamy-Pryce's may have been all-important. Strychnine has a nasty taste, and there seems to have been a full grain of it used. The average person after one sip would have set the glass down. We may conclude the charwoman had a blunted palate, or was too thirsty for gin to be put off by a peculiar flavour."

As to the purchase of strychnine, it simply could not be done without a physician's prescription. Mrs. Clover's panel doctor denied having ordered his patient any medicine with strychnine in it. The increasingly-frequent theft of doctors' bags from cars offered a possible solution, but the Clover premises had revealed nothing but patent remedies, all harmless.

"But have you seriously supposed it might be suicide?" asked Tommy in surprise.

"I had to rule out the chance of it, naturally. The husband declares Clover was of a cheerful disposition. He says she was feeling on the top of the world just then, having won fifteen shillings the night before on the dogs. No, it wasn't suicide."

"These restrictions about poisonous drugs don't apply to all countries. Gavin, don't forget, is just back from India. More, he's been right away from civilisation, in a region where he may well have carried his own medicine-kit."

"I dare say," retorted Headcorn dryly. "But do you imagine we'll find any strychnine in his possession?"

"Not now, certainly."

Tommy spoke bitterly. To his thinking, the police had been almost criminally negligent—for if not, could this murder have been allowed to happen? That the victim was who she was made it none the less excusable. No one aware of the facts could be of two minds as to what person might have been killed.

As though answering his censure, the man on the sofa said calmly:

"Gavin has been under observation since before this happened. I knew he had come home—if, indeed, he went away at all, which I can't yet prove. While he was out with his brother yesterday afternoon one of my men got in and went through his belongings, hoping to locate the Smith and Wesson revolver. It wasn't there. He saw a medicine-kit. A phial in it had contained nux vomica tablets—in other words, strychnine; but the phial was empty. So now you know."

"Oh!" Tommy was mollified. "And when you talked with the vicar late this afternoon did you hear where—ostensibly at least—Gavin had been, and for how long?"

"He hadn't specified. The vicar had dropped him a line to say he would be in town yesterday morning. Gavin rang up the hotel, mentioning that he'd just got back from a short stay in the country, and would come round in the afternoon. By this time the vicar had got into touch with his sister-in-law, who had assured him there was nothing whatever to worry about. He did, however, suggest that Gavin come with him to see his daughter at her place of work. I had to get at these facts very cautiously," explained Headcorn, "so as to rouse no alarm. Miss Bellamy-Pryce and her aunt helped me, by letting it all come out in general conversation. It really wasn't difficult. I may say I've rarely met a man so wholly unsuspicious as the Reverend Cuthbert Bellamy-Pryce."

"Then Gavin did know in advance he was going to a cocktail party."

"Yes, it's an important point," replied the inspector without enthusiasm.

"Could anything be made out of the finger prints found on the glass?"

"Nothing helpful. Out of the general blur I deciphered those of the actual victim, Miss Bellamy-Pryce, and Miss Tarrant, who had washed relays of glasses and replaced them for use. Gloves or not, there was probably no need to touch the glass at all. The tablets could be dropped in under cover of reaching for something beyond."

The detective drew discontentedly on the cigar he had lighted. Tommy, glancing at his watch, began to grow restless.

"Do you honestly believe an attempt was made to poison both these women?" he asked bluntly.

"I can't say." Headcorn seemed to be evading a definite answer. "One of them may be mistaken. If so, I don't think it was the young one. Do you?"

"She wasn't mistaken. She's too familiar with those glasses. You're satisfied, are you, that they're both in danger?"

"It's about all I am satisfied of," grumbled the inspector. "As to the agent—well, if it were still the aunt only who was being attacked, the information you've handed me about Sir Osmund and the nurse might be worth the inquiries I'm making now. As it's the niece as well, we are forced to look elsewhere—and, of course, we have the vicar also involved. Right or wrong, we've got to keep a sharp eye on Gavin."

"I should hope so," snapped Tommy. "Can't you arrest him?"

"On what grounds?" retorted the other. "Oh, he's got the motive, and I can't find any one else who has, saving only the vicar; but so long as his sister-in-law conscientiously refuses to identify him as the man who struck her down on Saturday—"

"But damn it all!" exploded Tommy, personally outraged. "The woman's sure of it—dead sure! Can't she see that by sitting on the fence like this she's paving the way to her own death and a couple of others?"

The inspector shrugged massively and drained his whisky.

"She won't, or can't, admit she's sure. That situation's unchanged."

"Then she's still shielding him. After this actual murder, she can't be influenced solely by the horror of scandal. There's another reason holding her back. What's your idea?"

After a moment's silence the Yard man asked: "What was that remark she made in your hearing to Captain Argus?"

"The one about her being considered of more use alive than dead?"

"That's it. Well, she appears to have forgotten ever saying it. Thinks inadvertently you misquoted her. I've tackled Argus, but he swears he hasn't a notion what she meant. Be that as it may, here's a possible interpretation: She was left bound and gagged while a certain search was conducted, in order that the searcher, not finding what he wanted, could extort information. I don't say it was a knife he was after. Suppose it was a paper of some description, the nature of which it would be damaging to have revealed?"

"She'd hardly keep anything of the kind, would she?"

"It all depends on what it was. I admit it's not easy to think of the right answer; but if we did know it, it might explain her being strongly opposed to bringing this man to justice."

The picture of Mrs. Bellamy-Pryce, decent, conventional, rose before Tommy. It was hard to credit a woman of her type with a seriously compromising secret.

"I see your objection," continued Headcorn. "But the damaging fact may concern her late husband, not herself. There was a quarrel in the boat-cabin. Several people heard it. If Gavin did try to get money out of his brother.... No, I don't yet see any means of getting at the truth. The cables from Colombo give both the Bellamy-Pryces an unimpeachable record, and in addition declare them to have been a singularly united couple. The clue may lie just there. Proving it's another matter."

"Granting all this," argued Tommy irascibly, "it still doesn't hang together. She was undoubtedly shot at. How can you account for that?"

"The shots may have been meant only to terrorise. I'll go further. Until this strychnine death occurred, I was beginning to wonder if murder was being contemplated at all. Oh, well!" The visitor planted his cigar-stump viciously in an ash-tray. "We'll have to have Gavin watched for a considerable period. His next move would almost certainly deliver him into our hands; but obviously that move has to be prevented. I don't want him to know he's under suspicion. The charwoman's inquest will be a formal affair, only medical evidence called, and a postponement secured. So that needn't alarm him. Will you, in future, keep right away from Lambs' Conduit Street?"

Tommy blushed. He had been back there only this afternoon, though only to stare up at a partly-opened window on whose grimed sill a lean, ugly cat had been lapping from a saucer. Gavin's familiar, romantic fancy might have called it . . .

"Right you are," he promised briefly. "Though I don't quite see why you want this scoundrel's fears to be lulled into a peaceful slumber. It seems to me to be asking for more trouble."

"Better ask for trouble we're prepared for than to have it plumped down on us after the vigilance has ceased. It would be nice to keep guard in Victoria Grove indefinitely, and have relays of men trailing this brother-in-law from now till he dies; but unfortunately the Yard funds won't run to it."

With this practiced observation Inspector Headcorn said good-night.

Tommy, gravitating towards the Shaftesbury Palace Hotel, felt the constriction of fright in all his muscles. Rosemary was in positive, perhaps imminent danger—and it seemed nothing could be done about it, except, for a limited time, subject her potential murderer to surveillance. He had known cases of this kind before. They had always galled him. In the present instance his agony was acute.

And the reason for this state of affairs?

Oh, blast it, that was an easy one! He had fallen in love.

CHAPTER SEVENTEEN

THE truth had come to him at ten thirty-five that morning, along the quiet reaches of Brackham Place. One sledgehammer sentence had done the damage. It still rang in his ears: *"That glass happened to be mine."* He would hear it re-echoing in his dreams—if he was lucky enough to sleep.

How badly was he taken this time? Examining his symptoms he feared the worst. Recovery, he foresaw, was likely to be a tedious, painful business; but that there was any alternative to fighting his way back to normal did not occur to him. How the hell could it? Juxtaposed to this girl he saw himself as shopworn, substandard. Who was he, an adventurer-journalist—better say hack-reporter and be done with it—no longer young, careless in habits, with next to nothing saved—yes, who was he to turn his eyes in her direction?

"Why, she wouldn't have me served up on a silver dish with watercress round!"

And supposing for one weak-minded moment he were to imagine she might consider him, had he the hardihood to suggest it? From his point of view there was a very awkward snag. In course of time she would fall heir to a fortune. No power could prevent that—or rather, no power save death. . . .

Fear gripped him again. Those clear eyes glazed, that voice which all-unmeaningly had called him darling silenced for ever while he lived on? The mere thought of it was torture—and the danger was real, not something conjured up by an exaggerated fancy. Headcorn believed in it. He knew her recognition of the glass was to be trusted. To use her term, she, like her aunt, was black-listed—and, as her death alone could not profit, so was her father. In short, the clean sweep was no longer an absurdity. That stark, grinning corpse found huddled under the wash-basin destroyed any false illusions. But for sheer fluke it might have been hers.

"My God! What's holding these English police that they can't make an arrest? And me—am I to sit twiddling my thumbs, waiting for that damned little viper to bite again?"

Apparently this was what was expected of him. Gavin was to be watched for a time—and then let loose to carry out his design. If he was clever enough to have eluded justice thus far, he would most probably elude it a second and even a third time. He would not have another go with strychnine. No, he would adopt different methods—and his safety would be partly insured by his sister-in-law's dread of a formal accusation. Somehow he had seen to that. . . .

What was it Boggie feared which made her take chances with her own life? He was to puzzle over this at intervals during the next hour, but no solution was to come to him.

In the hurly-burly of the hotel lounge he had little difficulty spotting his friends. They were, indeed, almost the only fair-skinned persons in a non-Aryan assembly, and as such stood out. No one, looking at them, could by the widest stretch of imagination, connect them with furs, tobacco, or gentlemen's outfitting—a distinct advantage from the searcher's angle. Tommy made for them as directly as could be managed—that is, in a series of zig-zags, halted at every third step when an intervening chair had to be shifted to let him pass through. Argus, he saw, was one of the party—ill at ease, from the look of him. The vicar's influence, perhaps; but at nearer range Tommy thought there was more to it than mere chastened restraint. The Australian, not mingling in the talk, was glowering into his beaker of Bass with an expression of fulminating fury. Something, obviously, had gone wrong.

The two women were being speciously cheerful. The vicar, a pleased smile on his face, sipped an orange-squash, and let his charmed eyes feast on the stimulating mob. At some quip from Boggie, Argus raised his eyes and for a second levelled at her a baleful glare. She countered with an amused challenge. "Well, what are you going to do about it?" was the message Tommy read. As he watched, the brief hardness of her glance melted to good-humour. She pressed Rosemary's hand with the staunch, exclusive gesture which means We Women Against the World, and asked for a cigarette. It seemed significant that Argus made no move to oblige her, and only after the vicar, hastily roused, had offered a shabby leather case did he churlishly produce his lighter.

Rosemary had now spied the new arrival.

"Oh, Tommy! I'm so glad you've come!"

The two men got to their feet, Argus with a bad grace, and Boggie beamed her welcome.

"How nice of you! Jack, another chair."

The murder, Tommy concluded from the warning touch on his knee, was not to be mentioned. The vicar, however, soon broached the subject in his own innocent fashion. He had fished up a newspaper, and with pleasant courtesy handed it over.

"Though I dare say you've seen it. Poor, unhappy creature, ending her troubles away from home, no doubt, to spare her family inconvenience! It seems strange and rather terrible to think that those who saw her performing her daily tasks can have had so little knowledge of her intention."

At the thought of Clover's mutely-borne woes Mr. Bellamy-Pryce grew quite noticeably saddened. A little vaguely he developed his theme. Frequently it was health. Cancer—or neurasthenia. An error to suppose the working-classes were immune from the latter complaint. He himself had never yet had a housekeeper who was not neurasthenic.

"Because you encourage them, darling," Rosemary murmured, stroking his hand.

Yet again, said the vicar interestedly, suicide seemed wholly the outcome of a sudden, mad impulse. What was the expression coined by Poe—it was Poe, surely? Oh, yes, The Imp of the Perverse. So apt a description of the obscure seizure which compels persons otherwise normal to cast themselves in front of oncoming traffic.

"I don't know why, as I'm saying this, the Westminster Cathedral should come into my mind," remarked the speaker, hazily groping. "Possibly because yesterday afternoon, when my brother and I had stopped rather unwisely in the middle of Victoria Street to admire the cathedral tower, I very nearly got run over by a 'bus. We had just dropped in to listen to the very beautiful plainsong. A pity our Anglican communion has nothing so fine."

Boggie's jaw dropped slightly. Rosemary, riveted, was gazing at her father with tense, anguished fixity. Both women might have been watching a young child chasing a ball over a live rail, terrified to call out lest he stumble and be electrocuted. Argus also was staring, his eyes angry with protest. Tommy himself for a fleeting instant wondered if the vicar should be left in total ignorance of his peril. That barely-averted accident so mildly mentioned! Gavin had been there. . . .

"Daddy's staying till the end of the week," announced Rosemary suddenly. "He's got shopping to do."

So this explained the situation observed before and rendered more acute by the recent remarks. The vicar had double-crossed them.

"Quite so," declared Mr. Bellamy-Pryce, amiably serene. "I've put it off for a long time. I really must not let the pleasures of London prevent my calling in at Margaret Street to be measured for a suit. I understand I'm badly off for surplices—yes, and a hat. Oh, it's all written down! Mrs. Pennylove, my factotum, very kindly prepared me a list. I'm afraid if I return home without the hat I shall be most severely reprimanded." Rosemary sent Tommy a look of mute, suffering appeal. For the life of him he saw no way out of the difficulty; but even as he racked his brain Boggie turned, pricking up her ears.

"Is that ridiculous little page calling us?"

In and out the jammed tables a beady-eyed little boy in a green uniform glittering with gilt buttons was weaving casually, bawling as he came, "Mr. Bellamy-Pryce! Mr. Bellamy-Pryce!"

Boggie touched her brother-in-law's elbow.

"It's you, Cuthbert. Boy!" she called. "Over here."

The emissary approached. "Lady for you, sir," he declared hoarsely. "Wyting in the lobby. Says it's urgent."

"Dear me!" The vicar looked startled. "Did he say a lady? Most odd. Why"—he consulted his old-fashioned watch—"it's nearly ten. Now, who can she be? One of the good women of the parish, I dare say, though even so it's—"

"Now, now, Cuthbert!" Boggie twitted him. "What's this you're hiding from us?"

She had a curious, perplexed glint in her eye; but Rosemary had risen with resolution.

"I'll go with you, Daddy. You never can make short work of these people. Tommy, will you come?"

The three wormed through to the clearer air of the foyer, floodlit by tubular pillars of sickly green composition—presumably made of milk. Rosemary cast a stony eye round the nondescript loiterers.

"I don't see any lady," she said shortly. "She's not here. Unless—oh!" She gave a subdued cry and drew Tommy back behind one of the columns of light. "Look!" she whispered. "If it isn't Nurse Claiborne! What on earth can she want?"

A tall woman of commanding presence had come forward determinedly and was holding low-voiced speech with the vicar. She had a stiff backbone, a fresh, hardy complexion, chill grey eyes above high cheekbones, and a chin that brooked no nonsense. Dressed in a severe, well-tailored coat and skirt and with a hat almost smart admirably adjusted over neat, mouse-coloured hair, she towered above the unassuming little man now listening with sober attention. Tommy noticed that though her figure was spare and flat-chested the hips tended towards what is commonly styled the middle-aged spread. Everything about her spoke of the woman who thinks well of herself and ill of other people. She could guard a secret, he decided, yet temper lurked in those pale, compressed lips, ready to flash out if her vanity were attacked.

"Lucid intervals," they heard her saying. "Quite impossible to tell how long it will be before complete coma sets in. However, I've just received word that he wants to see you."

"To-night? Dear me! Will that be possible?"

"To-morrow would be better. I, of course, am starting back at once. Shall I expect you about three in the afternoon?"

"Certainly! Oh, most assuredly! I am greatly obliged to you, Nurse. Did he mention my brother?"

"Not at all." The thin lips tightened, and red spots suddenly flared over the cheekbones. "Only you. He'll see no one else."

"Quite, quite! I will come."

Nurse Claiborne inclined her head stiffly, turned, and without a glance at the shoddy persons blocking her egress, left the hotel. Her straight back indicated contempt. Rosemary came forth.

"Well, well!" murmured the vicar dazedly, fingering his fading thatch. "Most surprising. My plans are altered, you see."

"I'll tell Boggie," said the girl in a relieved tone. "If you're getting an early start, you'll want to go to bed now, won't you?"

She found her aunt and Argus deep in conversation. An argument was going on, Boggie explaining and justifying herself. The couple looked up at her approach. She told them quickly what had happened.

"So that's it! Thank God!" Defensively Boggie met her companion's eyes. "So you see, Jack, all this nagging was for nothing. My brother-in-law's going home." Energetically she collected her bag and gloves, and ordered Argus to settle the account. "Does this mean a death-bed repentance?" she asked.

"Heaven knows. Whatever it means, we can't quarrel with it."

Tommy, when they regained the lobby, was speaking of trains.

"The best one, if I remember rightly, leaves Waterloo at ten-ten. I was suggesting," he said to Rosemary, "that I come along in my car and make sure your father doesn't miss it. I can also take him to Margaret Street—it's quite close—so he can at least buy his hat." Clearly the vicar shrank from facing his housekeeper minus the needed headpiece. He protested vigorously against giving Mr. Rostetter so much trouble, but his daughter cut him short.

"Oh, splendid, Daddy dear! Tommy, you're wonderful! Of course he doesn't mind, darling. He'll be here at nine sharp—won't you, Tommy?—and attend to everything. How well it's working out, isn't it?" Three of the party understood the joy in her voice. No gap was to remain during which the vicar could run any risks. Shepherded from the moment he left the hotel till the carriage-doors of the train closed on him, he could come to no harm.

"I should have liked to see Gavin again," ventured Mr. Bellamy-Pryce regretfully. "However, it can't be helped. Now, then—what have I done with my key?" He fumbled vaguely in pockets, while Rosemary examined his hat and pronounced it a disgrace. "Can I have been stupid enough to—"

"Didn't you leave it at the desk?"

"Yes, yes, to be sure I did! Over there, I believe."

"Darling, no! On the other side." Rosemary pulled her father back as he ambled confidently towards the tobacco-stall. "Wait, I'll get it." She addressed the sharp-featured clerk, was handed an immense key, and before yielding it up idly read aloud the number on the wooden tag attached to it. "Nine hundred and twenty. So you're up in the sky."

"Eh? Quite at the top, I believe. No view, as it happens, because my room, though most comfortable, overlooks an air-shaft; but as I'm seldom in it—"

"You'll lock the door, won't you?"

"Lock—? Oh, I see! One hears a good deal about hotel-thieves. I have nothing worth stealing except my watch, but yes, if you think it wiser, I will certainly lock my door."

He kept the magnificent lift waiting while he made his adieux, discovered he was being inconsiderate, and bolted in with incoherent apologies. The imitation bronze doors clanged to, the cage shot aloft, and the vicar's small legs, like the disappearing smile of the Cheshire cat, melted from view.

"Home, James!" sighed Rosemary, suddenly gone limp. "Oh, dear, so that's over!"

She squeezed Tommy's hand gratefully. A thrill almost painful in its intensity travelled up his arm and into the innermost recesses of his body. For a second he was a little drunk. His vision clearing, he saw that Boggie was mopping her forehead in whimsical relief, and that Argus was letting out a vindictive growl.

"Damned bit of luck, I say," declared the Australian. "No telling what might have come to him. Shall I nab a taxi?"

"If you don't mind packing in," said Tommy, "I think I can manage with my two-seater. It's just outside."

"That damned midget? Oh, don't bother about me. The tube's handy."

"Rubbish, Jack!" Boggie scolded her friend. "If we don't mind squashing, why should you? And you're on our way."

Argus shrugged, and followed Tommy to the parking-place.

"What gets me," he burst out, "is this: If the man's in danger, why can't he be told?"

Tommy made a placating gesture. To demonstrate to Captain Argus's intelligence just why it was impossible at this stage to warn the vicar seemed a task beyond his powers. He was beginning to understand, however, the cause of disagreement between the Australian and Mrs. Bellamy-Pryce, and he imagined the passage at arms was still going on when Boggie, stowed at the back with her antagonist, preserved a smug silence. If he turned his head he could just make out the two rather hard-set faces, lit now and then from the pulsing end of Argus's cigarette, smoked in angry, nervous jerks.

"I could hug my grandfather!" whispered Rosemary in Tommy's ear. "Oh, you can't think how awful it's been! We couldn't have kept daddy from seeing Uncle Gav—not possible. That 'bus in Victoria Street!"

A long shudder went through her. Tommy touched her hand.

"It was a nasty jar," he admitted. "But it'll be all serene now. Your uncle's being carefully watched. Headcorn's just told me. Still, I'm as glad as you are your father's going back."

"I'll come down to see him off. Yes, it's a heaven-sent mercy. We're safe enough, what with our plain-clothes man and a new maid in to-morrow. It was only him. . . . Look, Captain Argus will want to be set down at the little mews round the corner from us. I'll show you when we come to it. He's got a furnished flat there."

Argus, duly deposited, took a bad-mannered leave. When they had gone on, Boggie, from the rear, remarked hardily that he considered both her and Rosemary deplorable fools.

"Are we, I wonder? No, I don't see how we can act differently where Cuthbert's concerned. He wouldn't believe us, he'd only be shocked for no purpose." After a thoughtful pause she added: "And, of course, we may, after all, be mistaken."

Tommy said nothing. He was thinking that if Argus really had seen Gavin on the boat-deck his present attitude was understandable.

Boggie, it developed, was taking her friend's disapproval to heart rather more than she cared to admit. So Rosemary realised when, tucked in bed, she lay listening to the long telephone argument conducted from downstairs. Boggie had slipped down in her mandarin coat to ring up her friend Jack and establish her rightness. Once or twice she sounded almost in tears.

"But, Jack, you fool, can't I make you see the position regarding poor Cuthbert? He's a happy innocent—and he's simply devoted to that vile brother of his. Heaven knows why. We couldn't have done it. No, no, it's out of the question! What's that? . . . Oh, the poison! I quite see your point, but however sure you and I may feel the law's another matter. Do listen! What I'm trying to tell you is that after this Gavin will be frightened off. When his father dies, he'll pack off again and leave us in peace. A bird in the hand . . . oh, dear, don't say that! As though I weren't frantic enough already! . . . No, I've told you a dozen times I can't swear I saw him. I can't—so do stop badgering me!"

So it went on, the best part of half an hour, till the girl in bed drew the linen sheet over her head to shut out the sound. She knew now it was Uncle Gavin. She had been an idiot to think anything else. As for that stiff-backed Claiborne woman, why, self-righteousness was written all over her! Just the same, of course, she was glad the creature hadn't insisted on taking daddy back in the Rolls. One thing about that dreadful Shaftesbury Place, it was safe—safe as a great sanitary prison. Daddy would be asleep now, behind a locked door—had he remembered?—and in the morning Tommy would look after him. She must get to sleep herself, for she had an early start to make.

The day-clerk—twin brother to a weasel—eyed Tommy with a queer, shuttered look.

"Did you say Bellamy-Pryce?" A pause. "The clergyman, is it?"

"Certainly." Tommy was growing annoyed. "I don't suppose you've two of that name stopping here. Will you ring his room?"

The clerk held an inward debate. His narrow wedge of a face, pallid as that of some cave-dweller, grew more like a weasel's. Suddenly he turned and vanished through a door all but concealed in the wall behind the desk. Tommy, obscurely perturbed, ran his eye over the cleared spaces of the lobby and lounge. A few hatless females, clutching bags, emerged from the lift and made for the restaurant, doubtless to partake of the sumptuous breakfast, included in the room-tariff, which by a little management could tide one over nicely till tea-time. Nowhere did he spy the grey summer suiting and pancake hat of the man he sought—and now he noticed that the girl from the news-stand had stolen across to her colleague who dispensed tobacco, and was whispering with furtive glances in his direction.

It was at this moment that Rosemary came up the restaurant stairs. She looked fresh as a wild-rose in her trim, navy frock with its white organdie frills.

"Oh, there you are! Daddy's not been down. Think he's overslept?"

Before Tommy could frame an answer the weasel returned to his post, sent a swift look at Rosemary, and mumbled, "Would you mind stepping this way, sir?"

"Tommy!" She had paled a little. "Can anything be wrong?"

"No, no! I dare say he's gone out and left a message. Sit down, I'll be back in a jiffy."

Why this dryness of mouth and singing in her head? It was just what daddy would do—wake early, go off to some matins or other, and . . . Why were those two girls staring at her so hard? Silly! They were interested in her frock. It was rather a good model. Oh, here was daddy now! She dashed forward, and retreated, confused, as she saw that the small, grey-clad person she had accosted had an olive skin and a hooked nose. . . .

In a cubby-hole behind the desk Tommy faced a black-eyed personage who seemed to be the manager. He had a hesitant, almost accusing manner.

"I understand, sir, you're inquiring for Mr. Bellamy-Pryce. You're a relative, are you?"

Tommy explained. The black eyes held his, suspiciously, but with growing discomfort.

"I see. Well, I'm afraid I've some bad news for you. Possibly, though, you may be prepared for something of the kind."

"Prepared? What the devil do you mean?"

The manager coughed.

"Last night," he said detachedly, "at about eleven-fifteen it was, a most unfortunate accident occurred. The gentleman you're referring to fell from his window to the bottom of an air-shaft, and broke his neck."

CHAPTER EIGHTEEN

HE WOULD have to tell her.

It was Tommy's first sickening thought as he steadied himself from the blow. He demanded details, and as he took them in beheld in his mind's eye a vivid picture—the two brothers stopped in the swirl of traffic, and one nearly getting run down by a 'bus. . . .

The body, heard to crash, had at once been picked up. A doctor had been summoned, and the police, taking charge, had conveyed the remains to a mortuary, where they now lay. That was all that any one knew. It had not been possible to inform the family, since in no London directory did the name of Bellamy-Pryce appear. Naturally enough. Sir Osmund's telephone, as Tommy happened to know, was not in the London book, while Boggie's was listed in the house-owner's name.

"And you say it was an accident?"

The manager, always watching him, clicked his white teeth together and drew in a faint whistling breath.

"Or the other thing. It will be up to the coroner to decide, won't it?"

He made this remark with smug defiance, but the import was evident. Incidents like this were a calamity in the hotel business, and must, as far as possible, be hushed up and smoothed over. His manner was nervous and vaguely insolent. Tommy glared at him, and left the cubicle.

The next period was one he shrank from recalling. Never would he forget Rosemary's face, frozen with grief and horror, her extraordinary self-command, and the terrible question in her eyes. He got her home to her aunt, whose reactions to the news remained a blurred impression of woe, self-reproach, and the capable rising to the occasion he had known he could count on. He would have stayed, but Rosemary forbade it.

"No. Go back. Find out . . ."

Back he went, after telephoning the inspector, who was not in. Headcorn, in fact, was already in the victim's bedroom on the ninth floor of the hotel—had been for the past forty minutes. Learning this, Tommy insisted on being taken up. The manager accompanied him, and in the lift made a single observation.

"Mr. Bellamy-Pryce was a little . . . ?" He tapped his bald head meaningly.

"Absent-minded?" supplied Tommy, firmly misconstruing. "He was; but what's that got to do with it?"

The man shrugged sceptically and was silent.

The Imp of the Perverse. Could it be the mad impulse the vicar himself had mentioned had been responsible for this thing? Reason righted itself. No! The vicar as seen last night was a man in good health, placidly content with life, the prey to no morbid phantasms. Suicide was unthinkable.

Inside Room 920 Inspector Headcorn and a sergeant looked up as the door opened, and with set faces went on with their work. The manager hung about watchfully, and Tommy took stock of the room's meagre contents. It was a box-like chamber, small, buff-walled, and negative. The bed, turned down, had not been occupied. Across it lay the vicar's gaudily-striped pyjamas, and underneath were a pair of soft, round-toed black shoes. The vicar, it seemed, had met his death fully clothed, except that he had changed to slippers.

An open suitcase, on a stand, revealed a soiled shirt, a soiled clerical collar, a packet of picture postcards showing the Westminster Cathedral, and nothing more. On the glass shelf above the fitted wash-basin was a worn waterproof case alongside a safety razor and a few other necessaries. The chest of drawers displayed a pair of shabby hair brushes, a comb and a sixpenny packet of Virginia cigarettes, while from the mirror above dangled a pathetic object—the dusty flat hat its owner had meant to replace at the ecclesiastical outfitter's in Margaret Street. The opened wardrobe was empty. The vicar had travelled light.

There was one window, a sashed affair, wide open, and with the green damask curtains well parted. Close against the sill was drawn a straight chair with a plump, green-upholstered seat.

"Has this chair been moved?" demanded the inspector, turning.

It had not. The manager himself had remarked the position when he had entered the room directly the body was recovered.

"I dare say you've seen what fell out of his pockets? There was a fountain-pen, with the nib broken."

"Not injured by the fall," retorted the detective grimly. "Bone dry, and the cap in place. Here's what he used." He picked up an ordinary pen from the writing table, and pointed to the uncorked ink bottle. "He'd dated this postcard, but got no further."

The manager turned slightly green, and swallowed apprehensively. The blot with which the date ended seemed to show that the writer had left off in the midst of his task. Tommy saw that the table was fully six feet distant from the window, and that the only other chair, a low, cushioned one, was on the opposite side of the bed. If the vicar really had been writing immediately before the catastrophe occurred, he had been sitting on the straight chair which now stood by the window. For what reason had this chair been shifted?

He joined the inspector, now staring out on to the air-shaft, which was broken by other windows at every floor. He noticed that the sill struck him just above the kneecap. This meant that with the vicar, shorter by several inches, it would have come well up the thigh. A fall, then, looked virtually impossible; but at this moment he noticed something else—the white holland blind, run up to the top, and so tightly rolled that the cord controlling it had wound itself round many times. The inspector twitched at the cord, but the blind refused to descend. He then stooped over and examined the chair-seat. The rep surface was clean, but revealed two slight depressions.

"He was standing on it," spoke the manager in triumph. "Trying to get the blind down. That's been my idea from the first. Lost his balance, and fell out."

Headcorn grunted: "Fetch another chair like this one. We'll just make an experiment."

When the chair was brought and placed in the same position as the other, Headcorn sized up the heights of those present, and picking the manager as shortest, asked him to take his stand on it.

"Good!" he muttered, when the man had obliged. "Now raise your arms."

The manager did so; but by no stretch of imagination was he in danger of falling through the window. The back of the chair, rising a foot above the sill, formed a barrier.

"Couldn't have happened," declared Tommy in an undertone. "If he'd managed to tumble through, this chair would have slid back, or sideways, not stayed put as it is now. If he wanted to jump out, why, it's obvious he'd have turned the chair alongside, to avoid the back."

Headcorn grunted again. The manager got down and dabbed his damp face with a clean handkerchief. He was visibly shaken.

"One or the other it must have been," he insisted doggedly; but the inspector was not attending.

"These lights," he demanded. "Were they left on?"

"Oh, certainly!"

"And the time?"

"It was eleven twenty-five when I got up here. Say ten minutes before that the accident occurred."

The inspector seemed gloomily satisfied with these answers. He gave instructions that the names of those guests occupying the adjacent rooms and the rooms overlooking the shaft be supplied him, and then, as the manager was turning to go, inquired how many persons had heard the crash.

"Only some of the staff," replied the manager sulkily. "The ones at work in the scullery. It's directly below us, in the basement—where you see that iron rail and the steps coming up. Don't lean too far out," he cautioned unnecessarily. "Yes, the body seems to have struck that rail, and rebounded into the open space of the court. Our boys rushed up at once. You've seen the injuries, I suppose?"

"Neck broken by first impact," recited Headcorn, his gaze still roaming the shaft. "Compound fracture of skull, snapped thigh-bone, smashed elbow and bruises."

"But no marks of violence," reminded the manager cunningly.

"None that I noticed," returned the detective, grimly ironic. "That will do, I think."

When the manager had gone, Tommy asked how it had come about that Headcorn had so quickly been secured for the investigation. Had headquarters known immediately it might be his affair? Reluctantly the inspector answered that it had not happened quite in this way.

"One of our men picked up the brother at ten-twenty last evening, slipping out of the Lambs' Conduit Street house. He shadowed him all the way to the lounge of this hotel—and then lost him. His report reached me first thing this morning. I rang up to ask if the vicar was still here, and after some sparring got hold of the news."

"Gavin came here last night?"

Although cold to the marrow, Tommy saw in this circumstance a stupendous piece of luck.

"Not so good as it sounds," Headcorn informed him. "There's nothing as yet to prove he got as far as this room. There are two public exits to the lounge, one leading to the lobby, one at the side communicating directly with the staircase and lifts. Somehow he slid through the crowd without being noticed—or so it appears. Oh, we've found his finger-prints in here—one set, by that light-switch. We know they're his, because we've got several clear sets taken from his room; but it's known he came up with the vicar Tuesday evening. So that's no great help. If the interviews I'm planning to hold don't give us anything—well, there it is."

The big man sat down with an harassed expression. Plainly he was suffering from severe mortification.

"I'd better tell you," said Tommy, "what happened last evening . . . and he described briefly the vicar's conversation, laying stress on his cheerful spirits, and the sudden summons to his father's bedside."

"Westminster Cathedral!" mused the detective. "That's interesting. Now, will you repeat as accurately as you can everything that was said in the lobby, just before the vicar got into the lift?"

Tommy did his best to reconstruct the parting scene. The inspector wanted to know if many passers-by were likely to have heard the room number read out; but it was a difficult question. Possibly several had heard. Certainly the lift-operator and two women passengers must have caught the vicar's remark about having nothing worth stealing except his watch.

"The watch—a gold repeater—was on him," Headcorn said tersely. "It tumbled out and the crystal was smashed."

He got up, and returning to the window began studying, through a lens, the surface of the sill. Presently he handed the lens to Tommy.

"Just take a look. Notice anything here?"

Tommy made out two faint parallel smudges, close together, on the inner projection of the ledge. All they amounted to was a mere dimming of the glossy paint.

"It looks as though something's been rubbed against the sill," he remarked. "They're twin marks. Well?"

"Twin marks. Exactly. Tracks left by the fronts of leather slippers as they dragged upwards."

Tommy looked at his companion.

"I see. You mean that if he'd fallen or jumped out he couldn't have made marks like these?"

"He most certainly could not. Unfortunately the slippers are too battered and begrimed to show any corresponding smudges. I doubt if the coroner's jury will agree that the victim was hoisted bodily up from the floor just here by the window and thrown, like a sack of potatoes, down the shaft. A clergyman, you know. Makes all the difference in the verdict. However, we'll see what can be done."

CHAPTER NINETEEN

Another blow had been struck—and the C.I.D., amply warned, had been powerless to avert it. Could the individual who had committed this daring yet simple crime be apprehended? That was the question gnawing at Tommy's vitals when he went back to Victoria Grove to give his negative but disquieting report.

"I suppose Jack was right." Boggie wiped her reddened eyes. "I dare say we should have said something; but when I myself wasn't sure . . ."

Rosemary glanced at her, shut her lips, and remained silent. Tommy experienced a sudden overwhelming irritation. Again he wondered if Mrs. Bellamy-Pryce could have made more definite assertions if she had chosen to do so. It seemed to him—though it might be a harsh judgment—she was sticking, in self-defence, to her former attitude, and he believed the same thought was in her niece's mind.

"If that's the case," he said rather dryly, "you can have no reason to reproach yourself. I very much doubt if warning him would have altered the result. Besides, the thing may have been due to accident."

"Do you think it was?" asked Boggie bluntly.

"I've told you all I know, which isn't a great deal." She bit her lip and with working features left the room. Rosemary waited till the sound of footsteps had retreated up the stairs, then said quietly:

"Captain Argus will be here any minute. So I must be quick." She stopped, as though her breath were entirely spent. "You know what daddy said about looking up at the tower and nearly getting run over? He was speaking to Uncle Gavin about the sudden thing that makes people commit suicide. To us the example he gave was throwing oneself in front of traffic; but then he was always so vague. Do you see what I mean?"

"Not quite."

"Well, then, not very long ago a woman jumped off the top of that cathedral tower. It was almost certainly suicide he was talking about, only when he referred to it afterwards he got it mixed up with his own escape from the 'bus. I thought of it directly. So did my aunt."

In a flash Tommy saw. It was more than likely the vicar himself had supplied his brother with the idea later put into operation.

"Poor, darling little daddy!" Tears welled slowly to her eyes. "Oh, the horrible, ghastly shock of it!"

He begged her not to dwell on it. Whatever happened had been over in a twinkling—and death itself had been instantaneous. She winced and clung to his hand.

The gate clicked. She jumped up and fled to her room, leaving him to take care of the visitor, just arriving. There was no need, however, for Tommy to open the door. That service was performed by a staid, highly competent-looking maid, only that morning entered into the household. She showed the Australian in and departed upstairs to inform her mistress. Argus, hat in hand, his face lined and haggard, stared hard at his fellow-guest.

"You've been down there, have you?" he demanded in brusque, hushed tones. "I see. Well, and what's the verdict?"

"It's a bit early to say. I left the inspector searching for clues."

"Clues! Not much in that line, I fancy."

The captain made this comment with bitter scepticism not unmixed with triumph. He seemed to be savouring his own superior wisdom. Drawing a deep breath, he deposited his hat very carefully on a table.

"And what else is he meaning to do?" he asked gloomily.

"Interrogate people. Learn if any person was seen going in or coming out of the bedroom—or if any one saw the vicar fall."

"To be sure. Well, they may give us a break. What's your idea?"

"That it was not suicide."

"Suicide!" Argus scoffed. "Never in this world. May have fallen out, I suppose. You've seen the window. Think it's possible?" He waited tentatively, and getting no answer, burst out with an odd petulance, "I've never come across a man as . . . as woolly-head as that! Never, I give you my word. Oughtn't to have been let out without a keeper. Why, a man of his sort might walk in his sleep, take a header—"

"He hadn't undressed."

"Oh? Well, it's no matter. What I say is he was half asleep on his feet. Just plain brutality to let him loose on his own. The Society for Prevention would have something to say to it. In a case like this. . . ." Argus pulled himself up with an expostulatory sweep of his arm and a strange crack in his voice. "Why," he summed it up, "he put salt instead of sugar in his orange squash, and never noticed! That'll show you."

Without warning he broke into raucous, hysterical laughter. It had a shocking sound in that quiet house. Tommy jogged his arm.

"Here, this won't do. Take a drink to steady you."

"A drink! Yes!" Argus got control of himself and made for the sideboard. "It was seeing him only last night that's knocked me," he muttered. "And hearing about it just now. . . . God, I'm jittery!"

The whisky decanter rattled against a glass, the drink, a generous one, was jerked off at a gulp. For a moment Argus remained where he was. When he returned he had calmed down, and his brown eyes were hotly filmed. Tommy felt the distaste a certain type of clumsy mentality always roused in him. Parenthetically he marvelled that a man well accustomed to whisky should react with such speed. He inquired if Argus had eaten breakfast. The answer was long in coming.

"Breakfast?" A delayed spasm of disgust crossed the ruminant features. "No! Fact is, I was sick in the night. I'd not long dropped off when I was rung up with the news."

Tommy was noticing that he had dressed carelessly and not shaved. Glancing at the door, he moved a step closer and spoke in a lowered tone.

"Captain Argus," he said soberly, "I hope you won't take this wrong. I'd like to know if for reasons of tact you've not been quite open on a certain matter we once mentioned. I got the impression last night that just possibly you might have some explicit knowledge concerning Gavin Bellamy-Pryce. Is that so?"

The brown eyes, glazed but resentful, swerved round. "Me? God, no! Think I wouldn't have come out with it?"

"I wasn't sure. Another thing: On the boat, or in Colombo—you stopped off there between boats, didn't you? Did you come across any rumours to suggest any sort of danger threatening the judge and his wife?"

In a fuddled way Argus grew very cautious. It might be merely the habit of a somewhat dull mind to weigh with exaggerated suspicion what even remotely touched its owner.

"No!" he said again, too violently, Tommy thought. "They were strangers to me. I never heard 'em discussed—and on the boat, well, it was just as I've told you. I'll admit I've had my suspicions about the brother and so on, but it's been no business of mine. I've kept out of it."

"Still," Tommy reminded him, "you did advise Mrs. Bellamy-Pryce to hold on to the knife."

"Knife!" The captain's stare showed a curious slowness of comprehension. "Knife? What the hell . . . oh, the knife!" He gave a guffaw, quickly subdued. "Oh, yes, so I did. As a general precaution. I didn't know then what had happened, and I don't now."

He swayed slightly and smothered a hiccough as Boggie came into the room. Her swollen eyes regarded him shrewdly but with tolerance.

"Poor Jack," she murmured sorrowfully. "It doesn't make you happy to say I-told-you-so, does it?"

He grasped her hand in awkward sympathy. The strained relations of the evening before seemed to have melted away, leaving them once more good friends. All the same, Argus did know something, Tommy reflected, as he quitted the room; and Boggie likewise possessed more knowledge than she dared yield up. His thoughts flew back to the inspector's groping suggestions of a pressure brought to bear on the person first concerned, and he wondered if indeed there were two different but intertwined motive forces at work. It would require something of the sort to explain all the contradictions observable in this troublesome case. Possibly the two left behind in the drawing-room were in much the same position as himself—blindfolded, helpless, constrained simply to wait for events to unfold. If so, it was easy enough to understand the display of nerves on the part of Argus, who, though outside the circle of danger, was attached to these two women—in the case of the younger one, very much bound up. One would not have expected a man of his type, vigorous, unsubtle, even coarse-grained, to go to pieces in this hysterical manner. Why, just now he had cracked as men used to do under heavy gun-fire; and then the mysterious swiftness with which his faculties had dulled after one drink of whisky!

No, perhaps that wasn't mysterious. All it meant was that Argus had been drinking before, and on an empty stomach—started in, no doubt, the moment the news of the vicar's death was telephoned him. This latest drink had merely tipped the balance.

Rosemary called softly from the top of the stairs. Going up, Tommy found her preoccupied, trying pathetically to summon her ideas.

"If you could just call in at the shop," she suggested, "you might tell Joan and Cybele why I'm not there. You said there'd have to be an inquest. Do you know when?"

"Probably to-morrow morning; but I'll come back and let you know."

"Do. I . . . yes, I think that's all I wanted to say. No, I'll be all right."

He held her hands for a moment, realised the futility of speech, and left her. She turned, like a sleep-walker, back into her room.

If she had been less stunned, she would have seen, with her inevitable clear vision, that the loss of her father would not, in itself, greatly alter her life. Since she had first gone away to school she had spent little time with her remaining parent, and in no important way depended on him. To her he had been something very precious, something to be guarded and shielded, but not deeply essential to her being. Her existence—if indeed it continued—would go on much as before.

It was the manner of his death which dazed and crushed; the thought of his last, shocked moments, and the feeling, constantly haunting her, that she had been outwitted. Whatever was officially decided, nothing could uproot her conviction that crime, wanton and brutal, had robbed a harmless man of his life, and that the foul act had been committed by the brother once trusted and loved. She had foreseen the chance of it, and not been able to prevent its happening. It gave her a surging, bitter resentment against herself, fate, the police—most of all—was this possible?—against her aunt. It was a resentment she was as yet powerless to analyse, but the moment she became aware of its chief tendency her habit of fair-thinking made a mechanical rebellion.

"I'm a beast." Her lips moved without sound. "Boggie's not to blame. She's marked down, too—as daddy was, as I am. Why, she's *in* it! For all we know, she'll be the next to go."

What was wrong with her? It was as though her brain had for the time being turned crooked, preventing her arguments from exerting any force. In her throttled consciousness she kept thinking that till Boggie had arrived in England everything had run smoothly; that only since she had come to share her aunt's life had her peace been shattered, her mind grown murked with ugly suspicion and fear.

"That's quite unreasonable. I mustn't forget that the same boat that brought Boggie brought Uncle Gavin as well. She did try to warn me, that first day at her hotel. I stopped her. What was it, I wonder, she wanted me to know?"

No good, she could say all this, see the truth of it, but her inner feeling remained unchanged. That proved she was not herself. It was these ghastly pictures constantly before her eyes—her father, seized and hurled down the long, drab air-shaft; Clover, rigid and grinning, hunched under the wash-basin; her uncle, smiling at her, across the array of bottles.

Her aunt, she felt, ought to have known. . . .

Joan and Cybele, thunderstruck, poured out their sympathy. Oh, poor Ro! How too devastating for her! That sweet, little lamb of a vicar! Thus they chorused, knee-deep in the spuriously-labelled hats, going—because of the excitement here—like hot cakes. Tommy sidestepped their questions; and then, of a sudden, both girls ceased babbling and stared blankly at one another.

"Two tragedies," murmured Joan in a curious tone. "And both in this place. The victims, I mean. Is it . . . ? Can it . . . ?"

"Oh, Joan, what bilge!" reproved the flaxen-haired dean's daughter. "There couldn't be a connection. Whatever gave you that notion?"

"It's funny, though," declared Joan, her grey eyes narrowed. "I do wonder how he came to fall out. Or . . ." she leant forward, sinking her voice, "Did he jump?"

"Ass!" muttered her companion. "Of course he didn't. Why should he?"

"I was thinking of my grandfather," said Joan pensively. "He did—from the window of a Turkish bath, as it happened. Perfectly gaga, of course. All he had on was a chin-strap, and he weighed twenty stone, and collided with a fruit barrow."

"The vicar didn't drink," objected Cybele. "All he had here was one small glass of sherry. His brother's odd-looking, isn't he?"

"But Ro'll have money now," remarked Joan, brightening. "So lucky for her! My grandfather left only debts. . . . I say, do you know what the countess is hinting?"

"No, Joannie, don't!" Cybele nudged her.

"Why not? It's such marvellous fun. That smarmy Dago, you know—the one that keeps going after Ro. Well, the countess knows he's planning to walk out on her. She didn't tell that inspector-man, but she's got it all doped out about the strychnine. It was got ready for her by Ro and Grimaldi jointly—only something went wrong in the shuffle. Cyb, do stop pinching me!"

"Please, Mr. Rostetter, don't tell Ro," implored Cybele, scarlet to the roots of her pale hair. "She's got enough to bear, and long before she comes back the countess will have invented something else."

Tommy made his escape.

In the hotel he found Headcorn just returned to the bedroom after his first batch of interviews.

"No one saw anything," announced the detective moodily. "If Gavin did get up here, he used the stairs, and managed to escape notice. He could easily have done it, and once up he'd only to knock to be let in."

"The vicar would have let any one in," mused Tommy.

The inspector looked momentarily arrested by this remark. However, he merely asked if Gavin, whom he had not yet seen, appeared strong enough to have lifted his victim up bodily and tumbled him through the opening.

"It's hard to say," replied Tommy thoughtfully. "He's a meagre specimen, but sometimes his sort is capable of surprising feats. Much would depend on getting the other man in the right position—back turned, face to the window, and, of course, on taking him wholly unawares."

"That's how it happened," declared the inspector authoritatively. "Not a doubt of it, to my mind; though I warn you again we may get quite a different verdict. Even the matter of lights won't, I imagine, carry much weight in the coroner's court—and that I regard as the strongest evidence in favour of foul play. You see those two windows facing us?" He pointed to the nearest of those overlooking the shaft—one, indeed, exactly opposite. "Well, at the time it happened, that upper window had an old lady sitting just inside, knitting, with her curtains open to let in the air. In the other room—almost as good a view of us, you see—a travelling salesman was packing his bags. His curtains, too, were wide open; yet neither he nor the old lady above noticed any commotion or movement in here. They heard the thud of the body, and the man lower down saw something drop past, but that was his first intimation."

"But if they didn't notice a commotion . . ." began Tommy, puzzled.

"We needn't specify commotion. With this window a bright patch standing out against darkness, wouldn't a man mounting to the sill and falling or jumping out be pretty certain to catch the eyes of his neighbours? It's hard to conceive otherwise."

Tommy suddenly saw the point.

"So the light for a few seconds was switched off in this room!"

"I'm confident it was—and by the murderer. While the room was still dark he ran this blind up to the top, moved the chair over to the window, and stood on it, leaving the two dents in the seat. If he hadn't been too flurried to think clearly, he'd have placed the chair with its back at right angles instead of blocking ten inches of the space. That little carelessness reveals a lot, though I'm afraid it'll be hard to make a jury appreciate its importance. However, I've still got a few more guests to question. We can't afford to miss out any one. It ought to be in our favour this Gavin is such a singular-looking person."

Thinking of the large assortment of singular-looking persons assembled in the hotel last evening and every evening, Tommy felt downhearted. He took the lift to the restaurant, wolfed down some food, and hurried back to Victoria Grove.

The new maid admitted him. He walked into the drawing-room, and came face to face with Gavin Bellamy-Pryce.

CHAPTER TWENTY

THE sight of this man, quietly seated with his sister-in-law and niece, struck a blow straight between the eyes. It was the last thing Tommy had expected—yet after all, why not? Guilty or innocent, it would have looked odd for Gavin not to come here. Under the present circumstances he was not likely to commit a tactical error.

He was sitting with his back to the light and a full cup of black coffee on a small table at his elbow. As the door opened, he rose, a ragged, hand-rolled cigarette pinched between long, incredibly dirty nails, and although there was recognition in his glance, submitted to being re-introduced. He said nothing, but his deep-set, saturnine eyes, the whites stained as with coffee, had an expression of intense awareness. Indeed, his whole air was that of a man astonished at nothing, least of all his chill reception here. At the same time Tommy instantly knew that for some reason he was afraid.

The room, barred with bright sunlight, seemed abnormally still. Gavin, having resumed his post on the needlework piano-stool, sat hunched like a fusty crow, furtively regarding his two womenfolk. They in their turn looked down at the floor, Boggie tight-lipped and stern, Rosemary dead white and motionless, her hands gripping a newspaper. It was the older woman who at last broke the strained silence, addressing her remark in her brother-in-law's direction.

"So your father's been notified."

Gavin ground out his frayed fag and began deftly to roll another. His knotted fingers showed brown to the second knuckle.

"The police sent a wire," he replied, and his voice, singularly well-pitched and cultivated, was in amazing contrast to his appearance. "And I myself spoke on the telephone to the nurse. I doubt, however, if he knows. I was informed he had sunk back into a coma."

Complete silence engulfed his words. Boggie, for a second, let her gaze travel to his face.

"In that case, the end seems to be near," she presently observed.

"Not necessarily," retorted Gavin, with detached precision. "He has been in a similar condition several times before. The news, if he hears it, may finish him. And again it may not."

Slowly and maliciously he smiled, displaying long, crooked teeth. There was something very vulpine about them. He is like a wolf, Tommy reflected, but a wolf that's frightened. At this moment he's asking himself what report I may have brought. . . .

It was a bizarre, no, a nightmare scene. Four persons keeping up a masquerade of amenities despite the belief held by three that the remaining one had just committed a particularly vile murder, and was even now planning to remove two of those present! Tommy was thankful for his own poker-face, though Boggie alone, to his thinking, maintained the really perfect composure—every nerve-twitch buried deep under a skin in figurative as in literal sense extraordinarily thick. She was not even attempting to conceal the fact that her visitor was unwelcome—a pretence which would have betrayed her. Her behaviour was merely that of one member of a family towards another in habitual bad odour—stoical resignation enforced by good breeding. During the succeeding pause she went so far as to raise the silver coffee-pot at her elbow and motion casually to Gavin. He thanked her, but shook his head. His cup as yet had not been touched.

The conversation continued lamely and with a sub-current of sparring. Tommy announced that the inquest was definitely set for Friday. Gavin, attentive, remarked that as one session would probably end it, the body could be conveyed to Sussex on Saturday, and the interment be arranged for the following day. He seemed, as he said this, to anticipate dispute; but Boggie contented herself with inquiring coldly if he meant to attend the funeral.

"Naturally," said Gavin in his precise, well-bred tones.

His oblique glance met hers. Neither pair of eyes wavered. One might have said that a challenge had been delivered and accepted.

Suddenly Rosemary left the room. Tommy quietly followed, and found her in the small garden-room jutting out at the back of the house. She closed the door and leant against it, sick, desperate.

"Get him away," she panted. "I shall scream!"

"I will," he promised. "There's no need for you to go back."

"No," she muttered, and after a moment looked at him. "You're keeping something from me," she said. "What is it?"

"I'd rather not have said. It's still not known for certain that your uncle was in the bedroom. Headcorn, however, feels pretty sure about it. From one or two circumstances."

"I guessed it." Though her voice remained studiously even, her hands were clenched at her sides. "But they won't prove anything. You'll see. Listen!" She turned her head, her pupils dilated. "He's just going. If I'd known, I'd have stuck it a bit longer and not been such a coward. It's not fair letting my aunt bear the brunt of it, wonderful though she is, only . . . What are you going to do?"

"Get a few words with him," said Tommy determinedly. "It can't do harm, and I might trap him into some admission. I don't believe the inspector can object."

He overtook Gavin at the gate. The archaeologist, hearing his step, had turned and was surveying him composedly but with slight wariness. Under the shadow of a villainous black hat, profane travesty of his brother's clerical one, his yellow features and inky elf-locks had taken on a more evil aspect. Tommy offered him a lift. He hesitated, glanced at a cheap watch, and with unexpected civility accepted.

"That is very good of you. I should be glad of it. I am going in the Bloomsbury direction. Set me down where it is most convenient."

Was there a latent sarcasm in the speech? Tommy suspected it, and had a hunch that Gavin believed himself at all points prepared. Never mind, if he was guilty his armour could not be entirely perfect. One must just see in which spot lay the flaw. He held open the door, and Gavin got into the place beside him, disposing his hands—strangely stuffless, like a scarecrow's, in the wrinkled folds of the black gloves—upon his bony knees. His threadbare garments, exuding a musty odour, hung loosely over his emaciated frame.

While Tommy was considering how best to open conversation, Gavin took the reins into his own hands. Rather dryly he inquired:

"Have you known my two women relatives for any great length of time?"

"Only a few days," Tommy answered. "But it so happens I've seen them quite frequently during that interval."

The profile at his side revealed another wolfish baring of teeth—satyric, malevolent. Tommy waited, in full expectation of questions concerning the recent alarms in the house just quitted, but none came. Instead, with a complete abandonment of the topic, Gavin spoke without emotion of his brother's death.

"I understand you were in his company not long before the accident occurred. At what time did you leave the hotel?"

"About ten-thirty, I think it was."

"And you had just seen my brother into the lift. Ah, quite so."

It was clear enough why Gavin wanted to be assured of these things. The distinct lessening of tension after the last affirmative showed the anxiety till now lurking in his mind. As though satisfied, he lapsed into silence. Tommy in his turn took over the interrogation.

"I suppose," he hazarded, "you didn't either see or telephone the vicar after the time I've mentioned?"

Gavin remained immovable, hunched in his seat. It seemed doubtful if he had heard; but at last, deliberately, he made answer.

"No. I called for him this morning, hoping to take him with me to the Museum to look at some inscriptions. It was then I learned the news."

Now Tommy understood the long delay. Gavin had been debating the advisability of risking total denial. Satisfied anew, he had risked it, but there seemed little doubt he was lying. The smile played more openly about his lips, and suddenly Tommy saw what Boggie had meant when she spoke of him as Satan in the flesh. At this moment the warped creature sunken down at his side seemed less a man than a soulless poltergeist. No, that didn't quite describe it. He was an intellectual Pan, incapable of mercy or remorse, filled with black pride, greedy ambition.

The smile had become a sneer.

"My brother Cuthbert," murmured the smooth voice with its trace of Oxford accent, "was the one member of my family who sought my society. Why he did has remained a mystery I for one have never attempted to solve; nor, I imagine, did he."

There was something infinitely revolting in the cynical detachment with which this remark was delivered, but bad as it was Tommy could hardly believe his ears when it was followed by a low chuckle. Glancing to the left, he saw the whole ill-nurtured frame convulsed and vibrating with devilish mirth!

The tremors increased in violence, shaking the seat. The face by his shoulder had turned more lividly yellow, the black-gloved hands clutched each other as though in frantic effort to control the unholy emotion. But was it emotion? The chatter of teeth suggested some seizure. Good God, epilepsy! With the parenthetical thought that this dread disease would explain much, Tommy slowed the car. A palsied gesture bade him go on.

"Malaria," grinned Gavin with a ghastly rattle of teeth. "If you don't mind, Lambs' Conduit Street . . ."

Pausing only to snatch the rug from behind and bundle it round the shaking form, Tommy cut across the Park.

Further speech was impossible. At the bake-shop Tommy had to help his passenger out and hoist him almost bodily up the stairs—even unlock the door for him. Inside the room, the archaeologist collapsed on a meagre camp-bed and lay a shivering heap. Tommy covered him with moth-eaten quilt and a striped blanket, adding the motor-rug.

"Quinine," chattered the ill man. "Cupboard. Medicine-box."

There was only one cupboard, painted brown, and wedged in a narrow niche between fireplace and wall. In it Tommy saw a vast pile of manuscript, a few cooking utensils neatly arranged, some fragments of ancient pottery, and the medicine-box, of black japanned tin. This was locked, but a spasmodic hand indicated that the owner had the key on his person. In another moment the quinine tablets had been found.

"How many?"

"T-two."

There was water in a cracked jug on a corner wash-stand, and a thick tumbler. The sufferer grasped it with talon-like fingers, spilled some of its contents, but swallowed most. Tommy re-covered him, rescued the box from being shaken to the floor, and before putting it away took a good look at the labelled phials. Yes, here was the tiny bottle the official searcher had seen. It was marked Tinc. Nux. Vom., and it was entirely empty.

CHAPTER TWENTY-ONE

IF TOMMY had not previously witnessed the severities of a malaria attack he would have said as confidently as Lord Downside had done that the archaeologist's labours would never reach completion. Even so he found it easy to believe that a bout like this would soon end matters. James's heart had given way, and James, one imagined, had been a hardier man than Gavin.

Common humanity made him think of succour. Knowing that hot stimulant would presently be wanted, he filled the rusty kettle which stood on the gas-ring, lit the flame under it, and while waiting for the water to boil surveyed the room.

Underfoot lay a worn, cheap rug such as the natives of Syria weave for their own use. A mere patch, it left a wide desert of bare boards. Gas for lighting, supplemented by a student's oil lamp; a common deal table and chair, another chair of wicker, filled with sodden cushions, a small chest of drawers; a few discoloured maps on the walls, pipes and more broken pottery on the pinched mantel-shelf—this was all, save the books, which crowded to the ceiling between the two windows, and overflowed into dusty stacks on the floor. They revealed a catholicity of taste. Beside treatises on amulets, fetich-symbols and the Kabbala were shabby editions of the Greek, Hebrew and Sanskrit classics—even works in Egyptian and in Arabic. Neolithic culture jostled elbows with poetry, a monograph on the detection of palimpsests and a complete set of Stendhal sandwiched in Spinoza. The Manichean Heresy—yes, that would be here. Irenaeus, also, in his tattered glory of half-calf.

Finding the gas burning low, Tommy dropped pennies into the slot beside the ring, and although the June sun poured in at the windows, lit the miserable gas-fire with which the grate was equipped. He then chose a volume of Herodotus, and sat down by an inch-opened sash to fill in the time. . . .

"I shall get up, I think."

Roused from visions of royal crocodiles wearing jewelled earrings—barbarously interspersed with strychnine tablets and Smith and Wesson revolvers—Tommy looked across towards the speaker. The paroxysms had completely ceased. He unhooked a poisonous old dressing-gown from the door, got the recovering man into it, and helped him over to the wicker-chair by the fire. Grunting thanks, Gavin remarked that in addition to his recurrent attacks of malaria he was just pulling up from a touch of 'flu, which had confined him to bed for a number of days.

"You were ill here, were you?" asked Tommy alertly.

"From last Tuesday till my brother arrived. Oh, I was able to attend to my few wants," explained Gavin coolly but with intention. "I am quite accustomed to looking after myself. I prefer it, in fact."

"I understand you have been away. That's why I asked."

The sunken eyes met Tommy's with malicious humour. There was no doubt Gavin had perfectly comprehended the trend of the question.

"I told my brother that to avoid argument," he said simply. "He would have wanted to drag me down to the country, and my work necessitates proximity to the museums."

It was easy enough to see why Gavin was now contradicting his former lie. If called on to substantiate an alibi covering a certain period he would find himself in a tight corner. The partial truth on which he had fallen back might be unprovable, but with his present attack to back it up would sound at least plausible. As to his being confined to this room, witnesses might yet be found to swear the contrary. No matter on what charge, the great thing was to get him locked up where he could do no further damage.

There was tea in the cupboard. Tommy poured the bubbling water into the chipped brown pot, let the brew draw to suitable strength, and filled the one large cup he had unearthed. Gavin took his tea just as it came. Tommy was therefore puzzled to see him hitch his chair towards the half-pint bottle of milk fetched out for him and carefully decant some of its contents into the saucer. This he now carried to the nearer window, on whose pane a faint scratching sounded. When the opening was large enough, in stalked the ugly cat seen outside two days ago. It arched its back, rubbed against the ministering hand, and set to work to lap up the refreshment.

"My familiar," said Gavin, sinking back exhaustedly into his chair. His provocative glance, coupled with the use of the very term present in his visitor's mind, brought an uncanny suggestion of thought-reading. Tommy felt appallingly ill at ease. It was one thing to believe in a man's evil proclivities, quite another to see those beliefs stripped bare and held up for ridicule—for this, astonishingly, was what Gavin appeared to be doing.

"The ague's quite passed, has it?" inquired Tommy awkwardly.

"Quite. I'm beginning to sweat. Presently I may doze off, but not while the fever lasts."

Refilling the cup, Tommy noticed that the ailing man's temperature was soaring rapidly. Red patches flamed on the sallow cheeks, the burnt-out eyes had kindled with fire which was no mere reflection of the gas. Strangely enough, Gavin looked younger, less repellent. It was even conceivable that in a past not altogether remote he might have possessed some measure of good looks. His tongue, moreover, had loosened, and it wanted but the mere mention of the Indus to let forth a torrent of speech.

"That chain of buried cities—do you know what they mean to us?"

Tommy ventured some reply, but his host brushed him aside instantly to begin expounding, rhapsodising, riding his hobby at breakneck speed. From a side-pocket in the chair he dragged up a ragged map, and traced a course on it with his dirty finger-nail. Gone was cynicism, not a trace of the sneer remained. Tommy kept the cup replenished with hot tea. When the pot was drained, Gavin rolled his crude cigarettes, smoked them excitedly, and went on with his tale of civilisations dead and lost before the dawn of our era. He spoke of trade routes and social systems, of kingly orders and the Kassite period. Ever recurrently he dwelt on the slow evolution from animistic worship to riper forms which still were permeated by that predominating influence of all ancient peoples—fear of evil spirits.

"Lamashtu!" Leaning forward till his face was a foot from his listener's, he whispered the name gloatingly. "Goddess of calamities—daughter of Anu. The world moved in terror of her leopard's body, her lion's face, the feet like those of the Storm-God, Zu. And then the frightful Pazuzu—covered with scales, and with four wings. His hind legs have the claws of a bird of prey. Seven demons are lodged in him, each with a different beast's face—the ram, the ibex, the panther, lion, bird, serpent—and don't forget the wolf. Listen!" Monotonously he intoned: *"I am Pazuzu, the son of Hanpu, King of the evil spirits of the air. I go forth from the mountains raging like a whirlwind."*

Tommy, reluctantly fascinated, felt a chill steal into his blood. Gavin, through half-closed lids, was watching him. More quietly he continued:

"That's on a famous inscription. Indian pictographic writings are twin brother to the Sumerian ones; but India carries us farther back. Trace Gnosticism. You get Babylonian beliefs. Where did Babylon get them? Why, from the Indus valley!"

Suddenly, hardly descending from his rapt plane, Gavin broke into lamentations. He had himself earmarked a site which might yield the richest treasures yet to be found, and his great fear was that others might forestall him in excavating it.

"There it is, waiting—the pearl in the oyster. Waiting—but for how long? Any day I expect to hear it's been snapped up by some foundation. American whipper-snappers in horn-rimmed spectacles will maul it over and at night play jazz on gramophones. Do you see why I have to get back, and not with empty hands? The sun, the marshes—pah! That wasn't why I crocked up. It was the having nothing to go on with—the certainty that I could do nothing without funds. I got word that my father was dying at last. Oh, he's cheated me times out of number—and he may cheat me again. Still, there's the chance. I squandered my last penny getting back. Not that I shall secure the tenth part of what I require. What do you suppose holds up work of this kind for years, for centuries? Lack of money—only that. Money to pay wages, money to feed labourers, money to enable you when you've dug wrong to start again in a new spot. A fortune—and if you haven't got it, what happens? What you've dreamed of the other fellow finishes. Yes, when I'm rotting under the sod men alive and keen will be burrowing through to foundations, opening up tombs thousands of years sealed, piecing together records I'd sell my soul to decipher!"

The passion died down. Gavin shrank into the folds of his ragged dressing-gown, a figure pitiable in its despair, but by its spent lassitude betraying the force, god or devil, housed within. Gradually was returning that inhuman look which had roused repulsion. Seeing it, Tommy thought of James's timely heart attack which had brought his brother one step nearer the goal. James gone, now Cuthbert—and the money which would have been theirs ready to pass into other hands; but the whole of it not yet into Gavin's. For that to happen two more persons would have to be wiped out in satisfactory fashion. Still, what of it? Human lives in this man's estimation were only so much lumber to be cleared from his path. That was the meaning of the harangue just terminated. Gavin, by his own eloquence, had accused himself.

Again there stole on Tommy the feeling that his thought had been divined. His companion's eye was upon him, discerning, speculative.

"My sister-in-law," remarked the scholar's voice, at once rasping and suave, "appears to believe a certain dose of strychnine was designed for her consumption. Stop!"—as Tommy opened his lips to speak. "I gather my impressions in my own way, and this one was very clearly conveyed to me by the lady herself during my short session alone with her. Just why she chooses to infect my niece with her ideas is not so readily apparent; but then I have never pretended to fathom my sister-in-law's motives, nor, indeed, have I found them of interest. Be that as it may, one perceives she is being persecuted. If my brother Cuthbert had not felt convinced of it he would doubtless be living now. To be sure, at the first opportunity she took pains to remove his fear. That was kind of her—though possibly, shall we say, a mistaken kindness?"

Gavin began horribly to chuckle.

"One can't know what is behind it," he continued philosophically. "The most one can declare with certitude is that she is still alive. Yes, though twice shot at—we are told at remarkably close range—and once pounded on the skull and reduced to helplessness, she survives unscathed. One might almost say that she bears a charmed existence, or accredit her, like our feline friend here, with nine lives. Let us call her Lamashtu, of whom I spoke just now, and to whom at present she seems singularly akin. Round and below her calamity crashes, but never touches her. She rides triumphant above the storm."

How to deal with these outrageous words was a poser, but luckily there was no need to consider a reply. While still speaking, Gavin had shuffled to the cupboard and reaching something from within, stood looking down at it. Over his shoulder he said:

"You never knew my brother James, I suppose? The eldest of our clan—except Charles, who met an early death during my own childhood. I have no good likeness of James, but recently I discovered these snapshots, taken five years ago when I visited him in Ceylon. Would you care to glance at them?"

Tommy took the faded prints to the window and examined them. They showed two gaunt men in sun helmets on the deck of a sailing boat. In two was a third figure, a woman so shadowed by a wide hat that her face was a dark blur. Close scrutiny revealed her as Boggie. The smaller man was Gavin, the other, thin-lipped and with a death's head visage, slightly resembled him. James, living on quinine, stern in the performance of his judicial duties; but why was he being shown as an exhibit of importance?

All at once Tommy noticed that in each picture James held a line, dim in the sun-glare—unmistakably a fishing-line, equipped with a reel, and extending over the side of the boat. He raised his eyes and found Gavin wickedly leering at him.

"Yes," purred the surviving brother smoothly. "James was at all times a keen fisherman. Trout he preferred, but in Ceylon he took to heavy fishing. With that line I helped him land a small shark. I remember the cord, a remarkably thick one, terminated in a wire."

The speech ended in a cavernous yawn.

"I'll leave you now," said Tommy abruptly. "Shall I stow these pictures away for you?"

Nodding with drowsy indifference, Gavin accompanied him to the door. Once more he spoke, with drooping eyelids.

"My sister-in-law," he said, "dislikes me intensely. That is probably because I have always intensely disliked her. Thank you for your most opportune assistance. I wish you good afternoon."

He closed the door. Tommy heard the key turn in the lock.

"Pazuzu," said Tommy to Inspector Headcorn half an hour later. "He's a devil with seven faces, one of them a wolf's—and one may conclude has the nature of all the menagerie. I rather fancy Gavin at times tends to identify himself with this interesting person. I don't mean he's mad in the sense that he can be certified, only that there's more than a touch of fantasy about him. What really matters is he's a fanatic of the most dangerous sort. Do you know what he dreams of doing? Finance a whole research-expedition. Make it a one-man affair. Pure megalomania. It goes hand in hand with crime, doesn't it?"

Headcorn made a sour mouth.

"You seem to have spent several hours in his company. Is that all you've got to tell me?"

"Good God! Did you expect a signed confession?" cried the amateur, wounded. "I've said his whole manner convinced me he did it. In the beginning he was on pins and needles for fear he'd been spotted in the neighbourhood of that hotel room."

"He can be easy about that," growled the inspector. "As to his deliberately mentioning his feud with Mrs. Bellamy-Pryce, he simply seized the chance of discrediting any statements she may have made against him. Wait, though! If the vicar never knew what happened on Saturday . . ."

"I hoped you might notice that slip," interrupted Tommy dryly. "If it was a slip. Somehow I doubt it. I don't see Gavin making blunders of that kind. It's my belief every syllable he utters is calculated beforehand. I rather fancy Mrs. Bellamy-Pryce herself gave him the information, to watch his reactions. Better ask her."

"Humph!" grunted the detective with eloquent contempt.

"I entirely agree," said Tommy, nodding. "All you'd get would be another evasion. It's all very annoying."

He was thinking once more of the perverse stubbornness with which Boggie, the sane and normal woman, was flirting with death. A word from her would place her brother-in-law behind prison bars. One was tempted to believe she courted assassination; or was it true that like the fabled Lamashtu she brought catastrophe to those about her while she escaped scot free?

His companion's practical voice routed these fantasies.

"It was shark's line. It must at one time have had the attachment of wire meant to keep the shark from biting through after he's hooked. What the blue blazes has become of it?"

"Gavin's probably thrown it down a drain," retorted Tommy. "You don't suppose he'd mention it at all if it was likely to crop up? I'm telling you, this cat-and-mouse game amuses him. I rather wonder he didn't inform me his brother James owned a Smith and Wesson revolver."

For several moments Headcorn stared at him with wooden impassivity. Then he turned back to the papers on his desk, and Tommy, taking the hint, departed.

Boggie that evening indignantly denied having spoken to Gavin about the Saturday episode. Indeed, she seemed to think Tommy slightly mad to have assumed it.

"If he does know, there can be only one explanation." A look of nervous apprehension crept into her eyes. "Quick," she whispered, "before Rosemary comes in. This will give them grounds for an arrest?"

"By itself? Hardly."

"Pity," she muttered. "I was hoping it would." Had she been hoping it? He could not for the life of him be sure.

CHAPTER TWENTY-TWO

SEVEN beast-demons might be lodged in Gavin's gnarled body. If so, at the coroner's court the entire assortment was well battened down.

It was not that the archaeologist had made any improvement in his attire. His voluminous overcoat was unbrushed, his hair and ancient black stock vied with each other for greasiness, but when he stood to answer questions there was dignity in the features so oddly suggestive of an El Greco in an advanced stage of decay, and as his voice was heard the room became miraculously stilled. The coroner, re-adjusting pince-nez, accorded him an unwilling respect. A bishop in gaiters let his disapproving stare relax, while the minor clergy, who flocking together lent the occasion the air of a small oecumenical council, blinked and then listened as though one of their own number were addressing them. Breeding and a scholarly utterance were exerting their spell.

Only a sparse handful had attended. They included a few bored reporters, several old-fashioned persons whom Tommy took to be friends of the vicar's, various witnesses from the hotel, and a little, woebegone woman in black, who—Mrs. Bellamy-Pryce whispered this—was poor Cuthbert's housekeeper, Pennylove. To the left of the seats occupied by the family was Nurse Claiborne, well-dressed, with lips rigidly compressed and chill grey eyes never deviating from the front. To Tommy it seemed she was taking a far keener interest in the proceedings than her position warranted, and that the main object of her attention was Gavin. When the latter took the stand her hardy colour flared up, her chin grew more antagonistic. Her resemblance to a high-spirited horse, curbed by a tight check-rein, noticeably increased.

The coroner, badly afflicted with hay-fever, sneezed repeatedly, wiped streaming eyes, and finally asked if Mr. Bellamy-Pryce had known in advance of his brother's visit to London. Gavin gave a simple affirmative, and, pressed for details, continued:

"I had a note from him by the first post on Monday morning. I had been ill with influenza, but towards noon I felt well enough to go out and telephone the hotel where my brother was staying. I called on him after lunch, and we spent the rest of the day together."

"Did the note you received give any particular reason for his coming to town?"

"It mentioned some disturbance in connection with his daughter and sister-in-law, living together in Kensington. When I saw my brother, however, he informed me that he had been under a misapprehension, and was no longer alarmed."

Rosemary's hands clinched more tightly in her lap. Boggie's ragged brows drew together in an anxious furrow, and Argus, at the end of the row, made restive movements in a chair too small for him. Would the coroner delve more deeply into the matter? He did not.

"Should you say that the deceased was gravely worried over any cause?"

"I saw no sign of it," answered Gavin unhesitatingly. "He seemed in his usual quite placid spirits."

"You yourself know of no domestic or financial difficulties?"

"He mentioned none. I have never known him to suffer from either."

The coroner succumbed to another fit of sneezing, struggled manfully, and gasped out, "I now must put a rather painful question to you, Mr. Bellamy-Pryce. Should you say that at any time your brother exhibited a tendency to mental aberration?"

"Most decidedly not. I should describe him as a remarkably sane man."

"Not subject, then, to sudden attacks of depression?"

"On the contrary, he was of a very even, cheerful disposition."

In the front seats bewilderment grew. Tommy, who had confidently expected a different reply, hung on the next question. The coroner, consulting notes, brought it forth uneventfully.

"Mr. Bellamy-Pryce, did you visit the Shaftesbury Palace Hotel on the evening of your brother's death?"

"I did," answered Gavin readily.

"Indeed! Kindly tell the court what happened."

Turning slightly towards the jury, the witness made answer, "I arrived, without appointment, at about half-past ten o'clock. Failing to discover my brother in the lounge, where I had expected he would be, I concluded he had gone to bed. Not wishing to disturb him, I went away. I was in the building a few minutes only—possibly five."

"Always on the ground floor?"

"Certainly."

"You made no inquiries for him?"

"No. I expected to see him in the morning."

Gavin was allowed to stand down. Throughout he had maintained his customary composure, minus, this time, the arrogance. When he was reseated, however, Tommy saw him mop his face surreptitiously with a filthy handkerchief. His gloved hand shook, and for a few minutes he sat with closed eyes.

Rosemary and her aunt had already been gently interrogated, so that the nature of the "disturbance" just mentioned was not wholly a mystery. If nothing had been said about the third attack in Victoria Grove, that fact was due in part to the absence of a leading question, and more to the inspector's previous coaching of the two witnesses. Headcorn had strongly impressed on them that it was inadvisable to say more than was necessary. This was not a criminal court, and until foul play was definitely established, motive and unsubstantiated suspicions had better be left out of it. For a moment it had looked as though complications might arise over the daughter's connection with the hat-shop in which, some four days before, a charwoman had met death by poisoning. However, the brief flurry of excitement had died down when two additional witnesses—Thomas Rostetter and John Argus, of Sydney—both testified to the deceased's having been only mildly concerned and in no way morbidly impressed by the casualty. In short, a deal of thin ice had been skated over with remarkable success—which, it appeared, was exactly what the man in charge of things wanted.

Just why did he want it? Tommy himself was not wholly pleased with the manipulation of affairs, and it was easy to see that Argus was taking an even more recalcitrant view. The simplest explanation was that Headcorn hoped for an adjournment growing out of his own findings and the evidence he meant to call; but very soon it appeared that nothing useful was to be got from the hotel staff, who formed an iron-clad combine against the bare suggestion of foul play. A bell-boy, a lift-operator and several nervous but self-assured young women supplied instances of the deceased's vagaries, while the day-clerk, coming last, added a more striking quota to the tale of wool-gathering wits. The vicar on one occasion had gone out leaving change for a pound note lying on the tobacco-counter. He had left his spectacles in their case on the desk instead of his key, and had come very near having a nasty accident with the revolving doors. Only Wednesday morning the day-clerk had remarked to a colleague that the little clergyman up from the country oughtn't to be going about London on his own. However, the colleague had said there was no need to bother, this being the sort of person whom Providence always watched over.

In the audience various heads nodded wisely. "Children and fools," they seemed to say, and the bishop's cough had a significant ring. The coroner asked, "Did you receive the impression that this absentmindedness was the result of anxiety or depression?"

"No," replied the witness coolly, "but I did think at times he wasn't quite all there, so to speak."

Rosemary flushed hotly and leant forward. Tommy laid his hand on her arm and quietly drew her back. The day-clerk, further questioned, was saying with slight embarrassment:

"I'm thinking in particular of the Monday evening when I happened to catch a bit of conversation between the deceased and his brother. I'm not sure what it was they were speaking about. The brother said something that sounded like 'Coptic remains.' The deceased answered, 'Ah, yes! I'm told they do them up in gelatine.' I shouldn't have thought anything of it but for the way the other gentleman stared and then smiled. It gave the idea—well, maybe I'd better not say it."

The jury turned meaning glances on one another, and the foreman, a County Council schoolmaster, shook an ominous head. The witness was dismissed, and the coroner called on Mr. Bellamy-Pryce for elucidation of a remark seemingly irrelevant.

"It is fairly simple, I think," said Gavin, faintly smiling. "My brother was often irrelevant, owing to lapses of attention. I imagine he confounded gelatine with paraffin wax, which is sometimes used to preserve inscriptions from the deleterious effects of the weather. The moment before he had been speaking of some glazed pheasant he had enjoyed at a luncheon given by his Bishop. I could easily have ascertained his meaning, but the matter did not seem worth pursuing."

It was perhaps unfortunate that directly after this the housekeeper, Sarah Pennylove, should dwell lachrymosely on the vicar's vagueness. She had, she declared, been kept constantly on the jump, in a manner of speaking, to see her poor master committed no imprudences or mortifying mistakes—such, for example, as going to service in his bedroom slippers. Once, indeed, she had just caught him crossing to the vestry in an old dressing-gown. Last summer he had taken a bee-hive without proper protection, getting seriously stung, while worse still was his walking into an old well at the edge of glebeland and having to remain waist-deep in stagnant water till his shouts were heard. Not but what her master had been the most considerate man alive, never one to give trouble if he could help it—and as for open-handedness! Why, the lowest tramps and scoundrels could get money out of him! It was just that he wanted looking after more than most gentlemen—which was saying something, to be sure. In fact, Mrs. Pennylove's first wail on hearing the dreadful news had been, "There! Didn't I say he'd ought never to have gone up to London by himself?"

A tall frightened young curate and two stolid parish members gave a general confirmation of this idea, emphasising the happy nature on which cares had so lightly weighed. A family solicitor declared positively there had been no money difficulties, and indeed not one person interrogated had observed the least symptom of worry on the vicar's part. Accident began to loom large in most minds, and blocked the door firmly against any alien intrusion.

There could be no doubt that Inspector Headcorn strove hard to upset the comforting belief. His own witnesses, the two guests from the air-shaft rooms, were given a respectful hearing, the chair on which the victim had or had not stood was fetched into court and the objection to a simple fall logically demonstrated by means of a foot-rule. Photographs of two parallel smudges were handed to the jury, and a detailed description given of the rolled-up blind.

It was this last-named feature which defeated him. Instantly the blind was mentioned coroner and jury seemed to close their minds as an oyster its shell. As the coroner pointed out later in his summing-up, who at some time has not got up on a chair to struggle with a refractory blind? And with a man of fifty-five, what more natural than for sudden giddiness to follow exertion? To say that the chair tilted back by an over-balancing body would not subside into its former position was mere guesswork. On a carpeted floor the chances were it would return into more or less the same place it had occupied before the fall had occurred. If these nearly-invisible smudges on the paint could be proved to contain brown boot-polish . . . but they did not; and as for the somewhat fanciful idea of the lights having been switched off and then on again, there was nothing valid to uphold it. The two persons opposite had on their own admissions been busily engaged at the time, a fact in itself sufficient to account for their not observing the actual fall.

Implicit in the foregoing remarks was the reminder that the unfortunate victim was not only a vicar of the English Church, but could not by the wildest stretch of imagination have possessed an enemy in the world—two facts which spoke for themselves. Stronger arguments than those just produced would be required to outweigh them. The jury, of course, would form its own conclusion.

The jury, one may assume, did so, but the mass opinion was so transparent that the verdict when returned produced no astonishment. Death by Misadventure it was—and nearly all who heard it gave evidence of entire satisfaction.

As the room cleared Tommy buttonholed the inspector for a moment only.

"I warned you what to expect," muttered the latter, and could not be induced to add a word to his comment. He waited till Mrs. Bellamy-Pryce had passed through the door before speaking in a low voice to Rosemary. She made a slight gesture of assent, and moved on to join her party. Gavin had already disappeared, so unobtrusively that Tommy was reminded of the story told by Argus of the man seen for an instant on the boat-deck. He was not among the few who paused in the street for brief, hushed discussion, nor, as a backward glance showed, had he remained behind in the court. During the instant of time when Tommy had spoken to Headcorn he had melted from view.

The bishop, politely hiding his impatience at being detained by the nervous curate, was getting into a handsome Bentley. Nurse Claiborne, high-coloured but self-contained, pointedly avoided the vicar's family and sailed straight for her employer's Rolls-Royce coupe. One remaining car stood by the kerb. It was a span-new, strikingly-smart Alvis saloon, minus a chauffeur. As Tommy idly wondered whose it might be, Argus went towards it, ran his big palm caressingly over the glossy hood, and flicked a speck of dust from the shining wind-screen.

"Yours, is it?" inquired Tommy, surprised.

"Good guess," affirmed the Australian satisfiedly. "Delivered this morning. Decent model, what?"

In the undertone still obligated by the recent proceedings, he explained that the new purchase had about cleaned him to the bone, but that a bargain such as this was couldn't be missed. He held open the door for Boggie to get in, then looked expectantly at Rosemary. She shook her head.

"I'm going with Mr. Rostetter," she said firmly, and turned on her heel, leaving Argus to glower after her.

"Of course," murmured Boggie quietly, touching her friend's arm. "Never mind, we'll all meet at lunch. You'll come to the house, won't you, Mr. Rostetter?" The Alvis had already shot out of sight when Rosemary took her place in the humbler car.

"Well?" she whispered, as they drove off.

"I hardly know what to say." Tommy spoke cautiously. "On the evidence, I dare say it's a perfectly natural verdict."

"Yes." She drew a spent breath, slowly removed her gloves, and smoothed the fingers. "In a way, I suppose it is—natural; but is it true?" Before he could answer she pressed his knee with her clinched hand. "No, don't say it. I know what you're thinking. The inspector thinks it, too. That's why he did all he could to persuade the jury there was something wrong. And yet"—her forehead twisted into anguished indecision—"I don't quite know . . . If it weren't for other things, I could almost believe . . . No! I can't believe it was an accident! Not now. There's been too much happening. It's only that as I sat there watching my uncle and listening to him—oh, do you understand?"

"Perfectly. It was a sort of spell, wasn't it?"

"A spell! Yes. He forced one to believe he was telling the truth. I think he must be two people. There are cases like that, aren't there? That might explain it. I see now I must have been sort of hypnotised. Yet I wasn't the only one. They all believed him."

"There was no one to refute his statement," Tommy reminded her dryly. "If he did go up those eight flights of stairs, he did it without being seen."

"And he'd have known that, of course." She drew her hand over her eyes, as though against her will a delusion were being torn from her. "Still, that's not what matters most, is it? The real thing is there's no one else—no one—who could want to kill my father. That nurse couldn't gain by it. With Boggie it was different. My grandfather could do as he liked with Boggie's money—or most of it. He can't touch my father's. Why, though, did she come?"

"The nurse? I'm devilled if I know! She takes these family matters very much to heart, that's certain. Unless your grandfather sent her?"

She shook her head, worn out with futile speculation.

"Look here," said Tommy sensibly. "We may be sure of one thing: Nothing more is going to happen now. It would be suicidal to attempt it. The fact that your uncle can't yet be apprehended means very little. He's going to be watched every step of the way from now on."

"Watched! He was supposed to have been watched before."

"Yes, I know," Tommy had to admit. "But it's very seldom a Yard sergeant makes a bloomer such as was made in that hotel lounge Wednesday evening. The crowd lent itself to a disappearance. Don't you see how easy it would be once a man got through those doors to make a dive for stairs that are almost never used, and slide into a lavatory on an upper floor to wait? Headcorn knows this much: your uncle didn't turn up at his room for a full hour after he was lost from sight. He may have walked about outdoors, but equally he may have spent most of that interval hidden in the hotel. As I say, it was a damnable blunder letting him escape like that, but there won't be another set of circumstances of the same sort. There can't be."

"There's something wrong about all this!" she cried. "This inquest itself. Why weren't we allowed to tell all we knew?"

"I suppose we must trust Inspector Headcorn to know what he's about. Let's reason it out. What would have been gained by giving full details of, let's say, the attack on your aunt? Nothing—unless your aunt had been prepared to state absolutely that it was perpetrated by her brother-in-law. Which she emphatically isn't. An ugly suspicion might have been raised, but there it would have ended—and the same in every respect applies to the poisoning episode. Just suspicions, without tangible proof. We have to remember not one thing concerning any of these affairs has been proved. I have the inspector's word for it that every possible line of investigation has been followed up. They've all petered out."

"Then why does the inspector want to see me this afternoon?"

"Did he say that?" Tommy thought it over. "Only you, is it?"

"Yes—and I'm not to mention it to my aunt. That's another puzzle. I'm to go down to Scotland Yard at three o'clock. Oh, I shall just say I'm calling in at the shop to collect some things I've left there. Perhaps you'll drive me down?"

"Certainly—and call for you later. It won't be bad," he comforted her. "I expect he only wants to get an unprejudiced account of a few incidents, maybe caution you about being alone with your uncle during the next few days. That part's easy. I'm going down to Sussex, and I shan't budge till he's gone. I was even going to suggest your putting me up at the vicarage. There's a good excuse, because my brother has his wife's relations staying with him."

"Oh, if you would!" She turned grateful eyes on him. "Though, of course, Uncle Gavin will go to the inn."

Tommy thought there was no of course about it, but said nothing. Rosemary also was silent, presently to say how much she dreaded the family meal and the inevitable discussion of the inquest.

"Why go through with it?" He slowed his car. "There's no need."

"I must. I can't hurt Boggie. Besides, it's only putting it off. No, let's get it over."

Afterwards Tommy recollected that just at this juncture he experienced the disagreeable sensation known as some one walking over his grave. He could not account for it, though the immediate cause seemed to be the remembered expression he had noticed on Mrs. Bellamy-Pryce's face when the verdict was returned—an expression of overwhelming relief. Perhaps Rosemary also had observed it, and was wondering, with him, what it could mean. If so, he could see why she shrank from her aunt's company. The idea that Mrs. Bellamy-Pryce after what had happened and in the face of what might happen was still protecting a murderer was fraught with horrid possibilities. That no conceivable excuse for such an anomaly could be found merely increased the horror of it. Then, here was this fresh interrogation. It was Rosemary alone who was wanted, and her aunt was not to know. . . .

The sun, hot and brilliant, broke forth from a cloud, and the chill automatically passed. They turned the corner into Victoria Grove, got out, and were met by the new maid, Larke by name, who held open the door and eyed them in a curious, portentous manner.

"Don't be upset, miss," she said quietly. "But the fact is madam's just had a rather nasty mishap."

CHAPTER TWENTY-THREE

"STEADY on!" Tommy took hold of Rosemary, who had clutched his arm and turned ghastly pale. "What's happened, Larke?"

The next moment Rosemary was weakly laughing. Her aunt had merely cut her hand with a grape-fruit knife.

"That's all, miss. She was mixing a cider-cup; but it's her right thumb, and it's bleeding quite a lot. The captain's looking after her, up in the bathroom."

They ran upstairs. Red drops were spattering on to the waxed linoleum from a deep, jagged wound which Argus, inexpertly, was trying to stanch with cotton-wool.

"I told her to let me do it," muttered the Australian, scowling at a splash on his tie. "Here, take a look. Think it'll want stitching up?"

"Oh, nonsense!" Boggie jerked her hand away. "Just let's put something round it and let it go."

"Better disinfect it first," Tommy advised, examining the still bleeding cut. "No, I think it will heal without stitches, but it's a beast of a jab, all the same." He took the brown bottle Rosemary had reached from the small white wall-cupboard, soaked a pad of wool with iodine and warned the sufferer to brace herself. "This will hurt, you know."

"Oh, don't mind me! I've borne worse things in my time."

Mrs. Bellamy-Pryce did not flinch when the iodine stung the raw fissure. She even chuckled a little, repressing it quickly when she realised the sound of her mirth was out of place. Rosemary noticed that Tommy was eyeing her with almost scientific interest, as though he considered her a woman in a thousand when it came to bearing pain—which, of course, she was.

They went down to lunch—a rather silent meal. There was a little halting discussion, naturally, but less than Rosemary had feared. Argus seemed angry over the verdict, but did not express his opinion in actual words. Boggie's manner betrayed a mixture of thankfulness and apology. It would have been more remarkable if it had not been so like all her behaviour since disasters had begun happening. The uneasy glances she kept stealing at her niece showed very clearly that she appreciated to the full the awkward position in which she had been obliged to place herself.

How often must Rosemary keep repeating to her own inner censor that Boggie was in no way responsible, and that she could not in all fairness be expected to swear to an uncertainty?

"I must be nicer to her," the girl made new resolutions. "I suppose, without in the least intending it, I've seemed a tiny bit distant and critical. I simply couldn't help it, but I must try harder, that's all."

She took a bit of the omelette she had felt unable to eat, and made brave efforts to get it down.

"That's right," Boggie approved. "It's no good giving way, is it? We've still a trying time ahead of us. The funeral, I mean." Hastily she corrected any possible misconstruction of her remark, and looking at Rosemary's white cheeks with sympathy advised complete rest for the remainder of the day.

"I simply have to go down to the shop for a bit," said Rosemary. "No, Larke, I have finished. For one thing"—she bethought herself of a valid excuse—"I must get hold of a decent black hat."

"I'll drive you there and back," Argus promptly offered.

"Thanks so much, but Mr. Rostetter has promised to take me. It's almost on his way."

"Oh! Well, that's up to you, I suppose."

What foul manners he had! It was Tommy's expression, though, which caught her attention. His blue eyes, suddenly like steel points, were fixed on her aunt's face, which she now saw had reddened unbecomingly. Probably for the once Boggie was embarrassed by her protege's rudeness. The wonder was she didn't more often notice that Captain Argus wasn't quite out of the top drawer. Perhaps for her, as for the majority of women, his good looks and dominant masculinity blinded her to his lack of breeding. . . .

"The nurse?" Boggie was speaking acridly, answering some question Rosemary had missed. "Oh, I saw her! Extremely well turned out she is these days. I don't suppose one need ask where she got that silver fox. She ignored us, as usual. I quite expected it; but why she came at all . . . Still, one mustn't give her a black eye. When all's said, she's done her best to keep her patient alive when it can hardly be to her advantage."

Argus roused from the sulky fit into which he had fallen over Rosemary's refusal of his escort.

"Meaning she'll come in for a fat legacy?" he demanded.

The question had been put with all his characteristic suspicion. Boggie glanced at him in slight surprise.

"She must look forward to something substantial," she declared calmly. "He can leave her what he likes so long as it's been saved out of income; and you may depend on it she's run things on a narrow margin with just that very thing in view. You must have your coffee Ro, my child." She rang the bell. "Thank goodness it will be coffee, not the imitation stuff that wretched Vera used to give us."

Again Rosemary, on her way to her room, saw Tommy's alert glance and arrested movement. She knew what he was thinking; but it was useless, Vera couldn't tell him anything. She had gone well before anything had happened in this house. A nice, friendly little thing she had been, despite the dreadful coffee. More human than this machine-like Larke. Just another of the changes which made the atmosphere different. The whole of life till recently so jolly and comfortable had fallen under a cloud.

She herself, in her black last year's coat and black hat two seasons out of fashion, seemed in the glass an unfamiliar person. A good thing the coat could be wrapped round, for all of a sudden she had got decidedly thinner. Older, too. That, of course, was due to the dark smudges under her eyes which gave her a hollow-eyed look. Even her father, if he were here, would have noticed the alteration. She battled sternly with the lump in her throat and went down.

At the entrance to Scotland Yard Tommy suggested waiting for her.

"No, don't. I can't tell how long I'll be, and it would make me uncomfortable. I really do mean to go on to the shop. Suppose you pick me up there about four-thirty?"

He agreed, and with a nervous sinking of the heart she disappeared into the doorway.

Tommy, returned to his flat, made ready for his stay in Sussex. He had made Rosemary promise to take a taxi to Brackham Place, but in spite of this he did not like having to leave her. Which, of course, was entirely stupid. Whatever might happen would not happen now. It was altogether too soon. Gavin, he firmly believed, had just skinned out of a nasty situation, and would for the immediate present lie low. Besides, no plain-clothes sergeant was likely to make a mistake and let Gavin out of his sight again.

As he folded clean shirts into a narrowed compass, an aphorism he had frequently had occasion to quote came into his thoughts: "Neither the presence nor the absence of love can be long concealed." What a searching truth that was! No doubt, every bit as plainly as Argus and Rank, he was giving his emotions away to all beholders; but at the moment what prompted the recollection of La Rochefoucauld's famous words was something he had seen quite accidentally during lunch—Boggie's sudden flaming anger. There was no question as to what had precipitated it. It had been Argus's jealousy of himself. Her face had grown brick-red and swollen, her good-humoured eyes distorted with hate. In short, for the space of thirty seconds she had been the woman he had only once before seen, and then reflected in a mirror. The instant she had realised he was looking at her she had softened into her ordinary self.

In a flash of insight that startled without wholly astonishing, he had known the reason. It was really very dense of him not to have guessed all along that Boggie was in love with Argus. Possibly her serene acceptance of the latter's attachment to her niece had put him off the track—that and her frank middle-age, her scorn of beauty-aids and general unromantic outlook. Not till now had it struck him that she was stoically hiding her real emotions. It was as though for one half-minute, or less, a cheerful mask had fallen. Too bad. The man, quite patently, courted her society solely because of the chance it gave him to see more than might otherwise have been possible of the younger, more desirable object. She must know that. But did she?

"Oh, certainly she knows it! Why, it sticks out a mile. I merely happened to catch her off her guard." He picked up a batch of collars. "Stoic! She's that and no mistake. Look at the way she let me douse that gashed hand with iodine and never turned a hair! I've heard men curse a blue streak for less."

Come to think of it, it had been rather curious. The point was, there had been no involuntary recoil. None whatever. Truly remarkable. . . .

Laying down the collars, Tommy reached the volume into which he had been dipping the night before. It was one of the many specialised treatises, some old-fashioned, which Bromley, the owner of the flat, had collected over a period of years. Passages had been marked, probably for some topical interest they involved. To one of these he now turned. It was supremely irrelevant, but none the less intriguing. He had another hour to kill, so he might as well see what old Lombroso had to say. . . .

In Inspector Headcorn's plain office Rosemary was being put through the hoop in a way that puzzled and at moments offended her—though to do him justice, the inspector was using the utmost tact. She could not think why once again she was being questioned about matters already finished with, as, for example, the dismissal of Vera Coldbottom.

"I've told you all I know," she said rather desperately. "I liked her, but my aunt never did find her satisfactory. I suppose her getting ready to go out in my hat was just the last straw. Anyhow, I came home that afternoon—Monday it was—and found her already gone. She'd been given a week's wages and board money in place of notice."

The inspector did not probe further into Vera's shortcomings, which was just as well. Rosemary, home but little, had only vague ideas on the subject. The next minute, however, she was frowning again. What on earth was this about her aunt's taking something out of storage and fetching it home just before the Saturday attack?

"I'm sure you're mistaken," she insisted. "What she has stored are my uncle's things. If she had brought anything home, she'd certainly have mentioned it."

"You never, then, saw a bundle lying about? I had better explain. We have not been able to find any trace of a fishing-line having been purchased. I know Mrs. Bellamy-Pryce denies having seen the cord that was used to—"

"Fishing-line!" She could hardly believe her ears. "You thought it might have belonged to my uncle? Oh, what utter nonsense!"

"Don't be offended, Miss Bellamy-Pryce," said Headcorn, looking sorry. "You see, we now know that your aunt wanted very much to conceal a certain suspicion from us. In her anxiety to do this she might quite easily have declared she had never set eyes on that cord before when in actual fact she herself had brought it into the house on Saturday morning—meaning, we'll assume, to give it to some friend who was fond of fishing. I don't say she did, only that if this were so she would later on find herself obliged to stick to her statement, even if she were shown the flaw in it. Now, then, you saw the cord. Should you say it could be carried in a man's coat-pocket?"

"No," she admitted. "There was too much of it."

"Quite. It would have made a pretty bulky parcel, which your aunt could hardly have failed to notice when she opened the door. Perhaps now you understand my suggestion. Supposing this cord was already there, lying in full sight?"

"I'm positive it wasn't."

"Well! Be that as it may, you had better know this: When Mrs. Bellamy-Pryce was first questioned, she did not recall having noticed that the man she saw was carrying a parcel. Afterwards she recollected a vague impression that he did have a bundle of some kind, in his left hand, partly hidden behind him."

Rosemary turned hot all over. There was no need to underline the discrepancy in these two statements, one of which could not be true—but which? She was distressed and confused—mortified, too, over this new proof that Boggie had hedged and prevaricated. She wanted to defend her aunt, but could think of nothing to say. The dreadful part of it all was that Boggie would not have lied unless she had some very strong reason. That the lying was a bungling business might illustrate Boggie's essential goodness of heart, but it could, she knew, have other meanings to this coldly logical detective.

The dull blue eyes were watching her closely but with genuine compassion.

"I deeply regret having to trouble you as I am doing, to-day of all times," the inspector continued. "I have to do it because the gravity of the position forces me to attack matters boldly now, before you leave town. I have ascertained that your aunt did call at the Harwood Storage Depository on Saturday morning. It is true she was not observed to bring anything away with her except her shopping-bag, but as there was no reason to take especial note of—"

Rosemary stopped him eagerly.

"But of course!" she cried in relief. "She fetched away my Uncle James's revolver—a Colt's '45. If you'd only known, you were sitting on it that same afternoon. It was under the chair-cushion, only—"

She pulled herself up guiltily. "Oh, dear, ought I to be telling you this? She hasn't taken out a licence."

Headcorn's face was a comic study.

"Oh!" he said stiffly. "I see. Well, if you're quite sure—"

"Of course I'm sure. She showed it to me next day."

"And how large is her shopping-bag?"

"Oh, just ordinary. You must have seen it, because she always uses the same one. I don't think she has any handbag large enough for that cord to pack into."

He rubbed the big wart on his nose and reconnoitred. She had the breathless feeling of having by the simple statement of fact demolished a pet theory and at the same time vindicated her aunt from some mysterious and unpleasant imputation. It was a small point scored; but it did not greatly relieve her. Her father was dead, and both she and Boggie must still walk in fear. Thus far not one word had been said which could give the assurance her terrified consciousness craved.

CHAPTER TWENTY-FOUR

SPEEDING towards the shop, Rosemary tried to solve the riddles she had been too battered and dragooned to tackle while the inspector's eye was upon her. First, how had Headcorn discovered what storage place Boggie had gone to? Even she hadn't known. Uneasily she wondered if in their absence this morning the house had been searched. Most unlikely. The righteous Larke would have told them; yet she could not think how except through a storage-receipt the information could have been learned.

Again, why had she been cross-examined once more about a wine-glass? About every incident surrounding the time when the gin had been poured out? Above all, why had she been made to repeat word for word her telephone conversation with her aunt prior to the Saturday attack? When she had remembered saying to Boggie that she would be bringing Mr. Rostetter home in three-quarters of an hour, the man facing her had sat like an owl, making calculations—not very satisfactory ones, either, to judge by his expression. That, at least, was something. . . .

"But why do I say that?" she muttered, with a nervous start. "I suppose it's because he wanted to know whether I volunteered the information or simply gave it when I was asked how long we'd be. Boggie did ask, of course. She wanted to have tea all ready when we arrived—and there was double the amount of bread-and-butter to cut, because Rank was coming. She rubbed up the kettle, too. All in all, it must have taken her a good twenty minutes."

Yes, she had the feeling she had successfully scotched whatever ugly idea had been working itself up in the inspector's brain. Why, then, was she just as wretched as before? It was idiotic to ask. Clearing Boggie of God knew what only deepened the black shadow overhanging her father's favourite brother. For days now she had been hemmed in by two fires, afraid to move in either direction. The dimming of one sent the other flaring up the more hotly. Also, she could no longer shut her eyes to the widening breach between her aunt and herself, nor view with any tranquillity her life in Victoria Grove. The once-happy relationship had been spoiled. A thing broken may be patched up, but the mend generally shows.

"Is it because of the fibs she's told? She had what she believed was a good excuse. Altogether an unselfish one. Or was it her letting fly at me that one time?"

Candour compelled her to date the beginning of change considerably earlier. Though unable exactly to place it, she had grown conscious of it when her aunt let slip the fatal words, "black gloves." From then onward nothing had been quite the same as before. It was entirely illogical, and she must fight against her feeling. If she didn't surmount it she would be slumping from that standard of fair play which, without analysing it, she had always set herself. . . .

Anatol's was just being emptied of several aristocratic customers. Luckily the countess was not there, only the two weary girls, clamorous with sympathy. Even this was too much for her.

"Joan, darling, please let's not talk about it. You do understand?"

"Perfectly, my sweet! You want a hat, don't you? Look, here's the very thing. I've kept it back for you. Don't you want to see how it looks? Oh, well, it's charming on you, and only a guinea. I'll just rub off this spot."

Busy with the removal of a small portion of the countess's facial adornment, Miss Walford prattled on tactfully.

"I say, you know Minnie's, of course? Lousier than ever, I may tell you, but David and I happened to drop in last night, and who do you think was there being a little ray of sunshine?"

"Joan!" admonished Cybele Tarrant. "Poor Ro won't want to hear."

"It was your Australian heavyweight," continued Joan. "He'd got some weird pick-up in tow—the most dubious piece of goods; and, my darling, he was stinko. Absolutely paralytic."

"Oh?" murmured Rosemary, her gaze wandering.

"No, but you should have seen him! Doing a horrible rumba, shouldering couples off the floor—and then he turned ugly. Tried to pour rye down the saxophone horn, and when Jimmy, the band leader, wanted to stop him there was the filthiest row. Davy and I cut. We quite expected the police in, and after the stuff we'd seen circulating—"

"Don't you two want tea?" interrupted Rosemary. "If so, now's your chance, while I'm here."

"Angel! You're sure you don't mind? You'll have the place all to yourself for another half-hour. Talia's getting a new face-lift. So reckless of her—and I say, have you any notion what's become with those new scent sprays?"

"I'll have a hunt. Hurry along, you both look frayed to bits."

So did the stock, Rosemary reflected listlessly, when she was left in piece to start mechanically putting things to rights. Here were the scent sprays, never unpacked, under stacks of rubbishy flowers, and underneath, in a corner of the cupboard, a small object which brought a blur of tears to her eyes. Poor, forlorn Cuthbert! She couldn't leave him here friendless, with his gentle, trusting eyes. She tucked ten and sixpence into the desk-drawer, and slid the glass dog into her bag, wondering if she would ever again find delight in this hazardous but fascinating employment. She would not have to work now. A letter from her father's solicitor this morning assured her she could count on a small but adequate allowance. Still, she had been happiest in harness, with every minute of the day mapped out. If she thought of her former existence in terms of exhausting rush and brain-fag, the answer was that she was not quite normal. Why else this agitated longing to flee the premises, the mere sight of whose mirrored stools and silver stars threw her into a sick panic?

It was when she went into the tiny back room, dark as a cave, that she understood the real reason for this. All at once she saw the stark, repulsive body wedged behind the lavatory door, felt the paralysing stricture of her heart which had come with the realisation of her own purely fortuitous escape. Oh, let her get away, quickly, before she cracked to bits!

"That's simply stupid." She set her teeth. "I really must take myself in hand. Besides, Tommy'll be calling for me any minute."

Trying not to hurry, she collected the spare pumps, extra stockings kept for the days when she had to tramp about in the rain, all the oddments that might very well be left; but returning to the main room she took care to close the door, and finding by her watch she would still have some time to wait, decided to let Tommy know she was here.

But was there any use ringing him up? He might not be at his flat. With her hand on the white microphone she hesitated, wondering how it was she longed for Tommy as a frightened child longs for its nurse, and troubled a little to find within her another feeling less easy to pin down. She did not think it could be love, for the simple reason that love as it was understood by other people, as she herself supposed it to be, had never yet come her way. She had not needed it, not sought it. When it had been given her, unasked, she had buffeted it away, impatient—too frequently disgusted—it its demands.

There was something lacking in her, naturally. Her friends frankly said so—though they also said, so annoyingly, that she would feel quite differently once the right man came along. She, of course, knew better. There would never be a right man. The trouble was in herself. Somehow she had been made immune and self-sufficient—able to feel ecstasy in quite impersonal ways, over her job, over beauty, over the incredible adventure of life. Rapture transported her at the mere fragrance of daffodils in spring, a phrase of music, a dramatic moment—but never, oh, not once, at the touch of a man! Maybe it was true that an important ingredient had been left out of her. The rest of the world couldn't be wrong; but if she didn't miss this ingredient, could it matter?

It had never mattered till now, when she was overtaxed, jumpy of her own shadow, miserably—yes, miserably—*afraid*. . . .

For literally the first time in her life she had lost that feeling of self-completeness. She who had done the protecting now, of a sudden, longed to be protected. Oh, not to be kissed and mauled! That, from a little girl, she had hated. Just to be taken care of. Altogether unfair. No man wanted to give and not receive something in return. The test would come when Tommy Rostetter left her and went back to Paris. If by then she had stopped being frightened, how much would she mind his going? Quite honestly she did not know, but what she did know was that even this brief solitude was insupportable. She must tell him she was alone, waiting for him to come and comfort her! Let him think her a weak-minded fool, imposing on him, taking up his time with her woes. Anyhow, it was not as though he were in love with her or likely ever to be. If he had shown the least sign of it, she would have had to give up seeing him—as had happened with so many others.

She dialled the number—and replaced the receiver. A car had stopped outside the shop.

He had come! Here was his welcome figure darkening the doorway. Impulsively she rushed round the intervening hat-standards, both hands outstretched.

"Thank God!" she cried, almost sobbing in her relief. "Oh, darling, I did want you! I . . ."

She gasped, appalled by her mistake; but it was a little too late. She heard her name roughly whispered, and even as she took in the amazed gratification and another, muddied emotion in the hot, filmed eyes bearing down on her, she was crushed by powerful arms and felt a devouring mouth on her own. Outraged fury lent her extra strength. She wrenched herself free and dealt a stinging blow on her captor's sensual face.

"Keep away! How dare you do . . . that?" she blazed.

Argus smiled, drawing in on her again—and now she knew he had been drinking, and would in consequence be hard to deal with. She felt a physical nausea as she fended him off and retreated towards the wall.

"Dare?" he repeated. "And why not? You said you wanted me. Well, then, why all this fuss?" Arrogantly he pressed forward. "Own up you're glad I've caught you alone," he cajoled. "Come along, say it."

"Glad! *You?*"

Long pent contempt exploded in the two words. He continued to smile.

"Oh, don't think I haven't seen what's been holding you back!" he said fatuously. "But, it's not the case—understand? There's nothing to stop us, so get that into your head. I want you—have done, since the first day I set eyes on you. And you've wanted me, though you'd never admit it. Oh, I've known!"

"Stop! Get back!"

"You won't say that when I've kissed you properly. Listen! You and I are getting married—yes, you heard me, married—and the sooner the better. Oh, I mean that! Just you say the word, and leave everything to Jack. He'll fix it okay. Come along, now, this is on the level. You've shown me how you feel, so . . ."

"How I feel?" Backing steadily, she had crashed into one of the hat-standards. Hedged in by his advance, with another embrace imminent, she found voice to stab with. "Yes, I have shown you—and only a vulgar, unspeakably conceited fool could have misunderstood! Me marry you? I'd rather die first. You must be mad as well as drunk. No, leave go! I . . . I feel I want a bath."

His hands dropped to his sides. He breathed hard, and an ugly red flowed into his eyes. She had not meant to say quite those things. It was he who had forced them out of her, but now she had said them she could not be sorry.

"You call me conceited." He said it in laboured fashion. "And vulgar. Am I correct?"

The look in his face drove her on to finish the job.

"You're insufferable," she told him. "I've tried to be decent to you on my aunt's account; but I'm not used to your sort. You ought to know that."

"On account of your aunt!" He began to laugh raucously. "That's damned funny, that is. You've been frank about me. Now you'll have a dose of your own medicine. Know what I think of you?" Savagely he lurched forward, his breath in her nostrils. "You're a damned, cold-livered little bitch. A bloody, calculating . . ."

"Get out!"

Neither had seen Tommy enter. He stood before them, his blue eyes expressionless in a face paper-white. Argus jerked round on him, a bull enraged.

"You meddling swine! Trying to jump a claim, are you? Keep out of this! What the hell's it got to . . ."

"Get out!"

The sight of the Australian, fists doubled, his animal bulk looming upon Tommy's wiry slightness, brought a moment of acute panic. Rosemary saw the thick, shaven neck bent forward, every clean seam suffused with crimson, and uttered a prayer.

CHAPTER TWENTY-FIVE

AND then, miraculously, it was over. Argus, still with that look of a rage-blinded bull, had cannoned out of the shop, and Rosemary, suddenly weak, found herself in Tommy's arms. The hands which held her were iron-hard, the voice which presently spoke, was without humour.

"What happened?"

Trying to laugh, she detached herself and felt for her powder-puff.

"He asked me to marry him. Then he turned nasty."

The blue eyes were bleak. Though lightness had returned to Tommy's tone there was a rasping edge to it.

"I see."

"No, you don't." Now the tension had snapped she felt limp and slightly hysterical. "It was the things I said to him. They got under his skin."

"Oh?"

She glanced fleetingly at the set features.

"If you must know, he came in tight, and—and made a grab at me. It was partly my fault, because I—well, I thought it was you, and I'd gone all nervy with being alone in this place. I lost my temper, and told him a few home-truths. I couldn't help it. I was nauseated."

Tommy eyed the front window and straightened his tie.

"Your two friends are coming back," he said. "Shall we get off?"

Over tea, in a nearly deserted little place in Park Lane, she gave him a fuller account, noticing he was unusually silent.

"Oh, well!" she smiled wryly at him. "This has torn it a bit, hasn't it? Never mind. It does mean the finish."

"So he's done this before, has he?"

"Oh, not the honourable proposal! He's made the usual passes, if that's what you mean. That's why I've refused to go out with him. I thought I'd made things clear, but it seems he'd got the idea I was for some reason hiding my real feelings."

"Oh?" remarked Tommy again, still with that faintly disagreeable rasp.

She felt overpoweringly anxious to make him understand.

"Don't you see? He's just that kind of impossibly conceited fool. It's really not to be wondered at, when you think how nine out of ten women—young and old, all classes—simply fall on his neck. Oh, yes, it's true; I've seen it happening. He couldn't believe how I loathed him. He does now, though," she ended grimly.

"So that explains the gutter-language."

"Oh, that!" Rosemary shrugged. "I've heard worse. It did sound fouler, somehow, coming from him."

"It will be awkward," said Tommy, blowing careful smoke-rings. "Having to go on seeing him—as I suppose you will have to do, for a time?"

"It will. I'll just have to put up with it. There's this about it—Boggie won't ever know."

His real thought had been that this contretemps might furnish a good excuse for splitting forces. Very soon now he would have to return to Paris, and he would go more comfortably if he knew a certain living arrangement had been altered. Actually he should have gone yesterday. If he remained in London it was only because of his fear lest the bright, dangerous flame which held him, a hypnotised moth, should in his absence suffer extinction. This move of Argus's had done more than infuriate him. It had given birth to a new and alarming idea. The usual passes—but not the honourable proposal—*till now*. It wanted thinking over.

"What did Headcorn want?" he asked suddenly.

"I haven't an earthly. I'll tell you what he said."

He gave close attention. No, nothing very startling—certainly nothing to touch on this present affair. He had guessed the inspector would try to find out if by any chance the fishing-line could have been the judge's. What he did not know was that Rosemary, almost unconsciously, was glossing things over here and there.

"I hope," she said nervously, "I didn't make a frightful mess by mentioning that revolver. You don't suppose it will get Boggie into trouble?"

"Certainly not. Headcorn will probably help her obtain a licence. I shouldn't worry about it."

"And the fishing-line. Did you think it might have been Uncle James's?" she challenged him.

"Quite honestly, no." For some reason he was glad to be able to answer so sincerely. "I believe those snapshots I told you about were shown me so I would think it. By the way, was the house in Colombo given up or merely let?"

"Let for six months. It'll be sold now. Why?"

"Only because it's usual if a house is let to reserve a cupboard or two for the owner's use. There'd be no sense in bringing fishing-tackle of that sort to England."

"Of course. Things of that kind would certainly be left behind."

Tommy, however, was appending a clause to his own statement. If a person had no fixed abode, he might well cart about cumbersome fishing-tackle, on the chance of returning. Would Gavin do this? The difficulty there was that Gavin was no one's idea of a sportsman. It was unlikely he would own fishing-tackle at all.

Argus!

Suddenly Tommy felt he had hit on something. What if it was Argus's cord, left at the house earlier in the day? That would readily explain Boggie's refusal to identify it. Unfortunately, the theory did not carry one far—in fact, no distance at all. All the same, it would be as well to see Headcorn once more before getting down to Sussex. . . .

"Shall we go?"

"Oh, dear, I suppose we must." She looked reluctant to move. "It feels so safe here. So shut in, so—"

"It will be just as safe at Broughton-Elmtrees," he promised. "With me sticking to you like a burr."

"Yes, of course it will be all right. Thank God you're coming!"

She had a moment's quiver of the nerves when they arrived home to find the inspector with her aunt. What had he been saying? Nothing alarming, it would seem. It was Boggie who had a small shock to deliver. Only a few minutes before Mrs. Pennylove had rung up from the country to ask how many guests to expect, and had mentioned that a telegram just received from Mr. Gavin announced the latter's intention of spending the coming days at the vicarage.

"It's not possible!" cried Rosemary, all her returned colour gone in an instant.

"It's true," declared her aunt with tightly-set lids and a curiously triumphant glint in her eyes. "Poor old Pennylove sounded rather upset."

"Pennylove?" echoed the girl, frowning.

"Mr. Bellamy-Pryce is a free agent," remarked the inspector, letting an unobtrusive glance rest on her briefly. "We can't well prevent him going where he likes—or at least I don't consider it wise to raise objections. As I understand Mr. Rostetter is making one of the party, our main difficulty is solved. If he had not volunteered, I was going to suggest it. In addition, I have just been explaining to your aunt that a plain-clothes sergeant will be travelling down in the same carriage with you, and will put up at the inn close by as long as you remain."

Even more non-committal than usual, he stood looking down absently at the bandaged hand the older woman had laid protectingly on her niece's arm. Without a word Rosemary moved over to the piano and removing her new hat—it was very simple and smart—plucked unseeingly at its stiff ribbon cockade. Tommy went towards her, and when the others had left the room still in conversation, asked her if she were frightened.

"Frightened?" It had taken some time for his question to register. "Not of being killed. Not with this double bodyguard. It's the inspector's believing we need all this guarding. From Uncle Gavin. And Pennylove being upset. I suppose that's why she got away this morning without speaking to us. It makes it all seem so—so certain. Oh, Tommy"—she struck her hands together with a little, desperate movement—"if one could only know, know definitely, one way or the other! Anything, anything would be better than this!"

It was unendurable to see her suffering and be powerless to stop it. How, though, could he come out brutally with his own rooted conviction in her uncle's guilt? He had no absolute proof of it. He, too, had been influenced by Gavin's spell, only now that spell was removed he was seeing in it the ruse of a diabolically clever man to gain credence and sympathy. Gavin at this moment must be hugging himself in triumph over his ability to manoeuvre death in such a way as to outwit suspicion. If this were so, there was good reason to expect him to try his skill again, at the first propitious opportunity. Not for nothing did megalomania figure largely in his composition, and it was pretty pointless to argue that the next essay would prove his downfall. That had been said once, but in spite of it the vicar was dead.

As all this went painfully through the reasoner's mind a tenuous possibility raised its head. Even vainglorious Gavin might hesitate at the risk of two more crimes. . . .

"You've always believed your uncle was fond of you. Is that so?" Tommy asked tentatively.

"As fond as he can be of anybody," she said doubtfully. "It's things he cares for, not people."

"But with your aunt there's a very positive antipathy. Do you know of any concrete reason? He wasn't, by chance, an embittered rival for her affections?"

"Uncle Gavin? What an idea! Women don't interest him—unless they're mummified. For that matter, I don't think he even knew Boggie till years after she was married. She was a Miss Boggs, of Twickenham. Her father was a retired Indian Civil, and Uncle James lodged with them while he was toiling for his law degree. At that time Uncle Gavin—the little asp, Uncle James called him—was tutoring down at Margate, crocked up from rheumatic fever. Why he hates Boggie I can't tell you, any more than I can tell you why my grandfather hates her. It's just one of the mysteries there's no solving."

"Chuck something at me if you like," said Tommy, after thinking this over. "But are you still sure—dead sure—the glass with the gin in it was yours?"

Her eyes came slowly to meet his. Drawing a deep breath, she whispered, "It was mine, Tommy. Don't build any false theories on it, will you? And now, run along. I can see you want to talk to the inspector."

Headcorn was waiting by the gate. Catching him for a second off-guard, Tommy noticed symptoms of brooding anxiety—the expression a self-contained man wears when for once he is both apprehensive and baffled. It augured badly. Tommy invited him to climb into the two-seater, and though eager to impart his own news, waited for what might be forthcoming from the official side. There was not much of it, as it happened.

"You know my belief about the vicar," began the detective, when they had reached Knightsbridge. "You also appreciate that in the case of a clergyman there's a general conspiracy to give the benefit of the doubt. In all justice to the coroner, the evidence I was able to produce wasn't in any way conclusive. You may be sure if I could have proved anything I'd have let out more than I did; but as things actually stand, no one can say the affairs at Victoria Grove or the one at Brackham Place bear any relation to the inquest just held. They may yet reveal something. I only say they don't at present.

"Well! There appears to be just one individual who has anything to gain by killing off this family. We can't charge that individual with either murder or attempted murder—nor would it greatly simplify matters if we could, seeing our chief witness is unable—or unwilling—to give the necessary identification in court. We needn't go into that again," continued the inspector dryly. "Suffice it to say we're reduced to allowing Gavin Bellamy-Pryce a certain amount of rope—"

"On the chance he'll hang himself before doing damage to other people?" Tommy broke in, with slight sarcasm. "It seems to me that has a familiar sound."

"With you keeping an eye on him indoors," pursued the inspector unperturbedly, "and Sergeant Gibbon taking care of his outdoor movements, it's unthinkable he can bring anything off. Still, there may be some kind of attempt, prompted by this gathering together of the family—

probably the last occasion when the three of them will be assembled under one roof."

"Another alleged accident, making a clean sweep of the remaining obstacles?"

"Not necessarily an accident," answered Headcorn thoughtfully. "Don't be biased by any preconceptions. What I'm saying to you is, Look out—in every quarter, however unlikely. Keep close to those two women—and if a chance occurs pick up stray gossip and send it along to me, or, if you see fit, report it to Gibbon, taking care, of course, you're not seen doing it."

Tommy had already resolved to collect what rumours he could. He mentioned the fact that his brother was the village doctor, and as such might know something of interest concerning Gavin's history, medical or social.

"Quite," murmured the detective. "But chiefly I'd like to learn, if possible, how the vicar came to hear of the trouble at this end. The evidence on that point was, you may have noticed, singularly unrevealing. I don't say glossed over. Just a matter of not being known. The post from Friday onward consisted of only bills, circulars, and a parish magazine. No one called at the vicarage, and no wire or telephone message was received. Gibbon will do what he can, but you may stand a better chance. I would go down, but I have strong reasons for wanting to remain in town. And now," said he, turning in his seat, "What have you got to tell me?"

"Oh, so you've guessed, have you? Here it is, then. This afternoon Captain Argus proposed marriage to Miss Bellamy-Pryce—and was refused unconditionally."

A quickened gleam in the inspector's eye betrayed the anticipated reaction.

"I see. Well, let's have the whole of it."

Tommy gave further details.

"I dare say Argus meant to wait for a more suitable moment," he said in conclusion. "He'd been drinking, and a misunderstanding gave him false encouragement. At the same time, he's had ample opportunity for proposing, yet the fact remains he delayed doing so till the vicar was dead and Miss Bellamy-Pryce in the direct line of a fortune. You may recall I mentioned to you a long telephone conversation Miss Bellamy-Pryce heard taking place between her aunt and Argus at a very critical time on Wednesday night. Have you by any chance checked up on the call?"

"Yes," replied the inspector calmly, "but without success. Ordinary calls, as you well know, are not recorded. The night-operator at the Kensington exchange dimly remembers a rather lengthy connection between the two numbers in question, but can't state what evening it was. When I tried to pin him down he grew even more uncertain. I'm afraid nothing more can be done about it."

"Of course," resumed Tommy, arguing it out, "I see strong objections to its having been Argus. It would mean the connivance of Mrs. Bellamy-Pryce in the creation of a suggested alibi for him—and why should she do it? Her brother-in-law's death brings her no benefit. Also it's hardly reasonable to think Argus would commit murder on the bare chance of being accepted by the victim's daughter."

"You're sure it was only a bare chance?" asked Headcorn shrewdly.

"Not a doubt of it," retorted Tommy, flushing slightly. "I'm ready to swear he got no encouragement—though against that is the man's overweening vanity. It's distinctly possible he believed he had only to mention marriage to be snapped up. Here's a worse snag, though. The poisoning. Would he want to murder the girl he hoped to marry?"

"Had you at any time suspected Captain Argus of that particular crime?"

"Frankly, I hadn't. My God, what a muddle!"

Not for the first time did Tommy see this case in terms of his one hideous experience of flying blind in a fog, over the Atlas mountains. The horror of those moments were still with him. Again he saw the wall of grey mist pressing in on every side, heard the hum of engines which must not be stopped, felt the paralysing dread of rocky peaks wrapped in invisibility but near—near! At any moment the crash, the spurt of flame, and the long, twisting descent that would end in charred wreckage of what had once been life. So it was now—no flare to guide pilot or passengers, forced to go on, death hidden—but where?

Inspector Headcorn was speaking.

"I had to consider Argus," he said, "because I foresaw the possibility of the very event you have just described. The previous alarms might have been false ones, contrived to lay a misleading scent—though the poisoning took a serious turn for mere red herring business. Here is what I've learned: He was seen going into his flat at the time you set him down close to the mews-entrance—and he was not seen to come out again, as he would have had to do almost immediately in order to get back to the hotel by, we'll say, eleven-ten at latest. He was certainly at home shortly before midnight. The motor-mechanic who is his next-door neighbour heard him being violently sick."

"Which bears out his own story," muttered Tommy.

"And is not, it would seem, a unique occurrence, though as a general thing it happens in the early morning hours. I took the pains to make other inquiries. Argus gives rather riotous parties at his flat. Sometimes a woman stops on till noon next day. He's in debt to tradespeople, behind with his rent, always with the excuse of delayed remittances; yet on top of this he buys himself a fairly expensive car. Second-hand, to be sure, but practically new, costing—well, I happen to know the exact figure. The mechanic neighbour arranged the sale. The first payment, in cash, was made through him."

"Cash, was it?"

"He has no London banking-account, and the source of his remittances—said to come by registered letter from Australia—I've not gone into. Certain features of the car-purchase slightly intrigued me. The deal had been pending for weeks, and was closed with quite suddenly yesterday morning. All of which may lack relevance."

Totally, Tommy reflected with disappointment. He had just bethought himself of yet another objection to Argus's having a hand in the vicar's death. Single-handed, he could not have encompassed it—that is to say, he wanted Boggie's help over the telephone call which would indicate his presence at his flat during a given period. Was it conceivable a woman herself in love with him would lend him aid to commit a murder, the sole end of which was marriage with her niece? It was as absurd as supposing these two friends guilty of trying to poison the girl on whom all hope of financial gain depended. No, attractive though this new theory had appeared, it crumbled to dust when closely inspected. Argus was, because he must logically be, simply an outsider. The pun, of course, was unintentional.

The Houses of Parliament hove in sight, pearly grey in the late sunshine. When Tommy had driven into the narrow entrance to Scotland Yard, Headcorn, getting out, leant for a moment on the window-sill.

"You appreciate," he said gravely, "just why these next few days are so important? I've spoken of the unique opportunity they provide, but there's a second reason I'd better mention. The old man, Sir Osmund, is actually on the point of death. This time there's no fooling about it."

"Does that circumstance affect the issue?"

"It wouldn't, if one of our persons concerned wasn't champing at the bit to get back to India—only waiting, in fact, to secure all he can lay hands on in the way of money."

"I see. Impatience to return to his digging may make our archaeologist-maniac unduly rash."

"I certainly think it may bring matters to a head. If the father had a stretch of life ahead of him, whatever is meant to happen could be strung out over a wider space of time."

These parting words hammered ominously in Tommy's brain all the way along Whitehall, past the Cenotaph with its heat-fading garlands, and to the very base of the Nelson Column in Trafalgar Square. Something told him that Headcorn was right, and that whatever danger did threaten was close at hand. Not that delay meant the removal of that danger. Far from it; but unless some additional evidence was dug up immediately there was reason to expect speedy action. Every possible channel of information had been exhaustively dredged without result. He did not question the inspector's thoroughness. Was there no possible source that had been overlooked or considered unprofitable?

As he was turning into Pall Mall the inspiration flashed on him. Vera Coldbottom! Drat the girl, why must she keep sliding out of his mind only to pop back at inconvenient moments? He was sure Headcorn had discounted her. It seemed careless on the part of a professional. Never mind, there was still time to hunt her up. He had her new address in his pocket. Circling the monument, he took a course up Charing Cross Road, heading for Epping Forest and the county of Essex. Of a sudden his hopes had soared high. This dismissed servant-girl—she might well have seen something. If he cornered her and got hold of useful information, he would be one up on Scotland Yard. He made a list of the questions he would put to Vera when he had her alone. A good tip might work wonders. . . .

Vera had gone.

Three days ago, he was told—leaving no address. Simply walked out, there being no cinema closer than Loughton—though why these wretched girls ever took country places Heaven alone knew! Yes, she had stopped only till she had got her week's money. She wouldn't dare ask for a reference, that was certain. Her last was nothing to speak of, only one could no longer pick and choose, could one?

It was a cruel blow. Over cold beef and ale in a forest inn, Tommy bitterly told himself he had never properly estimated Vera's importance. She might yet be found, but further search must wait till his return from Sussex. Come to think of it, was this disappearance act significant? It had an ugly look. . . .

"Seen the evening paper, sir?"

Genially the landlord deposited by his plate a copy of *The Star*. Tommy thanked him and glanced down.

"DEATH OF TEA MERCHANT," he read, and below, *"Third of Family Dies at Eighty-six. Sir Osmund Bellamy-Pryce, nominal head of the celebrated tea-importers, passed away this afternoon at . . ."*

So it had happened. And now—?

CHAPTER TWENTY-SIX

"HARK to that ass of a bird!" said Peter Rostetter, feasting his eyes on his own sunny jasmine-trellis. "Jug-jugs all day now. Muriel's mother wants me to write to *The Times* about it. Got some notion I've nothing better to occupy me."

Across the well-laden breakfast table Tommy directed a glance of bleak contempt.

"Fine," he applauded. "I've put in six minutes on a first-class sensation happening, so to speak, on your own doorstep, and all I get is some blither about a nightingale's bad habits." He watched his brother help himself bountifully to bacon and eggs, then continued, "Has anything I've been saying to you got home?"

"I was up till six bringing unwanted twins into the world," returned Peter amicably. "Now I'm damned hungry; and from what I have heard, it's the concentrated essence of tommyrot. Ha, ha! Not too bad, is it? I'll tell you what's wrong with you, old son. It's living amongst excitable Latins." He shoved a copy of *The Times* over the table. "Seen the obituary stuff about Sir Osmund? You may care to glance through it. Yes, I was with him at the last. He never knew about the vicar. Stupid affair, that. Definitely accident, of course." He stifled a yawn. "Try some oi this brawn," he invited. "It's Muriel's own recipe."

Tommy surveyed his brother's scarcely-lined face, resting now on a chin comfortably doubled; the exiguous hair, the serious, kindly, unimaginative eyes behind circular lenses. He might have been looking at a vision of himself ten years hence, supposing he had smothered his adventurous instinct and remained rooted in native soil.

"And if I told you," he said acidly, "that Scotland Yard believes the vicar was murdered?"

Peter suspended the play of knife and fork, stared a little, and took a deep drink of coffee.

"Is this a leg-pull?" he inquired. "Who in his senses would murder Cuthbert Bellamy-Pryce?"

"The person who benefits by his death. If you'd been listening you'd know that this so-called accident represents one successful attempt out of five; that the fourth attempt resulted in death to a disinterested bystander, and that the whole indicates an organised scheme to wipe out all the Bellamy-Pryce survivors save one."

He had at last got Peter's ear, albeit a recalcitrant one. Indeed, as he plunged back into his recital, he was reminded forcibly of the horse which may be conducted to water but not induced to have any. Peter, showing patent resemblances to his equine parallel, was actually in the water now, up to the withers. His ears were almost visibly laid back, his eye anxiously roving, but his teeth remained clamped together with a stubbornness worthy of a better cause. Ultimately he stoked a pipe, laid it down unlighted, and from pure habit muttered that it was all undiluted balderdash. That he was shaken, though, betrayed itself in his first apprehensive question: "See here—you haven't wirelessed any of this to the boy?"

"Rank?" Tommy had virtually forgotten his nephew, still aboard the slow boat to Madeira. "Rosemary wouldn't have him told. Afraid he'd turn round the minute he landed and come back."

"Good girl!" Peter's tension relaxed. "Sensible head she's got on her shoulders. That's the only thing that worries me," he added. "Neither of those two women is an alarmist. No, there's no hysteria there."

"So you do know the aunt, do you?" asked Tommy, with interest.

"Mrs. James? Certainly I know her. Have done for years, off and on. Level-headed, matter-of-fact—plays the smartest bridge-game I've come across, barring a few Indian majors who've put their boys through Sandhurst on their winnings. Yes, we saw quite a bit of Mrs. James when she was down here in March. Bearing up remarkably well, we thought; but I always understood James was none too easy to live with, so perhaps that's why. Took a great interest in the garden. I'd say she's a reed country-woman at heart," Peter declared, as though stating a virtue of the highest order. "Muriel and I are rather hoping now the money's hers she'll settle near us."

"Never mind her. What about Gavin?"

Peter's uneasiness had returned. Very little that could be depended on was known about Gavin. A strange chap, yes—devilish peculiar in his habits, but he was rarely here, and Peter in a medical capacity had never had a chance to study him.

"Loony he may be. I wouldn't swear the contrary; but murdering off an entire family connection for money—! It's too tall an order by half. Particularly Cuthbert, who'd never antagonised him. Wasn't in him to offend any one. Vague, I grant you, but happy as a sandboy with his peace-offerings and his chorals and his belief in every impostor—"

"You've said it." Tommy leant forward. "Don't you see what that trusting spirit could lead to?"

Peter, after a startled glance, vigorously protested. No, no, he for one wouldn't hear of it! The inquest verdict was quite correct. The vicar climbed on a chair to pull down the blind, and suffered a sudden attack of vertigo. Things like that happened every day, so why make a song about this instance?

"Revolver shots," said Tommy softly. "And strychnine. Do they happen every day and in the same group of persons?"

"Pooh; totally unrelated incidents!" Peter crossly flung down his napkin. "Seriously, my boy, Gavin's not the only queer one knocking about. The shots were fired by a stranger labouring under a misapprehension—or a genuine lunatic with a grudge against Mrs. James. Probably the latter, in view of that third attack you spoke of. As for the poisoning, well, there seems to have been plenty of rotten sub-normal chaps in that Countess What's-her-name's outfit. Come to that, what's wrong with plain suicide? Slum-women do kill themselves. One wonders they don't do it oftener—and any one can get hold of poison by pinching a doctor's bag. Why, mine was pinched—"

"When?" fired Tommy.

"Oh, two years back. Nothing came of it. I just mention it to—"

"Gavin," said Tommy dryly, "had owned strychnine. I myself saw the bottle."

"And why not? He'd use it as a tonic out in the wilds. The malaria, now, interests me. Incomprehensible for a man of his education to let it go on when it can easily be cured."

"I was meaning to ask you," said Tommy. "For how long at a time would a malaria attack incapacitate?"

"Depends on the type." Peter on professional ground was rock-firm and showed it. "Which has he got? Or don't you know?"

"A diabolical type while it lasted. I took it for an epileptic fit. Came on like a thunder-clap—teeth rattling, utter exhaustion. . . . He rallied after the quinine, but—"

"Lord," Peter chuckled, "that's only the benign. Looks nasty, but you should see the worse variety. Quinine, eh? I thought so. What he should have is atebrin. German discovery. Knocks the plasmodium clean on the head inside a week."

"Suppose he had attacks four or five days running?"

"Couldn't happen." The doctor spoke dogmatically. "Tell me this: Is it tertian or quartan? Must be one or the other, you know. Tertian means alternate days, quartan—"

"I've been to school, too. Every fourth day."

"Wrong, every third day. You take the count from the first set-off. It's immaterial which. The point is, between bouts he recovers completely. And here's another thing: the attacks will occur at the same time of day—invariably. You can set your clock by 'em. The most usual time is from three to four p.m., and the duration roughly is three to four hours. After rest and sleep, the patient's able to get out, do what he likes."

Gavin's attack had occurred shortly after three o'clock. If this dope was right—and Tommy did not question it—there was no need for the sufferer to have been laid low as late as ten o'clock on any evening. It was true 'flu had been mentioned, but that was doubtless fiction. The Saturday affair, however, had taken place at just the time when, if it was the right day, Gavin would have been shaken to atoms. A little counting, first two day intervals back from Thursday and then three-day ones, brought a reliable conclusion.

"I see what you're figuring," said Peter challengingly. "Does either way give him a clean slate for the Saturday?"

"No. Whether tertian or quartan, it works out the same—a free day."

"Not proof," muttered Peter, adding that Mrs. James could not be wholly satisfied it was her brother-in-law she had seen, or else she would not hang fire over accusing him. His forehead, nevertheless, had broken out in a mild sweat, and his eyes strayed in a manner Tommy was quick to interpret.

"Better not speak of this to Muriel," the younger brother warned. "If I drove down early it was only because I hoped you might have learned something about Gavin up at Black Gables, and after this morning I shall be too occupied to hold any lengthy talks. In half an hour the three of them will be arriving. I'd like you to come with me to meet them, and see if your medical eye can spot any abnormalities in this bird. To my thinking there are more than enough. Now, listen: In the compartment with Mrs. Bellamy-Pryce and Rosemary will be a plain-clothes sergeant. He—"

"A—a what, did you say?"

"You heard me. A detective to watch Gavin. Man, can't you get it into your skull this is a life and death matter?"

Peter Rostetter stumbled from his seat.

"Dashed close in here," he muttered. "Let's go out."

The nightingale ceased jugging while they passed under the starred jasmine. Peter, rubicund but disturbed, scanned the distant rose-garden, satisfied himself that his tweed-skirted wife was on the warpath for green-fly, and voiced the load on his mind. It was, in a word, Rosemary. If she really was in imminent danger—not that he believed it—it was a most appalling state of affairs, involving personal responsibility.

"On the boy's account," he explained. "Oh, I don't say anything's settled! At least, we hope not—though I don't know, all considered, if it mightn't be a good thing if some such dependable girl took him in hand. We thought it a hopeful sign her egging him on to take this job. The sooner he gets on the quicker they can. . . . What's wrong?" he inquired. "Tooth want attention? Oh, I see, a bit of gristle from the brawn. Muriel won't like that. Rosemary'll have money, of course. Not to be despised. What matters, though, is the splendid young woman she's grown into. Her mother's looks and practical sense into the bargain. Toned down a bit since that time she squashed the ripe plum down your back. Ha, ha!" Peter guffawed. "Not forgotten that tragedy, I suppose?"

"My God!" cried Tommy weakly. "That wasn't Rosemary?"

"Was it not?" Peter rumbled. "Little spindly thing, all legs and freckles. I can see her now, hot-footing it over the lawn after messing up your new flannels. You'd dropped off in the old hammock we had slung between those two cedars. Yes, she was wild as a colt in those days. No one to curb her. Not that it's done her any harm. . . ."

So that small demon with the sun-blistered nose was she who at present writing enslaved his every thought and impulse—controlled, in fact, his whole destiny. Tommy eyed the heavy-limbed cedars of Lebanon breaking the placid landscape and saw far more than his brother had seen. He saw a date stamped on himself, plain as the purple marking on one of Muriel Rostetter's breakfast eggs. He and this girl belonged to different generations. While he had been dozing over Proust, smugly content with his first Savile Row suit, she—well, she had been getting Rank down in wrestling-matches and planning deviltry with superannuated plums. The exquisite rapture with which he had been contemplating these coming days of close proximity turned to ashes. The dream he had stupidly drifted into vanished like a soap-bubble. He was awake now, brutally so, and once more realising the improvement manifested in Peter's eldest son—an improvement, no doubt, underestimated by his avuncular eyes . . .

"Charles," pursued the voice at his side, "seems to have been the pick of the bunch. You remember him, of course?"

Charles? Who the hell. . . . Oh, Charles Bellamy-Pryce!

"See here, Peter," barked the younger Rostetter, stung. "What vintage do you think I am?"

"Quite right; Charles was before your time. I remember him, though. Fine, upstanding chap, Oxford Blue. He'd brains, too—and by the same token he was the worst knock-out to old Osmund's pride. They say the old boy kept hoping till the last that Charles would knuckle under. When he'd the cable saying the lad had gone under in some God-forsaken hole overseas, he never spoke for a week. It was the first intimation he'd had that Charles had been bed-ridden nearly a year with a gunshot lodged in his vertebrae. They didn't do much bone-surgery then. The War brought that to the fore."

"He had a wife, hadn't he?" asked Tommy absently.

"Yes, some Colonial girl who died later on, after finding herself another husband. Never came to England. I . . . Oh, blast!"

Peter's face had fallen. Seeking the cause, Tommy perceived, just beyond the privet-hedge bordering the premises, a lean and scraggy female peddling purposefully towards them on—yes, it was no ocular delusion—a tricycle. Beneath a child's straw hat wreathed in black daisies were gimlet eyes close set and false teeth bared in a terrible smile.

"Miss Gosmartin," muttered Peter. "Ever run foul of her? Well, you will now. Be devilish careful what you say."

The spinster on the tricycle minced and bridled over the introduction, but after a few airy remarks on Paris—visited, it seemed, on a Cook's tour in 1912—confined her efforts to the doctor.

"I thought you'd be interested to hear that the funeral is arranged for to-morrow. The first of our funerals, that is," she explained with relish. "Sir Osmund's, I understand, is set for Monday—the Bishop, of course, officiating at both. Poor, poor vicar!" Miss Gosmartin sighed, fixing greedy eyes on Peter's face. "I'm wondering, doctor, if his death—that is to say, the circumstances of it—struck you as at all peculiar?"

Peter made disparaging noises, out of which "vertigo" stood clear. Miss Gosmartin watched him as a hawk watches a chicken, breathing tensely through pinched nostrils.

"I do sincerely trust you're right," she mused insincerely. "The coroner should know, shouldn't he? I was only thinking of the—the opportuneness, if one may so put it. Coming on the very eve of Sir Osmund's death, and so very soon after that of the judge. . . . When did that sad event take place? It can't be more than three months, for it was the first week in

Lent we had Mrs. James in our midst. H'm—yes. A most strange coincidence, wasn't it, for Mr. Gavin to have been on the same boat with them?"

"Was it coincidence?" asked Peter, harried.

"Now, that was my question!" cried Miss Gosmartin cunningly. "I should have been tempted to call it a most odd coincidence indeed, but I may not be competent to judge. Mr. Gavin, I'm told, will be staying at the vicarage—with his sister-in-law and niece. Not often he honours us with his presence. Except for that one glimpse of him in the spring. . . ." She coughed and fixed Peter again. "You've no word from Mrs. James and Miss Rosemary, I suppose? None at all? Well, no news is good news. We may take it, I dare say, that they are both quite well—allowing, of course, for grief and shock."

Here the speaker enlivened her discourse with another repellent smile and remarked that it would be delightful to see Mrs. James again.

"If I do manage to see her," she continued uncertainly. "Mother, you know—how is she? Oh, most cheery. Hardly any sensation in her legs now. I've wheeled her into the little summer-house with her tatting, and now I'm hurrying back to take her my bits of news. Which reminds me: Two of them, wasn't it? What a surprise-packet! I don't think, though"—judicially—"that Mr. Entwhistle should say quite so loudly that misfortunes never come singly. Not in the High Street. I fancied a few of the passers-by took his remark to mean something quite different from twins. The two deaths, you know; but I see you're watching the time. It's the good train they're coming by, isn't it?"

"It's due now," mumbled Peter desperately. "Tom, we must dash!"

"Oh, doctor!" Miss Gosmartin made a determined clutch. "I was rather wanting to ask how Nurse Claiborne was taking it?"

"Taking Sir Osmund's death? Why, how should a sensible woman take a fully-expected event of that kind?"

"Oh—ah. That's not quite what I meant, but never mind, let it go. Give Mrs. James my warmest sympathy—and the little daughter-in-law to be. Aha, you mustn't mind my teasing! Say I stopped by to leave notes of condolence and just a few of my best irises, but that owing to mother's condition I may not be able . . ."

In the road Tommy muttered between his teeth, "That ghoul of a woman knows something."

"She knows a deal too much, always." Peter, hot and bothered, dusted his windscreen. "Got her knife into Gavin, that's certain, though why this interest in Nurse Claiborne. . . . See here, am I to take Gavin back in my car and leave the women to you?"

"That's it. Step on it, we're late."

In what way, reflected Tommy, on the two-mile rush to the station, could this Gosmartin creature have got wind of what was happening in London? There had been a leakage, which it was his job to look into; but how did it connect up with a village pest when the vicar himself had divulged neither its source nor content? He thought of Gavin's evil suggestion. It had not been required to point out the likelihood of the vicar's having been lured to London for a definite purpose, but it was in keeping with Gavin's malicious audacity to impute to another person an action presumably his own. Yes, it must have been Gavin who found means of drawing his victim's attention to the London trouble—and somehow Miss Gosmartin had managed to tap the message. How, though, to prove it?

When the two brothers reached the platform the ticket-collector and solitary porter were just abandoning their game of draughts to range themselves in readiness for the line of dingy carriages at that moment drawing alongside. Boggie alighted, sober and dependable, with Rosemary behind, steady-eyed, but fine-drawn in her black spring coat. Neither glanced at the very average man in plus fours who transferred his suitcase and golf clubs to the lone Daimler outside, and the latter did not flicker an eyelash at the wizened, caped form emerging from another third-class compartment. Tommy, however, was keenly alive to Gavin's well-posed approach. He missed nothing of the greeting, on one side awkward, as Peter stepped forward and relieved the archaeologist of his dilapidated Gladstone bag, and a second later, his notice falling on the two station functionaries, he observed an arresting phenomenon.

Forgetful of duty, this pair had drawn together and were staring fascinatedly at Gavin. Both heads gave a slight nod. Said the porter, *sotto voce*:

"Aye, he's come, right enough."

"I said it," returned the ticket-collector, barely audible, "so you can blinking well hand over that bob."

CHAPTER TWENTY-SEVEN

THAT this demonstration was no isolated affair was proved by the knots of tradespeople all along the High Street, posed to stare silently and ominously at the caped figure in the doctor's Austin, and by Sarah Pennylove, whose lugubrious welcome held a distinct tinge of fear. As the arrivals entered the vicarage—Elizabethan, small-windowed, with a superadded Victorian ell—the housekeeper backed nervously against the wall, avoiding Gavin as though he were a plague-victim, and babbling agitatedly that she had given the two ladies their usual rooms on the main landing, while the gentlemen she was putting farther along.

"Farther along" meant through a baize door on the upper floor in the Victorian addition, where the male guests found themselves ushered into two small, stuffy bedrooms and precipitately deserted. Tommy opened his casement window, partly dislodging a swallow's nest clinging to the eaves, and looked down on the churchyard. Directly opposite rose the squat stone-and-flint Norman tower, from whose dog-toothed arch a decrepit verger peered forth like a turtle from its shell. All around were graves, some sunken, some covered with modern stones and railed in. In corners the grass grew long, and ten yards distant a hole with a mound of freshly-turned earth marked the spot where the vicar was to lie. The body was due to arrive that afternoon and rest in the chancel. It was a saddening thought. Tommy withdrew his gaze and, quitting the room, paused beside the open door alongside.

Gavin was unpacking his disreputable bag—containing, apparently, little but manuscript. Turning, he locked some unseen object in a drawer, pocketed the key, and only then—though he must have been well aware he was being watched—looked round with his slow, sardonic smile. It was singularly difficult, confronted by those omniscient eyes, to frame any remark. As on a former occasion, it was Tommy who suffered from discomposure.

"Feeling better?" he asked lamely.

"Thank you, quite as usual." The archaeologist inclined his head and added blandly, "Your brother has very kindly offered to procure a remedy for my complaint. Something new and highly efficacious."

So that is what Peter had done!

"I know, he mentioned it to me. He says you'll be cured in a week."

"That would be of inestimable benefit."

The simple rejoinder gave the effect of peculiar irony. With the unaccountable feeling of being bested, Tommy walked on, and as the baize door swung to behind him, muttered to himself, "Pazuzu—King of Air-Devils . . ."

On Peter, just departing, he vented his wrath.

"You're a prize chump!" he exploded through the car-window. "Who the hell wants that scoundrel cured?"

"He's a case," retorted Peter, perfectly restored in aplomb. "And see here, my boy, you're backing the wrong horse."

"Is that so? And what horse," demanded the younger Rostetter scathingly, "are you prepared to back?"

"Not Gavin, anyhow," declared the doctor stoutly. "Hang it all, it's impossible. He's a scholar and a gentleman."

Tommy turned away. What difference did it make if Peter reverted to the comfortable view? After all, he had expected it. Gavin, when he chose to exert it, had charm, and from the outside viewpoint all these close-knit facts might be disjointed and neatly demolished. The village, though, had its own opinion, however obtained. It was as though every man, woman and child in Broughton-Elmtrees had its eye on Gavin, and was watching with bated breath for the final act of tragedy to unfold. Headcorn was probably right. Here, where the vicar had lived, might lie the key which would unlock the mystery and perform the reverse operation on a prison-cell. Could he lay hands on it? That was the question. It must not only be done, but done soon.

In the house again, he entered the oddly-shaped little drawing-room, filled with faded chintz, family portraits, and Victorian ornaments—nothing changed, he imagined, since Rosemary's mother died. Boggie was there, reading a note written in a prim backhand on mauve paper. She glanced up with a deprecatory smile.

"Gosmartin!" she mused. "What a ridiculous name! Who she is, I've no idea, but evidently some well-meaning creature I met in the spring. Very good of her to leave flowers for us," she added, touching the handsome purple irises on the mantelshelf. "Though one can only hope to be spared visitations. I see she's written Ro, too. I must take it up to her. Are you all right?" she asked meaningly, and then in a lower tone: "What does your brother say about Him?"

Tommy told her that the doctor declined to connect Gavin with the various sensations, and held to the accident theory where the vicar was concerned. Mrs. Bellamy-Pryce looked gravely at the dim-figured carpet, nodded as though unsurprised, and gave a stoical shrug.

"And he may be right. Who can say?" she murmured, as she left the room.

Tommy would have liked to have a closer view of the notes left by Miss Gosmartin. She had taken both with her, however, and though he made a movement as if to call her back, he thought better of it.

A moment later Rosemary joined him, her eyes fixed and far-seeing. She looked unutterably tired, but rigid, some interior purpose holding her taut.

"Tommy," she said, closing the door and coming close to him, "I've been talking with Ted Sprocklehurst—daddy's curate, you know. He doesn't know either how daddy came to hear about our disturbances, but I'm sure of this, that whatever it was happened just after the evening service last Sunday. You see, he was all right before, but when he went to take off his cassock Ted found him in the vestry in a sort of daze. When he woke up he simply said he had decided to go to town next morning. After a moment he explained he had better see the organ people in person. One of the foot-notes kept sticking, and the choir-boys would giggle. He didn't want Ted to know, of course, his real reason for going."

She finished with her last remnant of breath and a strained look in her eyes. Tommy made her sit down.

"It couldn't have been Uncle Gavin," she continued. "At least not directly. Daddy wouldn't have wanted to consult Uncle Gavin if . . . oh, if only I'd kept daddy's letter. Still, I'm sure of what he said." She sank her bright head on her knees. "Tommy! Who told him?"

"Tell me," he said, slipping his arm round her, "about this woman called Gosmartin. I met her this morning at Peter's, and she seemed bursting with information."

"Aggie Gosmartin?" Rosemary glanced up incredulously. "How could she have anything to do with it? She never goes to London. She wrote to Boggie, but Boggie can't even remember her. There's one of her sort in every village. Daddy dodged her whenever he could. See, here's her note to me. Just smarmy sympathy, nothing to suggest . . ."

Tommy read the unrevealing lines and tucked the mauve sheet into his pocket. The girl at his side, forgetting Miss Gosmartin, had begun to tremble.

"Every one here believes Uncle Gavin murdered my father," she whispered. "I saw it coming along. So did Boggie. What makes them think it wasn't accident? For they do, a fool could see it."

The luncheon gong sounded a subdued roll.

"It's all part of what we must find out," he said quietly. "See here, need you come to the table? You don't have to, you know."

Already, however, she was smoothing her hair.

"Oh, I must! It's not decent to Boggie to leave her to cope with him alone. Come along, let's get it over."

Gavin and his sister-in-law were standing stiffly by the dining table, not looking at each other. The four sat down, and made what pretence they could of eating the overdone cutlets set before them.

Never out of a long experience could Tommy recall a more ghastly meal. It seemed to him that Rosemary, already at breaking-point, must crack under the strain of it; but he had not reckoned on the massed force of British conventionality. Boggie brought all her training to the fore, and whether from superb tact or sheer imperviousness—did it matter which?—showed herself mistress of the situation. As she sat there, solid and four-square in her black tailored clothing, alone able to command a flow of impersonal remarks, Tommy paid willing tribute to all she stood for in a rocking world. For the time being he lost sight of the exasperation she had caused him and remembered only her sterling qualities.

Suddenly a nasty incident shattered every one's false composure. Pennylove, bringing the coffee, stumbled on Boggie's bag, and burst into dithering apologies. Good-humouredly Boggie said: "Not at all, Pennylove. See, we'll put it here," and rescuing her property—heavily charged, as all could see—plunked it down on the table with a sinister, metallic clang. The housekeeper turned pale, and spilling the coffee, bolted to the kitchen. Rosemary looked sick. Tommy glanced at the fourth of the party. He was gazing with narrowed eyes at the bulging bag, while over his yellow-parchment features a twisted smile played. A moment later he declined the cup of coffee passed to him, excused himself, and quietly withdrew. In the passage he could be heard fumbling with the sticks in the hat-stand. Presently the front door closed quietly, and Boggie, along whose neck a little brickish-tint had spread, heaved a sigh.

"Thank God!" she exploded.

She made no reference to the revolver in the bag by her plate, merely lit a cigarette with a contented expression, as though she had accidentally come off best in an encounter. Rosemary said nothing, but rose and moved towards the door, and Tommy, believing she wanted to resume their talk, followed her into the drawing-room.

She was standing by the front window, which commanded a view of the road winding southward towards the green slope of downs. Some distance along this her uncle was trudging in a crab-like fashion against a breeze which sent his voluminous cape flapping like the wings of a bat. In the foreground, from nowhere, a second figure had bobbed up. It was the man in plus fours, innocently exploring the countryside, but taking the same course as the less congruous pedestrian ahead.

"Going to the Black Gables, I suppose," murmured the girl tonelessly, and then, with a spasm of unhappiness crossing her face: "Will he guess he's being followed, I wonder?"

All at once her finger closed convulsively on the window-frame.

"Why, oh, why," she whispered miserably, "must she make things worse by bringing that revolver to the table?" Instantly she had said it, she looked covered with shame. "I . . . I'm not myself," she apologised. "I suppose all this is getting me down."

Tommy, as it happened, was thinking of a different matter.

"Two-twenty," he murmured, glancing at his watch. "So there'll be no attack to-day."

Her pupils dilated in panic.

"You weren't expecting one to-day?" she whispered.

"Good God, not that sort of attack!" Tommy hastened to assure her. "It's your uncle's malaria. I've something to tell you about it."

It would, he was reflecting, cause a slight distraction. She took his hand.

"Let's slip into the church," she said quickly. "We'll be quiet there."

It was her first admission that she preferred excluding her aunt from their conferences. He understood her feeling about it. Boggie, whatever her avowed belief, was a hopelessly prejudiced person. This constant carrying of a weapon proved it beyond a shadow of doubt. He wished from his heart that for the niece's sake things had been otherwise. Civil warfare was always the most horrible sort.

In the gloom of the little church nave, pungent with mouldy cushions and ageing prayer books, Rosemary reproached herself again.

"If it is my uncle, it's better he should know we suspect him. After all, the inspector wouldn't go to these lengths without good reason. This malaria—what about it? Can it give him an alibi?"

Tommy explained what he had learned from Peter. She listened despondently, but on hearing that Dr. Rostetter was undertaking to treat her uncle for the recurrent malady showed a slight relief. "He'll stay here for a bit, and we can get off. Boggie will want to stop on for my grandfather's funeral. She has very conventional ideas about these things; but after that . . ." She broke off nervously, turning in alarm towards the vestry door. "S-sh! Did you hear a noise in there?"

Tommy also looked in the direction of the slight sound. The heavy worm-eaten door was cautiously opening, and round its edge peered the face of Mr. Sprocklehurst, the curate. It was a rather beautiful if empty face, doe-eyed, and furnished with a milk-and-roseleaf complexion many a woman would have envied. That complexion now was curiously curdled, while the soft brown eyes betrayed a glint of fear.

"Ted!" whispered Rosemary sternly. *"What's wrong with you?"*

The curate converted a gasp into a cough and creaked diffidently towards them. In his trembling hand was a slip of paper.

"In the pocket of your father's old cassock," he stammered. "Yes, on the whole I think you should see it. I . . ."

"Give it here!"

It proved to be the long-detached fly-leaf of a hymnal. On it in block capitals was printed:

> *"The writer feels you should know that two attempts have been made by shooting to end the lives of your daughter and sister-in-law. They do not want to frighten you, but there is reason to think they are in serious danger. Say nothing about this, and destroy the message without delay."*

CHAPTER TWENTY-EIGHT

THE vicar, of course, had forgotten to destroy the note. For once his absent-mindedness might bear useful fruit.

"But who brought this to him?" demanded Rosemary, suddenly more haggard than at any time since her father's death. "Ted, can't you tell us?"

Mr. Sprocklehurst could only shake a troubled head. He had absolutely no idea on the subject. There were the usual handful of people at the three Sunday services, no strangers among them. One knew their faces so well. . . .

"And yet I think I know when and where he found this paper," he faltered eagerly. "Yes, I could almost swear it was between the pages of the lectern Bible, at vespers, and that that is why your father made the sudden pause during his reading of the second lesson. I had put the markers in for him after the morning service, and there was nothing there then; but it certainly happened that just as he turned over a page—it was in the third chapter of the Gospel of St. John—he came to quite a noticeable halt. I looked to see if his glasses had broken again. They were rather insecurely mended with a bit of wire; but it wasn't that. He seemed to be staring hard at something, and though he went on again his attention throughout the service very definitely strayed. More than was usual, that is to say."

"You say only the habitual congregation was present," said Tommy, pinning him down. "Out of them were there any who were in the church before the service began?"

Mr. Sprocklehurst on this one occasion could not say. There were a number of devout ladies who made a practice of coming early, mainly those who undertook the renewal of flowers for the altar-vases, but he had been late Sunday evening, and had barely time to get into his vestments before the processional started. Asked to name the prowlers and potterers, he gave a hesitant list which included Miss Gosmartin.

"But one can hardly suspect any of them of a thing of this sort, can one? So underhand, so . . . Oh, no! Really, it's an impossible thought!"

Rosemary stood with her eyes glued to the crumpled flyleaf. She had assumed her father had received a verbal intimation, though now she thought it over he had not definitely stated it. There was something very ugly about this block-printed message—of all anonymous communications, as she well knew, the most difficult to trace. Beyond question, the writer wanted to keep his identity secret. All he was after—why did she use the masculine pronoun?—was to induce her father to go to London. Well, he had succeeded.

"The flowers," Tommy was saying. "Were there any fresh ones for the evening service?"

"N-no," wavered the curate, glancing at the brass vases heading the dim chancel. "They were renewed in the morning. And yet"—he puckered his smooth brow—"let me think . . . Dear me!" He struck the arm of a pew a feather-light blow. "The purple irises!" he exclaimed, "quite fresh that evening. I distinctly recall noticing how they repeated the colour in the one bit of old glass Cromwell left us. Especially fine ones, from Miss Gosmartin's garden. But surely you can't suppose—?"

"I'm supposing nothing," replied Tommy, wooden-faced. "The great point is, can any one get into the church on Sunday between services?"

"Oh, yes, any one!" The vicar had held strong views on the locking of churches, even after the third rifling of the poor-box; and as the verger was often absent for long stretches of time, a person entering could do what he chose without being seen. Still, in a small community like this a strange face was usually noted at once. If an unknown visitant had been in the village, it would soon be mentioned.

"And I have not heard of it." Mr. Sprocklehurst, looking younger than ever in his embarrassed bewilderment, swayed from one long leg to the other, and goggled the question he dared not utter. Finally, unencouraged, he murmured, "I am greatly distressed to be of so little assistance,"—and with another deprecatory cough faded back into the vestry.

"No," said Tommy slowly. "Miss Gosmartin's part in this is easily accounted for. Poking her nose into the Bible—God knows why—she came on this note. She couldn't say she had found it, for that would be giving away her unholy inquisitiveness; but she did drop a few mysterious hints, just as she's doing now, and it's those hints that have given rise to the general suspicion present in the village. I rather expect for some time past there's been a feeling against your uncle, though I may not find it has a better basis than your grandfather's feud with him. As for the person actually responsible for this vile message—"

"Well?" she prompted with dry lips, letting him take the paper.

"Well," he repeated grimly, "I don't imagine Headcorn will discover any significant fingerprints on it; but one point we can settle. Can you dig up an A.B.C.?"

They crossed the long grass and entered the vicarage by way of the side door. Boggie, Pennylove informed them, had gone to her room for a short rest, and there was no one to interrupt their study of the battered timetable found under a butterfly-net in the hat-stand. It told Tommy what he wanted to know—that a traveller from London could have got here on Sunday at three-twenty by the branch line most people used for Broughton-Elmtrees, or, if he wished to avoid recognition, he could have come by the main line to Tipchester, arriving at three-fifty, and returning the distance of seven miles across the downs.

"If it was Uncle Gavin," Rosemary objected, "it's hard to think some one didn't notice him. Maybe he could manage it; but wait! Was Sunday a clear day for him?"

"It was. I worked that out while the curate was talking. It must be the three-day type of malaria, and that leaves Sunday free. As for his being seen, well, he may have been. I rather suspect that fact's contributed to the attitude towards him. When I've posted this note to the inspector, I'm going to have a chat with the landlord of the pub at the corner. He's the fount-head of local information, and from the look in his eye as we came along he knows something worth telling. I'll keep watch on both roads, and if I see your uncle coming I'll be here before him. Meanwhile, hadn't you better follow your aunt's example and rest for a bit?"

She was standing motionless as he had so often seen her do lately, her arms at her sides, her eyes staring straight into vacancy. When she spoke her voice lacked expression and seemed to come from afar off.

"Yes," she said evenly, "I'd like to be alone—to think."

She turned and walked up the stairs. Tommy followed her with troubled eyes, and when her door had closed went to his own room to prepare a rapid precis for the inspector's benefit. In it he enclosed not only the fly-leaf but Miss Gosmartin's note to Rosemary. Between the block-printing on the one and the back-hand writing of the other he could detect not the faintest resemblance.

In his opinion, as he had said, there was little use searching for any; but Headcorn must have all the cards at his disposal. He directed his letter without official prefix, and addressed it to the inspector's home in Balham, lest P. Ashdown, grocer, or the young woman who presided at the pigeon-hole post office in the shop, draw unnecessary conclusions. Then, having posted it, he repaired to the side yard of the Sheep For Shearing, where, as he had hoped, he found the gargantuan landlord stretching his colossal legs in the shade of his crimson Maytree. He was greeted as an old friend, and found it easy, by a few deft inquiries about trade, to open conversation.

Beer, he was told, was not what it had been—nor, worse luck, were thirsts. The missus was saying only this noon as how she'd little thought they'd see the day when they'd be thankful for a chance week-ender, down for a blow, like; but there it was, taxes had done it, and there was no good grousing. The new chap seemed a decent, chatty sort, no side about him, and quite pleased to hear about the vicar, Sir Osmund, and that. Off for a stroll, now, and not put out by there being no golf-course handy, for all he'd fetched along his sticks.

"I see you're up there with the family. Friend of the widow's, I take it?"

Stomaching the guileless affront, Tommy assented. Mr. Budge, achieving archness, declared that Mrs. James was a fine one, no nonsense about her, and well deserved the bit of money she was coming to. No doubt she'd earned it—though it was not for him to be passing such remarks. Like as not Mr. James had been a better husband than he was publicly accredited.

"All I mind is the nasty way I heard him telling her off one morning—two years back it must have been—right out here in the High Street. I says to my missus at the time, 'There's one woman that's got a deal to put up with; and just look at her,' I says, 'turning it off with a jolly laugh!' Some I could mention would have rounded on him like a snapping-turtle—naming no names, you understand."

Digging a large thumb into his visitor's waistcoat, the landlord indulged in asthmatic chuckles, then sobering he jerked the same thumb towards the red Tudor chimneys of the vicarage and edged closer to ask:

"And this here rum one? The brother. Going to put him in the loony-bin, are you?"

Tommy knocked his cigarette-ash against the rain-barrel beside the officially closed bar.

"Think that's where he belongs?" he parried encouragingly.

There was a prolonged stare and a volcanic shrug. Looking cautiously round, Mr. Budge swelled for a confidence.

"That or another place," he began cagily. "Maybe you can tell me: Is it or is it not a fact that this party we're speaking of has set out to wipe off the family? Because that's the idea hereabouts, and right or wrong, there looks a deal to support it."

"What, for instance?" inquired Tommy, with tact.

"Oh, one thing and another." Mr. Budge cast a second wary glance towards the High Street, and sank his voice to a lower rumble. "What about him scaring the judge to death aboard that there steamer, and coming straight here to try the same dodge on the old man? Next, there's the vicar. You may guess what stories have got going over that, verdict or no verdict; and then other things—shots fired at these two ladies, up in London. I don't mind telling you, soon as we heard you was putting up at the vicarage I says to my missus, 'Mr. Rostetter's here for a purpose—and a rare comfort he'll be o' nights to them two marked down victims.'"

It was more than optimism could have expected. In fact, information had come in such a bombardment of missiles that it was hard to know which item to deal with first. Keeping a composed face, Tommy asked how it was Mr. Budge had learned of the shootings.

"Now, let me think." The landlord scratched an immense, cropped head. "First I heard was on the Monday evening, in this here bar. Chap I was serving with a double bitter says to me, 'So vicar's gone to London?' 'Yes,' I says, 'by the nine-seven.' 'Ah!' he says, 'and for why?' 'To make a row about the organ,' I says. 'Organ!' he says, 'no bloody fear. It's to give an eye to his girl,' he says; 'find out who's bin firing guns at her.' 'How'd you get that?' I asks. 'Never you mind,' says he, 'but I got it straight, so don't you go swallowing any stuff about organs, bad as ours is.'"

Tommy offered his packet of Players, and inquired who the landlord's informant had been. Mr. Budge accepted a cigarette, pinched it doubtfully, and pursed his lips.

"I dare say there's no harm putting a name to him," he conceded, "seeing as how a dozen more heard him same as myself. 'Twas Alf Swain—him as works for Barker's, down your brother's way. Missus says he got it from the young woman he walks out with—her as does for them two Gosmartins, old and young. Not so young, neither, if you've had a good squint at her," Budge rumbled again.

"Miss Gosmartin, I suppose, gets hold of a good deal."

"She does that—and the old lady being stone-deaf, the girl hears her telling about it. How she gets hold of it's more than the Almighty Himself could say. I know for a fact she ordered in five London papers, but that was after; and there was nothing in 'em about shootings, for I saw 'em before she did, only stuff about the inquest."

Thus far it merely strengthened Tommy's own theory; but the tale about the judge? This proved a matter on which the landlord was rather hazy. It might in the first instance have emanated from Black Gables, in which case it was understandable the vicar's not knowing of it. Depend upon it, the vicar had not known, else he'd have thought twice about asking his brother Gavin down for that week-end six or seven weeks ago. This was the time the vicar had got ill of gastric 'flu—if it was that. There had been some discussion about it. Anyhow, the housekeeper had been in a rare state. It was she who, against the vicar's wishes, had called in the doctor.

As Mr. Budge was evidently waiting on tiptoe for a leading question, Tommy willingly obliged him. Why was it believed that Sir Osmund also had been singled out for a scare calculated to put an end to him?

"Now, sir, that I can answer." Triumphant, as one about to cite chapter and verse, the landlord hoisted his vast bulk still nearer and hoarsely proceeded. "This same week-end I'm speaking of—a Sunday afternoon it was—the young person what acts as parlour-maid up at Black Gables was cutting across the spinney joining on to the west paddock, making for the Tipchester 'bus, it being her time off. Well, then, out of sight of the house, in amongst the trees, she comes bang on a small, dark man in an old cape and a hat nearly like the vicar's. He's got such a crazy look she don't like to pass him, so she draws back to see what's he's up to with the thing he's got in his hand.

"All of a sudden, *Crack!* goes a shot, plunking straight into a tree-trunk. She's afeerd to stir, and there she stands while four more bullets is fired, two hitting near the same mark. Then the chap squats down, as she thinks to reload—but instead he begins laughing. Yes, sir, laughing—or so she believes. No noise, but shaking like a jelly. It seems that put the wind up her worse than the shots, particularly when she sees his eyes gone glassy and foam coming out of his mouth."

"Foam!"

"Yes, sir, it's some kind of a fit. He's a dangerous lunatic, and her all alone with him. More than that, he's spied her. He's grinning, teeth rattling like hailstones—and then what do you think he says, very polite, all in the midst of his shaking and frothing? Now, sir, this will clinch it," declared Budge portentously. "He says, 'It's all right. My watch stopped. I'd mistaken the time.' There! Those was his words, just as the poor girl repeated 'em when she come tumbling in at our door, turned the colour of that there wall over your head. The missus give her a drop of brandy to quieten her down, and we got the whole story. Oh, she'd no notion who he was, and even we wasn't sure; but next morning she knew, only she never said nothing except to the missus and me, on account of maybe losing her berth."

"Why next morning?"

"Because she opened the door to him. Bold as brass, and quite the gentleman, for all he'd gloves on you and me'd have chucked in the dustbin. She's half minded to bang the door on him, but the Big Pot—pardon, that's our private word for the nurse—comes along, sees who it is, and makes short work of him. Tells him straight out Sir Osmund's not fit to see visitors, same as she's done with all the family, except now and then the vicar. This time we'll say she was within her rights, having got Dolly's tale about the revolver. Oh, he never got past her! There's not many that have done. Faults she may have, but—well, talk of the devil!" Mr. Budge suddenly sat up in his Windsor chair and motioned towards a dark Rolls coupe gliding smoothly past the yard opening. "There *is* the Big Pot now—still lording it, I see. It'll be a fine come-down for her, we're thinking, with no more staff at her beck and call. Just a plain wage-earner she'll be, same as she was when she first come here."

Sure enough, through the Rolls window, showed the commanding profile—chin up, above restrained but handsome mourning attire. Tommy, however, was no longer interested in this woman, except for an idle speculation as to how far she had fostered her patient's animosity towards his kin. All his thoughts centred on the revolver story. One thing it proved—there had been a revolver in Gavin's possession some six weeks ago. Of what make? All at once he recalled the quiet locking of the drawer on something concealed from him. That drawer must be examined without delay. If it contained a Smith and Wesson revolver, what a stroke of unbelievable luck! Gavin could be arrested, and danger was over. He had decided long ago that the failure to find such a weapon in the Lambs' Conduit Street room meant less than nothing. It was ridiculous to imagine it would be left for any one to find. Of course, he carried it with him. Easy enough, under that flapping coat . . .

Mr. Budge was quite positive Gavin had never shown his face in the village since the famous week-end.

"Not he! Why, I'd have known it within the hour. No, what we say is he decided the old man could be left to die natural; but these survivors is another pair of shoes." The landlord spat on the rose-red carpet of fallen May-petals, and cast a gloomy eye on the vicarage. "The vicar never owned a revolver," he said weightily.

"If so be it you doubt my word, ask the old girl up there. She'll tell you. That means it's his—same one he's tried to shoot his womenfolk with. And he'll try again, if he can get hold of a way to cover up the traces. Fire would do it, with a bit of luck. Them old timbers would go up like matchwood. If you'll be warned by me, sir, you'll look careful to your petrol."

Back at the house, Tommy quietly collected all the keys the ell could muster, and tried them one after the other on the absentee's locked drawer. The eighth fitted. With smothering excitement he pulled on the knob—and saw with infinite disgust that he had been sold a pup.

The sole object he stared down at was the black japanned medicine-box. It also was securely fastened.

CHAPTER TWENTY-NINE

WHAT galled him almost as much as the disappointment was the feeling of having been deliberately hoaxed—yes, played upon, by the same Satanic humour which, even in the throes of an ague-attack come on in the open, had found vent at a terrified parlour-maid's expense. Locking this drawer when he knew he was being spied on was of one piece with those mad-sounding words, *"My watch stopped. I'd mistaken the time."*

"I suppose it's damned funny."

For once, however, he could not laugh. He was too obsessed by the rage the honest poker-player feels when his money crosses the board to the sharper he cannot foil. Instinct urged him to seize this joker by the neck and throttle him out of his self-satisfied security; but what would come of third-degree methods? Gavin, fully justified, would lodge a complaint, and it would be the hot-headed journalist who found himself behind bars.

No, this room contained nothing in the way of a weapon. He had made certain of that. It must therefore be in its owner's pocket. To-day—but what about this time to-morrow? The course then was obvious. He would get Peter to support him, and while the sufferer dozed the sleep of exhaustion he would comb those execrable garments, turn them inside out—having previously, of course, assured himself that Gavin was given no chance to park his revolver elsewhere. Unless the thing was found, lie would say nothing to Rosemary. To do so would only add to a torment already insupportable. For the moment let her go on thinking her uncle could not, as Budge had said, penetrate the village of his birth without being observed. That was nonsense, naturally. Not for nothing had Pazuzu a serpent's head as well as a wolf's. When it came to cases, Gavin might have been noticed at Waterloo, or else at Tipchester. Headcorn would institute proper inquiries. The whole foot-journey could have been managed over open country, while the actual time spent in the church need have been only a few minutes.

For the rest, what chiefly impressed him was that the landlord—in other words, the village—knew nothing of the Saturday episode. It argued that no regular channel of information existed, and that suspicion here rested on two rumours—one spread by Miss Gosmartin after finding the note left in the Bible, the other traceable to the maid from Black Gables. However, it might well be that Boggie herself had unintentionally prepared the ground during her week at the vicarage in March. Was it not likely she had dropped some remark about the incidents aboard-ship—rather more than she had done to her niece, who, he remembered, had cut short the confidences? For a second, it occurred to him to sound her on the subject, but straightway he decided against it. In view of her other suppressions, Mrs. Bellamy-Pryce would hardly, at this late date, admit that sort of imprudence—if imprudence it was—and the matter was not of vital importance.

Hearing no movement from Rosemary's room on the main landing, he went down again and out into the old-fashioned garden. As he prowled between the rows of wallflowers and sweet-william just coming into bloom, another thought struck him. All he had heard at The Sheep for Shearing would seem to have travelled, as it were, underground—the gossip of working people. Peter evidently had learned none of it; but Peter, he imagined, did not often frequent bars, or if he did would not be regaled with this type of story.

He came on Boggie, under a ragged rose-arbour, enjoying a solitary tea. She had not seen him yet, and for a moment he stood thoughtfully regarding her strong, matter-of-fact profile. Some of his old irritation returned. How infinitely simple it might be if only he could get from this woman a few straightforward answers! Was it really the case that she knew no more than she had said, or was she still, from motives concealed, keeping back some essential? He could not for the life of him decide. She gave him at all times the impression of temporising, banking on the fortuitous solution. It might be she was protecting her dead husband's honour. He could not think it was her own she was jealously guarding, for that seemed an absurdity. Whatever the facts, the result was a deadlock which now as before prevented him making her party to his conjectures.

With the air of repose and well-being seldom absent from her manner, she lit the inevitable cigarette. As she turned her head to shield the match-flame from the breeze she saw him and smiled cheerily.

"The tea's still hot," she said. "May I pour you some?"

While he drank a cup standing, she explained that she had sent Rosemary's up to her.

"I've had visitors," she continued, with a rueful grimace. "Four of poor Cuthbert's parish ladies, and I shouldn't wonder if more came along. I can't have the child bothered with them. I thought it better for her to keep out of the way and let me deal with them. I only wish she didn't feel obliged to attend the funeral tomorrow, but I suppose one can't spare her that."

She was genuinely kind, Tommy reflected, ashamed of his recent annoyance. One could rest on her as on a thick cushion—just what the nerve-racked girl needed now.

"Thank goodness this won't last long," she remarked, tucking in a stray end of gauze from her bandage, which, he noticed, showed a slight bloodstain. "I'll get her away the first moment she'll consent to go. I've been wondering—though you may think me silly. You don't think he has any weird Eastern drugs that could be sneaked into our food?"

"If he has," said Tommy shortly, though it was hard to say why the suggestion brought back his exasperation, "I'll know to-morrow when I give him his quinine. I'm going to get my brother to overhaul the medicine-box he's got with him."

"To-morrow?" She looked shrewdly at him. "So he has an attack then, has he? I didn't know. And his medicine kit's locked, I suppose." It was not quite a question. "I'm glad Dr. Rostetter will be here. I've not lived in India for nothing, you know. They've vegetable stuffs out there we know nothing about—and one's told they can't be traced."

Her eyes strayed towards the kitchen premises, and she said no more. Tommy moved away, thinking he would go along to the grocer's and telephone Peter to warn him he would be wanted the next afternoon; but as he reached the gate Peter himself came chugging along in his Austin.

"I've just passed your suspicious character," he said as he stopped. "He wouldn't let me give him a lift. Pity that atebrin had to be ordered from London. It won't be here before Tuesday, which means another attack."

"Save your sympathy," advised Tommy, "till you hear what Budge has been telling me about him."

The doctor seemed highly diverted. Target-shooting, eh? Good Lord, couldn't a man take pot-shots at a tree without branding himself as a potential murderer? And if Gavin, spending half his life in unbridled regions, wasn't entitled to a revolver, who was?

"Servants' tittle-tattle—bah! He's an eccentric and a *poseur*; but so was Disraeli, in a more cleanly way. And what's this nonsense about the vicar's crocking up while he was here? Chill on the liver. I attended him. Watch stopped! Very natural, though it makes me laugh to hear you tell it. Chancey business, all the same, getting caught out in a howling spring gale. I wonder he kept so quiet about it. Seems to be his method."

"Method!" repeated Tommy dangerously. "Doesn't it occur to you Gavin's known all along about this German medicine, and that he may not be keen on getting cured? No, I mean just that. He may consider it damned useful to hang on to his malaria. It keeps him so puny it's not easy to connect him with crime—and it might even serve as an alibi. Think it over—and be on hand to-morrow, at three."

Peter drove on with a snort, and almost directly the returned wanderer hove in sight, edged past Tommy with a quiet smile, and entered the house. About to turn after him, Tommy descried Mr. Budge's guest sauntering aimlessly towards him across the lush meadow opposite.

"Beg pardon," called the latter politely. "But have you a match on you?"

Tommy obliged him, and as the tweed-clad stroller moved on let his palm close on the scrap of paper neatly transferred to it.

In his own room he examined his communication. It read:

> *"Wireless message from boat definitely states that steerage-steward saw Smith and Wesson '45 in passenger's possession during malaria-attack. If possible, make thorough canvass and report at once to inn."*

CHAPTER THIRTY

DURING the funeral service just concluded, two distinct schools of thought had been noticeable. One, embracing the rank and file, manifested itself in a gruesome expectancy, covert glances at the surviving relatives, and a suppressed tendency to nudge. The other, headed by the bishop who had attended the inquest, and taking in the "county," stuck steadfastly to reactionary principles and regarded the vicar's end as the natural outcome of habit so wool-gathering as to border, if truth be told, on the half-witted. One had only to look at the tactful, superior faces to read their thoughts. In the opinion of the classes, Cuthbert Bellamy-Pryce, lovable man that he had been, should never have been allowed off leading-strings.

Yet one figure standing by the open grave, clothed in strange garb and wearing a curious, fixed smile, might—indeed probably did—carry at this very moment the weapon which had twice attempted the lives of two others present.

Tommy looked at Miss Gosmartin. Her beady, close-set eyes dwelt with horrific fascination on the archaeologist's yellowed features and twitching, vulpine lips. Once or twice her gaze gravitated to the niece and sister-in-law, but always to dart away as though afraid of being caught. Stiffly she stood, her hands in their black fabric gloves, picking continuously at her black shirt, a tendon in her stringy throat flexing nervously. Nor did she linger, as other parishioners did, when the ritual was finished, for hardly had the last sonorous syllables rolled to silence when she made an awkward dive towards Boggie, squeezed both the latter's hands vigorously, and bolted like a rabbit from the churchyard.

Her flight was the final support needed for Tommy's belief. Miss Gosmartin had read the vicar's message, and it lay heavily on her conscience that she had done nothing about it—though what she could have done was a problem.

Rosemary, dry-eyed and with a dignity which seemed part of her semi-dazed suffering, slipped at once into the house. Tommy moved after her, and under cover of the rose arbour leading to the side entrance found Gavin, just consulting his Ingersoll watch. At this precise moment the church clock chimed the quarter after three.

Gavin's sunken eyes met his fellow guest's. Again, with secret malice, they smiled. Very courteously the vicar's brother stood aside for his companion to go first, and thus it was that both men caught the bursting whisper of a stout matron just approaching Mrs. Bellamy-Pryce.

"Well, Mrs. James! I dare say you, as one of the family, will have been informed?"

"Of what?" demanded Boggie, low-voiced, evidently puzzled.

The matron swelled. "You don't mean you haven't heard? Dear me! Why, about Sir Osmund and the nurse. Married this three months! *Lady Bellamy-Pryce* it is now. Quite a surprise for us, isn't it?"

Surprise was a mild term for what leapt forth from the commonplace eyes of James's widow. The news which jolted Tommy had dealt in this other quarter a knockout blow. It was ably mastered and in a second Boggie's mottled colour flowed evenly again, her thick brows went up with a humorous twist.

"You don't say!" she murmured, with a good show of indifference. "Well, well, that's most interesting. To be sure, it doesn't at all affect me."

Perfectly true, it didn't. That flash of unedited emotion could represent only the annoyance most women feel when a subordinate member of their sex steps suddenly into position and fortune. The bitter resentment of all union supporters towards the blackleg . . .

Gavin had slid into the dusky passage. In another moment Boggie had disposed of the sympathetic queue and joined Tommy in the doorway.

"What a tremendous joke!" she whispered, though her wide bosom still rose and fell tumultuously. "A sharp woman, that Claiborne. I, for one, take off my hat to her."

In the faded drawing-room she let herself go.

"The slyness of it!" she exploded. "This explains it, of course."

"Explains?"

She ceased her drumming on the table by her side to stare sharply at him. Understanding, she gave a short, dry laugh.

"Oh, not our trouble! Her conduct I was referring to. You don't mean to say you thought she had a hand in this?"

"I might have done," he admitted guardedly, "if I'd known there was a marriage. There's a clause in the will—ineffective now, of course."

Unheeding, Mrs. Bellamy-Pryce pursued her own thoughts.

"It will cut into Ro's money," she mused, "and his. They could, perhaps, contest it. Undue influence, you know, mental incompetence?"

Thunderstruck at the suggestion of the uncle and niece combining forces in a law-suit, still more baffled by her calculating tone, he could only stare back at her. She had stripped off her gloves and was fanning her flushed face.

"And why not?" she retorted defensively. "To think of that scheming creature's coming in for a full widow's share! She's no right to it. There's something funny about it. Don't we all know the old dodderer was completely gaga for years past?"

"I question it."

It was Gavin who had spoken. He had come in like a twisted shadow, and was regarding them in sardonic amusement, which to Tommy seemed a mask for a more genuine reaction. He and his sister-in-law gazed at one another steadily. The third of the group realised with a shock that he was witnessing the last phenomenon he would have expected—a common ground for grievance. Almost it formed a link between them. Gavin, for a better reason than Boggie, was feeling tricked and cheated, but he, as his words indicated, had no wish to make a fight.

"Then you mean to let it go?" demanded Mrs. Bellamy-Pryce in a curious tone.

"Certainly. To do otherwise would be throwing good money after bad." Gavin's chill suavity was impudent, odious. "My father knew quite well what he was doing. You, however, seem concerned."

"Me?" Her fingers twitched as though with the desire to scratch, and the red of sheer anger coursed down her neck. "And what, pray, has my father-in-law's marriage to do with me? It's natural, surely, to feel annoyed on my niece's account. Does that astonish you?"

"Very little," returned Gavin composedly, "astonishes me."

He walked away, and, his narrow shoulders convulsed by some interior cataclysm, mounted the stairs.

"Really!" muttered Boggie. "That he, of all people, should dare!" She battled with her feelings, got the upper hand of them, and remarked in her usual tones: "Oh, well, I suppose I'd better break this to Rosemary. Poor child, it seems about the last straw, doesn't it? I hope it won't upset her too badly. I thought just now she was looking far from well, though it's not to be wondered at."

Tommy was thinking that the time for action had now come, and that he had best get to Gavin's room as quickly as possible. As he followed Mrs. Bellamy-Pryce into the hall, Peter arrived for his professional visit. He had attended the funeral and driven home to collect his bag. Leaving him to exchange greetings with the sister-in-law, Tommy sought the upper floor, and found Rosemary standing in the door of her room. She had a dream-bound expression, almost that of a sleep-walker.

"I heard," she said absently. "I don't know that it really surprises me so very much. Boggie mustn't worry about me. A little less money—what does it matter?" She seemed overcome with fatigue. "I think I'll lie down again," she said in the same disinterested voice. "My head aches, rather."

He knew there was no pretence of indifference over the re-division of property. Her total lack of mercenary spirit was one of the many things which endeared her to him; but he distrusted the flatness of her speech and manner. This, he feared, was how people behaved when on the ragged edge of a collapse. It was agony to him to be able to do so little for her. He had to remind himself that if his approaching task succeeded the situation automatically would resolve.

Even as he pushed open the baize door the ghastly rattle of teeth assured him the attack had begun on the dot. Seeing Mrs. Pennylove, come up to change from her funeral attire, he asked for a hot-water bottle. Her swollen eyes rounded in sudden dismay.

"Oh, sir, not for Miss Ro?" she gasped.

He explained, and her apprehension subsided. It was both irritating and disturbing, though, to find her jumping instantly to such conclusions. The slight sniff with which she departed on her errand showed very clearly she put small faith in Mr. Gavin's indisposition.

Some time later Peter took a final look at his patient, lying with closed eyes and sweat-glistening features under a mound of quilts.

"Good, we'll leave him to sleep it off. I just wanted to watch this one attack. Quite typical, as I expected. Send his dinner up to him. He won't want to crawl out this evening."

Tommy hung a tattered undervest over a chair and cast a baleful glance at the sunken lids which even in slumber seemed to hide a wicked triumph. Without argument Gavin had allowed himself to be divested of his clothing and put into the warm flannel pyjamas taken from his dead brother's store. During the past minutes every article he possessed had been meticulously ransacked. The revolver had not been discovered.

Had it been hidden elsewhere in anticipation of this turn-out? Probably—but where? For hardly a moment had he been free from observation from lunch-time onward, and every crevice he might have visited had been searched, even to the topmost ledges in the bathroom. Yet it did not seem reasonable to suppose he had got rid of his weapon altogether . . . unless, to be sure, he had abandoned all idea of shooting, and was maturing some other diabolical scheme. Suddenly Tommy believed this was so, and that it would account for Gavin's serene docility. The medicine-box! He spoke quietly to Peter and motioned him into the passage.

"You went over those bottles," he said. "Anything in them?"

"Rubbish! You saw me taste 'em. Just what they're labelled—and half of them empty. What's eating you now?"

"You know very well. Can you look at that face in there and not think there's something up his sleeve?"

Peter grunted intolerantly and taking up his bag walked back to the main landing. Tommy returned to the bedroom, ran a last reluctant glance round its meagre appointments, and for the second time stood gazing down at a letter laid beside the tumbler which had contained the quinine. It was a square envelope of thick, white paper, excellent quality, and bore a broken seal of green wax, displaying what looked like a crest. The superscription was typed, the postmark so badly defaced that all he could decipher was an L followed by an e, and the termination of the county, —lts. He had noticed it on the hall table yesterday evening—so it had come by the last post. Hesitating, he looked down at the sleeper. Yes, sound as a church, not a doubt of it, and from the livid pallor of his skin utterly exhausted.

Tommy picked up the envelope—and laid it down again in disgust. It was an empty shell. Contents destroyed? No letter was inside the sodden wallet, deposited with the Ingersoll watch and handful of crumpled cigarette papers. The hearth, though . . .

Bending over, he poked the minute heap of blackened ashes he had just seen. Crushed to dust, not a fragment worth salvaging. To his warped imagination it seemed that the slumbering man smiled. . . .

Outside Rosemary's room he came on his brother in earnest conversation with Boggie, whose face betrayed grave concern.

"It may be nothing," she was saying in an undertone. "But you'd better just make sure, I think. I don't quite like this pain she speaks of, particularly as I've been feeling a little wonky myself."

"Pain?" Tommy grew cold along his spine. "What's this? When did it start?"

"During the funeral. We neither of us ate much for lunch, did we? And it was all very plain. I can hardly see how . . ."

He waited for no more. On the instant he was in the bedroom, stooping over the girl who lay flat on her back, her pale gold hair outspread on the small pillow, her dry eyes staring up at the ceiling.

CHAPTER THIRTY-ONE

THERE was nothing wrong but nerves. Peter was dogmatic about it.

"Not a trace of temperature. It's this cursed hullaballoo that's caused it. Oh, I'm sending her along a mild sedative, so she can get some sleep, but what she really wants is a peaceful mind."

Tommy hung on to the departing Austin.

"Then you'll stake your professional reputation she's been given nothing?" he demanded.

"Good God, man! Think I wouldn't know! Just to satisfy you, I've been over all you had for lunch—swallowed cold bits out of the larder—and I'm telling you it's stark impossibility. I know that girl. She's sound as a bell, but too highly geared. Suppresses things. Good fault, but it takes toll of her body. See here, there's just one thing for it. She must be got away. Clean away—you understand?"

"I entirely agree. Away from her uncle—but how can that be managed so we can count on it?"

"Away from—? Oh, well, since this damned idea's got firmly rooted, I suppose we must give in to it. Yes, obviously. I can tell you how. I'm going to keep Gavin here for ten days at least, undergoing treatment. He's agreed to it, hasn't he? Now, then, that'll fit in nicely with a very sensible suggestion Mrs. James has just been making. I shall advise Rosemary to fall in with it. A short motor-tour, just the two of 'em together—doesn't matter where they go, so long as it's dead out of this. Get Mrs. James to tell you about it."

"Motor-tour? But Rosemary won't feel like driving a car, and I doubt if her aunt can. Have you noticed her thumb?"

"She showed it to me. It's healing nicely, and when it comes to that it won't do the girl any harm to take the wheel for a bit. I wouldn't raise any objections. Let them lose themselves for a couple of weeks. Best possible solution till common sense re-establishes itself. If I'm any judge, it soon will."

Peter set his engine going, but lingered for a parting injunction.

"Don't be fool enough to say anything about that Smith and Wesson revolver being seen on the boat. You've no proof it was that one that did the shooting, and if you don't want this girl to have a serious breakdown you've got to keep her calmed down."

The proposal outlined to Tommy sounded sensible in the extreme, but somehow failed to exhilarate him. For one thing, would Rosemary take to it? As he stood meditating in the hall, Boggie came down from the bedroom and spoke to him in her cheerful, matter-of-fact way.

"Well, has Doctor Rostetter told you the plan? It's just pure good luck Jack's handing over his car. Such a good one—and we can have it at once. To-morrow, if Ro's fit enough."

"So Argus is lending you his car, is he?"

"Oh, no, selling it to me."

"But he's only just bought it."

"You don't know him as well as I do. All enthusiasm one moment, down in the dumps the next. I got a chit from him last night. He declares he's fed up with trying to land a job, and going straight back to Australia. It was a wild extravagance buying a car at all. I told him so at the time, but when I couldn't argue him out of it, I offered, when my father-in-law died, to take it off his hands if he went away. I'll be wanting a car, and this one is a great bargain."

Argus had gone entirely out of his mind. He wondered now if this sudden decision to leave England resulted from Rosemary's refusal. What amazed him was not so much the Australian's vagaries but Boggie's placid acceptance of his departure. To judge by her face, she was quite genuinely undistressed. Either he had been mistaken about her feelings, or those feelings had abruptly altered.

"It's up to me to take care of Ro," Mrs. Bellamy-Pryce continued hesitatingly. "And myself, of course—though that part doesn't so much bother me. I feel I've a deal to answer for where she is concerned. For all I know, I may have dragged her into this horrid mess—and without meaning to, God knows, I've made things rather worse with my tarra-diddles and general alarm-making. You've thought that, haven't you?"

"I didn't suppose you could help it," Tommy protested, disarmed by the direct challenge.

"You must have thought it," she said philosophically. "And I certainly can't blame you. Still, though I don't stress it, it has been my danger as much, if not more than hers. Actually I may be the only one who needs to watch out."

From her viewpoint she had a perfect right to make this assertion. It was she who on the two occasions had nearly stopped a bullet. Headcorn himself had never questioned that fact; and it was she who had been stunned and tied up. If one accepted the official verdict in the vicar's case—the reverse seemed unprovable—then every attack but one had been directed exclusively at her person. Possibly even the hat-shop affair was no exception. If there had been some mix-up over the glass . . .

"See here," he said with a last, faint hope, "are you still unprepared to state it was your brother-in-law you saw?"

"If only I could!" A thoughtful expression came into her eyes. "It might have been better if I'd simply said it was. I was trying to be honest. Unless one is absolutely sure one hasn't the right . . ."

"No, no, of course not," he cut in, with slight impatience.

The feeling that some vital detail was being withheld died hard in him; yet there was a look of frankness and anxiety to justify herself in her plain, wholesome features, and such abundant good-humour that any criticism seemed unworthy. He was about to add something to soften his remark when the gate opened and the young woman from P. Ashdown's came up the gravel walk with two telegrams, both for him. He read them, stuffed the more disturbing one in his pocket, and gave the other to his companion. It was from the inspector, and reported that a passage to Bombay had been booked and paid for, the date of sailing being June 23rd. No name was mentioned, but the inference was clear.

"Only a fortnight from now!" Mrs. Bellamy-Pryce whispered it with satisfaction. "That's the best sort of news. If Ro will agree, she and I can take the car and simply disappear—till he sails. What could be simpler? After that, we'll neither of us have anything to be afraid of. Oh, we'll let you and the inspector know where we are, but not another soul. If he can't locate us, he'll have to give up. If he does know and can get at us—well, you see, don't you, what this narrow margin of time will mean?"

For a second Tommy wondered if they were meant to draw this rather obvious conclusion. It might be a ruse to lull them after the coming fortnight into a false sense of security. Sailings can be cancelled. On the other hand, Gavin's perfect tranquillity hinted that his plans were well laid. He might feel confident of accomplishing his design, whatever it was, in the immediate future. If he failed to leave the country, Headcorn would know at once, and meantime every moment spent within his reach was a definite risk.

"If he does go back to India?" murmured Boggie. "The climate will probably finish him. I doubt if we'll ever see him again."

"You're right," Tommy conceded slowly. "Yes, on the whole, I can't think of a wiser dodge than this motor-tour, especially as my brother means to hang on to him for a bit and pump medicine into him."

"I'm glad you do see it," she answered in evident relief, "I, for one, should feel perfectly safe. It will get us off your mind, won't it? I dare say you won't be sorry for that."

Would he? The other telegram in his pocket clamoured for attention. He had been offered a big new consignment, demanding his speedy return to Paris, with Spain as the objective. Already he had let one tempting job slip through his fingers. If he said good-bye to this one—well, there were plenty of eager men waiting for the chances he turned down. . . .

"Going up, are you? Our little meal will be ready any minute now. If he's asleep, don't wake him, will you? He can have his food later."

Gavin still slept, yellow and limp in his roll of coverings. Rosemary also had dropped off, so her aunt informed him when he joined her in the dining-room. He began to feel more easy about her—and about Boggie too. He saw now that his idea about their altered relationship had been quite formless, not worth weighing against peace of mind and a guarantee of safety. As for Gavin, the police-vigilance would continue right up to the moment he sailed. All the same, the wire he dispatched at nine-thirty was a tentative one. He would make no cut and dried decisions about this consignment till he had seen Rosemary and talked with her. Let it wait over till morning, after she had had a good rest.

Stepping in at the pub bar for three minutes he heard an illuminating item of news. The new Lady Bellamy-Pryce had yesterday afternoon refused to see her son-in-law who had called, and directly afterwards had driven straight to the residence of Colonel Grayce, Chief Constable of the district. She had remained closeted with the colonel for a good half-hour, as those who had seen the Rolls in front could attest; and if this didn't mean yet another party was watching her step, where was the good of eyes?

Catching sight of Sergeant Gibbon, Tommy managed a private word with him.

"You don't think he could have stowed that revolver away somewhere when he was out yesterday?" he asked.

"Not unless he dropped it in a rabbit-hole—and I followed so close my only fear is he twigged something. And he didn't get rid of it at his father's house. He never got inside the door, and the maid who answered his ring stood yards away from him."

Having mentioned the projected sailing and Gavin's decision to undergo medical treatment, Tommy slipped into the dark village street and walked quickly back to the vicarage.

Rosemary, meanwhile, lay on her back in the little enamelled bed with ducks painted on it which she had occupied all the years before she had launched out on her own—lay in a state bordering on stupor, but possessing none of its advantages. Through her dulled consciousness half-thoughts darted, visible to her in the form of mis-shapen shadows such as a candle-flame casts when blown about in a draught. Each as it appeared sent her heart beating with trip-hammer blows. Every blow hurt, though whether mentally or physically she could not have said.

That interior discomfort she had experienced—it was passing now—was a symptom of emotional distress. She had needed no doctor to tell her it was purely a matter of overwrought nerves. Indeed, no other explanation would ever have occurred to her if it had not been for Boggie coming in and plying her with rather tense questions. That was because

Boggie also had been feeling queer, ever since lunch, though in her case the sensations had been less severe.

No, it was just nerves. She had very nearly reached the limit of her tether, and although too healthy-minded to consider the possibility of a real breakdown she did sense the peril of her condition to the extent of knowing, for her own good, she must shut herself off from the outer world till her balance was readjusted. Complete and rigorous exclusion of every face, everything, connected with the recent period would be her remedy—and that, worse luck, she could not achieve. At this particular time those about her—even Tommy—would think it madness to indulge her craving for isolation. Merely to mention it would raise a storm of protest she dared not face.

Yet oh, if only they would all stop worrying about her—just let her get off somewhere, anywhere, by herself!

She seemed to have been lying here a very long time—how long she could gauge only by certain sounds which came to her. She heard Tommy go down to dinner and presently leave the house. That meant her uncle was still sound asleep—for Tommy would not venture out otherwise. It was still not really dark, only too dim to see the room clearly. She longed for the night, with its entire cessation of noises, and the assurance of being left undisturbed. Maybe, as she had had her Bengers' Food and her sedative, she need fear no further incursions; but no, she was wrong, for here was Boggie again, peering cautiously in the door.

She closed her eyes and made her breathing regular. Even so, though her aunt took the hint and withdrew, her silly heart had started thumping worse than ever, and it took an age to quieten it.

She heard Boggie go down—so Uncle Gavin must still be sleeping. This malaria was very convenient. It came to her that if she wanted to carry out the wild plan lurking in her mind now was her chance. She could get up, throw on her clothes, and make a bolt before any one knew. Why not? She had five pounds in her purse. She could escape, get clean away, send a wire to relieve every one's anxiety. . . .

What was wrong that she could not make the effort? Some spring broken, it seemed. In a moment the precious opportunity would be missed—and there might not be another; but she could not stir. No, here she must stay, struggling to compose the chaos of her brain, and to-morrow, as to-day, cringe painfully from even the most ordinary encounter. To-morrow! It meant that tolling church-bell again; the bishop's hateful intoning voice, the choir, slightly off-key, rending her sick nerves. She would not be present at this other funeral, but she might as well be, up here in her room.

Smarting tears burned her lids and slid into wells at the corners of her eyes. They blurred the faded watercolours on the walls, set the glass eyes of her Cuthbert-dog blinking, turned the oval mirror that still reflected the sunset into shimmering iridescence. A fly lit on her nose and stuck there, drinking her tears. Fretfully she turned her head to get rid of it, and as she did so noticed the door. Very slowly and silently it was being pushed inward.

She stared hard. Had she been mistaken? No, it had been shut before, and it was now open about a foot. The aperture was blocked by something dark. Tommy? Boggie once more? Why didn't they come in?

Suddenly her mouth went dry, the hair on her scalp rose. A face narrow and furtive was looking in on her. She could just discern the eyes, muddily-dark, with their bloodshot whites—and they were fixed on her face. An arm covered by a threadbare cape slid inside, then the whole body. She tried to raise herself, but a sort of nightmare paralysis chained her to the bed.

Her uncle, still without sound, closed the door behind him and moved towards her.

CHAPTER THIRTY-TWO

ALTHOUGH she had exchanged not three sentences with him since their arrival here, she could have sworn no thought of hers had been unknown to him. That was her feeling now. It was this, superadded to her uncertainty, which had set up her agony of conflict.

Uncertainty! That was gone. With a violence which stunned she saw her most hideous beliefs confirmed. With vile cunning, choosing the moment when he was believed asleep, he had got up, dressed himself, even to the shouldering on of his horrible caped overcoat and the donning of his greasy gloves, and come into her room. Here he was, edging inexorably upon her, with evilly-amused eyes never wavering from her own. There was a click in her brain, and stark terror took hold of her. She opened her lips, but the sound she uttered was only a dry croak.

He was less than a yard away—and still she could not leap up. Besides, he was keeping between her and the door. To make a dive and be caught—!

She could smell the musty odour of his clothing, make out the shiny patches and frayed hems. Midway down the front of his overcoat a bone button dangled from a single thread—a button in other times she would have sewn on for him. Now, to avoid his eyes, she glued her gaze to it and kept it there. Round that lone button the whole darkening room seethed in a dizzying whirl. There was a singing in her head. Then her vision cleared slightly and some of her terror receded.

Reason had told her that whatever her uncle's intentions might be he would not risk putting an end to her now. The thing must be made to look like an accident—or else suicide—an impossibility with other people within call. At a pinch she could put up a respectable fight, scream the house down. She had also noticed how desperately weak he appeared. He seemed hardly able to stand up. Why, then, was he here?

He was speaking, his voice even, faintly ironic—and cold. It sent shudders through her.

"You seem to be ill," he stated, always watching her. "Has the doctor visited you?"

She nodded, voiceless. He continued.

"I see. And what does he say is wrong?"

She managed to mutter, "Nothing. I want to be alone."

"Oh, yes." A long pause, while his features twisted themselves into a sardonic grimace. "I understand," he said softly. "Oh, quite; but don't be ill here. I shouldn't advise it. Get back to town. You have friends there? Then go to them—now. Get your friend Rostetter to drive you back in his car. To-night."

Although his tone and manner remained satiric, he was visibly hanging on her answer. All at once she saw why. Of course, he wanted to get her removed from her protective circle—among strangers, or better still on her own. If she went, he would follow. What he wanted to do could not with impunity be done in this house.

"You don't value my advice?" he asked, and when she continued mute he nodded twice to himself. "No," he resumed dryly; "that does not astonish me. I was afraid to offer you counsel. Still, I am doing so. You won't consider the idea of going away?"

The effrontery of it took her breath. Did he seriously suppose her witless enough to be influenced by his suggestions? He must, for he had bent over her, his sunken eyes probing into her own. It flashed on her that he might have hypnotic power, and that he was trying to use it. She stole one look at him, and saw that despite the coolness of his speech those eyes held an excited, inhuman gleam such as she had sometimes seen when he used to spin her tales of heathen devils and odious practices. Even in those days it had repelled her. She forced her gaze back to the button.

He seemed to give up. A chary movement of his arm sent the hem of his cape against her cheek. He noted her instinctive recoil, and smiled with bitter scorn.

"I find myself peculiarly hampered," he said detachedly. "I still say you would do better to leave here, but if I cannot make you listen . . ."

What exactly happened she did not know. She heard the rasp of something against the headboard near her pillow, and instantly felt herself smothered in stuffy folds of material. Horrible—oh, worse than all her imaginings! Too late she had grasped his meaning. He had been offering her a more comfortable death and by refusing she had got—this.

Frantically she struck out. Sound burst from her, but died to nothing in the stifling cloak which seemed to weigh a ton. Her strength ebbed in a single wave, and with a curious, far-away chuckle in her ears she slipped over a dark precipice. . . .

Only a faint?

She had opened her eyes on a room grown black. It was her own room, though, for here was the familiar bed under her, and close to her ear she could hear the small, busy ticking of her watch.

Her uncle had gone. So had the cloak, as she presently discovered by feeling furtively along the covers. Had he tried to smother her and been interrupted? Not likely. In such a case she would not wake to find herself alone.

Besides, how could that sort of death be made to appear natural? It might, of course, have been something other than choking or smothering which had been attempted. Killing her by fright, perhaps. If her heart was weak as her Uncle James's had been. . . . Was it? It had certainly been acting queerly this evening, bumping and thumping. . . . Another thought struck her. She explored her arms, her throat, but could find no tender spot where a needle might have been jabbed in. No, that was out too. It would have left a smarting place.

Incredible but true, she seemed none the worse except for mere giddiness and exhaustion. Then she thought of how Boggie had been attacked and left to survive. It must be—there could be no other explanation for it. Her uncle was mad.

Emboldened, she turned on the lamp beside her and looked at the time. Nine forty-five. So it had not been very long; but what was that rasping noise as the cape closed down over her face? Not a revolver. He would never have dared shoot her, however mad he was—and it hadn't sounded like metal. More of a dull scratch.

Close by the bed, lying on the faded green carpet, was a small, dark disk. Only a button? Like lightning she remembered. This was the loose button that had hung from his coat. Somehow it had got torn off, probably by entanglement with the bed-post as he leant over her. How stupid she was! This had been no attack. In freeing himself her uncle had accidentally let his cape tumble down upon her.

She began weakly and uncontrollably to laugh and straightway, the thing righted in her mind, resolved to say nothing about the ridiculous misadventure. Oh, no, it would never do to make a stir about it! Breathe a word and she would have Boggie in here, sleeping on the sofa, to-night and every night. That she could not bear.

Yet ought she to remain wholly silent? She decided to tell Tommy the first portion of the incident, keeping back the fainting part. Anyhow, she felt so crushingly ashamed of that cowardly act. Losing her nerve through sheer, insane panic! It was the sort of thing she had never supposed she could do.

Strangely enough, she was much steadier now than she had been for some time. In an odd way the atmosphere seemed to have cleared. She got up, put on her blue dressing-gown, and was just tidying her wild locks when she heard Tommy's tread on the stairs. Opening her door cautiously, she beckoned him inside, and not at first noticing that he was a bit dishevelled and out of breath gave him her abridged account.

He had taken her hands and when she described her uncle's bending over her his grip on them hurt. However, he made no immediate comment, only looked at her oddly.

"And then he just went away." The finish sounded lame. "He wanted very badly to make me leave here and go back to London, but more than that I simply can't tell you. What do you make of it?"

She had rather feared he would question her closely, but to her relief he did nothing of the kind. After his first searching glance and a long breath that spoke of tension relaxed he stood there, still holding her hands, his black brows drawn together over the pure blue of his eyes. He appeared, she thought, to be striving with a hopelessly-knotted problem which was no longer a desperate one.

At last he shook his head.

"I don't think it need trouble us," he said. "The fact is, your uncle's cleared out."

CHAPTER THIRTY-THREE

ROSEMARY had a blank feeling. Could she have dreamt all this?

"What do you mean—cleared out? When? Where?"

"About twenty minutes ago it was. I was coming up the hill when I met the station taxi just turning into the High Street with your uncle inside, looking like death. Till he'd whizzed past I couldn't believe who it was."

"But how—"

"I've not an idea. He may have nabbed the car as it set off to meet the up-train, or he may have made previous arrangements to be called for—though it's a puzzler to think when he managed it. The driver got off before we could catch him—Gibbon and I, that is. I dashed back to the pub for him and we followed in my car hot-foot to the station. The London train had just pulled out." For a second more she remained transfixed. Then quite suddenly and quietly she began to cry. A tear splashed straight down and plopped on to the crimson nail of her largest toe where it stuck from the open front of her blue sandal. She stooped to dab at it, muttered brokenly, "How utterly silly!"—and found herself in Tommy's arms, sobbing without restraint.

"I—I—oh, please don't think me a complete fool!"

"You're not a fool. Go on, get it over. Think I don't understand?"

Thus he soothed her. She tried to laugh, wept afresh, and wiped her nose against his shoulder. It was as if a dam had given way and nothing could mend it—or perhaps she did not want it mended, not while these hands kept stroking her hair, and this cheek, firm and comforting, pressed her wet one. How strangely different these caresses from the ones she had indignantly repulsed not once but many times from other men! Only they sapped her will-power, turned her into a baby.

It wouldn't do, she presently realised. Poor Tommy must be hating it. Embarrassing him in this stupid fashion. Hadn't she already imposed on him more than was decent? She withdrew, swallowed down her remaining tears and tried to command her thoughts.

"How was it no one heard him leave the house?" she asked.

"Your aunt—" he began; but Boggie herself, just entering, took up the tale.

"Your aunt was a miserable imbecile," the latter said crisply. "I'd gone back into the kitchen for a word with Pennylove—never dreaming he wasn't still asleep. Why, I'd looked in on him barely a quarter of an hour before! He was shamming, of course. Oh, well, it's one trick we can't quarrel with! He's taken all he brought with him," she announced with satisfaction. "What he means to do now remains to be seen; but it was the Waterloo train, so for the moment we're rid of him. He didn't stop for his father's funeral—or for his treatment."

Her tone indicated that nothing her brother-in-law could do was calculated to amaze her.

Rosemary had gone to the glass and was surreptitiously flicking her powder-puff over her face. She did not want Boggie to guess she had been crying.

"I suppose the excitement woke you up," said her aunt tentatively. "Now it's all over and we can breathe again, what about a cup of tea? I've just told Pennylove to make some."

"Thanks most awfully," murmured Rosemary, but did not turn till her aunt had gone out. "Don't," she whispered hurriedly to Tommy, "mention what I've said. There's no point in it now, is there? And it will only start more fuss and bother."

"Right you are," he agreed, but eyed her curiously. "By the way, your aunt told me that just after this happened she poked her head in here and found you asleep. You were asleep, were you?"

For one weak moment she was tempted to own up about fainting; but she bethought herself of an excuse, valid enough, if applied to an earlier occasion.

"I was shamming too," she confessed naively, and regretted it, seeing she had conveyed the wrong impression. "That is," she explained hastily, "I simply couldn't bear having to talk to any one at all. I haven't wanted even to see any one . . . except you, which isn't the same."

"I know," he answered softly. "It's entirely natural."

She wondered if he did understand when she herself was in such a muddle. Was it possible her real motive in wanting to keep a certain incident hidden from her aunt arose from a lingering desire to give Uncle Gavin the benefit of even a shadowy doubt? In any case she could not let Tommy know how Boggie's mere presence played havoc with her nerves. A feeling so senseless as that must soon evaporate. While it clung it was far better to say nothing.

Tommy had picked up the glass dog and was examining it absently. His attitude told her there was more than she yet knew. She went close and took him by the shoulders.

"You're not fooling me one bit," she whispered. "Quick! What else has come out about Uncle Gavin?"

Startled, he collected his rather different thoughts. Should he tell her about the Smith and Wesson? No. It was not as though the thing had actually been seen by him.

"Nothing vital," he put her off. "Let's forget it."

"It is vital—or you think it is. At least tell me this: Is it proof?"

"Technically, no. At the same time, I fancy he knew it was bound sooner or later to come out, and that this explains his cutting off. All in all, it looks very much as though he'd decided to give up the game. For that matter, this new mother-in-law puts another rather formidable obstacle in his path, doesn't it?"

"You mean he may content himself with the extra income he'll get through my father's death and let Boggie and me go?"

"He'd be mad if he didn't. I shouldn't at all wonder if he hasn't realised he's being trailed. That in itself would put the wind up him. Here comes your tea. Drink it up and get a peaceful night's rest."

He stayed till he had seen her tucked up again by Boggie's competent hands, then in his own room took stock of the altered situation. Before he could do this, however, he had to allow a rather devastating emotion to simmer down. Not while he continued to re-live certain moments in the immediate past could reflection take a sober trend; but he was helped somewhat rudely by the termination of those moments, very sharply etched on his memory. As he thought of them he wrenched of! his collar and flung it angrily from him.

"She won't want me once this is over. In normal times she's not looking for a shoulder to cry on—or if she is, it won't be mine. Well, I haven't really kidded myself. It might have been worse."

Now, then! With matters in their present state, was not his particular rôle played out? As far as he could see it was. Sergeant Gibbon was now racing by hired car to London, having first telephoned the inspector that Gavin had taken a through ticket to Waterloo and was on his way. This meant another plain-clothes guardian would be waiting, ready to take over. It might be Gavin would be placed under arrest this evening. If not, then from now till his date of sailing vigilance over him would be redoubled. All would depend, Tommy supposed, on what discoveries Headcorn had made these last two days; but either way would serve, especially if for the coming fortnight the two women went into temporary hiding.

"Yes, it's a water-tight thing—unless there's a catch somewhere, and I can't think of any. All in all, what's to hinder my pushing off to-morrow on this new job?" Nothing save a stubborn reluctance to quit English soil—and a feeling hard to analyse, which he believed had little connection with his own personal equation. After all, he would have to leave Rosemary soon in any case. She would send him away—so it couldn't be that. No, it seemed to centre round Gavin's latest move, which tended to confuse all logic. Hard to say why. The reasons he had given himself rang sound enough surely.

"Damn it, they are sound! The chances are he was never fool enough to contemplate more than the one murder—leaving James out of it, for that death may have been a happy accident for him. I'd say he made tries in various directions as the opportunities presented themselves, and that he didn't much care which of his family he killed. He brought one try off with remarkable success. Would a man of his brains wreck everything by over-reaching things?"

Even megalomania, he argued, has some limits. Notwithstanding, he passed a bad night, to find in the morning that matters had rather magically resolved themselves. He saw Rosemary, looking rested and very young in a filmy blue bed-jacket, and after talking over the plan of action Boggie had already outlined to her, apprised her of his Spanish consignment. She bade him close with it at once. It would make her utterly wretched if he let anything slip on her account, and besides, there was no longer the slightest excuse for monopolising his attention.

"I'm so glad. You'll be crossing to-night, won't you?" Thinner she had certainly grown. He noticed it now her arms were uncovered; but after this one tranquil night her eyes had recaptured their clear lustre, her voice some of its enthusiasm. In fact, he found her resilience most depressing.

"I may be kept in London for a day or two, on preliminary interviews. I shall try to wangle it. If so, you can keep me posted as to your movements—assuming, of course, you do carry out this motoring scheme."

"You'd like me to, wouldn't you?"

"I'd feel happier, certainly—on the off-chance."

Very slightly hesitating, she said: "Then we'll call it settled. It was practically that anyhow. I suppose it is a good idea. Boggie has a list of country houses she wants to look at with a view to buying. That will be our ostensible object; but she's told you, hasn't she?"

"Oh, yes, last night at dinner." Tommy paused and looked closely at her. "You do like this idea?" he demanded abruptly. "We could devise something else, you know."

"Could we, on such short notice?" She shook her head. "I doubt it. I certainly don't want to be in London now; and here's just as bad." She also paused to add, "I supposed it was the dodging about feature which was the main point. It's so clever of Boggie to think of it, I'd hate throwing cold water on her plan."

"None of which is answering my question."

"Silly!" she retorted with spirit. "Of course I shall like it . . . and it's not for long, anyhow. I'll admit I don't terribly rejoice at having to see Captain Argus again, but he's only fetching the car down and going straight on to Southampton. So that's no great hardship."

"Why Southampton?"

"Oh, some notion of having a last flutter at Deauville. He's picking up his boat at Marseilles—or so I understood. I can't say I'm interested."

Nor was Tommy, any more than he had been in Boggie's description of the rural life she was looking forward to, and her hope of finding a nice, old-world house replete with modern conveniences in the heart of some picturesque region. At this, their last free moment together, there must be better topics to discuss than the future existence of either Argus or Mrs. Bellamy-Pryce; but what topics? Invention ran strangely dry. All Tommy could think of was that when he saw this girl again she would probably be married—to his nephew, or to some one else—what did it matter? The door now merely closed would be padlocked and doubly-barred . . .

"Hadn't you better be sending your wire to Paris?" she reminded him.

"What? Oh, yes! Perhaps you're right."

It was his dismissal after services rendered. He accepted it, and within the hour was speeding back to town.

At three in the afternoon—Argus, he reflected would just be turning up with the car—he received a message which puzzled him. For what possible reason did Inspector Headcorn desire him to come at once to Victoria Grove?

CHAPTER THIRTY-FOUR

Rosemary, for a few blessed minutes alone, pored unseeingly over the station bookstall. Far down the platform her aunt and Captain Argus had stopped deeply engrossed in conversation. At any moment the train would arrive, and the man who had been such a thorn in the flesh would be removed utterly and ultimately from her horizon.

It was a welcome thought—though she had to admit this final encounter had not proved difficult. Argus had driven up just as the second funeral was over, and she had not been obliged to see him till, dressed for her own journey, she had found him in the drawing-room, arguing with her aunt over last business details. Rising, he had barely touched her hand and not looked at her at all. A vast relief; but her one glimpse of his face, iron-hard with indifference, had shown her in a flash just why he was leaving England so suddenly.

Odd she hadn't thought of herself in connection with it—yet here was the truth, staring at her. Overnight, as it were, he had indulged a wild hope of landing a girl with money. Cheated of the prize he had fatuously believed would be his for the asking, he had turned sour, lost his interest in her and her aunt, and in the language of the schoolroom was not going to play. Yes, he resented her—bitterly. That explained his refusal to meet her eyes—a vast relief, incidentally. She had known at the time that she had wounded him beyond forgiveness, but, though tender-conscienced as a rule, she couldn't in his case feel the slightest compunction. She had only to think of his handsome, drunkenly-confident face surging lustfully upon her to feel all her ruthlessness revive.

None of which was very interesting. Here was the Southampton train, steaming round the bend. Just say good-bye, wish him luck, and draw the curtain over a disagreeable episode.

The absorbed couple had wheeled about and in the business-like manner which had marked all their behaviour this past hour were moving towards the pile of miscellaneous luggage. All Argus's—a battered but strong cabin-trunk, three stout suit-cases plastered with labels, a tennis-racquet in a canvas jacket, a crammed golf-bag. Having seen these articles apportioned between van and carriage-rack, the owner removed his brown Homburg hat and with the air of performing an irksome duty extended his hand. Rosemary, when she took it, was struck again by the stiff absence of response—less surly, she thought, than stubbornly detached. She delivered her little speech. Argus made sounds by way of reply, and very markedly turned to her aunt.

"Well," he said carelessly, "you never know, do you?"

"Oh, I dare say you'll be back one of these days," returned Boggie with light heartiness. "Meanwhile, a good voyage—and don't lose all you've got at the tables."

"Darned likely, what?"

He bared his teeth in a challenging grin. Boggie's subdued laugh answered him as he swung into his compartment and slammed the door. That was all, except that once Boggie waved her gloves, and Argus, face glistening in the sun and red sparks glinting in his hot, brown eyes, jerked two perfunctory fingers aloft. Even now he did not glance towards the girl standing listlessly by her companion's side, but it seemed no calculated avoidance. In fact, Rosemary had the queer feeling that she in the flesh was not there at all, only her invisible wraith.

Now she thought of it, this same feeling had come to her while Argus had been instructing her aunt about gears and gadgets, and again on the short drive here. Deliberate ignoring she was prepared to expect, but this almost unconscious discount of her existence was a mildly intriguing phenomenon—less remarkable, though, than the exceedingly casual parting between these two intimates. That did astonish her. Why, for over three months—nearer four—they had been seeing each other almost daily—playing bridge together, living in each other's pockets! Once or twice, on her aunt's side, she had fancied a sentiment warmer than friendship—though that idea hadn't gone far. Anyhow, they were close comrades, yet now when they were separating, possibly for ever, they were behaving as nonchalantly as though in a few weeks they would meet again. Matter-of-fact people, both of them. From neither would she have looked for emotional display, but all the same . . .

"Well, shall we be getting along?"

Boggie's voice roused her. It sounded different, it was not easy to say how. Brisk and pleasant, it yet had an impersonal ring. It reminded her of the jog one gives a car whose radiator has gone cold. Another matter too unimportant to dwell upon. It did, however, add its bit to the quota of things which made to-day just a little peculiar, as though from the moment of waking it had got twisted askew.

Boggie, already through the gates, sent her a reassuring smile. It recalled the talk they had had early that morning, when subtle misconceptions had become righted.

"I'm a fool," Rosemary chid herself. "It's my mind that's gone crooked. I must get it straight again, that's all."

She smiled back, but did not speak, having nothing to say. Taking her place beside Boggie, she heard the engine whirr, and in another moment was seeing the familiar landmarks slide past and be left behind. In her heart was the dull prayer that she was also leaving behind the miasma which had been poisoning her thoughts.

Miles were covered, and still on both sides the silence persisted. The roads were dry, the car went marvellously, and not once did Boggie, competently steering, complain of her hurt hand. Once, indeed, Rosemary remembered it with remorse and suggested changing over, but Boggie shook her head.

"Still going strong, old thing. When it does turn bad on me you shall have your innings."

It had not occurred to Rosemary to inquire where they were going. No doubt Boggie had worked out something from the road-maps she had been studying all morning. The direction was westerly, veering north, since the sun, at first in their eyes, soon slanted in on the left. When it had sunk low Rosemary woke to the fact that they had crossed Sussex and were well into Hampshire. As there seemed purpose in the steady forty-five to fifty they were keeping up she finally asked if the houses they meant to visit lay far afield. Boggie did not immediately answer. She was squinting straight ahead, her brows knit in consternation.

"Houses? Oh, yes, all of them. Wiltshire, you know."

"Wiltshire?"

"I've always had a fancy for it since I spent holidays there as a girl. As I was saying last evening to your nice Tommy, I've been collecting a little list of possible places, more or less in the same district. I thought we'd press on quickly to get well out of our own neighbourhood, after which we can potter."

"Oh, yes, quite."

Noticing her limp tone, Boggie patted her knee encouragingly.

"Not interested, are you? Never mind, you can leave everything to me. I've given Tommy our first stopping-place—The Black Bull, Salisbury—so if he doesn't cross to-night he may ring you up. Drat those cows! Why must the man take the middle of the road?"

She sounded altogether the same Boggie whom Rosemary had met in March and instantly liked. Lately that first grown-up impression had got rubbed dim, but it had come out vividly again this morning during their frank little talk. Nothing new had come out, of course, but Boggie had shown very clearly not only her own awareness of her equivocal behaviour, but her wretchedness at seeing the effect this had had on her niece.

"I know quite well I've told fibs—or seemed to," she had admitted ruefully. "But who wouldn't, in my shoes? It's been so hard to know where my responsibility lay. What right had I, an outsider, to charge in and crash to bits your faith in your own uncle? It wasn't as though I had anything really substantial to go on. I know only too well just what that inspector had been thinking of me. I don't worry about him; but I do feel rather dreadfully about you. It hasn't been easy. I've been terrified, too—and after that knock-out I was so confused! Do you know it wasn't till the middle of the night that I remembered—"

She had stopped and stolen an uncertain glance at the girl in bed.

"About the bundle he was carrying?" Rosemary had supplied.

"Oh! So you've guessed. Well, all of a sudden it did come back to me. Just another of those hazy impressions. There, let's not speak of it. What good does it do? I dare say if we can get over these next two weeks we'll both of us be out of the woods. When I've settled in the country, you will sometimes come and see me, won't you?"

Boggie's chin, now and then a thought too dominant, had suddenly grown wistful. If there had been any direct appeal for clemency Rosemary would have felt less ashamed of her unspoken deflection. As it was, there had been something so sporting about her aunt that she had been covered in mortification, seen humiliatingly how she and she alone had been small-minded, and been seized by anxiety to atone in the one practical way—that of agreeing at once to the measure proposed for their joint safety. After all, it was so small a concession! In a lifetime, what did two weeks count? And then it was a sensible idea, one which appealed to her own reason if not to her inclinations. Tommy's consignment, naturally, had tipped the balance—for in that quarter, too, she had an uneasy conscience. . . .

Well, she had squared two accounts, and they were off on their Hegira, their well-being all but an accomplished fact. If she could not immediately rouse up and show a better spirit—was it because the lead weight still weighed on her, or had it to do with this aching emptiness she had been feeling ever since Tommy drove away? Tears kept filling her eyes. Maybe to-night, when she was quite alone, she would let them come unchecked. Now she must fight them back, or poor Boggie would think she hadn't wanted to come. . . .

Cool, luminous dusk, with Salisbury Cathedral rising out of a green hollow. Here they were in the narrow old streets, stopping at the rambling hotel, once a coaching-inn, with a cobbled courtyard and a great curtain of purple wistaria cascading from a low balcony. Scents of roast beef and draught ale came out to them. They put up the car, washed, and ate dinner in an ugly dining-room, almost deserted, for it was long past eight. Then a long hour in the lounge, also deserted—Boggie smoking thoughtfully, Rosemary dog tired, propping open her eyelids only because if the telephone rang it might be for her. There seemed scarcely anything to say. Never before, indeed, had she realised how few interests she and her aunt had in common; but then in London there had been so much to do, and seldom for long had they been thrown exclusively on each other's society.

The call came. Up she sprang and raced to the box in the hall.

"Darling, how too good of you! Yes, I'm quite all right, only fagged. So you've not gone yet?"

"To-morrow or maybe next day I'll get off. I've seen Headcorn. No, much the same, nothing for you to bother about. See here, what's your next stop?"

She didn't know.

"I'll try and wire you. Sometime to-morrow. Yes, our rooms are together. Argus? Oh, out of it, thank goodness. It wasn't so bad. He's on his boat now, going to Havre. Oh, Tommy—" Here, none of this! She had been on the very verge of saying how terribly she missed him. She changed it to, "What a blessed angel you've been! But don't trouble about me any more, will you? Really, there's no need."

"Sleep well. . . ."

On her way back she was melted to tears again, but the lump in her throat was of the pleasant variety. That last "Sleep well" made her live anew certain delicious moments of last night. After them she had slept well. She would again, if only she could get by herself quickly before the spell of Tommy's voice could fade.

She pushed open the lounge door and stopped stockstill, staring hard at the table where her aunt was seated, idly turning out the contents of her bag.

"Where," she muttered hoarsely, "did you get that button?"

Boggie jumped, poked guiltily at the small, dark disc lying amidst assorted rubbish, and laughed.

"That? Heaven knows! I never can resist picking up stray pins, buttons, rubber bands. Anything wrong with it?"

Rosemary continued to stare mutely. Boggie thrust the pile of 'bus-tickets and general debris into an ash-tray and pushed it from her, button and all.

"Of course!" she exclaimed. "It was on the floor in your room this morning. I thought it was Tommy's, and meant to give it to him. It is his, I suppose?"

"Maybe." Rosemary had gone limp again. Wearily she yawned. "I think, if you don't mind, I'll turn in."

"Oh, I shall, too. Pray God there are decent beds."

Idiot that she was to get wrought up over just nothing! Why else than from the habit they had so often joked her about should Boggie salvage a stray button? Funny not to notice Tommy's Burberry was fawn, not black; but most people were unobservant. . . .

It was in the forenoon next day that Rosemary became really aware of the alteration in her aunt. Probably she was the unobservant one now, or she would have sensed it sooner. Still, the degrees were gradual and so subtle that she questioned her own judgment. Over-sensitised—that was her trouble. It was unreasonable, surely, to feel at moments increasingly-frequent as though the woman at her side were a complete stranger.

Boggie had taken off her hat and settled down to her driving with a gravity almost stern. Even more silent than yesterday, she not only failed to volunteer remarks, but when addressed seemed scarcely to heed. She was looking for one of her houses, evidently, for there were numerous halts to study the section-map, and on several occasions they turned back to try an alternative route. They were choosing byways now, through what was mostly barren downland, very desolate, the villages widely-spaced. Once, topping a ridge, they sighted Stonehenge, looming lonely and unimpressive out of its vast plain, but though it would have been natural to pay it a visit Boggie merely frowned and reversed in a southerly direction.

"Lunch," she snapped. "No inns about here."

At an almost isolated tavern they paused, and Boggie made a hearty meal of the villainous food. Against her will Rosemary kept glancing at her. Her ragged brows were still knotted over eyes wholly self-absorbed, and with her crinkled hair dangling in dry wisps—the henna-dye tipped only the ends now—and the pores of her skin coarse from sun-glare and lack of powder she had entirely parted with the spick-and-span tidiness with which she had started out. Her vigour, though, was truly remarkable. Since nine o'clock she had driven without a real break, despite which she seemed supercharged with energy. In the London days Rosemary had found this quality a tonic. Now, inexplicably, it had the opposite effect, leaving her physically and mentally depressed, as though her own vitality were being drained out of her in great draughts by the more seasoned, less nervous body at her side.

It was perhaps perverse that she should suddenly think of her Uncle James. Had he, too, at times, suffered a little from his wife's excess of buoyancy? Till now she had seen quite a different equation. There was this about it, though. One had no need to exert one's self.

"While you're finishing," she said, "I'll get some cigarettes."

Boggie gave a bare nod, and helped herself to a second big wedge of Cheddar. Rosemary got up and walked towards the bar. As she reached the door she heard her aunt call to the landlord for the bill, and while she waited for her change caught the two voices conferring over a direction. Vaguely she listened. Thus far she had not been able to discover just where they were heading. Boggie herself seemed undecided. Maybe this conversation would enlighten her.

"You did say Ledbrook?" asked the landlord. "Well, now, you won't find that on no signpost, not till you're on top of it. Unless that map of yours is an extra-sized one. . . ."

Through the open bar entrance, quite close, was a little all-in shop, with Post Office on a sign jutting out. Rosemary went across to it, scribbled a telegram and handed it in. Then, with some bottles of ginger-beer under her arm, she returned to find Boggie making a rough toilet and looking well satisfied.

In the car again they steered back into the unbroken country. Towards Ledbrook? There was nothing to indicate where they were going, and Boggie's manner made it difficult to put any more questions. They had begun once again their rather aimless wandering, under a blinding hot sun, with a wind blowing furnace-gusts, and to add to the discomfort a steady succession of army trucks, heavy grey affairs, churning up dust-clouds which choked the lungs and hung low over miles of landscape. This was Salisbury Plain, of course, and army manoeuvres were in full blast. Distant volleys of shots reverberated. They passed scores of encampments, and even along lanes normally peaceful motor cyclists ground swiftly past. What a lot of them there were! Nearly all go-between messengers, robot, unidentifiable figures in goggles and dust-coloured coats, bent low over machines that exacerbated the ear with their dentist-drill noise. Oh, to be rid of them for half an hour!

To crown the unpleasantness, Boggie's hand was giving trouble. At their stop for tea Rosemary found it broken open and bleeding. From now on it was she who took the wheel, with a good will but diffidently, for her driving experience was small. They looked at one house, wholly unsuitable, and when they went on Rosemary, fully occupied, relinquished her last pretence of interest and simply did as she was bidden.

All day she had told herself that this was her aunt's show. Now as evening approached and she directed the car wherever the terse voice ordered her, she could, if she had chosen, have put it more strongly. Yes, ridiculous as it would sound, she felt no more than a pawn on a chess-board, pushed about this way and that, but always—this was the most absurd part of it—with some quite definite purpose.

CHAPTER THIRTY-FIVE

"WHAT the hell's going on here?" exclaimed Tommy, pausing in the door of Mrs. Bellamy-Pryce's bedroom.

"Never mind me," returned the inspector, stripping off the loose cover of the sofa and prodding in the corners. "I got your message saying you were back and had more to tell me. What is it?"

Actively observant of the room's disorder, Tommy described what he had heard from Rosemary. Her uncle, just before his unceremonious departure, had tried to persuade her to go back to London—unable, naturally, to give any reason, and making a definitely poor show of it. One imagined the marriage of his father had put a bad spoke in his wheel, and that from now on he was abandoning matters.

"As a general precaution—" Tommy was continuing when the detective's conduct drew from him another exasperated query. "What price this servant downstairs?" he demanded. "Won't she report the mess you're making?"

Headcorn, now busily hauling covers from the bed and exploring every inch of the plump mattress, merely grunted. "Stands to reason it's here. Go on. I'm listening. When will they be home?"

"Not before the twenty-third. I was going to say they've taken over Argus's car and are off on an unpublicised tour. Best possible notion, don't you think?"

The inspector, surrounded by mauve blankets, gazed at his informant with singularly dull eyes.

"I see," he said thoughtfully. "And whose notion was it?"

"My brother's, in general. He ordered the girl away. Her nerves are in pieces. Mrs. Bellamy-Pryce worked out the details. She and I talked it over last night, and as far as I know they made a start this afternoon. In a couple of hours I mean to ring up Salisbury, where they're stopping the night."

"Oh, so you know that much, do you?"

"I do, certainly, but no one else. If I go to-morrow, they'll keep you posted day by day. With their whereabouts kept dark and Gavin under your eye . . ."

"Gavin!" Headcorn roused and returned to his task. "I should have told you at once. He's given us the slip."

"The devil he has! For God's sake, why didn't you say so?"

For a second Tommy felt as though an iron fist had landed him below the belt-line. So this return journey was a feint, and he had been taken in by it. . . .

"There are three stations where he could have got out," explained his companion calmly. "The last for Waterloo express trains is Wyebridge Junction, where the branch line to Newhaven cuts across."

"You think he may have crossed to Dieppe?" asked Tommy, with a ray of hope.

"It's possible; but he couldn't have made the night boat. Hand over those pillows, will you? I've had one go at them, but I'll look again."

Gavin on the loose—and the officer in charge of the chase put in his time ransacking premises for God knows what!

"But, man, don't you see what this may mean? I've told you in my opinion Gavin has something very close to second sight. How do we know he hasn't got on to this motoring project? Even the first halt, though I don't see how . . ." Tommy drew in his breath and smote his thigh a resounding blow. "He may be on to it," he cried. "Yes, it's quite possible. . . ."

"How?"

"Mrs. Bellamy-Pryce and I were discussing it at dinner last night, just about the time he sneaked off. He may have heard and planned accordingly."

"Could he have heard enough to be of any use?"

"We mentioned The Black Bull at Salisbury," said Tommy slowly. "And there may have been more. I can't say I paid very close attention, as the rest wasn't fixed."

"You don't think the Australian went with them?"

"I almost wish he had done. No, he was catching the Southampton-Havre boat. All of a sudden he decided to go back to Australia."

"I knew he'd given up his flat," remarked the inspector, running a frowning eye over the other furniture. "I'm calling there presently, if you'd care to come with me."

"But surely you'd washed Argus out?"

"That is so. All the same, I'd like to see if anything's come of the instructions I left with the mechanic neighbour. I don't hope for anything. That's why I'm concentrating here."

"Perhaps some time you'll tell me what it is you are hunting for," suggested Tommy, heavily sarcastic. "But only if it doesn't inconvenience you."

"That's easy. It's a paper."

"Oh! What paper?"

"Unanswerable till I've seen it. I imagined you agreed it was a paper the person who rummaged in the brief-case expected to find."

"Then you entirely discredit the knife story?"

"Don't you?"

Tommy considered. It was true, he had felt doubtful on this subject. He could even place the exact moment when scepticism had taken root. It was when Argus, fuddled by whisky, had seemed so completely blank. . . .

"All I say," Headcorn went on, "is that the steerage steward noticed no knife among Gavin's effects, though he had the run of them twice at least before Gavin paid his known visit to the judge. It's taken me several wireless messages to clear up the point, but it is clear now. He handled the Smith and Wesson revolver, but no other weapon."

Light was breaking.

"You believe Gavin was after some document his sister-in-law was, or is, holding? That in some way this may explain her refusal to identify him?"

"Be that as it may," returned the inspector evasively, "we don't require proof of her not wanting to put Gavin in jail."

"I could understand that if Gavin had got the paper—if it is a paper," objected Tommy. "Not if he failed to get it—and I don't think she was fooling me. There was a look of triumph one couldn't mistake."

"That's just what I'm banking on—your power of character-reading. I trust you value the compliment. If that one detail is wrong . . ."

Headcorn broke off. The new maid, without knocking, had come into the room.

"Can I help you, Inspector?" she asked pleasantly.

It was her conversational tone which gave Tommy his second shock. For the first time he noticed her intelligent eyes, and the fact that her demure ecru cap seemed out of place with them.

"You can put everything back as it was," answered the detective, replacing the mattress. "And tell me once more why you think the article I'm searching for hasn't been found."

"What I'm going by," said Larke, "is the way he banged the door."

"Who?" exploded Tommy, fed up with mysteries.

Larke smiled at him commiseratingly. The inspector, in a brown study, blinked and woke to the situation.

"My fault, Mr. Rostetter. This is Mrs. Gladys Potter, one of our employees for delicate jobs. Go ahead, Potter, you can repeat what you told me. Saturday morning, wasn't it?"

Mrs. Potter, having bowed, delivered a crisp statement.

Tommy, feeling a hopeless fool, listened with increasing bewilderment.

"Not long after the two ladies had gone," said the Yard assistant, "Captain Argus called in to say Mrs. Bellamy-Pryce had sent him back to fetch the pass-book she had left behind and post it on to her. He had been advised where to look for it, so I gave him the run of the house while I, with his permission, went out on an errand. I came in at once, very quietly, slipped off my shoes, and hid in this room opposite—leaving the door ajar."

"Argus?" repeated Tommy, bemused. Where on earth was this leading?

"He had come in here and closed the door," continued Mrs. Potter. "I heard him flinging things about and swearing hard. He took about twenty minutes over it, after which he had a go at the lower rooms. When I made my official return he was helping himself to whisky with a very black expression. Finally, as I've said, he went out and banged the front door."

"And the pass-book?" inquired Tommy.

"Oh, still in that pigeon-hole," replied Mrs. Potter, pointing to the small writing-table. "Where it had been all along. If you're going out, Inspector, I can do this room later on."

When she had withdrawn, Tommy remarked somewhat coldly that Argus must have supposed his visit would be duly reported to Mrs. Bellamy-Pryce.

"Oh, I dare say," admitted the inspector absently.

"In that case, aren't you making a fairish number of bricks without straw? Pass-book or not, need we conclude he wasn't commissioned to look for something she had left behind?"

"No, perhaps not."

"I'll go further," argued Tommy. "What does this incident prove except that—as I for one have always believed—Argus is more deeply in Mrs. Bellamy-Pryce's confidence than we are? Mind, I hold no brief for the fellow. It's just that he appears to stand completely outside the whole affair. In no conceivable way can he hope to benefit by any death in this family. He may once have hoped it, but he can't any longer."

"Coming?" asked the inspector, leading the way downstairs.

Mutely protesting, Tommy followed, and together they drove the short distance to Argus's abandoned residence. All very well this putting a spy in the Victoria Grove household, if results justified it; but did they? It appeared that the professional on the case was taking a vast deal for granted, in addition to keeping his own counsel in a manner little short of infuriating. The amateur began to suspect him of making blind casts, for small reason, and to little purpose. It was not what one had been led to expect from Scotland Yard.

At the second door out of the mews they were met by a thin, shrewd-faced man with blackened nails and grease-streaked features. He conducted them up a flight of linoleum-covered stairs to a fair-sized living-room, into the centre of which a heap of litter had been raked together.

"This is the lot, sir," declared the mechanic. "And I asked the wife about the thing you mentioned. She's seen nothing of the kind."

"I was afraid she hadn't."

Moodily the inspector turned over the empty bottles, twisted tubes of shaving-cream and torn-up letters. Among the debris lay a dead orchid, a cracked mirror, and a grimy powder-puff. After a cursory examination he stowed all the flotsam away in an attaché-case, and having ordered the rooms to be left as they were, clumped down to the pavement. Here, looking despondent, he seemed desirous of parting company.

"If you get on to Miss Bellamy-Pryce this evening," he said, "I should not say anything about her uncle's disappearance, merely try to secure some idea of where they mean to go next. If you want to get in touch with me, I shall be back at the house."

"Having the carpets up, I suppose?" suggested Tommy dryly.

"It's already been done," returned the other, maddeningly mild. "Still, I may think of something."

"See here; what makes you so certain this paper, if it exists, is hidden in the house?"

"Because it is not among Mrs. Bellamy-Pryce's stored belongings, which I've taken the liberty to search. And she has no private deposit-box at her bank."

"Otherwise, I take it, you'd have searched that too. But if you don't know what this document is, how can you swear you haven't come across it?"

"Possibly I have. However, I think not. Yet if it has neither been destroyed or taken with her . . ."

"And why not, if it's so important? No, I get you. With Gavin at the vicarage she wouldn't have risked it. Oh, well, you know your business best. If it was left to me—but I'd better not say it."

"Not at all. What would you do?" inquired Headcorn with a very courteous interest.

"I should go all out to locate Gavin, then put him under arrest."

To Tommy's astonishment the inspector gave a slow nod.

"When I do locate him," he said gravely, "I shall probably do that very thing."

He turned on his heel and walked rapidly away.

CHAPTER THIRTY-SIX

BACK in the bedroom, now tidily restored, Inspector Headcorn disposed of the meal his assistant had brought him and lit a thoughtful pipe. As he did so the downstairs bell rang, and a moment later Mrs. Potter came up to say that the young person he was expecting had arrived.

"Show her up," he instructed, and rose to receive the guest whose nervous giggle presently sounded on the stairs.

In the doorway she stopped—a girl of full-blown and slightly unfinished prettiness, flushed with embarrassment, and agog over her entry into the limelight.

"Come in, Miss Coldbottom," said Headcorn kindly. "Sit down, won't you?"

Vera Coldbottom subsided awkwardly on the extreme edge of the Sheraton chair. Her hands, large and conspicuous in chalk-white fabric gloves, smoothed her navy skirt over her robust knees, her china-blue eyes glanced round in a manner half-frightened, half-defiant. She gulped twice, and meeting a friendly gaze broke into a broad smile.

"That's right," said the inspector comfortably. "Now, then, Miss Coldbottom, just understand that all I want is a few straight answers. They won't affect you in any way, and as I mentioned in my letter, I shall make it worth your while to be frank. First of all, do you recall the occasion some six or seven weeks back when a gentleman, Mrs. Bellamy-Price's brother-in-law, paid a call here?"

"Oh, yes, sir! Who wouldn't remember him?" Vera gasped over her own impulsiveness and added primly, "What I mean to say is, he did look so odd."

"Did you notice anything in particular while he was paying his visit?"

"Well, sir"—the tone was doubtful—"I didn't see much of him. It was soon after lunch, and I brought up some hot coffee for him. Madam could always do with a second cup. I did notice the gentleman never drank his, for his cup was full up when I took it down. And I noticed most of the talk was between him and Miss Ro. That's the young lady, you know. I thought Madam seemed stiff like."

"Did the ladies show him over the house?"

"Oh, no, sir!" The question evidently surprised her. "At least, they couldn't have done without me hearing. He didn't stop long. He and the other gentleman that was here that day went off at the same time. I saw them walking off together, along the street."

"And this other visitor was—?"

"Why, sir, Captain Argus," said Vera Coldbottom simply, though with a trace of reserve.

"Oh, yes, Captain Argus! He was a fairly regular caller, wasn't he?"

"I'd say the only regular one. No, I'm wrong. There was a nice young man—red hair he had. I can't just say his name, but he was sweet on Miss Ro. Madam had some lady visitors, people she'd known out East, I think; but not many. And Miss Ro saw most of her friends outside. They was both out a lot."

"But Captain Argus came frequently?"

"Treated it like his 'ome," said Vera shortly and shut her lips in a trap.

"He was pleasant to you, I suppose?"

"Yes, sir," replied the girl woodenly but with a hard glint in her eye. "Very nice indeed, always."

Was she tempted to add something? The impulse Headcorn detected in her passed, leaving her expressionless.

"Now, then," he resumed. "After this one occasion did you ever see Mr. Bellamy-Pryce again?"

"Oh, no, sir! That was the only time."

She spoke quite naturally, and it was clear on this subject she was keeping nothing back.

"Good! In that case, I'd like you to cast your mind back to the day Mrs. Bellamy-Pryce took possession of this house. You arrived just after she did, I hear. Did you help her unpack?"

At ease now, Vera launched on a rambling account of her first afternoon here. As soon as she had got into her uniform and an overall to cover it she had come up to this room to lend assistance with the trunks. The captain had turned up, too, and seemed to be getting on Madam's nerves. Anyhow, he was sent round to Harrod's to fetch in some gin and whatnot for cocktails; but only, as Vera could see, to get rid of him.

"Miss Coldbottom," said the inspector, stemming the flow, "on that first afternoon your mistress managed to mislay an important paper.

She thinks she put it away so carefully that she forgot the hiding-place. You know how that sometimes happens?"

"Oh, yes, sir, often! Why, only last Friday—"

"Quite. We all do it. What I want to know is, did you see her with a paper of any sort—in or out of an envelope—in her hand?"

"A paper, sir? No, I can't say as I did. I was in here right along, but for the little time I had to run out to get curry powder."

"It may have been then. Still, try to remember what she did during the time Captain Argus was out. I say then," explained Headcorn, meeting her puzzled look, "because he knows nothing about it, and that's why, as they are both away, I've been called in to help. Understand, it's a thing that couldn't possibly interest any one but Mrs. Bellamy-Pryce herself—just a family document. It was simply stored away somewhere. You are quite sure you didn't see anything being hidden?"

"No, sir. Nothing of that kind."

"And you didn't hear your mistress mention losing anything?"

"Not no paper, sir." Unexpectedly Vera giggled. "Now, if you'd 'a' said nail-file, sir, I could 'a' told you how she came to lose that—and where it is now. But that's not a paper, is it, sir?"

"Oh, so she lost a nail-file, did she?" asked Headcorn indulgently.

"Yes, sir, right down that crack." Vera's gloved finger indicated a section of wainscoting beneath the back window. "Let it slip out of her hand, she did, and it fell in there and slid right to the bottom. You can't see now, because we pressed it back, but that wood used to stick out a bit beyond the sill. It's like that in lots of these old houses."

"And the file's still there, is it?"

"Must be. How I knew was hearing her say Damn!—like that, when I was in the bathroom putting out clean towels. I offered to try fishing it up with a skewer, but she said, No, it was only a Woolworth's one, so it was better to leave it than maybe ruin the panel."

"Well, well, accidents will happen. It's too bad you don't know anything about the paper, but it can't be helped. Now, one more question—a rather personal one, which I hope you won't mind." Headcorn's manner became more tactful. "I hear you were dismissed without notice, but that you were given a reference. That's so, isn't it?"

The girl on the Sheraton chair sat up more rigidly, with warmed cheeks and a mutinous air.

"She couldn't refuse me a character," she muttered. "Not as things was she couldn't. And so I told her, straight out."

"Suppose you tell me your side of it," encouraged the inspector. "I'd like to hear, and I can promise you it will go no further."

In the same tone Vera continued, gulping a little. "She knew and I knew me trying on that hat—it was going to be mine anyway, when Miss Ro was done with it—hadn't nothing to do with sending me away. Oh, no, that wasn't the reason! Given an hour to pack my things and get out! Just so I shouldn't be here when Miss Ro come home from her work. I might 'a' said something. Not that I would; but she couldn't know that. So out I had to get. Wicked cruel it was!"

"And the real reason," said Headcorn, bending slightly nearer. "Can you tell me what it was?"

"What I'd seen," whispered Vera ashamedly. "I'd rather not say."

"I won't press you," said the inspector, and seeing disappointment registered changed it to, "That is, you needn't go into detail. Just give me an idea."

"It was my afternoon off," murmured Vera, not averse to yielding up her secret. "Only I had to mend my costume, so I was a bit late starting. Thinking Madam had gone out, I had a fancy to see how Miss Ro's blue hat looked on me when my hair was done proper—so in I popped. Then I couldn't seem to get a good light on it, that room being north. I opened this door, thinking I'd take a look in that big glass." She dropped her eyes, painfully self-conscious. "How was I to know who was in here?" she continued, barely audible. "Her and the captain. I hadn't heard a sound."

"Maybe you were mistaken," suggested the inspector gently. "If you only glanced in—"

"Me mistaken?" she flashed indignantly. "Oh, no, sir, not me! And besides, if I was, what made her fly at me with a string of names I wouldn't soil my lips by repeating? It was a bit of luck for her me having that hat on my head. She'd got her excuse; but she'd have found another, trust her for that!"

When Vera had gone Headcorn pushed aside the dressing-table and pried at the loose-fitting panel. Next, with his ear close, he pressed the wood and listened. Something at the back faintly rattled. He rose, an excited gleam in his ordinarily dull eyes, and going to the landing thundered down:

"Potter! Fetch up a screw-driver, or a chisel—anything of that sort. A carving-knife will do, but be damned quick about it!"

CHAPTER THIRTY-SEVEN

"GOT what you wanted?" asked Mrs. Potter, fingering a rusted nail-file.

The inspector did not answer. Squatting amidst dust and splinters, he was poring greedily over the stained sheet of foolscap which, twice-folded, had been snugly posed against the inner boards. He read it through twice, and examined the three signatures, appended to which was an official stamp. Then, still without speaking, he got up and clumped heavily down to the telephone. On his face was a look very rarely seen. His subordinates would have read its meaning, but they would not have commented on it in his hearing.

As he reached the bottom stair the telephone rang. Fiercely he ordered Mrs. Potter to answer it, but when the receiver was handed him and he heard his journalist friend's voice he had his usual control.

"Good," he grunted. "I see"—and after a few terse questions hung up. He then rang the Yard, issued rapid commands, and with the document in his wallet quitted the house.

Subterranean blasphemy broke from him as he hurried by taxi to his office, and at one and the same time his thoughts raced in two separate channels. In the first he was saying that Gavin had got to be found immediately and asking himself how it was to be done. In the second he was envisaging his own endangered prestige. If what he foresaw materialised, would only explanations exonerate him from blame? They would not—nor would an unbroken series of future successes ever remove the stigma of a failure so crushing.

Yet he had wasted not a moment, neglected no inquiry however indirect, and if he had committed the fatal error of silence it had been done with the best of reasons. From first to last he had been working in a thick fog, streamers of which still impeded full vision. Even now, with the crash close upon him—oh, he saw that clearly enough! he could not think how he could have acted to better advantage. Two persons it was his duty to safeguard were being hurried headlong and blindfold to their doom, and at this late date only miraculous intervention could pull them back. A singularly perverse fate had stolen a march on him; but who would take that into account? These two deaths when they happened—as they would happen—would be laid at his door.

"The girl, of course, may manage to send that wire."

But could she? Before opportunity came she might be dead. How was it possible to rescue victims not only ignorant of their imminent danger but ungetatable? Broadcasting in this case would be worse than useless. One fact only held out a dim hope. What was planned would not take place to-night in the populous city of Salisbury, nor yet—one would imagine—during daylight to-morrow. If, as he believed, darkness was chosen, it promised a brief respite.

The hope, however, was nearly extinguished when by the late afternoon of Tuesday no information concerning Gavin Bellamy-Pryce had come in. It seemed impossible that the archaeologist could so genuinely disappear, but there it was, he had contrived it. Sergeant Gibbon, under a heavy cloud, was moving heaven and earth to retrieve his reputation. All he had learned was that a man answering Gavin's description had gone through the gates at Wyebridge Junction on Sunday night and handed over a ticket to Waterloo. From that exit the man had been swallowed up, and meantime the hours were rushing by towards the night Headcorn dreaded. Rostetter, as it happened, was still in town. He had heard nothing further from the two motorists, and thus far it had seemed pointless to alarm him; but now, in sheer desperation, the inspector rang up the Albany flat, and finding the journalist waiting in on the chance of a message, went round to see him.

His gloomy expression assured Tommy that nothing vital had been discovered at Victoria Grove or elsewhere. Obviously the hunt for a paper—purely hypothetical, anyhow—had come to nothing. It was satisfactory to learn that every possible step was being taken to trace Gavin, but that no progress had been made in this direction cast a bad slur on official machinery. Tommy himself was acutely uneasy. That was why he had risked losing his consignment by loitering in London.

"Job or no job," he said shortly, "I can't leave while this scoundrel's on the loose. How far is Wyebridge Junction from Broughton-Elmtrees?"

"By road, twenty-four miles."

"Hum . . . Well, he didn't get back there before they left, whatever he meant to do."

"We don't know if he did mean to get back. See here, is there nothing that happened over the week-end that could give us a lead? I know he called at his father's place on Saturday afternoon, but he saw only the maid and spoke to no one during his walk. Did he receive any messages—wires or letters?"

"One letter, I think," said Tommy, suddenly recalling. "I saw it by the bed; but only the envelope. The enclosure had been burned. Oh, I looked at the ashes in the grate. They were knocked to powder."

"But the envelope. What was it like?"

"Good-class, typed address, sealed with some cipher or crest. The place-name on the postmark was blurred, but it began with Le, and the county ended with—Holy snakes!" Tommy leapt up as though a red-hot needle had been jabbed into him. "Wiltshire! Of course it was. What other county abbreviation ends in 'lts'? They're there. He may be, too. Not that it makes sense. . . ."

The inspector also had sprung up.

"Got an A.B.C.?" he demanded grimly.

Tommy had reached the time-table and was already ripping through its pages. He slung the book away in disgust.

"Not in it," he muttered. "We'll have to look on a large map; but is it conceivable he can have followed them on such a remote chance? Getting a letter from Wiltshire doesn't connect up with going there for this purpose. Wait . . . I think I can guess whom the letter was from. I may be all out, but it's one thing I can settle."

He had his hand on the telephone when Headcorn checked him.

"One minute. You mentioned a conversation between Mrs. Bellamy-Pryce and yourself during dinner Sunday evening. What precisely did she say about this tour?"

"You're right, it all rests on what Gavin could have overheard. My God, what did she say?"

Tommy savaged his hair. The truth was, Boggie's remarks had bored him. His own thoughts had been on the girl upstairs. If Wiltshire had been mentioned, he could not recall it.

"Still, she must have mentioned it, because Salisbury's in Wiltshire. She may even have dropped the name of some village in connection with one of her addresses. We were both so damned sure that black-guard was asleep—"

Headcorn had taken a sheet of stiff notepaper from his pocket.

"Look at this," he said tersely. "I found it in Gavin's room."

The typed communication, dated April 3rd, contained these lines:—

"DEAR BELLAMY-PRYCE,—In June, weather permitting, we propose opening up the last of our barrows. As I should much value your presence, I take the risk of renewing my invitation. Let me know if you will come, for my place will be let, and the accommodation I have arranged is strictly limited.

"Yours sincerely,

"DOWNSIDE."

It was at the engraved address that Tommy was staring hardest: Moorlands, Ledbrook, Wilts.

"Exactly," muttered Headcorn. "Now make your call."

A brief talk with Lord Downside's secretary elicited the fact that Lord Downside himself was in Aix, but that before leaving he had given the speaker a letter to be addressed and posted to Mr. Bellamy-Pryce in Sussex. As no reply had come there was no way of knowing if Mr. Bellamy-Pryce was accepting an invitation already twice declined.

"But the excavation is going forward, is it?"

"I imagine they'll start work this week, though I can't tell you which day. I only know that arrangements were being made when I was there with Lord Downside last Friday. It was then I posted the letter. What inns are there? Oh, only the Downside Arms in the village, which is a mere handful of cottages. It's a fairly miserable affair."

"Would Mr. Bellamy-Pryce be stopping at the inn?"

"Either there or at a temporary hut Lord Downside has had run up near the barrow. It's about a mile to the north."

Headcorn had heard every word. Instantly Tommy hung up he dialled the Yard number, and at the answer to his first question stiffened to attention.

"Hold on," he barked. "Let's get those details clear. You say Gavin Bellamy-Pryce hired a car at Wyebridge, and the chauffeur, just returned, says he drove him to a small place in the Wiltshire downs called—what's that—Ledbrook! Yes, I've got it. Left him at a sort of army hut, out of the way but surrounded by barbed-wire entanglements. I know, manoeuvre stuff." He rang off and turned to his companion. "Can you dig up a map?" he demanded.

Tommy by now was clattering down to the court where his two-seater stood. In another moment he was back with his section map, and the two heads bent over the county of Wiltshire. Here it was—Ledbrook—a tiny dim dot in a lonely waste of downland, remote from anything important. The journalist's face slightly cleared. With an entire district to choose from, was it likely two wanderers would seek out this insignificant village? Not unless there was previous reason—which, of course, one could not know.

"I suppose," said Tommy tentatively, "it won't do for any of those known to him to follow on. Will you send along a new man to prevent him from doing damage?"

What he was thinking was that if some misguided objection prevented this very essential step, he himself would take on the job; but even as he spoke he noticed an expression on the detective's face which roused violent alarm. Uncertain, harassed, it hinted at defeat.

"Might be a false move," Headcorn answered with a shake of the head. "Till we've definite knowledge of those two women it's a tricky business; and yet"—consulting his watch—"our time may already be too short."

The fall of these last words quickened Tommy's understanding. If Headcorn hesitated, it was because this three-fold journey into Wiltshire might still be coincidence. If this were so, he was afraid to chance an action which not ending in capture would leave the criminal free to ensnare his victims at some future time. At the same time he was even more afraid of allowing events to proceed without intervention—for had he not admitted that in the next few hours the trap was likely to be sprung?

Till this moment the failure to hear from Rosemary had seemed natural enough. She herself probably did not know where the day would end up—and that argued the lack of a previous plan. Yet, supposing there had been a plan and her uncle knew of it? It was now six o'clock. Had the sending of a wire been forcibly prevented?

"I'm going, anyhow," he announced. "If they're not there, well, I shall stick close to Gavin—if he hasn't skinned out when I get to this village. God, if I'd had the wit to listen as he must have done! And yet"—he paused midway the room—"I'm still utterly mixed over the workings of this! Surely it's an extraordinary bit of luck for Gavin to have this legitimate reason for getting into the same region? Relatively the same, that is. Wiltshire's a large area."

"Luck!" grunted Headcorn, eyeing him.

Tommy attacked him roundly.

"Inspector, in God's name, what have you got up your sleeve? Don't tell me Gavin's a hypnotist, able to put notions into people's heads and steer them where he wants them to go. I'll believe a lot, but not that. What's the answer?"

There was a flaw in his own logic, instantly perceived. Ledbrook might be only a convenient vantage point from which to make sorties and to which Gavin could return. That desolate country! Too well he knew the wide, uninhabited stretches. In his mind came a vision of a car in flames, burning up and destroying its human contents together with all evidence of crime. So horrible yet so possible did it seem that, not noticing his question had been unanswered, he strode again towards the door.

At this very moment the telephone gave a prolonged peal, and the despaired-of message came over the wire. As the operator repeated it the blood in Tommy's veins turned to ice, then to galvanic energy.

"They are in Ledbrook—or will be, this evening. Can I make it before they do?"

Hardly a chance, even with a powerful car, the securing of which would lose vital minutes. Go he must, though, and hope that the lingering June twilight would guarantee some protection.

"We'll wire back and warn them," he was saying, when a hand like a ton weight clamped down on his shoulder.

"No!" commanded the inspector, suddenly turned into a battering-ram. "You can come, if you like, but you'll go in my company, and do as I say. This is the Yard's affair."

Pinioning Tommy's arm, he lumbered out of the flat.

Shortly after this a high-powered Humber glided in and out the Hammersmith traffic. In the front were two sergeants in mufti; behind them Tommy and Headcorn chafed at the impeded progress and longed for the open roads, most of all the long levels of Salisbury Plain, where speed could be made up. A long drive lay before them—very likely too long. Oppressed by the thought of it, the two at the back spoke little and jerkily.

"Tuesday," Tommy broke silence. "It's a clear day for him."

"Does it signify?" was the grim retort.

No, not after nightfall, as Tommy knew to his cost. Another idea occurred to him. Bending over his map, he said:

"That wire, late as it was, was handed in at two-thirty, at a place called Duck's Corner—just here. As the crow flies, it can't be more than twenty miles from our objective. What if they've missed out Ledbrook, after seeing what it's like?"

"They'll go there," stated the inspector with ominous certitude. "Though it's not saying we'll find them when we arrive."

Tommy glanced at him curiously, but there was that in the stern features which checked further question. Whatever it was Headcorn knew or guessed he was not going to share it—nor at this stage did it matter, with every nerve strained on the one end of reaching a far-distant spot before darkness settled down. So many miles to cover, and no assurance that calamity had not already forestalled them!

Midway the great highway the man at his side spoke again.

"Mrs. Bellamy-Pryce may find trouble in driving," he remarked. "How, by the way, did she injure her hand?"

"Slashed it with a grape-fruit knife," replied Tommy, watching the speedometer. "Still, it was four days ago."

"Her right hand," commented Headcorn, with so little emphasis that a full minute passed before his companion registered what was said.

Her right hand? So it was. Queer, now it was mentioned, for Boggie, not a left-handed woman, to jab a knife into the hand which held it. One would expect it to be the other hand, steadying the grape-fruit, which would receive the cut. Queerer still how at agonising moments such profitless speculations should hover and stick, like flies on an open wound. . . .

CHAPTER THIRTY-EIGHT

WITHOUT warning Rosemary's door opened. Against the dim-lit passage outside showed the solid shape of her aunt, fully clothed.

"Get up!" ordered the brusque whisper. "Get on your things. We've got to leave here—now."

Rosemary threw off the flimsy cotton sheet under which, for perhaps an hour, she had lain, wide awake, dully revolving the unpleasant monotony of the day and dreading the similar ones to come. Her aunt's peremptory command jarred rudely on her.

"Leave this inn? But why?"

As she slid her feet to the slimy-feeling linoleum Boggie gave a subdued bark of a laugh and jerked a beckoning hand.

"I'll show you why," she said in the same harsh, low tone, and with a curious glitter in her eyes. "Come with me—but don't make a noise."

Huddling on her woolly beige coat, Rosemary followed into the passage. It was only a few feet across, and most of it taken up by the grained balustrade of the stairs. By this Boggie was standing. With a gesture almost cruel in its triumph she bade her niece look over into the cramped hall below, where a hanging gas-lamp made a flood of hot glare.

Rosemary looked—and drew back with a gasp. Then, doubting her eyes, she stole another look. Down there, engrossed in a dirty map pinned to the wall, was a stationary figure. She saw a flat, greasy hat at some former period black, a slinking cape dangling over a greatcoat, and emerging from its folds one stuffless gloved hand. The head turned half towards her in a listening attitude. No, she could not be mistaken. That pinched, yellow profile, livid in the gas-light, was her uncle's.

Panic in her eyes, she turned to find her companion closely watching her. At once she was seized by the arm and hustled back into her room—a wretched cubby-hole, stuffy and low-ceiled, with brown, discoloured wallpaper and cracked toilet articles which did not match. Boggie thrust on her an armful of clothing.

"Exactly," she snapped, with a stern jut of chin. "He's followed us. How? Don't ask me now. Dress!"

"Wait!" Rosemary felt she must get some understanding of this. "You say he's followed us. I simply can't see how, unless—"

"You can't? Well, I can. If you must know, I've been afraid this might happen. You may have noticed how quiet I've been. I came near skipping out this place, only I'd meant to come here, and it was such a remote chance—"

"How did he find us?"

"That's easy. I've two addresses near here. I spoke of it to Tommy over dinner Sunday evening. As I've told you, we both could have sworn he was too ill to creep downstairs, but—"

"You mean he came to the dining-room door and listened?"

"Why not? He was able to get about. Oh, he heard right enough! And he came to waylay us. Is there any other excuse for his choosing out of all England this wretched little spot we ourselves wasted hours hunting for? Never mind that now. It's too late to play about. He'll have seen our names in the register. What we must do is to watch our chance to slip out and get right away."

"His name isn't registered," objected Rosemary, passing a bewildered hand over her forehead. "Somehow this doesn't seem—"

"You saw him, didn't you? And you wouldn't surely expect him to use his own name." It was said with such scorn that all opposition was crushed. "Oh, he's no fool, if your aunt is! Well, anyhow, we're warned in time. Hurry! I'll be back in a moment."

Boggie disappeared, closing the door, and Rosemary with shaking hands pulled on the garments she had so thankfully taken off a short while before. Her heart thumped horridly and a loathsome, sick feeling was lodged in the pit of her stomach. A nightmare had come true. The vain, childish hope to which she had stubbornly clung was finally demolished—yet, though she did not blame her aunt for what had happened and ought, by rights, to be grateful to her for this timely discovery, she was conscious chiefly of a leaden resentment. Boggie should have told her. For once this trying to spare her had gone a little too far.

Where would they go now? Back, she supposed, to the more civilised village they had rushed through a quarter of an hour before reaching this miserable hole. It did not matter so long as they got away—right away—from here. The lock on her door wouldn't work, the rickety casement window opened out on a lean-to shed in which they had garaged their car, while all out there was dark as Tophet with its stunted cedars and clustering laurels. Any one could climb into this room and get out again with no human being the wiser. If robbery and murder took place during the night, who would connect them with another transient guest? Yes, they must go quickly and quietly, sneaking out like thieves; but oh, that the truth should be this!

Her face was still sticky with cold cream. She gave it a scrub with the sleazy towel and jammed on her hat to save combing her hair. Just as she was cramming her last belongings into her case Boggie stole back to announce that the coast was clear.

"I've settled the bill, and found there's a short cut back to Wynch. That's the place we passed through. Ready, are you? Then perhaps you'll lend me a hand with my straps. Of all stupid times to have this beast of a thumb!"

In the room next door Rosemary asked what had become of her uncle.

"I saw him go into the bar. We'll take another look before we venture down."

"Do they think it's queer our leaving like this?"

"Not much!" Boggie chuckled. "I told the landlady we'd seen something we didn't like spending the night with. She thinks it's the beds."

Rosemary could not share in her mirth. Strangely enough, this crisis seemed to have gingered up Boggie's spirits. As they tiptoed forth into the passage there was again that elated glitter in her eye, and the defiant thrust to her chin which showed her indomitable courage but somehow struck the wrong note.

The hall below was deserted. Down they crept and in a rush attained the door; but though the gamut was run the first step into darkness like a black wall seemed a plunge into a worse peril than the known one left behind. Beyond the few twinkling lights which presently would show lay the invisible downs—vast, rolling, desolate. Off and on all day they had been skirting them, and now night had come and no moon was yet risen the utter loneliness of the region played tricks with the imagination. Instinctively Rosemary had halted. Though the air was cool, her face streamed with sweat.

"What are you stopping for?" came her aunt's sharp whisper. "Do you want him to see us? Quick, follow me!"

How warm, how comforting those red bar-curtains, the open door through which gushed odours of ale and tobacco smoke! As she stumbled over the uneven ground she could not see the drone of slow West

Country voices came out to her. Some one in there was playing a piano-accordion—*Where my Caravan has Rested*—unctuous, a little wrong in the bass. The last link to security . . . but what a mad fancy! She shook herself free of it and groped her way into the shed.

Boggie, already seated, motioned impatiently.

"You'll have to drive again," she whispered. "Mind that beam. Can you see your way out?"

Once they had tottered across the yard there was but one course to take—the dirt lane, so narrow they had shot past it that evening and had had to turn back. From the few thatched cottages hugging its sides dim lights trickled into the gloom, showing wallflowers and scented night-stocks which yielded forth fragrance. Then the black wall closed in again and the village was swallowed up.

"Cross over the main road," ordered Boggie. "Keep straight ahead."

"Up there? Why, that old track will land us nowhere, in the middle of the downs!"

"Wrong. It will lead us presently into the good road to Wynch. It's the short cut I spoke of. Don't forget our petrol's running low. I didn't want to stop to fill up." Boggie was well-informed. After preliminary bumps the lane, though it mounted steeply and quickly degenerated into a grassy run, showed signs of usage and offered fairly decent going. Certainly it would not have done to draw attention to their departure, while almost as bad would be to fizzle out of gas miles away from a filling station. At the same time Rosemary was wretchedly uncomfortable. This flight in the night had an element in it which disturbed her in a way she could not quite place. Perhaps it was Boggie's rough manner—due, no doubt, to really petrifying alarm. For Boggie, in spite of her bold rally, was evidently very serious about this, not yet easy in her mind. Else why did she keep that rigid attitude, head constantly turned towards the huddle of cottages now blacked from view?

The headlamps blazed a path so dazzling that one could almost pick out the separate blades of drought-faded grass. The upland air grew dank, and Rosemary, beginning to shiver, found her coat hauled up from the rear and bundled round her shoulders. It was a thoughtful act. Was it the business-like way in which it was performed which set going one of her odd, unpleasant thoughts? Her brain must indeed be twisted awry if she kept seeing herself as a pawn shoved about at another's will. It was horrid to feel like this towards a companion who was so kind to her. If she could not conquer it, she had better first thing in the morning say she was too tired to continue. Make a stand for freedom, take a train back to London.

Freedom! There she was again. Why should she think of herself as a prisoner and her aunt as jailer? Really, she was a fool. . . .

"Stop!"

Startled, she pulled up. Confronting them was a fork, one branch leading up the slope, the other down into a deepish hollow, dotted, she thought, with clumps of bracken. Looking her inquiry, she saw her aunt with furrowed brow, intently listening—for what? All she heard was the faint, distant hum of a motor-cycle. Louder it surged, then ceased. Along the main road it would be; but Boggie, still straining her ears, spoke absently.

"Not a car," she said. "And we turn to the left. Don't go fast. There may be another fork."

Slowly they moved down into the hollow. After, a hundred yards the smooth slopes rose round them in an amphitheatre. Boggie had sounded sure, but still she bent forward a little to the side, staring fixedly into the surrounding darkness. All Rosemary could see of her was the hunched line of her shoulders and the rear view of her neck.

What was it about that thick throat with its deep horizontal crease of flesh and the clipped hair ending above it which filled her with sudden repulsion? Till now it had seemed to her comfortable and jolly. Her own eyes must have suffered change. So had her associational centres, for never before had the sight of this throat reminded her of the vile libels in her grandfather's letter. They were libels, as she had always known them to be—preposterous, fantastic. And one was safe in a car, even in this black waste of desolation, so long as one wasn't . . .

What was that sound just ahead? Involuntarily she slowed.

"Keep on!" commanded her aunt crossly. "It's a rabbit, of course. Good God! What's this?"

Midway their path a man had risen up. Rosemary jammed on her brakes barely in time to avoid collision with him. For one second he stood mutely confronting them, then he moved quietly to Boggie's side; but the brief glimpse had shown her a broad bulk encased in a cyclist's coat and a face virtually blocked out by the flaps of a leather helmet and great, concealing goggles. Nor was this all she had seen. On the ground nearby lay something dark and muffled. To her distorted fancy it appeared the headless trunk of some victim. A dumped kit-bag, of course! And the man was yet another of those cyclist-messengers.

"Is he wanting a lift?" she whispered doubtfully.

"I can't imagine. . . . *Look out!*"

Rosemary ducked, for she too had seen the winking object levelled in their faces. With a rush of terror she sent the car lurching forward, only to find the wheel rudely wrenched from her grasp.

"You fool! Do you want to be shot?" shouted Boggie, and surging upon her shut off the engine with such force that she was thrown violently forward and the breath knocked out of her body. Rough hands had seized her and were shoving her over the wheel.

"Down!" Boggie hissed. "Down, down!"—as though to a dog.

In the confined space her aunt seemed to swell and tower to grotesque proportions. She had a confused impression of a face grown puffy and splotched with eyes retreated to pin-points of hate—and then, just before the folds of her woolly coat descended over her vision, she caught the glint of metal hovering aloft. Was it in the bandit's hand? It must be—for there the creature was, looming in on them; and it could not be Boggie who . . .

The thought was never finished. Something crashed upon her head, and amidst blinding pain she slithered down into utter darkness.

CHAPTER THIRTY-NINE

Two ladies in a car? They had been here right enough, but now they were gone on to Wynch, other side of the downs.

This was the news which greeted the occupants of the Humber car when, after maddening search, they pulled up at the Downside Arms. Very sudden it had been, so the somnolent landlord told them, and a bit odd, come to look at it. Seemed as how they got the wind up over a gentleman having his bite of bread and cheese in the coffee-room. Quick as a wink they'd paid their account and got off.

"They saw some one who is staying here?" inquired the, inspector, keeping a tight grip on his companion's arm.

"Not stopping, he isn't. Walks over for a snack, like. No, there was only them two."

"Where is this gentleman now?"

"Oh, he cleared off, too, near about the time they did. Maybe ten minutes ago. Might be longer. The missus was just telling me; but here she is, you can ask her." The woman without teeth who joined them made a garrulous thing of it. The young lady, fagged out she'd looked, had gone up to bed, but the older one—the mother, was it?—came down for cigarettes, took a peep in the coffee-room, and turned white as a sheet.

It wasn't but a minute after that she was in the office wanting to know all about the farm road to Wynch. This gentleman? Who he was they didn't know, but he'd been dropping in these last two evenings, having his supper and slipping off again. Could he have caught what was said in the office? Well—he could have done. Just afterwards he was in the hall here, studying the big map, but when she'd looked again he was gone. He was an odd gentleman and no mistake—very different from other friends of his lordship's, though he must be one of that scientist-lot, seeing as how he was sleeping in the hut over by the old barrow.

Headcorn nodded. "And this short road you mention—does it pass in the direction of the barrow?"

"Oh, no, right away the other side. Over the downs it leads, and it's that way they took, or meant to."

"How do we find it?"

"You can't miss it if you follow your nose. Clean opposite it lays, when you pass the end cottage. When it forks you take the left turn."

Tommy could bear no more.

"Let's push on," he muttered. "In a small place like Wynch we can't fail to find them—if they've reached there," he added under his breath, for a sick feeling had smitten him.

He guessed that the inspector was a prey to the same apprehension from the stern signal made to the sergeant-chauffeur and the acute watchfulness with which he leant forward the moment they were mounting the upgrade. It was as though even now he were trying in every direction to pierce the thick gloom pressing in on them.

"Can't we put on more speed?" urged Tommy, irked by the moderate rate of going. "You can't surely expect to get a glimpse of them thus near the village. Why, they've had a quarter of an hour's start, if not more!"

The only response was a grunt, and Tommy, thrown on his own reflections, tried to formulate the means Gavin would use to attain his purpose. He might have damaged the car while, it stood in the garage. He might have gone ahead and thrown down broken glass, or there was always the old idea of a hold-up, covered by conflagration. If such a thing happened there would be no reason to connect him with it—or would not have been if Boggie had not betrayed the reason of the flight from the inn. Luck, this evening, had played marvellously into his hands—if luck it was. Contrivance was probably a better word for it. Still, there was hope of failure. All around was unbroken calm, no glimmer of light, still less a red flare on the horizon.

He began to breathe more easily. It looked very much as though the two fugitives had got safely to their destination. Why, then, this snail's pace?

"Keep a sharp watch on your side," the voice of his companion shattered his assurance. "Any sign of a motor-cycle? There'll be one, somewhere—if it's not already removed."

A motor-cycle! Such a solution had never entered Tommy's mind. Would Gavin make use of a motor-cycle? It seemed wholly ridiculous to suppose it, but before the matter could be pursued the sergeant at the wheel slowed tentatively and spoke over his shoulder. They had come to the fork. Were they sticking to directions?

"To the letter. Left it is. . . . Hold on. What was that?"

Twenty yards along the engine ceased, and the four men leant out to listen. Tommy heard nothing, but his scalp twitched, and when Headcorn got out to walk softly ahead he was quick to follow. Side by side they reached the summit of the spur and looked down into the hollow below. At the same instant both started, and Tommy swore. In the black, scooped valley at the bottom, only a few hundred yards distant, gleamed a fixed point of red light. Without doubt it was the tail-light of a car, stationary, with its engine and headlamps shut off.

A deadly nausea took hold of him. The stillness, the lack of movement, pointed to but one conclusion. The plan had succeeded. In that motionless car two dead women would be lying—and he, God help him, was responsible for their deaths. Yes, he, crass blunderer that he was—for was it not his advice, his wish, which had over-ridden the shrinking—intuitive, perhaps—one victim had felt towards this tour?

He stirred stiffly, like a man half-paralysed. Then blindly he set off down the slope—and again halted, his breath chopped in two. Out of the pall of silence had rung a volleying report. So wholly unexpected was it that the inspector as well as he remained momentarily spellbound. Not for long, however. The latter raised a shout to those behind, and in another instant all four men were dashing at full speed towards the red beacon and the pendant smoke cloud obscuring it.

Although Tommy alone was unarmed, the fact did not graze his thoughts. Well in advance he sprinted, obsessed by a single idea. One shot only. There might yet be time; but now from the hollow a second report crashed. Almost at once the ruby tail-light vanished, and with a whirr the dim shape of the car moved on, gathering speed.

"After it!" thundered the inspector. "Aim for the tyres!"

Tommy took his meaning. It was the murderer who had commandeered the car and was making off alone with his victims. Evidently that was it, for as shots began peppering the ground in the wake of the receding tyres the unseen driver abandoned the road to launch a drunken course over the turf. Immediately, however, two shots in swift succession shattered the theory. One of the sergeants doubled over with a blasphemous yell, and all eyes saw a wraith of pale smoke rise above a covert of bracken close by.

The truth was now plain. In the foreground a sniper was concealed, bent on picking off the pursuers. One he had lamed, and a third shot had dug up the earth just behind the inspector. What possessed the lunatic detective that he should continue after the car, still shouting orders? Only the women could be in it—one of them able to drive. This panic-stricken flight meant utter confusion on their part. They were taking rescue for a concerted attack.

The uninjured sergeant did not share his chief's delusion. Crouched low, he was creeping, gun in hand, round the dark mass of bracken. Tommy closed in on the other side, doggedly determined despite the bullet which sang past his ear. A foolhardy decision, but better be plugged by a Smith and Wesson '45 than to allow this sniping devil to escape. Towards the dispersing smoke he moved—and took an ignominious header over a bruising obstruction.

It was a motor-cycle, prone on its side; but hardly had he made the discovery when a panting form stampeded him, an iron fist caught his jaw, and he and the aggressor rolled together on the turf.

His first reaction was pure amazement. Anticipating a puny resistance, he found himself tackling an opponent heavier of build than himself and savage in strength. Under a rain of punishing blows, nearly crippled by a powerful kick, all he could manage was to fasten his hold on the thrashing right wrist to prevent the shot which would finish him. This thug in leather helmet and goggles the frail archaeologist? All his bearings were lost. Twice he was upheaved, twice metal touched cold against his skin, and then, by the grace of God, he had thrown the struggler and was lying atop of him. His free hand groped for the other's windpipe. The stiff, upturned coat-collar protected it, but he tore open the fastening, got a grip on the strong muscles. With might and main he squeezed, though his forearm was being twisted into a pulp. . . .

"Good work! Drop him!"

In unison with the words spoken out of the darkness above came a sharp snick-snick. Dizzy, blinded with sweat, Tommy extricated himself and through a rapidly-swelling eye beheld the sergeant in the act of hauling the heavy motor-cycle across the captive's legs. Swiftly they removed the belt of the trench-coat and strapped it round the protesting ankles; but as the sergeant was about to drag away the helmet and goggles twin explosions rent the air, and from a distance came a stern summons.

High up the slope the car was halted stock-still, but with vibrating engine. Both runners knew that a tyre had been struck, for the second report had had a peculiar timbre. It was strange, though, that so little progress had been made—a fact understood only when the inspector pointed towards a shadowy, interlaced mass into the thick of which the car's bonnet had jammed and stuck.

"Barbed wire," he said shortly. "So you've landed one of them, have you? Well, we've more trouble ahead of us. Now! Close together for a rush—and keep well behind the body of the car. There's a gun in there that won't want reloading."

Boggie's revolver, certainly. But what deterred Headcorn from giving a shout of explanation? Suddenly Tommy believed he understood. The man they had captured was some paid accomplice—a common gunman. It was the last thing he had expected—but what of it? Gavin was still the principal—and Gavin was in that car, cornered, but the more desperate, closeted along with the women in all probability now dead. Two shots had been fired before the scramble began. This sinister silence could have but one interpretation. . . .

Stealthily the three edged closer till they were shielded by the rear of the car. The Inspector jerked his hand. The sergeant, revolver gripped in readiness, darted to the right side and with a wrench at the door dodged quickly to cover.

Just in time, as it happened. In the dark aperture loomed a figure of menace—Mrs. Bellamy-Pryce, blood-drenched, her Colt's out-thrust, and her pale lips drawn back in a snarl. The total reversal of expectations completed the chaos in Tommy's mind. She, then, had been directing this crazy flight ending in disaster! Wounded, near death, perhaps, she had battled on, escaping from what she had taken for a company of bandits—but Gavin? Where was he? Was it a gross and garbled mistake on their part? Impossible to think he did not come into it at all, and yet—

All this careered through his brain in an instant of time, with but one sane notion to steady it. She must be reassured—at once, before that weapon of hers wrought havoc. Ignoring the restraining pressure on his arm, he stepped forward into her range of vision—and received a knock-out shock. She had seen him. Under the tangled wreck of her hair small hazel eyes met his with recognition and animal hate. Simultaneously her revolver-muzzle turned full in his face and the red forefinger compressed the trigger.

Was the top of his head blown off? Deafened by the roar, choked with cordite fumes, he regained his footing. Then he knew that the arm flashing past him had been Headcorn's, that the Colt's had been violently dashed to the ground, and that the bullet destined for him had ploughed a furrow in the dry grass. He had a nightmare picture of blood-stained nails fending something off, and then another metallic click sounded as handcuffs snapped on the thick wrists and Boggie, swaying and cursing, toppled headlong in their midst.

"Shot through the shoulder," reported the sergeant, bent over her. "Bleeding quarts. Seems to have passed out."

"One move in her game," grunted the inspector callously. "Tie her up—and fetch the car."

He caught hold of Tommy, who already was surging into the dark doorway.

"A bad business," he said gravely. "You'd best be prepared."

Tommy brushed him aside. Now the full hideousness of his blunder had come home to him, he knew full well what to expect.

"Yes. Leave me, will you?"

She was here, slumped into the far corner. He spoke her name, but she did not stir. The face he gently raised was dabbled in blood—but the wound? Not in her breast, nor in her body. He switched on the light, held her in his arms, and explored the soft surface of her throat. Then he pressed her heart. Beating!

Delirious with hope, he kissed her damp hair, her cheek, her lips. A small moan came from her, and the fingers of her right hand, unclasping, let fall an insignificant object which tinkled dully to the seat. He saw what it was, but it bore no message to him.

"My head," she murmured, a spasm of pain crossing her face; and then her lashes lifted, the pupils beneath widened with a rush of terrible memory, and both her arms closed in a stranglehold round his neck.

"Tommy!" she chattered. "Don't leave me! Oh, darling, you're here, you're here. . . ."

"You're alive," he whispered brokenly. "But not thanks to me."

He lifted her out and carried her down into the hollow where a pool of radiance marked the arrival of the Humber car. Cowered against his shoulder, she did not see the supine mass of her aunt as they passed it by, nor did she look up till they had reached the shadowy group at the bottom. Two of the three men were conveying a not-heavy burden wrapped in dark material and bestowing it carefully in the rear seat. Tommy stopped, for as the glare of the headlamps fell upon it he had seen a yellow, shrunken face and closed eyes—a death-mask in wax. Thank God she had not noticed. This must be broken to her at a better moment. Not that he understood. . . .

"There!" she muttered, holding more closely to Tommy's neck. "Who is he?"

It was the prisoner Tommy had helped to take. Against the running-board he balanced, ankles still bound, helmet and goggles still in place above a hard mouth and an upper lip swollen from recent shaving. Of his whole person only these small portions were visible, and even these he seemed trying to hide within the fronts of his coat-collar.

The inspector examined the revolver just handed him by his aide.

"The Smith and Wesson," he muttered with a nod, and slipped it into his pocket. He turned and played a torch on the stubbornly-averted head of the captive. In matter-of-fact tones he said, "And now, in the name of the law, I arrest you, John Frederick Evans, for the murder of Cuthbert Bellamy-Pryce and for murderous assault on . . ."

John Frederick Evans?

Tommy moved for a better view as the sergeant pulled away the disguising obstructions. He stared, and the girl in his arms gave a gasp.

The bloodshot eyes avoiding hers were those of Captain Argus.

CHAPTER FORTY

It was in her room at the inn that Rosemary first remembered her uncle.

"He was here. I saw him. Oh, what's happened to him?"

"He's in the room next yours," said Tommy gently. "Our other casualty was looking after him in the back as we came along."

"Dead," she whispered with dry lips. "Why don't you tell me? I know, you see. It was his body I saw on the ground."

"Not dead, I think. Just living. Like you, he was stunned as a preliminary measure; and the shooting was hurriedly done. They'd heard us coming."

"She—she meant to shoot me," said the girl in a stupor of horror. "Of course, I see it now. Or a bit of it. What stopped her?"

"A mix-up over revolvers," answered Tommy grimly. "The general stampede. She could only do it with the Smith and Wesson—and Argus had got it. Her only chance lay in making off while he kept us at bay till he could overtake her on his motor-cycle. It nearly came off. I had the luck to stop him—and then there was the barbed wire."

"What's been done with them?" she asked, not yet taking any of this in.

"They're in the nearest lock-up—or soon will be. We left our unhurt man to guard them till the car could get back. Mrs. Bellamy-Pryce," he added, "will want medical attention—and I think we'll find the bullet in her shoulder came from your uncle's revolver, which somehow they'd got hold of. We already know it was her Colt's which got him. Oh, there's not much doubt as to her game! Killing her brother-in-law was to be interpreted as an act of self-defence. It would have been taken as that, too, with you dead and herself wounded. Argus, of course, would have made off before anything was known."

"But why?" She frowned dazedly. "What could either of them have got by it? And this Argus—or Evans. Which is it—and who is he?"

"There you have me," he admitted. "We'll hear all about it soon, I dare say. Oh, I've made a rotten showing in this business! Don't think I don't know it. That'll do now. I want you to lie down. The doctor's just come, and he must look at you."

"No, at my uncle. I'll be all right. Tell me quickly how he is."

Like an automaton she stood while his fumbling hands unfastened her frock and got her dressing-gown round her. The nearness of her and the incredible bliss of her being alive still rendered him light-headed; but awkwardness was fast descending. Already he was remembering the gap in their ages, the money she would have—oh, a number of regrettable things which in the first moments of mad ecstasy had been forgotten. He had best clear off now before embarrassment took hold of them both. . . .

The Downside Arms was in a strange state of upheaval. On the landing doors yawned and shuffling forms cast weird shadows. Downstairs Headcorn was busy telephoning. The doctor summoned from Wynch was heard making disparaging grunts over the worst of his patients, the odour of disinfectant stole on the air, and presently a nurse padded in and out on mysterious errands. Tommy, a chunk of raw beefsteak clamped to his damaged eye, rendered aid in various quarters, moving in a waking dream in which deep humiliation fought with resentment. Ever and again, however, these feelings gave way to a joy that left him slightly drunk. Rosemary, whom he had believed dead, was alive. She had lain in his arms, clinging to him, begging him not to leave her. Whatever happened now, those brief moments were his for all time.

At a late hour the inspector beckoned his friend into the bedroom assigned for their joint use, settled his weary limbs into a chair, and eyed with relish the thick beef sandwiches and coffee waiting for consumption.

"And now," Tommy burst out, "why the hell didn't you explain?"

"And what good would that have done?" retorted Headcorn, helping himself bountifully to mustard. "Without a cool head you'd have been no use to me. Besides, I got my own proof only last night. Till then—"

He broke off. The door had quietly opened, and Rosemary, in her crumpled blue dressing-gown, slipped in to join them. Her cheeks were flushed. Her hair made a bright nimbus in the gaslight, and her eyes had the frosty brilliance of stars on a clear night.

"You've got to let me in on this," she announced. "I can't sleep till I've heard."

The inspector eyed her dubiously. Tommy picked her up bodily, ensconced her against the pillows on the bed, and poured her a cup of coffee.

"Good!" she nodded. "And now, this proof you speak of?"

Headcorn took a typed paper from his wallet and spread it before her.

"Saves a lot of talking," he grunted. "It's a copy, of course. The original document's at headquarters."

Tommy sat on the bed and together they read the following lines:

"Barriscombe Farm,
New South Wales,
Oct. 7th, 1903.

"MY DEAR JAMES,—As you know, with this broken spine I am doomed to peg out, the only question being when. I therefore feel it my duty to acquaint you with a piece of knowledge which may one day affect you and the others, though I sincerely hope it won't. I rely on you to say nothing about it, unless necessity arises.

"Just prior to my marriage, Eileen, my wife, gave birth to a son, whose father is John Frederick Evans, a builder of Sydney. I brought her here among strangers, and am calling the boy—now aged ten months—by my name; but Evans continues to exert a strong influence over Eileen, and as he is now a widower will probably marry her when I am gone. What I fear is that he may be unscrupulous enough to put forward a claim for his boy at some future date, representing him as a legitimate heir to the Bellamy-Pryce estate. He could easily do this, for the child's birth was not registered, and apart from our three selves only two persons now alive are aware of the facts. These two—Prentiss, the doctor who attended Eileen, and Douglas Pyffe, her cousin, through whom I met her just after little John was born—are with me now, and are appending their signatures as witnesses to this letter, which I am having stamped by a notary to give it some legal status. Please understand I do not believe my wife would lend herself to any such fraud as I mention. I am doing this simply to guard against the possibility of her pre-deceasing my father.

"Your affectionate brother,

"CHARLES ROSS BELLAMY-PRYCE."

Tommy swore softly. Rosemary continued to stare at the array of typed signatures.

"But why Argus?" she asked bemusedly.

"The name he took when he ran away from home at sixteen and joined the overseas forces," Headcorn explained. "In those days it was no unusual thing to falsify names as well as ages, and few questions were asked. Eileen Bellamy-Pryce did re-marry. Her son—Evans's son—was given his own father's name, and the past was wiped out. As both parents died during the son's long absence from Sydney, it is quite possible young Evans—or Argus, as he now was—knew nothing about his infant name of Bellamy-Pryce, courtesy-given, till a comparatively recent date. This, of course, we don't know. His father may have told him, or he may later on have learned it from some neighbour who had known him in early childhood. I think, though, he believed he had discovered the true facts of his origin hitherto kept from him. Certainly he came to England this time for the express purpose of pressing his claim—having read in the papers that the man he supposed to be his grandfather was about to die. I think he deliberately broke his journey at Colombo in order to continue on in the company of the judge, whose acknowledgment of his pretensions would have been of great help to him. As for the other claimant's boarding the same boat at Bombay—well, he also had the report of Sir Osmund's serious illness. All three men had the same reason for wanting to be on hand."

"Yes," said Rosemary eagerly, "and then what?"

"Complications," replied the inspector tersely. "The first was that Mrs. Bellamy-Pryce became speedily infatuated with the man she knew simply as Captain Argus. One may suppose that a surreptitious affair between them developed, that Argus confided in his mistress, and found in her a valuable ally. That relation, continuing, has formed the corner-stone of our whole series of crimes. Incidentally it has caused fully half the dust thrown in our eyes."

Electric with interest, Rosemary gave an understanding nod. Now she had been thus baldly told of the intrigue between the woman she had called aunt and the Australian ne'er-do-well she felt she must always have known it. What a self-blinded fool she had been!

"And Uncle James?" she prompted.

Headcorn warned her that much of his reconstruction was of necessity guesswork. However, as every essential was later substantiated, it may be given forthwith.

"Your aunt," he said, "was an embittered woman. She had married James Bellamy-Pryce solely for his expectations, and she had spent years trying to induce him to knuckle under to his father's will. It was true he had risen to a judgeship, but what was that to her ambitions? Not a drop in the bucket beside the larger dream she had entertained of London in the season, a country house in a hunting district, shall we say, and freedom from the dull restrictions of a colonial post. Now, in her middle forties, she saw herself tied to a querulous invalid soon to retire on a pension. Though more money would come at her father-in-law's death, all it would mean was settling down in a humdrum place like Cheltenham. That was the intention, I take it?"

"She'd have hated it. I do know that. Though I couldn't blame her."

"Your grandfather," resumed Headcorn, "probably understood her real character better than any one else—except, perhaps, James himself. It was doubtless typical of him to detest his daughter-in-law for scheming to overrule her husband, even though, paradoxically, he couldn't forgive the latter for striking out on his own. I dare say he knew her for the greedy and self-seeking woman she was, and that this true reading of her inspired his rather wild assertions about the part she played in his son's death. Actually I see that event happening something on these lines:

"Taking counsel with the wife, Argus decided to choose an auspicious moment and confide his identity to the judge. With this in view, he followed him to his cabin that evening, and there and then tackled matters. We may picture the invalid man giving cynical attention only, at the end, to drag to light his brother Charles's long-guarded letter and blow the pipe-dream to atoms. Argus had violent passions, but some shrewdness. No doubt, even in his blind rage and mortification, he saw that but for this paper and the ailing judge, his chances for establishing his claim were every whit as good as when he had believed them valid. So they were, if, as seems the case, the few in the know were now dead and he had found persons ready to swear that till his mother's re-marriage he had been accepted as a Bellamy-Pryce. His story was that Evans, of Sydney, had married a widow with a son, which son Evans had called by his own name. He decided on the spot that this story must stand. He went for James—and here we get the second complication.

"At the moment, we'll say, that James was succumbing to what was soon seen to be a fatal heart attack—little or no violence would have brought that on—his wife entered the cabin and took in the situation. She had no wish to prevent what was going on—in fact was glad enough to assist it; only in the confusion it was she who got hold of Charles's letter. You may imagine what she saw in it. Here in her hands was the means of bending her lover to her will now and for all time. She intended to marry him—and just so long as this document was in her possession he must form a permanent alliance with her or else forego his fraudulent claim. We needn't suppose she put the thing into words. She just quietly held on to the letter, and the moment her husband was dead gave it to the purser for safe-keeping.

"Argus was now in her power, and the next step shows us the two miscreants banding together in an ambitious scheme of mutual benefit—that of wiping out one by one the remaining claimants. I fancy the woman took the lead, because hers is the bolder and more calculating brain; but Argus, with one death safely accomplished, must have been readily persuaded. They agreed to divide the labour between them, not only for plausibility, but in order that neither could skin out and leave the other in a hole. The judge's widow must at once have seen that if three of the same family were to be removed within a short space of time there was small chance of making all, or indeed any of the deaths, appear natural affairs. One or more was certain to be recognised as murder. Well, then, let that happen, and provide a scapegoat to whom blame in each case could easily attach."

"Uncle Gavin." Rosemary was beginning to take it in. "So from the outset they meant every one to think he was the criminal!"

"Undoubtedly—and circumstances favoured the plan. Gavin was a queer one, he and only he would benefit by family deaths, and by sheer luck—obviously it gave them the idea—he was aboard the boat, and a few days previously had quarrelled with his brother James. This incident they proceeded to capitalise. Despite the certificate of death from natural causes, they took pains to drop damaging hints. Argus invented his story of having seen some one very like Gavin on an upper deck, and Mrs.

Bellamy-Pryce, arrived in England, adroitly developed the same theme, first with you, and later with the villagers in Sussex. She was preparing the ground, you see, for what was presently to come.

"She, of course, stood well outside the range of suspicion. It was impossible for her to gain by any one's decease, saving only her father-in-law's. And there could be no reason for connecting Argus, a fellow-traveller who had befriended her at a trying time—with money motives. This enabled Argus to remain in the open—more convenient than holding secret meetings with him and perhaps rousing talk. The idea was that at the right moment he was to clear off completely, back to Australia, there to resume the name of Evans and lie doggo till advertisements for heirs to the estate began to appear. Then only would he put in his claim, very discreetly, through a Sydney lawyer, who would conduct the whole business for him. Having got everything on velvet, he would meet his accomplice somewhere abroad and marry her. If at some later date the two chose to return to England, they could have done so without serious risk. All concerned would be dead, and Gavin, the last to perish, would be held responsible for the deaths of his relatives. A few people, if they ran into them, might remember John Bellamy-Pryce as Captain Jack Argus. But what if they did? No harm could come of it. Futile gossip doesn't penetrate a thick skin.

"Here you have the plan as originally mapped out. Daring, but perfectly feasible. In the working out, however, there were deviations—and it was these, on top of the absence of apparent motive, which were to tie us all—me included—into hard knots. I dare say you realise that early on our two confederates started in to double-cross each other?"

"One moment," interrupted Tommy. "You say this Smith and Wesson revolver really did belong to Gavin. What I'd like to know is how Argus got hold of it?"

"I learned that detail only an hour ago," answered the detective frankly. "Argus stole it from Gavin's room the afternoon he and Gavin met at Victoria Grove and went off together. He made a pretext of discussing James's death, accompanied his new acquaintance home, and was present when a malaria attack came on. Some days later Gavin discovered his weapon was missing."

"And he said nothing about it?"

"Would you suppose him likely to make a song about it? At first he didn't even connect his visitor with the theft. When he did make deductions he was already under grave suspicion of murder on one, if not two, counts. This was no moment to draw attention to his recent possession of firearms. He could only lie low and hope for the best. Unwise of him, maybe, but natural, you'll agree.

"As for the stealing of the revolver, it was no doubt that which determined the first line of attack. I think, incidentally, that on this same occasion Argus got a glimpse of Lord Downside's invitation. When I found it, it was lying in full view on the table, thick with dust—untouched, I should say, since it arrived, which was just before this visit occurred. If Argus did read it, he and his fellow-criminal would have been advised of a possible move which later materialised in Gavin's journey to this place. I'll say more of that presently."

"I see it now!" exclaimed Rosemary. "Uncle Gav must have guessed some bit of this. He tried so hard to warn me, and I—" She bit her lip, and tears dimmed her eyes.

"He was certain of being misinterpreted," said the inspector. "Long before Sunday evening your mind was packed with suspicion against him; and he was unable to supply any cold facts for you to check up because he himself had only a formless mistrust. He was in a singularly helpless position—a desperate one, when he began to see a whole cart-load of guilt dumped at his door. Yes, he guessed what was in the air. A remarkably astute man, he had worked it out that you and he were safe only so long as you were separated. His flight from the vicarage was the one thing he could devise towards preventing the catastrophe designed to engulf both himself and his niece. It was his plan to remain in hiding till he sailed back to India."

"But," she said, frowning, "I still don't get all of it. That Saturday attack on her—was it a complete fraud, just to put every one on a wrong scent?"

"Quite. It could not be wholly a success, for to achieve that your aunt would have had to be killed outright. Arranged on the spur of the moment when you rang up to say you were bringing Mr. Rostetter on the scene, it had glaring flaws as most impromptu affairs have, but it did serve one highly useful purpose: By means of it Mrs. Bellamy-Pryce was able to furnish, under great pressure and with convincing show of reluctance, her purely fictitious description."

"One wonders," remarked Tommy pointedly, "why Argus, with such a magnificent opportunity, didn't finish her off on the spot."

"Do you mean he wanted to?" Rosemary gasped. Quietly the inspector explained that a shot fired in mid-afternoon would have been courting detection. Stabbing, of course, meant a welter of blood.

"It may be Argus simply funked it—though personally I think we have the clue in the lady's own remark to him, made in Mr. Rostetter's presence. She said that possibly she was considered of more use alive than dead."

"Meaning she knew he wanted to kill her? Surely that's a tall order."

"Is it? I imagine she had thought of it after those two shooting fiascos and used some lurid language on him. He smoothed her down, but when, tied up and gagged, she heard him go up to her bedroom her misgivings must have revived. She knew he wanted Charles's letter destroyed. She also knew, too late, just how her own wily manoeuvre had played into his hands. She had refused to give up that bit of ruinous evidence. Now was his chance to get hold of it, or failing that to threaten her into revealing its whereabouts. What saved her was the shortage of time. He had to clear off, lest he be found when the coming party turned up for tea."

"So she couldn't resist that dig at him—after which, I suppose, he pretended he'd gone up only to wash his hands."

"An infatuated woman is easily placated," observed the inspector dryly. "When it came to strangleholds they were quits. She wanted him, I should say, rather more than she wanted the money—and at any price she was going to have him."

"Who," demanded Rosemary, her thoughts straying. "put that note in the Bible?"

"A tongue-wagging woman from your father's parish. Your aunt in March had purposely cultivated her, planting in her mind a general suspicion of her brother-in-law, Gavin—which suspicion percolated throughout the village, right up to the exclusive Miss Claiborne, who at the inquest very clearly showed her notions regarding the accredited snake-in-the-grass."

"So it was Aggie Gosmartin. . . ."

"Just so—privately apprised by a confidential note from your aunt, a note enjoining absolute secrecy, but hinting that some kind soul ought to acquaint the vicar with the facts. Needless to say, if Miss Gosmartin had failed to oblige, other means would have been found of bringing the vicar to London. As it happened, she did not fail."

"And the strychnine," interposed Tommy, swift to note the distress on Rosemary's face. "How was that obtained?"

"I'd say from the ship's doctor, with whom both confederates seem to have been on friendly terms. A few tablets taken from an eight-inch bottle are not likely to be missed, especially when the man in charge is, as is the fact in this case, easy-going and a heavy drinker. It was well to have the tablets on the chance of a suitable occasion cropping up. They couldn't, to be sure, be used in ordinary circumstances; but the cocktail party offered the ideal opportunity. Probably Mrs. Bellamy-Pryce suggested that Argus take on her niece's murder. He refused; and that refusal, coming after the two faulty aims and the attempt to steal Charles's letter, decided her to do the job herself, without consulting him. Gavin's presence was a bit of unforeseen luck. She had meant to go ahead this time without trying to drag him into it. Jealousy is a sharp spur."

"So that's why she flew at me that night when I turned up safe and sound!" cried the girl. "All those long hours she'd been waiting for news that I was dead." The inspector looked at her with annoyed reproach.

"That's something you never told me," he complained. "Always the same in these family affairs!"

Already, however, Rosemary's mind had leapt to other things. The Westminster tower—had that given them the idea about her father?

"Very probably—and his sudden decision to return next morning forced them to act at once, rather than submit to an indefinite postponement. While he talked with the nurse they held a hurried consultation, later supplemented by some signal unnoticed. Mrs. Bellamy-Pryce undertook to ascertain their victim's room number—"

"Only I saved her the trouble," broke in Rosemary bitterly. "No, I know what you'll say. They'd have got it somehow. All these things," she added wonderingly, "which we ourselves saw and made nothing of! Why, we had double your advantages, Inspector! Please tell us. Whatever put you on to it?"

CHAPTER FORTY-ONE

"I WAS having a stretch of blind flying myself," admitted the inspector modestly. "First through this total lack of apparent motive save where your uncle was concerned, and second as the result of Mrs. Bellamy-Pryce's most evident anxiety to hide the truth—or rather what she wanted us to believe was the truth. Very well, all that hedging and self-consciousness. It gave her story, when we did get it, the real stamp of the authentic—precisely as she intended. She overreached herself a bit, and there were unforeseen moments when emotion betrayed her—which moments were just about all I had to build on. In case Mr. Rostetter here is feeling a scrap downhearted, I'll say now that my most valuable clues—indeed almost the only ones—came to me solely through him. I wish to congratulate him on his acute powers of observation." With a wry smile Tommy muttered: "Thanks for small mercies; but I'd rather keep to my back seat."

"There are times," declared Headcorn, generously, "when a back-seat driver prevents a smash-up."

"And other times," retorted the journalist caustically, "when he causes it; but we'll waive the point. Are we going to begin with that famous Saturday afternoon?"

"On that occasion," resumed the detective, "several things clamoured for attention. Some I saw, others were reported to me. You, Miss Bellamy-Pryce, were upset for some reason which did not appear. Your aunt was still very clumsily trying to pull the wool over our eyes, causing painful embarrassment to those assembled; and Captain Argus, manifestly interested in you, took care to keep well behind his hostess's chair. That last item might be irrelevant; but I bore it in mind.

"Later, Mr. Rostetter's account was enormously suggestive. Although Mrs. Bellamy-Pryce had said nothing to me about the brief-case having been searched, she had most unnecessarily taken Mr. Rostetter with her on her tour of inspection! Was that an act of stupidity? It might have been a deliberate contrivance, performed on the assumption that all she did would be reported to me. If this was so, it meant she wanted me to cross-examine her from a definite angle—and it gave the wiping-off of the brief-case a high significance, especially when coupled with the removal of cigarette-ash from the bath-room floor. If the man had worn gloves, why do away with possible fingerprints? Though undecided—her action might have been mechanical and thoughtless—I queried those gloves; and if the gloves were invented, then the entire description might be a sell. Already, you must know, I had some doubts about the bona-fide nature of the attack itself. Why? Chiefly because the victim said that her hat, worn at the time, had mitigated the effect of the blow.

"I made her put on her hat. It had a wide, stiff brim, and a large ornament directly over the bruise on her temple. I did not believe the blow would have left so bad a mark through such an obstruction—and she distinctly declared the hat had been knocked forward, not back. I tentatively wondered if the hat had been jammed on her head after the attack, to suggest she had been taken unawares. That, of course, would mean the attack was committed with her consent; and as she could not have tied herself up in the fashion Mr. Rostetter described, it argued the attacking party was an accomplice.

"Who was this person? Not her brother-in-law, unless he and she were playing a joint game—and what game could it be if she were trying to incriminate him? I thought of the wholly spontaneous anger she had shown when she opened her dressing-table drawer and of her saying there was no need to examine the interior of the brief-case, because the thing searched for was not there. These were the illuminating flashes which in time led to my own hunt for a paper—for, as Mr. Rostetter knows, I did not feel convinced over the knife-yarn. It was the sort of explanation which could neither be proved nor disproved. That Captain Argus vouched for it made me wonder if he were the accomplice in whom I was coming to believe, and if he had seized the occasion of his partner's helplessness to gain possession of some object kept from him.

"If the third attack was a hoax, why not the preceding ones? I concluded—tentatively as yet—that they, too, were in a sense frauds, only that each time murder had been intended, the victim being the older woman. It was now that the double-crossing feature occurred to me. Argus, or whoever it might be, had tried twice to shoot Mrs. Bellamy-Pryce, and next, though sparing her life, had attempted to steal something from her. Yet I saw both these people on the best of terms, uniting to blacken the name of a third person! For the life of me I couldn't make sense of it. If it was not Argus who had done these things, why was he bolstering up his friend's stories? Then take the people themselves: Mrs. Bellamy-Pryce not only bore an unimpeachable reputation, but stood to gain not a penny by killing off her late husband's relations. Yes"—in answer to a questioning look from both listeners—"I thought it possible the sniper from outside had been supposed to take aim at the girl, but for reasons of his own had tried to pick off the aunt instead. Still, why? Argus—if it was he—had no discoverable connection with the Bellamy-Pryces. He was to all intents and purposes a mere boat-acquaintance who had become a friendly associate. I was left no choice but to settle on Gavin and have him watched, learning what I could about his recent movements. My inquiries netted me nothing at all beyond the establishment of the first-class motive already handed me, as it were, on a plate.

"The same with the shark-line. I could not trace its purchase, or locate the wire or chain cut off from the hook-end. Gavin was not my idea of a sportsman, and Argus was. But where did that get me? Nowhere. I resolved, however, to get to the bottom of the relationship between Mrs. Bellamy-Pryce and the man I felt convinced was her confederate, if not in actual murderous attempt, then in some other hidden enterprise involving the brother-in-law. All I could think of was that if the article searched for had not been found a second search would probably be made. By a little wire-pulling I managed to have the new maid engaged by Mrs. Bellamy-Pryce one of our own women-workers."

"Larks?" cried Rosemary incredulously.

"Quite so. I was not disappointed when the first days passed without any report from her. For the moment we'll dismiss her, and speak of the other maid, Coldbottom, about whose dismissal I was curious. She had been discharged summarily just before any of these events occurred, and the two accounts I had of her did not exactly tally. I wondered if she had made some awkward discovery. It might merely be that the kitchen looked out on the spot from which the shots were to be fired. Either way, I wanted badly to get hold of her; but she had drifted from place to place without leaving an address. So again I was stalled.

"We now come to the poisoning episode—a disheartening muddle. I had to satisfy myself that neither Countess Rakovsky nor her Italian friend could have fired the shots, and then look into the movements of Sir Osmund's nurse, at that period in London. I effectually proved that the latter had spent every evening and all day Saturday with her ill mother, in Ealing. Maybe she had an accomplice; but I got no traces of a secret love affair, and that she would rely on a paid assistant was most unlikely. Who in that Mayfair assemblage could link up with Nurse Claiborne? Besides, she was not the woman to lay herself open to future blackmail.

"Meanwhile, my private theory, though grounded on thin air, was too provocative to ignore. Given two criminals, each bent on outwitting the other, how many puzzles became soluble! It would explain Mrs. Bellamy-Pryce's eagerness to visit the hat shop next morning—for if it were she who had put the strychnine in a certain glass, and she knew her intended victim had escaped unharmed, she would naturally be on tenterhooks to learn what had happened. Yet her being the murderer on this occasion in no way conflicted with Captain Argus's fondness for the girl she wished to remove. It simply suggested she had stolen a march on him, as he, by the direction of his shots and his search of her room, had tried to do on her. On discovering the victim to be a charwoman, what more natural than for her to claim the glass as hers, thus driving home the idea that she herself was the proposed victim? You see, I accepted your story, Miss Bellamy-Pryce, in preference to hers.

"It all fitted in—but as before, though she was eager for me to believe her brother-in-law the culprit, she stopped short of committing herself to a positive identification. Slowly it was forced on me that it was no wish of hers to have Gavin Bellamy-Pryce actually arrested. What could account for this contradictory attitude, so at variance with her ostensible interests? Here was my answer: She knew that she, anyhow, was in no danger of being murdered. More crimes were to follow, and only when the series was complete was the trap destined for Gavin to be sprung. It was a horrible thought that unless I quickly secured proof against some one the slaughter begun with an accidental victim was to continue unchecked. The curious part of it, of course, was that the next victim might be Mrs. Bellamy-Pryce herself! For, whether or not she realised it, she was playing with fire just so long as she retained possession of Charles's letter.

"In regard to this feature, all I will say is that Mrs. Bellamy-Pryce is a strong woman, who was fully aware of her lover's weak character. She did possess a hold over him, and no doubt she argued that once a certain feminine attraction was removed he could quickly be brought to heel.

"To get back, here I was, with a theory that wouldn't serve, and nothing more; and I was still in this state, up to my neck in the hat shop investigation, when the first of the anticipated deaths occurred. It was a crime so successful as to be officially designated as accident; and as it's so painful a subject, I shall pass over it now and come at once to Argus's proposal of marriage. That incident was of immense importance, since it confirmed an integral portion of my belief. I said to myself that Argus was electing from now cm to play safe; that if he had been accepted he would have got rid of the older woman, whose disclosures could have prevented his marriage. His risk in this would have been slight. If the death were recognised as foul play, it would be almost certainly attributed to Gavin. However, he had not been accepted. Therefore the original plan would go on. This time it would be the niece who would be murdered—and it would happen very soon.

"Why did I see that event as imminent? Because her uncle, a necessary adjunct, was unlikely to waste time in England once his old father was dead. It might mean a delay of some weeks, but hardly more. During this interval I foresaw danger only when three persons—murderer, victim and scapegoat—were brought together. If there were two murderers—and I believed there were—the one bearing no visible connection with the family need not be present. I thought he would be, to render aid, but that he would disappear before he was seen by any living eye save that of his accomplice.

"The funeral—it turned out to be two of them—in Sussex presented a ready-made opportunity. I accordingly took all possible precautions. Argus, as I had expected, remained behind, and I had him followed, without learning his intentions, except that he was giving up his flat. Meanwhile Mr. Rostetter forwarded me interesting information, which further bolstered up my theory. I was not surprised to find the damaging rumours about Gavin. It was all part of the scheme. When I heard about the note found in the Bible and later in the vicar's cassock pocket, I knew who was responsible for luring this particular victim to London. That Gavin could have gone to a tiny village where every one knew him and come away again without being spotted was simply inconceivable. The note must have been planted by some one familiarly seen in the church.

"In short, my super-structure was complete to the last brick, the trouble being that it was based on nothing. What action could I take? None, beyond the preventative measures already adopted. Not only had I no shred of positive evidence against any one, but in the case of my two suspects I had still discovered no reason for their wanting to commit murder. My theory was a fundamental absurdity. As far as I could see, no motive except Gavin's existed—and I was further hampered by the inquest verdict. If accidental death is given out, I am not supposed to prod under the surface tor a criminal. I was still working on the poisoning affair, but getting discouraged.

"I said to myself that a motive must exist. Coming to grips with it, I argued that since Mrs. Bellamy-Pryce could not possibly hope to benefit, I must look more deeply into her partner. Again I asked, Who is this Argus? I kept the Australian cable-lines hot, got into heavy water with my chief over a 'phone call to Sydney—and still got nothing. A list of the local builders for forty years back did not show the name of Argus. Had Argus taken another name? As I had definitely established he had never in Sydney been called Bellamy-Pryce, this idea did not greatly help. I had traced Charles to Australia, but could not find that he had left issue. There were no others of the name in the whole of the continent. Australia House knew Argus only by his enlistment name—so they were a washout. Once more it was stalemate—worse now, because at any moment the crash might occur.

"On the Saturday I had word from Victoria Grove that soon after the occupants had departed Captain Argus had come with a plausible excuse and ransacked the premises—going away empty-handed. Here I was handed one solid fact. I went at it tooth and nail, hoping it would supply me with what I wanted. In the midst of my hunt more news arrived. I learned that on Friday morning Mrs. Bellamy-Pryce had withdrawn from her bank two hundred pounds—a sum just exceeding the cash payment Argus had made, that same morning, on his car. I gave instructions to secure the numbers of the notes issued, and cabled the former owner of the car asking for the numbers of the notes he had received. Somehow

I felt that the car itself was designed to play an important rôle in the forthcoming crime.

"On Sunday evening Gavin's departure and disappearance were reported to me. All to the good. It gave me more time; but on Monday afternoon Mr. Rostetter arrived to say that two-thirds of the triangle had gone off together in Argus's car! Nothing more ghastly could have happened. To my mind this move meant not flight from Gavin, but pursuit of him—and it was my fault for leaving Mr. Rostetter in the dark. As a desperate measure I resolved to arrest Gavin if I could locate him. I did not see how else I could at this stage avert a double catastrophe. But could I get hold of him in time? Even if I did, prevention was not cure. When he was again free the same danger would recur. Yes, up till yesterday evening I had drawn nothing but blanks, and had only one more card to turn over—Vera Coldbottom. I had small hopes from the girl, but having at last got in touch with her, I decided to see her."

The inspector here gave the events already described—the last-minute discovery of Charles's letter, the tardy receipt of the telegram, and the long, possibly futile, race over half England. Rosemary, as she listened, saw poignantly all these two men had suffered on her account; saw, too, with admiration how the detective's mind had made order out of chaos, even to the prophesying of the final details.

"Why," she asked, "were you so certain it would be to-night?"

"Because to-morrow means a malaria attack. Your uncle would probably not stir from that hut. I argued that he would be caught after dark, somewhere along the mile walk to this inn, then stunned and conveyed to some chosen spot not too near the barrow, lonely, but on the route you were to take. I quite expected you to be gone, also that your aunt would have said the direction you would take—in order, you understand, that it could be assumed your uncle had overheard. Failing to-night meant waiting till Thursday, by which time other scientists would be here, and your uncle would have company on his walks."

"But how could she know all this?"

"From Lord Downside's letter." Headcorn took from his wallet the envelope Tommy had seen by Gavin's bed. "I found it on Argus, who, of course, took it out of Gavin's pocket, after he had dealt the blow which your aunt later on was to say she had delivered, in self-defence, with the butt-end of her revolver. See that seal? Chipped in the re-sealing process. What your uncle burned contained all the information about the hut, the inn and the date when the digging would begin—all of which your aunt took down before letting the owner have it. Obviously she could not know if Gavin really came here, but that's where Argus comes in, with his motor-cycle, hired at once in Southampton. He rode here, did the required scouting, and turned up early this morning in Salisbury to make final arrangements."

"Is that guesswork?" demanded Tommy keenly.

"Oh, no! I had telephoned the Salisbury police to keep watch on the hotel. About nine I got word that at seven-thirty this morning Mrs. Bellamy-Pryce went out, met a man on a motor-cycle along a side-turning, and held a talk with him. I could not find out where he went afterwards, but I knew it was Argus—and I had anticipated the motor-cycle. Speed—and the costume, which not only furnished a disguise, but allowed him to become in this region almost a part of the landscape. If matters had gone as planned, he would now be back in Southampton, if not actually aboard his boat."

"Wouldn't the fact that Gavin had a legitimate excuse for being here have knocked a hole in the story?"

"Gavin would have been dead," said the inspector tersely. "Whatever might have been argued by his defenders, the fact remained that he had come here days in advance of the time stated. Besides, there would have been you to prove that Mrs. Bellamy-Pryce had spoken of her plans at a time when Gavin could have listened in."

"It's what she said to me!" cried Rosemary. "And I, poor idiot, believed her."

"Most vital of all," continued Headcorn, "her brother-in-law had the recognised motive, had been present in the hotel near the hour when his brother met his death, was twice examined by me, and was actually being trailed. Her motive, on the contrary, would never have appeared—nor, as I have shown, would Argus's. Oh, she was on very firm ground!"

Rosemary's eyes darkened.

"I'd begun to hate her," she whispered, "and to be afraid, without knowing why. When I saw her with that button . . ."

"Button?" echoed Tommy with a quick glance at the inspector.

She told them, in some embarrassment, all that had happened.

"I didn't want any one to know I fainted, particularly when I'd realised that coat tumbling down on me was only an accident. It was then the button got pulled off. It was funny her saving it."

"Not funny at all," Tommy said grimly. "You had it to-night, clutched in your hand. The final proof, you see."

When the tide of horror had diminished Rosemary spoke again.

"But that she could sit there and let herself be shot! How is such a thing humanly possible?"

"Much is possible," replied the inspector sententiously. "When a big enough stake is being played for. Her position would have been immeasurably strengthened if she had been found injured. Still, we must not suppose we are dealing with any ordinary woman. There's much to indicate that Mrs. Bellamy-Pryce is blessed, or cursed, with a very low degree of sensitivity. Physically she suffers extremely little; and, like others of her type, she's inordinately vain over what she considers a mark of superiority to her kind."

"We've all seen that," declared Tommy. "I, as it happened, was thinking of it only a few days ago in connection with a book I'd picked up. Not that I saw any relation between the callousness of certain habitual criminals and this ultra-respectable woman."

"Lombroso and his crowd." The inspector nodded. "We're apt to scoff at them these days, but it does seem as though a large number of abnormally insensitive persons turn easily to crime. Be that as it may, when I heard the lady had gashed her right hand while cutting a grapefruit I suspected the wound was self-inflicted—and for a purpose. Now we know what that purpose was. At the crucial moment her victim could be made to drive the car, and thus be at her mercy."

It was long past midnight when Tommy and Rosemary softly turned the knob of Gavin's door and looked in. The nurse dozed in a chair. On the table a night-light flickered, casting tongues of shadow on the yellow face of the injured man. Covered to the chin, he lay like a corpse; but as the watchers anxiously lingered his cavernous eyes unclosed and fixed on them the old, sardonic scrutiny. His lips moved. Tommy bent over to catch what he said.

"Lamashtu," came the faint murmur. "Goddess of disaster. So we find her human after all."

"Human enough to stand trial for murder," returned Tommy with an answering gleam. "But don't lose sight of the fact that you're our star witness for the prosecution."

"Highly annoying." The archaeologist's brow puckered fretfully. "Her final deviltry, chaining me here when I want to be gone . . ."

"He'll pull through," declared Tommy with assurance as he reclosed the door. "I knew that when I heard his only concern was having to cancel his passage."

Rosemary gave an unsteady laugh—her first sign of relaxation. Inside her room, however, she clutched tightly at his lapels.

"Don't go!" she begged. "I keep seeing their horrible faces. Hers is the worst."

"Well, then, I'll stay; but we must talk of other things."

What other things? When she had cuddled down on her bed, neither seemed able to speak. Night silence wrapped them round. This fag-end of darkness, their isolation amidst strange surroundings, and the spent pause that comes after cessation of terror, all combined to knit them very close; but words would not come. Tommy found himself swallowing an obstruction in his throat. She on her side was experiencing a similar difficulty.

"Tommy," she said at last, "to-morrow, I suppose, you'll be crossing to Paris. That's so, isn't it?"

"Do you want me to go?" he asked quietly.

"Yes. No. Oh, why do you ask me?"

Tears slipped from under her lashes. Her white hand lay limp within his reach, but he dared not touch it. His bruised eye throbbed.

"And Rank?" he asked dryly.

"Rank?" She looked at him, surprised. "Well, what about him?"

"Only what he told me." Tommy's voice was hard. "That you hadn't given him a definite answer, one way or the other. Since that moment I've been on the rack to know—well, just what you did say to make him so damned hopeful."

"You can't mean when he asked me to . . . to marry him? Oh, goodness, I suppose you must! Let me think. What did I say? Oh, I remember! I told him to go put his head under the cold tap. I . . . What's funny about it?"

"Oh, nothing. Maybe one day I'll explain." He took her hand lightly, his manner again grave. "And you," he said under his breath, "don't know what love is. No, don't say it. I know."

"It was true," she answered indistinctly. "It's not any more."

His grip tightened.

"What do you mean by that?" he demanded hoarsely.

She fended him off in a panic.

"Oh, Tommy, I'm such a dud! It's not fair on you—really it isn't! Think! Is it worth while?"

"Worth? . . . Oh, my darling!"

She had been so desperately afraid. Afraid of his not wanting her—or, if he did want her, of cheating him; but now, with his lips on hers, all those fears seemed silly, schoolgirl affairs. So must Galatea have felt when she ceased being a stone image. Miracles did happen . . .

At the window, Tommy looked out on the fast-waning night which had brought him humiliation, keenest agony, and now perfect rapture. The moon had risen, a fragment of pale shell, and all the rolling downs lay silvered in its light. Beyond their revealed splendour flowed the Channel—and beyond that lay France, the old life, once full, now—were he to resume it alone—pointless and barren.

Had this change really happened to him? He had to look back at the sleeping girl to assure himself he had not dreamed the whole of these twelve days, from the moment he had struggled against embroilment in another adventure to that other moment just past when the hand clasping his had loosened its hold.

"No more adventures," he whispered without regret. "From now on, safety first."

The landscape under his eyes was subtly altering. Cool air wafted in, and the horizon became flooded in the soft rose-wash of dawn.

He drew in a deep breath. His soul was at peace.

THE END

CPSIA information can be obtained
at www.ICGtesting.com
Printed in the USA
BVHW071707070622
639117BV00003B/139